MONSTER
in his
EYES

J.M. Darhower

This book is a work of fiction. Any references to historical events, real people, or real places are used fictitiously. Other names, characters, places, and events are products of the author's imagination, and any resemblance to actual events or places or persons, living or dead, is entirely coincidental.

ISBN-13: 978-1497585362
ISBN-10: 1497585368

To anyone who has ever believed they found their Prince Charming,
only to realize he wasn't the hero you thought he'd be.

This is for you.

Prologue

A single finger slowly traces the curvature of my spine, leaving a trail of goose bumps in its wake. Despite my best attempt at pretending to be asleep, I tremble at the feather-light touch, unable to contain my reaction.

My breath hitches.

Why must he do this to me?

I hate myself for it, almost as much as I hate him. And I hate him... boy, do I hate him. I've never hated something or someone so much in my life before. I hate his hair, his smile, his eyes. I hate the words he says to me and the raspy tone of his voice. I hate the things he does, the man he is. I hate the way he treats me, the way he affects me, the way his hands inflict the worst kind of pain before somehow igniting a fire within me. It burns deep, raw passion and desire mixing with the purest agony.

I hate it.

I hate it.

I fucking *hate* it.

Once he reaches the small of my back, his finger pauses, before tracing a line along the waistband of my panties. I can feel my body coming alive, heating, like he's expertly kindling a fire, one only he knows how to stroke.

I want to douse myself in gasoline and set myself ablaze, melting away in the flames just to escape these feelings, but I know it's useless. Even as a pile of ashes, I'd never get away. He's a force of nature. The wind would carry me right back to him.

The air feels thick, like it's filled with the blackest smoke, or maybe my lungs are just too stiff, strained along with every muscle in my body. I want to scream. I want to pull away.

I want to *run* away.

But I don't, because I know he'll just catch me if I do.

He did it before.

He'll do it again.

I keep my eyes closed as his finger trails up my spine again, willing myself not to feel it. It doesn't exist, I tell myself. I'm asleep. He's asleep. This is nothing more than a dream. Or is it a nightmare?

He's not *really* touching me.

Except he is... I know he is. Every traitorous cell inside my body is coming alive from that touch, every nerve ending sparking like live wires. If this isn't real, nothing is.

I almost wonder if that would be preferable.

His finger reaches the nape of my neck and once again pauses, this time for longer. Five, ten, fifteen... I count the seconds in my head, waiting for his next move, trying to think ahead, as if this is a game of chess and I can plan a counter-attack.

It's pointless, even wondering. He's already captured my king. *Checkmate.*

Once more, his finger follows the path of my spine, making it halfway down before deviating. It explores the rest of my back, going every which way, making shapes and forming patterns along my warm skin like I'm a living canvas and he's an artist.

Despite myself, curiosity gets the best of me, and I wonder what he's drawing. It feels random, nonsensical, but I know this man.

Everything he does is for a reason. There's always method to his madness, meaning behind every word, a point to his actions.

And it's usually never good.

I squeeze my eyes shut tighter, trying to make sense of the movement of his finger, as it seems to dance along my back. Is he drawing me a pretty picture of a life he once promised, trying to make the lies seep through my skin? Could he be writing a love letter, swearing to do better?

Or maybe it's more like a ransom note.

I wish he would draw a rope so I could pull it from my flesh and hang him with it. I'm sure he deserves it.

I pick up on the pattern eventually, noticing his finger following the same continual trail, looping and curving. I envision it as he does it, realizing after a moment that he's spelling out a lone word in cursive.

Vitale.

His full name is Ignazio Vitale, although once, not so long ago, he urged me to call him Naz. And it was Naz who charmed me, who won me over and made me melt. It wasn't until later that I got to know the true Ignazio, and by the time I met Vitale, it was far too late to just walk away.

If I ever even could've...

7

Chapter One

"Ugh, that's it." A book slams closed across from me, so hard the entire table shakes. "I can't take it anymore. I quit."

I don't look up, my eyes scanning a section of text, only vaguely absorbing the words. I've skimmed through it a dozen times, the book glued to my side the past few days, like maybe the information will sink in through osmosis.

"This is just way too complicated," the voice continues, interrupting what little focus I'm struggling to keep. "Half of it doesn't even make sense."

I flip the page in my book as I mumble, "Sometimes the questions are complicated and the answers are simple."

"Who said that? Pluto? I'm telling you, Karissa, that shit's not even in my book!"

Those words draw my attention away from my work. I glance across the little round table at my friend, Melody Carmichael, as she rocks the wooden chair back on its hind legs in frustration. "It's Plato, not Pluto."

She waves me off, making an, 'oh, who really fucking cares' face. "What's the difference?"

"One's a philosopher, the other's a cartoon dog."

If she can't keep that straight, she's screwed come test time in, say, oh... thirty minutes.

"Yeah, well, I'm inclined to believe the damn dog makes more sense than the old planet-y bastard," she says, shifting through her thick stack of notes. Philosophy, our last class of the day, our last mid-term as freshmen at NYU, and she's reached her breaking point. Typical.

"I mean, listen to this shit," she says, reading from her notes. "Many men are loved by their enemies, and hated by their friends, and are friends to their enemies, and enemies to their friends. Like... what does that even mean?"

I shrug. "Means people are people, I guess."

My gaze goes back to my book, my eyes scanning the text again.

"And it wasn't Plato, by the way," I say, answering her earlier question. "It was Dr. Seuss."

"Seriously?" she asks. "You're quoting Dr. Seuss now?"

"He was sort of a philosopher himself," I say. "Most of his work dealt with logic and reason, society and human nature. You can learn a lot from his books."

"Yeah, well, I prefer a different philosophical doctor," she counters, dropping her chair back onto all fours, the loud thump echoing through the small cafe. "I think Dre put it best when he said bitches ain't shit but hoes and tricks."

Her dead serious tone makes me laugh. "And here I thought you worshipped at the altar of Tupac Shakur."

"Now that man put Pluto to shame," she says. I refrain from correcting her this time, not sure if she really can't recall which is which or if she's just being a smartass at this point. "A coward dies a thousand deaths... a soldier dies but once. That's deep."

"That's Shakespeare," I point out. "Straight out of Julius Caesar."

"No way."

"Yes way."

Melody's eyes shoot daggers at me as she exaggeratedly reopens her book. Despite declaring she'd quit, she goes back to work, doing some last minute cramming. She's damn close to failing philosophy and needs to do decent on the mid-term to bring up her grade. Anything less than a C and she's skipping down the path of probation, straight toward suspension.

Me? While I may not be in danger of failing, per se, my scholarship is a different story. Not all of us come from the loins of wealthy Wall Street bankers like Melody and can afford to piss around. My mother's in no position to help me, seeing how I'm not sure how she's surviving as it is. And my father, well...

Not all of us have one of those.

If my GPA dips any lower, I'm on my own. And if I'm on my own, I'm fucked six ways to Sunday. Something tells me NYU won't take an IOU as tuition payment.

"Whose bright idea was it to take this class, anyway?" Melody mutters, dramatically flipping through pages.

"Yours," I reply. "You said it would be easy."

"It's supposed to be easy," she argues. "It's philosophy. It's like, opinions; there are no wrong answers when it's someone's opinion, right? I mean, it's supposed to be rational and logical, things that makes sense, not this existential science-y bullshit."

"Ah, it's not so bad."

Truthfully, I like philosophy, all bullshit aside. If it weren't for our professor, I might even love it.

"Not so bad? It's way too much thinking."

Rolling my eyes, I close my textbook and sit back in my chair. The words are all bleeding together into a sea of nothingness, bogging up my thoughts and weighing down the stuff I do remember.

I glance around the cafe, trying to clear my mind as I pick up my chocolate mint tea. It's still warm, despite it having sat here for over an hour, ignored.

"Only you, Karissa," Melody says, shaking her head. "We get a freak seventy degree day in March and you still order hot chocolate and wear a goddamn scarf."

Shrugging, I take a sip of my drink, savoring the rich creamy chocolate flavor. I blend in usually, with my normal getup of skinny jeans and sweaters and tall boots. It's not my fault we get one warm day and everyone else acts like it's summertime in the Caribbean.

Melody's personal plan seems to be to see how little she can wear without getting nailed for public indecency. She's currently toeing the line with some tiny shorts and a crop top. I feel obscene just looking at her.

"What's wrong with my scarf?" I ask, reaching up and running my hand along the soft material. It's my favorite.

"It's all pink and stripe-y and scarf-y." She waves my way dismissively as she grimaces. "Pretty sure it's what Aristotle was talking about when he said 'how awful the truth is when there's no helping it' because there's definitely no helping that scarf."

I burst out laughing, so loud it disrupts the people trying to work near us. I cast them apologetic looks as I correct Melody. "Sophocles said that."

Or something close to it, anyway. How dreadful knowledge of the truth can be when there's no help in truth...

"You're sure?"

"Positive."

Melody groans, slamming her book closed for the second time and throwing her hands up. "I'm going to fail this damn test."

〜

Sixteen multiple-choice questions, five short answer problems, and a two-page essay, all within an hour.

I'm in Hell.

Figuratively, of course, although it feels quite literal every time I look up from my exam to the front of the room, my eyes drifting to the sign hanging above the old school chalkboard.

Abandon hope, all ye who enter here.

It's a quote from Dante Alighieri, the inscription found at the gates of Hell in The Divine Comedy. Professor Santino clearly thinks it's funny, but it confirms my suspicions...

The man is Satan.

I bullshit my way through the essay and finish a few minutes before time is up. I turn my exam over, leaving it on the desk, and slouch down in my chair. Santino has a 'keep your asses in your seat until everyone's finished' policy, like we're kindergartners learning to follow rules for the first time.

Moving slowly so I won't be noticed, I reach into the front pocket of my backpack and pull out my cell phone. Concealing it in my lap, I find some mindless game to pass the rest of the time. No sooner I get it open, the gruff, stern voice echoes through the room, startlingly loud after hearing nothing but woeful sighs for the last forty-five minutes.

"Reed."

At first I think Santino is commanding us to read something when I glance up and meet his beady brown eyes, peering at me through a pair of thick glasses. Despite me sitting in the back row of a class with nearly a hundred students, I realize he's talking directly to me—Karissa Reed.

Oh shit. "Sir?"

"Put it away now," he warns, "before I take it."

He doesn't have to tell me twice. I instantly let go, the phone slipping from my hands and dropping toward my backpack without me breaking eye contact. He nods stiffly, satisfied with my compliance, and looks away to call an end to the exam.

As soon as the papers are collected I jump up, grabbing my bag and jetting for the closest exit.

Melody's waiting by the hall, her expression vacant, like there's nothing left inside of her to offer. It amazes me, how the pursuit of wisdom tends to turn people into shells of their former selves.

"How'd you do?" I ask.

"I made out about as well as Dante did with Bernadette."

"Beatrice."

She waves my way. "Well, there's your answer."

We shuffle out of the building and into the bright Manhattan afternoon. Melody's expression shifts once we're outside, the shell-shocked look fading as she puts it behind her.

I admire her ability to brush everything off.

Tilting her head back, she closes her eyes and smiles, bathing in the warm sunlight. "I need a drink. We going to Timbers tonight?"

I scrunch up my nose. Melody reopens her eyes, catching my expression.

"Oh, come on!" she says. "It's gonna be bitchin'."

"Like, totally," I mock. "Gag me with a spoon."

Melody laughs, elbowing me. "I'm serious, we have to go."

"Why?"

"Because it's eighties night!"

"So? You weren't even born then."

"All the more reason to go."

Ignoring her, I pull my bag off my back. I look through it, shifting books out of the way as I seek out my cell phone to give my mother a call to check on her. She wanted me to visit this weekend, but I'm in no mood to take the long trip... not to mention the lack of money for bus fare. I unzip the little pockets, searching, my stomach sinking when I don't find my phone anywhere. "Shit... shit... shit..."

"What's wrong?" Melody asks, pausing when I stop, dropping the backpack to the sidewalk to root around for it. "Lose something?"

"My phone." I groan. "Santino yelled at me for using it so I dropped it in my bag, but it's not here."

"It didn't fall out, did it?" Melody asks, looking behind us, down the block toward the building. "Maybe you left it in the classroom."

"Maybe," I say, zipping my bag back up and slinging it over my shoulder. "I'm going to go look for it. I'll meet you back at the room."

I'm off before she can even respond, taking the same path we took. I keep my eyes peeled to the ground in case it fell out during the walk. I slip back into the building, navigating the hallways on my way to the classroom. I approach, about to walk right into the room, when Santino's voice rings out inside. "I know what you're here for."

Brow furrowing, I step into the doorway, words on the tip of my tongue. He has my phone? He's sitting at his desk, the stack of midterms piled up around him, pen in his hand as he stares down at some unlucky bastard's paper, assaulting it with red ink. *Please don't be my test.*

I start to speak, the words 'my phone' slipping from my lips when another voice cuts through the classroom. "Good, because I'm in no mood to have my time wasted."

The voice is all male, deep and raspy, the kind that commands attention, each and every syllable oozing coolness. I immediately silence, my gaze sweeping through the classroom, seeking out the source. A man lurks near the corner at the back, not far from the only other entrance. Everything about him matches the huskiness of his voice—tall, broad shoulders, not bulky but undoubtedly solid, like the thick, sturdy trunk of a gorgeous redwood tree, a black suit perfectly hugging his frame. Although formidable, there's a sort of ease to his stance. He doesn't just sound confident.

He knows he's in control.

I take a step away, slinking back into the hallway when the man's calculated footsteps start through the classroom, toward where Santino sits. I consider leaving, maybe coming back later, not wanting to interrupt whatever this is, but man... I really need my phone.

And damn if curiosity doesn't have the best of me. What does this man want?

"I don't have it," Santino says, his voice casual, like the intimidating man doesn't at all affect him. "I haven't gotten my hands on it yet."

"That's not the answer I wanted to hear."

Before Santino can respond, a soft buzzing resonates through the quiet room, vibrating the floor. My gaze darts that way, spotting my phone under the desk I sat in to take my exam. Relief washes through me at the sight of it, replaced quickly by a swell of anxiety. The man turns his head toward the sound, giving me a brief glimpse of his profile. He seems to pause that way for a moment, listening to my phone buzzing, before turning around completely to face the doorway.

To face *me*.

I dart out of sight, not wanting to be caught eavesdropping.

Strained silence passes until my phone stops buzzing, whoever it is hanging up.

"I'll be back for it," the man says after a moment.

"I know." Santino's voice is so quiet I can hardly hear it. "I know you will."

Footsteps start through the room again, heading my way. Panicked, I turn, trying to tread lightly as I bolt down the long hallway, turning the corner and pausing. Contemplating, I hunch against the wall, bending down to absently shift through my backpack, pretending to be occupied with something. I hear him as he makes his way down the hall toward me, toward the front doors, my heart thumping hard in my chest at the sound of his calculated footsteps.

He leisurely rounds the corner near me. My eyes shift that way, staring at his shiny black dress shoes, my stomach sinking when they slow before coming to a dead stop right in front of me.

"Yours?"

I glance up, catching a glimpse of his face for the first time. Holy fuck me, it's not what I expected, yet it's everything I ever anticipated from someone so striking. He's older—thirty, at least, maybe pushing forty—but his skin has a youthful glow. There's a dusting of hair along his jaw like he hasn't bothered to shave in a few days. His brown hair isn't short, but it isn't long either, a tangle of wayward curl pushed back on his head. He either spent a long time perfecting it, or he rolled right out of bed that way.

Either way, I'm impressed.

Despite maybe, possibly (but hopefully not) being a hell of a lot older than me, I have to admit he's drop-dead gorgeous. So good looking, in fact, that I can hardly stop myself from ogling him, my eyes meeting his bright blue ones after a long moment of practically eye-fucking him every which way imaginable.

He cocks an eyebrow at me. It would probably be comical if it weren't so goddamn sexy.

"Yours?" he says again.

It isn't until he repeats the word that I even realize he's holding something. I freeze, spotting the familiar cell phone with the pink glittery case in his palm. His hand dwarfs the phone, his fingers strong and sturdy, the tips calloused, the skin scarred. I don't know what this man does, but he uses his hands.

A lot.

"Oh, uh, yeah." I reach for my phone, hesitating before taking it from him. "How did you—?"

I don't finish my question, and he doesn't answer it. Instead, a small smirk tugs the corners of his lips, revealing a set of deep dimples as he drops his hand. He stands there for a moment, staring down as he towers over me, at least six inches taller. He's staring at me intently, as if there's going to be some kind of test he's studying for.

He might pass it, as hard as he's looking.

Shaking his head, the man turns and strides away, not saying another word.

"Hey, it's me," I sigh into the phone after the beep. My mother's probably the last person on earth with an old school tape recording answering machine. "I was just giving you a call back. So, uh, ring me when you get the chance. Love you!"

Melody laughs when I hang up. She's standing in front of the mirror, fixing her hair, already dressed for the night at Timbers I still haven't technically agreed to. She looks ridiculous, covered in neon, a headband on like she just stepped out of an Olivia Newton John music video. "How's Mama Reed?"

I shrug, tossing my phone down on my desk. She was who had been calling when my phone was in the classroom.

Melody doesn't wait for any sort of explanation, turning to me as she changes the subject. "What are you wearing?"

"Uh..." I glance down at myself. "Clothes."

"Not now. I mean tonight."

"Clothes," I repeat. What the hell else would I wear? "Probably some jeans and—"

"Jeans?" She gasps, interrupting me. "Oh no, no... that's not gonna work."

She goes straight for my closet, sliding the door open to root through my clothes. There isn't much in there—at least, not compared to her side. I have to do laundry every two weeks or I'll be naked, whereas I'm pretty sure she has enough clothes shoved in her closet to last all year.

The dirty laundry surrounding her seems to confirm it. Less than ten feet separates her bed from mine, her entire half of the room a mountain of belongings haphazardly strewn wherever there is space, whereas my half tends to be little more than an open trail leading her to the door.

It's not possible for us to be any more different. Melody's an F5 tornado, and I've easily settled into my roll of playing National Guard and cleaning up her messes.

It's hard to believe we've only known each other for a few months. We moved in the beginning of freshman year, complete strangers, acquiescing to live together in a virtual walk-in closet.

Melody did it for character building, she says. I did it because I had no other choice.

Where else would I find a place to live in Manhattan for four thousand a semester? *Nowhere.*

"You have, like, nothing in here," Melody complains, moving from my closet to my dresser. Much to her disappointment, there's even less in there. Giving up, she retreats back to her side, opening her own closet to fight the avalanche of fabric. "Lucky for you, we wear the same size."

I have quite a bit more ass and thighs, but she scoffs when I bring that up, like I'm bragging. Melody is downright gorgeous, sleek blonde hair and unnaturally green eyes. She looks like she belongs on a Victoria's Secret catwalk.

When she doesn't look like Neon Barbie, that is.

She pulls out clothes and flings them across the room at me. I grimace. Spandex. "You're just prepared for everything, aren't you?"

"You have to be," she says, turning her focus back to the mirror again. "You never know what life with throw at you."

Those words take me back an hour, to the hunk of man I'd encountered at the philosophy classroom. I don't mention it to Melody. I'm not sure why. Maybe because it was nothing.

Or maybe because I wish it could have been something.

Either way, I keep it locked in my head, sealed inside of me, where it's only mine. Talking about it meant rationalizing it, when I prefer to let it simmer instead.

The reality is never as fascinating as the fantasy.

Hours later I'm standing in front of the mirror, the skintight black spandex bodysuit making me feel like sausage squeezed into the casing. Over top of it I'm wearing an oversize hot pink shirt, falling off one shoulder, the outfit complete with a pair of blue leg warmers. It might've passed for gym attire had I not been wearing pointy black high heels, my wavy brown hair teased to unfathomable heights, my face covered in makeup.

19

"I look like bozo the clown," I whine, gazing at my reflection in the mirror. Bright blue eye shadow and hot pink lipstick does not go well together, no matter what Cyndi Lauper might've thought back in 1983.

"You look hot," Melody says, smacking my ass as she struts past, heading for the door. She has changed again, for probably the fifth time, settling on what looks like a frilly blue prom dress. "Come on, the party awaits!"

I grab my things, stuffing it all in my bra since I have no pockets, and head out after Melody before I have time to change my mind. Timbers is just down the block from the dorms, a few minute stagger home at four in the morning. It's dark out now, the air starting to cool from the sun going down, the more typical March temperature creeping it. It doesn't seem to faze Melody, but I shiver.

My footsteps stall. "I should grab my scarf."

"Puh-lease," Melody says, slipping her arm around mine to yank me on. "It doesn't go with that outfit."

"Nothing goes with this outfit," I point out.

She laughs, casting me an amusing look as we stroll down the street. Music pours out of the door of Timbers, already alive with activity at a quarter after nine. We get in line, waiting along the grungy brick building as Melody fluffs her hair, fixing the gigantic bow she's using as a headband. When it's our turn, I pull my ID out of my bra and hand it over to the bouncer at the door, a big burly guy with a thick Long Island accent. He glances at it, and looks at me, before handing it back over.

As I slip it back to safekeeping, the man pulls out a permanent marker and yanks off the cap with his teeth. The noxious fumes burn my nostrils as he waves it my way, and I hold my hands out so he can mark big black X's on my skin.

I glare at them as I step aside.

Melody, on the other hand, gets a lime green wristband. She smiles, holding it up to show it off to me. She's only nineteen, not much older than I am, but her fake ID puts her at the ripe ol' age of twenty-one.

I stick my tongue out at her as she laughs, slipping her arm around mine again and dragging me inside. The bar is decked out in an array of eighties memorabilia, movie posters affixed to the walls as The Breakfast Club plays muted on a giant television.

We make our way to the dance floor, where New Kids on the Block bumps from the speakers. We get lost in a sea of color, crimped hair and leather jackets, surrounded by wannabe pop princesses and douchebags in black sunglasses.

The music shifts and continues as we infuse ourselves into the crowd to dance. From Vanilla Ice to MC Hammer, Madonna to Poison, the bass flows through my veins like blood, spiked with adrenaline as the lyrics wash over me, shouted out enthusiastically from the overeager not-born-in-the-eighties-but-fuck-if-we-don't-still-love-it college crowd. It's like stepping back in time, back into another decade, and leaving our imprint in a moment we never got to touch before.

Melody gets drinks—drink after drink after drink—some paid for; others bought for her by guys in the club hoping the night won't end here. I'm not sure where half of them come from, or even what they are, to be honest, but I sure didn't pay for them, so I don't care.

I steal sips when nobody's looking, needing the boost as I dance my heart out, spinning and jumping, laughing and trying to stay on my own two feet as the alcohol seeps in.

I'm a sweaty mess, my feet on fire, the shoes pinching my toes when I eventually lose track of my friend. Last I saw her she was talking to a pseudo-Maverick, straight out of Top Gun, the two of them hot and heavy, halfway to the danger zone.

I stand there for a moment, breathing heavily, and wipe my sweaty forehead with the back of my hand. The black marks there are still going strong, not even the least bit smudged, but I've long ago given up the façade of not drinking, a half-full cup of something in my hand, bought and paid for by Maverick.

He didn't look happy when I swiped it from my friend.

I glance around as I sip it, moving through the crowd, seeking out the frilly blue prom dress, but it's nowhere to be seen. She's not on the dance floor, not at the bar, and not in line for the bathroom. The air is thick and stuffy, and I feel light-headed, like I'm not getting enough oxygen. Sighing, I chug the rest of the drink and toss the cup as I make my way to the exit, moving past people to push my way outside.

I take a deep breath as soon as I'm out on the sidewalk, the night air so cold it feels like tiny little needles jabbing my skin as my body adjusts to the abrupt change in temperature. It's late... one, maybe two in the morning from what I can tell, the streets still alive but the line to get inside down to only a few.

Melody's not out here, either.

The bouncer eyes me peculiarly. I step away from the door, away from him, as I reach into my bra to grab my phone to call Melody. It slips from my hand, along with my ID, both falling to the ground. I hold my breath as the phone hits the sidewalk with a loud crack.

"No, no, no," I chant, crouching down to snatch it back up. I glance at the screen, grimacing at the long jagged scratch right down the middle of it. "Oh, fuck."

Frowning, I reach for my ID, but before I can grab it someone else gets to it first. Brow furrowing, I look up, expecting it to be the nosey bouncer.

What I see nearly knocks me on my ass.

It's *him*.

Him, all six-feet and some change of his glorious frame, still clad in his all black suit, looking exactly as he had hours ago. I should be alarmed, but I only feel a slight tingle trickle down my spine, a vague sense of awareness that in a city of nearly two million people, the odds of ever running into him twice are slim to none, much less twice in one day.

Maybe it's fate.

Or maybe I'm in trouble...

He stands there, glancing at my ID, before his blue eyes shift to me. I stand up again, swaying, my head swimming, everything around me delayed. It's hard to think straight, the alcohol kicking in. I've been drunk before, but this... this isn't the drunk I'm used to. I'm dizzy, and sweaty, and damn if I don't feel like I might puke.

Please don't puke.

"That's a terrible picture," I mutter as his eyes shift once more from me to the ID. He gazes at it for a moment—a moment that feels like an eternity as I try not to pass out on the sidewalk—before he holds it out to me.

"There's nothing wrong with the picture, Karissa."

I take the ID to slip it back away as the alarm finally sinks in. "How do you--?" I shake my head, the motion making me even woozier. My vision blacks out for a second, a second where I fear it won't come back. "How do you know my name?"

My voice comes out as a strained croak, and although my vision's blurred, I see his forehead crease with confusion. "It's on your license."

Oh. I mean to say it out loud, but I can't seem to get my lips to work anymore. I blink rapidly, trying to take a deep breath, but it's senseless. No amount of air will keep me afloat when I'm already falling. My knees give out, everything fading to blackness.

BAM

Chapter Two

Musk.

It surrounds me, infiltrating my senses as I creep toward consciousness. It smells earthy, woodsy and aquatic, all male with just a hint of sweetness. It seems to waft around me in a slight breeze I can feel against my skin, warm, and fragrant, and...

Oh God, it's cologne.

My eyes drift open when that thought hits me, the scent stronger as I come around. Blinking a few times, I stare up at a foreign white ceiling. A fan spins round and round right above me, the setting so low my eyes can follow the blades, the air blowing against my face. The room is dim, faint light streaming through a window.

Close to dawn, I gather, from the soft orange glow that bathes part of the floor.

Or is it dusk?

My heart races in my chest, each beat painful, as it seems to reverberate through my body. I'm achy, my head pounding in rhythm with my heartbeat. Panic bubbles in my gut that I try to ignore, to push back, but it's no use. I have no idea where I am, no idea how I got here, or how long I've been in this place. I'm confused, sore, disoriented...

And my bladder feels like it's about to explode.

Slowly, I sit up in the bed. It's fit for a king—way bigger than any bed I've ever owned. The mattress feels like fluffy clouds and the intoxicating scent clings to the pillows and the sheets. Everything is bright white, crisp and clean, and I'd think it was a hotel room, with how impersonal it feels, if it wasn't for the fact that there's no goddamn bathroom in the vicinity.

I strain my ears to hear, but it's dead silent, except for the soft sound of air swishing from the fan. My panic eases a little when I see I'm still fully dressed, wearing the god-awful eighties clothes from last night.

That was last night, right?

As I contemplate what to do, I hear footsteps off in the distance, calculated and exaggerated as they grow near. I hold my breath when the knob across the room turns, the door opening.

Oh shit.

Oh shit.

Oh shit.

What have I gotten myself into?

The moment I see him, memories start to trickle in. The bar, dancing, drinking, stepping outside as I search for Melody but somehow find him there instead. I remember looking at him, talking to him, and then there's nothing.

I'm drawing a blank.

He's wearing the exact same thing as last time I saw him, though, having still not changed.

Or maybe black suits are all he owns.

He hesitates in the doorway when he sees me sitting up, his hand still grasping the knob, but after a moment he lets go of it and takes a few steps toward me. Instinctively, I grab the blanket and pull it up, shielding myself, despite the fact that I'm still clothed.

The act makes him hesitate a second time. He pauses, and stares, but he doesn't speak.

I'm not sure what to do, or say, or how I should feel or even what to fucking think, so I just stare back. *Awkward.*

After a moment the corner of his lip twitches, revealing the deep dimple. "You're awake."

"I am."

Ugh, my voice sounds like sandpaper and feels just as raw.

"I was worried," he says. "You've been out for a while."

"Where is this?" I glance around the room anxiously. "Where are we?"

"My place."

His place. Oh, God... "How did I—?"

"You were drugged."

Those words stall me as my stomach sinks. I gape at him. Drugged? I was *drugged*? That panic surfaces again so quickly that I can feel it viciously rising, bile burning my throat. "You drugged me?"

His expression shifts, all amusement dying away at my question. His jaw clenches, his eyes narrowing, his nostrils flaring as he regards me with an anger that makes my blood run cold. "I did nothing to you."

"I, uh... I didn't mean..." Pulling my legs up, I try to fold into myself, slinking away from his tone. "I didn't know."

"You were slurring and struggled to stand up when I ran into you," he says. "Your breathing was shallow, your eyes distant, and you were confused, couldn't keep ahold of anything. You went unconscious on the sidewalk, and your pulse was slow. You were practically wearing a sign, sweetheart. Drugged."

The word 'sweetheart' slips from his lips with ease, but there's little warmth to it. The cold tone makes a chill creep down my spine. The man's intense.

"So you, uh, brought me to your place?" I ask incredulously. "When you saw I was drugged?"

"What else was I supposed to do?" he asks, arching an eyebrow in question. "Take you to the hospital, to the police, after you'd been drinking... underage, none-the-less."

"You could've taken me home."

"I could've... had I known where that was. You were alone, and your license lists a PO Box upstate. I couldn't very well drop you off at the post office in Syracuse, now could I?"

"No," I say. I didn't think about that. I never bothered to have my address changed. I haven't lived in Syracuse since right after I got my license at sixteen.

"So I brought you here," he continues, "because I couldn't in good conscience leave you out there."

I stare at him as those words sink in. Ignoring the fact that I'm in a stranger's house, in a stranger's bed, with no memory of getting there, I feel a peculiar sense of relief. If what he says is true, that makes him my savior... my knight in shining armor, even if I refuse to buy into being the damsel in distress.

"Thank you," I say. "I'm, uh... I'm Karissa."

He knows my name, but it feels like the right thing to do, to introduce myself. Maybe it will be slightly less awkward if he isn't a complete stranger to me anymore.

"My name's Ignazio."

My brow furrows in confusion at his unique name, my reaction causing his hardened expression to break. He smiles again, this time letting out a light laugh.

"You can call me Naz, if you prefer," he says.

"Naz." The name sounds weird on my tongue. "I've never met a Naz before."

"I like to think I'm one of a kind."

He stares at me, and once again, I'm not sure what to say. I feel like a fool, just sitting here, wrapped up in his sheets that smell so masculine, like I imagine he smells if I get close enough to inhale the scent of him. Although my heart has slowed down, my anxiety lessening, my head hurts like a son of a bitch.

And not to mention I still have to pee.

"I, uh..." I feel my cheeks flushing. "Do you have a bathroom I can use?"

He nods, breaking eye contact, and turns toward the open door behind him. "Just down the hall, last door on the left."

I climb out of the bed, my legs wobbly as I stand up. Geez, how long have I been out? Ducking my head, unable to look at Naz, I scurry past him, down the hall. The bathroom is massive, everything bright white just like the bedroom, the marble floor cold under my bare feet. The light burns my eyes when I flip it on, and I squint, trying to adjust to the brightness. I take care of business, groaning when I catch sight of my reflection in a mirror afterward.

I look like death.

My eyes are bloodshot, makeup streaked all over my face, a big smudge of color marring my skin. My hair is little more than a tangled rats nest perched on top of my head, and I'm still wearing the godforsaken spandex.

Grimacing, I try to fix myself up, splashing water on my face and running my fingers through my hair, but it does little to help. Giving up, I head back out, my steps unhurried.

I'm in no rush to face him again, knowing how I look.

He's still standing just in the doorway of the bedroom, his hands in his pocket, his stance full of ease. He's not at all uncomfortable having a strange girl in his home... in his bedroom.

Does anything bother him?

He turns, catching my eye when I approach the doorway, but I stop there, not going back into that room.

"I don't usually look this way," I say, motioning toward myself, feeling the need to explain my disaster of an appearance.

He smiles again. He has a nice smile—the kind that's warm but not overly friendly. It's genuine, nothing forced about it. He smiles like he means it. I don't know much about this man, but he doesn't

29

seem like the type to do anything needlessly.

"I figured," he says, his eyes scanning me, making my cheeks flush again. "Eighties night."

"Yeah."

"As a man who was around back then, I can tell you that most people didn't dress that way."

"Ugh, I know. Acid-wash and shoulder pads were all the rage, right?"

"Yes."

I eye him peculiarly, trying again to guess his age. When he smiles, his eyes crinkle, but I don't spot any wrinkles. "So you remember the eighties well?"

"Well enough."

"How old were you then?"

That's nicer than asking how old he is now, right?

A look of amusement flashes across his face that tells me he's on to me. "How old do you think I was?"

I hesitate. "A teenager?"

"Close."

My stomach sinks. Ugh. "Older?"

"Younger."

Whew.

"So that means you're about..." I try to do the math in my head, but there still seems to be a fog settled over me. "Forty-ish?"

Jesus, he's forty.

"I'm going on thirty-seven."

Thirty-six, then. That makes him eighteen years older than me.

Ugh, eighteen.

He's twice my age.

"Well, thanks, Naz," I say quietly, feeling inadequate. He's all man, and I'm probably nothing more than a silly, helpless little girl to him. "Really, I appreciate it."

He merely nods.

I look away from him then, glancing around the room, searching out the belongings I'm missing, but they're nowhere to be seen. The room has significantly lightened the past few minutes, swaddling everything in the soft glow. It's still early, but Melody has to notice I'm missing by now.

"Do you know where my phone is?" I ask.

He nods, pulling it from his pocket. "You seem to make a habit of losing it."

"Yeah, I guess I do," I say, taking the phone from him. "How did you know it was mine, anyway?"

"You had it with you."

"No, before that," I say. "In Professor Santino's classroom."

"Ah. I heard you ask for it."

"You heard me?"

"I did," he confirms. "You stepped into the doorway and said 'my phone'."

I look at him incredulously, clutching my phone, running my thumb along the jagged scratch down the screen. I hope like hell it still works because I can't afford to replace it. I can barely afford to pay the damn bill. "You must have great hearing."

"I do," he says, walking toward me. I stand still as he steps past, his arm brushing against mine, the familiar cologne wafting around me, clinging to him just as it clings to his bed. "Not much slips past me, Karissa."

He walks away, and I watch as he disappears through the hall and down a set of stairs. Looking down at my phone, I try to turn it on but it's dead, the screen staying black.

With a sigh, I look away, having no choice but to follow Naz downstairs.

The two-story house is large and mostly vacant, fully furnished but scarcely decorated. My eyes scan the rooms as I trudge through them. I spot my shoes in the living room and slip them on. Now all I need is my ID.

"Here," Naz says, picking up my license from a table and holding it out, as if he'd read my mind. "I think that's all you had on you."

"It was," I confirm, taking it. "I, uh... I should go."

I nervously turn toward the door when he clears his throat. "Do you want a ride?"

I hesitate. "A ride?"

It doesn't strike me until then that I could be *anywhere*.

"Yes," he says. "I can take you back into the city."

Jesus, I'm not even in Manhattan anymore?

"Uh, yeah, sure. Okay."

It turns out we're in Brooklyn, an upper-class neighborhood in the southwest corner of the borough. Naz's place is bigger than most others on the street. I wonder what he does for a living to be able to afford it. I don't ask, though. I feel enough out of place without having to know my Prince Charming is an actual heir to some sort of throne.

A sleek black Mercedes is parked in the driveway, roaring to life when Naz hits a button on his keys. He fits the car beautifully, both impressive and downright gorgeous. I feel even smaller sitting in the passenger seat, not speaking as he drives us through Brooklyn.

"Are you hungry?" he asks eventually, not giving me time to answer before he whips the car into a Starbucks drive-through. "What do you want?"

I want to say nothing, but my stomach is tearing up, and I'm pretty sure he can hear it. It sounds like grinding gears. "Just whatever you get, I guess."

He cocks an eyebrow at me. "What if I get nothing?"

"Then get me something else... something chocolate."

He laughs, rolling down his window to order—two coffees, loaded with cream and sugar, and a chocolate muffin. I thank him when he hands me mine, but he shrugs it off like it's nothing.

"So where am I taking you?" he asks when he pulls back into traffic.

"NYU," I say. "I stay in the dorms."

It's a twenty-minute drive into our part of lower Manhattan. I pick at my muffin and sip on my drink and try to think of something—anything—except for the reality of what I'd gotten myself into.

By the time we make it there, I'm feeling insignificant, little more than a charity case that has been picked up off the streets. He pulls the Mercedes around the corner and into an adjacent parking garage, stopping there and slipping the car in park, blocking the entrance.

"Thank you again," I say nervously, unfastening my seatbelt and reaching for the door handle. "Really."

I don't give him time to respond... this is uncomfortable enough without forced conversation. I step out, clutching my coffee, and slam the door behind me. Before I can walk away, the window rolls down, and his voice calls out. "Karissa."

I turn around, wondering why he just can't make this easy on me, and freeze when I see the pink object in his extended hand.

My phone.

Really?

Sighing, I step back that way and reach through the open window, taking it from him. I try to pull away but he grasps my hand, clutching it tightly. It doesn't hurt, but it locks me in place, his skin warm and rough to the touch.

"A word of advice?" he says. "Be careful who you trust. There may not always be someone there to save you."

"I, uh..." Those words are chilling. I have no idea what to say. "Okay."

He lets go, his hand grasping the gearshift to put the car in reverse. I back up a few steps, away from the car.

"Call me sometime," he says. "It would be nice to see what you look like out of those clothes."

"Karissa, it's your Mom... sorry I missed your call..."

"Hey, kiddo, call me back when you get the chance!"

"It's been a few hours and I haven't heard from you, honey. I hope everything's okay. Call me."

"Karissa, I'm starting to worry... call me, please."

"I swear to God, Karissa Maria, if you don't call me back right now—"

"That's it. You're grounded. Forever."

Sighing, I hang up and stare at the screen of my phone. It still works, thankfully, once I got it plugged in and charging. It sprang to life with a whopping thirty-two missed calls—a few from Melody, wondering where I was, but most from my mother. She went from asking to pleading to threatening all within the span of a few hours.

I'm surprised she hasn't called the police to report me missing.

On second thought, she probably did.

If they ever gave out an award for overprotective mother of the year, Carrie Reed would win it, hands down. For eighteen years she kept me on lock down, always two seconds away from a mental break whenever I was out of her sight for too long. I was a bubble wrapped package marked 'fragile'—do not bend, do not break. We moved around so much it was hard for me to keep friends. She was restless, always needing to move on to something else—a new town, a new hobby, and new people—while I just wanted nothing more than to have somewhere I could call home.

Despite migrating and starting over practically every year, homeschooling in a lot of the places we lived, my application and SATs were enough to get me on the waiting list at NYU. I figured it was hopeless, and nearly gave up, when at the last minute a spot opened up and I was offered admission.

She cried when I told her. I thought she would be happy, but she sobbed and pleaded, asking me to reconsider moving to New

York City. I told her I had to follow my heart, follow my dreams. She eventually backed off, but she never full accepted my leaving.

Abandonment issues, I guess. My father walked out on her when she was pregnant, and I don't think she has been the same since. I only vaguely remember seeing a photograph once, a flash of a mustached face, like a faded old Polaroid with a name scribbled on the bottom: John. It doesn't bother me—I can't miss someone I never had, can't mourn someone I don't know—but I know she feels the loss.

I know it, because I've heard her cry, muttering to him when she's in her bedroom, like he could hear her wherever he was.

She can't have him, so she overcompensates with me.

I lay back on my bed, too exhausted to do much more than move. My bed smells faintly like laundry detergent, but I smell like him. The scent lingers on my clothes from sleeping tangled in his sheets. It's half the reason I haven't bothered to shower, or change... the other half is because I can hardly think straight to function. My mother's messages are already slipping from my mind as Naz's words creep back in, replaying over and over, like a CD skipping.

It would be nice to see what you look like out of those clothes. I just gaped at the car as he drove away, disappearing into traffic. He'd seen me wearing something other than his ridiculous eighties get-up... the first time he saw me I was dressed normally.

It wasn't until I was in the elevator, heading up to my thirteenth floor room, that the double meaning behind those words hit me. *It would be nice to see what you look like out of those clothes.*

Holy shit, did he mean naked?

I'd been so startled I dropped my phone. Of course.

Sighing, trying to push it from my thoughts, I turn back to my phone and scroll through my contacts. I need to call my mother before she really does call the police. I make it to her name, *Mom*, when my finger hesitates, my eyes drifting to the name right below it. *Naz.*

I stare at it. He put his number into my phone at some point yesterday. I don't remember it happening, but that isn't surprising, considering I don't remember most of last night. I wondered how I was supposed to call him and shrugged the entire thing off, but now something stirs inside of me—anxiety, mingling with excitement. Butterflies tear up my stomach. I want to scream, to squeal, to puke. Before, it was harmless flirtation, but now... Jesus, now I can call him.

Oh God, no... I can't. I can't call him.

Can I?

I'm locked in an internal debate, trying to rationalize those feelings, when my phone starts ringing, my mom's name popping up before I can press the button to call her. I answer it, bringing the phone to my ear. "Hey, Mom, I was just about to call you."

"Karissa, where have you been? I've been worried!"

"I'm sorry. I, uh..." I went out drinking last night and was drugged and woke up in a strange guy's bed with one hell of a hangover. You know, all those things you worried would happen to me when I moved to NYC, but I told you only happened in the movies. "I dropped my phone yesterday and messed it up. I just got it working again."

That's true, at least.

"I thought something happened to you!"

"I'm fine, Mom," I say. "I just talked to you the day before yesterday... or the one before that. Nothing's going to happen to me."

She lets out a deep sigh. She doesn't argue with my words, but I know they don't reassure her. Switching the subject, I ask her how everything's going in Watertown and how things are working out at the flower shop she opened.

Watertown is where we lived the longest, the place that finally started to feel like home. We moved there from Syracuse right after my sixteenth birthday and she hasn't left yet.

Yet.

She's rambling on and on about how spring's coming and the flowers will soon bloom, and I'm trying to pay attention, but the words are fading away into a fog. The door flings open after a few minutes as I'm humming in acknowledgement to something my mom says, Melody appearing in the doorway. She does a double take when she sees me, her eyes wide. I can see the questions written all over her face and know, in about twenty seconds, an interrogation is coming.

"Mom, I need to go," I say, not wanting to be on the phone when it happens. "I'll call you later, okay?"

"Okay," she says, hesitating like she doesn't want to hang up. "I love you, Karissa."

"Love you, too."

I hang up with my finger still touching the screen when the dam breaks and the questions start flooding out. "What happened to you? Where did you go? Where have you been? Why haven't you called? And why the hell are you still wearing that?"

Rolling my eyes, I sit up. My head is still throbbing, despite the handful of pills I popped when I got to the room. I've had hangovers before, but this is more. This is a fuzziness I can't seem to shake.

"You first," I say. "What happened to you at Timbers?"

"I met a guy. Your turn."

Melody stares at me, awaiting some sort of response as I try to get my thoughts together and decide how much to tell her.

"Same," I respond. "I met a guy, too."

Her eyes widen. "Really? Who?"

"He's nobody," I say, not believing it even as the words leave my lips. That man is indisputably *somebody*. "So did you leave with the douche in the flight suit or what?"

She eyes me for a moment in silence, as if debating whether to push me for more, but she thankfully shrugs it off. "Yeah. His name's Pat or Pete or something, I can't remember. Maybe it's Parker? We made out and then passed out."

"Same," I say again. "Except for the whole making out part."

"So you went home with a guy and... passed out?"

"Pretty much."

"Well, that's disappointing."

I let out a light laugh as I stand up and stretch, setting my phone down to let it finish charging. "Yeah, it made for one hell of an awkward morning. So tell me about Pat-Pete-Parker-whatever."

She shifts the subject, going back to talking about whatever his name is, as I gather some clothes to take a shower. I don't mention Naz any more. She'll have more questions—questions I don't have answers for.

"Ugh, I have one hell of a hangover," Melody says eventually. "How are you feeling?"

"Like hell," I say. "I think there was something in one of those drinks last night... a roofie or something. I don't know. It's fuzzy."

She looks at me, horrified. "That's scary. Are you sure?"

"Pretty sure." I hesitate. "I think it was the last one... the one you got from whatever-his-name is."

"No way," she says. "He was totally a gentleman. It must've been another."

"Yeah," I mumble. "Maybe, but be careful, you know, just in case."

Chapter Three

"Are you sure you can't come?" Melody asks, exaggeratedly frowning as she sits across from me, clothes piled high all around her—this time on purpose. An empty suitcase sits on the floor by her feet, waiting to be filled.

"I'm sure," I say. "If I could, I would, but I can't."

"If it's about money, I—"

Before she can even finish that sentence, my eyes narrow and I cut her off. "I can't go."

She makes a face at me, somewhere between annoyance and pity. I know she's feeling both. It's Sunday, and tomorrow is the official start of spring break. With midterms behind us, we have nothing to worry about until classes start up again next week. Melody's off to Aruba with some old friends from high school—girls I've met but wouldn't recognize if I ever ran into them on the street. Melody's the only one in her group that stayed in New York for college.

So while she's at the beach, celebrating freedom and soaking up the sun, I'll be here alone. It is about the money, yeah... I could never afford to keep up with her lifestyle, even if she insists on including me whenever possible. I'm gracious when she buys dinner, or drags me for a night on the town, but I draw the line at a Caribbean vacation. There's a thin line between accepting help and being a charity case, a line I felt myself toeing earlier in the weekend.

But it's more than that, too.

I *can't* go.

"I told you I don't have a passport."

"Well, I told you we could go to Florida instead."

"And I told you I won't let you change your plans because of me," I say. "So go, have fun. I'm just going to hang around here, maybe panhandle, you know, make a little money."

She laughs as she starts tossing her clothes in her bag. "You don't want to go see your mom?"

"No, I'll see her in a few weeks for Easter."

Melody finishes packing, cramming more clothes into suitcases than I think I even own, before she walks over and flops down on my bed beside me. She lets out a deep, theatrical sigh, wrapping her arms around me. "I'll miss you, Kissimmee! Don't have too much fun without me."

I laugh at the nickname. She overheard my mother say it one day and completely ran with it. "I'll try not to. Might be difficult, though, with all this excitement going on around here. You know... empty halls and vacant classrooms and closed libraries."

"Sounds like Heaven," she says. "Too bad I can't stay."

"Yeah, too bad. You're gonna miss all the fun."

Melody plants a playful sloppy kiss on my cheek before getting her stuff in order, shoving a few last minute things into her bags. She's ready just as her phone rings, alerting her that a car is waiting down by the curb to take her to the airport.

"I'll call you every day," she says. "Every hour."

"Please don't," I reply. "My mother already does that."

With a laugh, she's out the door, hauling her luggage with her. To be honest, I don't expect her to call at all.

Once she's gone, the door clicking closed behind her, I toss my book aside and lay back on my bed.

A whole week.

Seven days of nothingness.

Melody hasn't even been gone a minute and I'm already bored out of my mind.

I clean, and read, and clean some more, and read some more, before my stomach starts growling. I grab a pack of Ramen noodles from the cabinet in the room, making my way to the small kitchen everyone in the suite shares. Most of the building is empty, save for a few wayward students like me who stayed behind. I fill a pot with water and put it on the stove. As I'm waiting on the water to boil, I pull out my phone and scroll through it to call my mom.

No answer.

Sighing, I leave a quick message. For someone who freaks out when I don't answer, she sure sends my calls to her answering machine a lot. Hanging up, I lean back against the counter and stare at the screen, my eyes drifting to the name beneath hers.

Naz.

I could call him. I mean, he put his number in my phone and told me to call him. He wouldn't do that if he didn't really want me to, right?

But what would I say? Hey, remember me, girl you picked up from the sidewalk, drunk as a skunk, high off her ass without even knowing it? You know, the one you felt obligated to take home with you because there was nowhere else to take her? Yeah, her, the one you bought breakfast for the next morning, the one who didn't offer to pay for her own because she didn't have a penny in her pocket?

You remember her?

I'm so, so sorry if you do.

Groaning, I cut my eyes at the pot of water. There are only a few tiny bubbles on the bottom. It needs to hurry up.

My gaze goes back to the phone, back to his name. It would be

41

rude not to call, though, wouldn't it? He helped me, after all.

Another glance at the pot. Still not boiling. *Dammit.*

When I turn back to my phone again, my finger hits his name. I press the call button before I can talk myself out of it, because I know I will if given the chance.

I bring the phone up to my ear and listen. The first ring seems exaggerated, like the sound echoes through my body, twisting my insides into knots. I feel like I'm going to puke and need to sit down, my eyes darting around the kitchen but the chair that's usually in here is gone.

Goddamn thieves.

I'm shaky, and edgy, and about to hang up when the line clicks, shutting off mid-ring. There's a pause of silence that feels like it drags on forever before his voice breaks through. "Hello."

Oh God, oh God, oh God... what was I thinking?

"Uh, hey... it's, uh..."

"Karissa."

My name sounds like Heaven from his lips as he says it in his rough, low tone. I want to ask him to say it again, and again, and again. "You remember."

"I do," he says. "How are you?"

"Better." A lot better than when he last saw me. "I just wanted to, you know, thank you."

"I'm glad you called. I thought maybe you lost your phone again."

"No, I still got it," I say. "For now, anyway."

He lets out a laugh, the sound making me smile, easing some of my anxiety. "Good."

"So yeah, like I said, I wanted to thank you again, for everything you did... you know, at the club, and the ride, and my phone. I appreciate it, really, and if I can ever repay you—"

"You can."

I stall at those words. "I can?"

"Yes," he confirms.

"Uh, how much?" I ask. "I don't have much money."

He laughs again, this time a little louder. "I don't want your money, Karissa. I have plenty of my own."

"Then what do you want?"

"You."

He says the lone word so confidently that I just stare straight ahead, unable to process it. "Me?"

"Let me take you to dinner," he says. "Then we'll call it even."

"I... I don't know what to say."

"Say you'll be ready in thirty minutes."

"Now?" I ask incredulously.

He wants to take me to dinner right now?

"Why not?" he asks. "No better time than the present."

I can name plenty of times better than now... times that don't include me wearing Oscar the Grouch pajama pants and fuzzy pink slippers, my hair a scraggly ball on top of my head. "I don't know."

"I'll tell you what," he says. "In half an hour, I'm going to pull up at the entrance to the parking garage, right where I dropped you off. If you're there, I'll take you wherever you want to go. If you're not, I'll go on my way."

Before I can respond, the line goes dead, my phone beeping. Call ended. I stand there, hesitating, contemplating, before turning around. Once again I don't give myself a chance to talk myself out of it. I switch the stove off, leaving the pot of freshly boiling water on the burner as I bolt from the kitchen and sprint to the room.

Thirty minutes. That's all I have.

I tear through my closet, throwing clothes around as I search for something to wear, pulling shirts off hangers and holding them up in front of the mirror before tossing them aside. I blast through everything I own, demolishing my side of the room in less than five minutes, putting Melody's mess to shame.

I move from my closet to Melody's, taking a deep breath before diving in. Her clothes are trendier than mine, more revealing... more her and hell of a lot less me. I shift through what's hanging up before scouring through her drawers, changing a few times before settling on a black long-sleeve sweater dress I fish out of the back of the closet.

It'll have to do, because I'm down to fifteen minutes. I let my hair down, running my fingers through it. It's wavy from being up all day, but there isn't anything I can do to straighten it. I swipe lip gloss across my lips and put on a coat of mascara, barely having time to spritz myself with perfume before slipping on my boots.

Sitting on the bed, I glance at the clock and tense. Time is up already.

I practically sprint out, taking the elevator downstairs and jogging outside, breathing heavily by the time I round the corner to the parking garage. My footsteps falter, and I pause when my eyes come into contact with the sleek black Mercedes idling there.

Something inside of me soars, the butterflies taking flight, like they'd just discovered their wings for the first time. My feet move again as the driver's side door opens and Naz steps out. He's wearing another suit, all black with a blood red tie, my eyes drawn to the pop of color on his broad chest.

Naz strolls to the passenger side, opening the door for me.

The stories got it right, I see.

Prince Charming has manners.

I offer him a smile, trying to get myself under control as I slip into the seat, taking a deep breath when he walks around to get back in. He hesitates, his hand on the gearshift, as his gaze sweeps along me. I can feel my body flush from the attention and curse my lack of makeup... I know my nervousness is written all over my face.

He meets my eyes, his blue ones bright, twinkling with satisfaction. He says nothing about it, though, turning away to put the car in reverse.

"Where do you want to go?" he asks, easing into traffic.

"Anywhere," I say. "Wherever you go."

"You sound uncertain."

"I guess I do."

My response makes him laugh.

"I just have no preference," I explain. "I was going to eat Ramen noodles tonight, so anything is an upgrade from there."

"Why would you eat that?"

"Because that's all I had in the room," I say. "And besides, they're not so bad. They cost like, twenty cents. You can literally survive off them for a dollar a day."

He cuts his eyes at me, looking not nearly as impressed by that as I am.

"Have you tried them?" I ask curiously.

"No," he says. "Can't say I've ever had the pleasure."

"I'll have to make you some."

He raises his eyebrows, regarding me peculiarly. "I'll hold you to that, but not tonight. I'm taking you out instead. You can treat me another time to your gourmet noodles."

I'm so embarrassed I can feel my face heating. What's wrong with me, babbling to this man about freaking Ramen noodles? I want to slink away, disappear into the cool leather seat and never again resurface. "Just ignore me. I'm an idiot."

"No, you're not. You're just nervous."

"That obvious?"

"I'm just good at reading people. It kind of comes with the territory."

"What territory?"

"Work."

"And what is it you do for work?"

"A little of this, a little of that," he responds. "I'm a freelancer."

I stare at him. That didn't answer my question at all.

He cuts his eyes at me again, and my confusion must be easy to see… or maybe he just is that good at reading people… because he chooses to elaborate for me.

"Let's say a company needs something done... like, say, they're downsizing and need to fire people. Some of them choose to bring in someone else to do it, so they don't have to do the dirty work themselves. They like to keep their hands clean. So they hire an independent contractor, someone with expertise, to handle it for them."

"And what's your expertise?"

"Dealing with people," he says. "Finding things."

As soon as he says it, it takes me back to Santino's classroom and the words I heard that afternoon. 'I know what you're here for.'

"What were you looking for from my philosophy professor?"

A legitimate look of surprise crosses across his face that he wipes away just as quickly. He doesn't answer, shaking his head after a moment as his focus remains on the road. "I can't talk about my work."

Fair enough.

He takes me to a restaurant near Central Park, the kind where you have to make reservations weeks in advance. I've never been—I don't think even Melody has been, the atmosphere too rich for even her upscale tastes—but I've heard of the place. Naz valet parks the car and I get out, glancing around nervously, feeling severely underdressed even in a dress.

I start to point out to Naz that we'll never get a table here when he leads me inside, past couples waiting. The hostess looks up. "Do you have a reservation, sir?"

"No."

"We're fully booked for the night," she says, flipping the page in her reservation book as if double-checking. "Rest of the week, too."

"Do me a favor," he says. "Run and tell the chef that Vitale sends his regards."

The hostess looks like she wants to say no, but it's hard to argue with someone who sounds so confident. She reluctantly excuses herself, disappearing into the kitchen. Less than a minute passes before she returns, grabbing two menus and flashing a forced smile at Naz. "I was mistaken. We have a table for you."

"I figured," Naz says, pressing his hand to my back and motioning for me to follow the hostess. I oblige, not wanting to make any more of a scene than he just caused, everyone waiting already regarding us like we'd come with bombs strapped to our chests.

I slip into the chair the hostess pulls out while Naz sits down across from me.

I gape at him when she walks away. "How did you do that?"

"Do what?"

"Get a table so quick?"

"I called ahead."

"So?"

"So I know the chef," he replies. "Called in a favor."

I'm quiet for a moment as the waiter appears, asking what we want to drink. I mutter "water" under my breath as Naz interjects. "Bring us a bottle of your best champagne."

The waiter looks between the two of us, and I'm just waiting for him to ask me for my ID, but he doesn't. Instead, he scurries away, walking off to fulfill Naz's request. It's fascinating, watching people react to him, while at the same time it's alarming. Is there anything this man can't get his way with?

"How'd you do it?" I ask. "Really."

"I just told you."

"How'd you call ahead? I didn't see you."

"I did it before I picked you up."

I shake my head. "But you didn't know where I'd want to go."

"Didn't I?" He raises his eyebrows questioningly. "I told you, Karissa. I read people. You have a tendency to just go with the flow and see where the wind blows, so I picked somewhere decent for you to land."

I'm flabbergasted as he picks up his menu and casually relaxes in his chair, his attention on it. I barely know anything about this man,

47

and yet he seems to know me in ways no one ever has before, predicting what I'll do before I even do it.

The waiter returns with a bottle of champagne and tries to fill our glasses, but Naz takes it from him, insisting he do the pouring. I pick up my menu then, glancing at it, my stomach clenching as I scan the list of items.

I don't know what half this shit is.

I'm still staring at it when the waiter returns a second time, ready to take our order. Naz gazes at me from across the table, his lips twitching with amusement. He takes the menu straight from my hand and turns it over to the waiter along with his. "We'll just have the tasting menu."

"His and hers?"

"No," he says. "I don't care which, but make sure there's no difference in the plates. I'd rather the chef not know which is mine."

The waiter nods and disappears as I regard Naz curiously. "Why don't you want the chef to know?"

"Because if he knows which is mine, he might poison it."

I let out a sharp laugh. "Paranoid much?"

"Not paranoid," he responds as he picks up his glass of champagne and takes a sip. "Merely cautious, which you should also be. You can't trust people, Karissa. Haven't you learned that?"

"Yet you want me to trust you?"

"I never asked for your trust." He smirks. "I only asked you to go to dinner with me."

Dinner's a four-course meal of seafood and steak, salad and some other things I can't begin to name. There's even caviar on the table. Gross. I'm stuffed by the third course but I don't decline desert, savoring the rich chocolate soufflé. Naz ignores his, instead sipping champagne.

We've almost drained the entire bottle. Naz has kept our glasses full. My head is fuzzy and my body feels like it's made of air. I'm floating sky high.

I never want to touch the ground again.

"Is it good?" he asks, watching me intently. I'm too intoxicated for the attention to fluster me anymore.

"Amazing," I say. "Best soufflé I've ever had."

"Have you had many before?"

"Nope. Never."

He smirks, pushing his across the table toward me. "You can have mine, too."

"I'll pass."

"Full?"

"More like it might be poisoned."

I'm joking, of course, but he shrugs a shoulder like he really thinks it's a possibility.

I set my spoon down, unable to take another bite. The check comes, and he turns it over, eyeing it as he pulls out his wallet to pay. I sneak a peek as I take a drink, nearly choking on the champagne.

The check is over twelve hundred dollars. *No fucking way.* I gape at him as he pulls out a wad of cash, paying in strictly hundred dollar bills, not even seeming bothered by the cost.

"That's nuts," I hiss. "I could eat for like a year off of that much money."

"Three years if you just eat your noodles," he points out.

"Seriously. Why's it so expensive?"

"Good food usually is."

I scoff. "You could've taken me to Taco Bell. I would've been happy, and you would've saved a thousand bucks."

"Everyone should indulge at least once," he says. "You enjoyed it, didn't you?"

"Yes."

"Then it was worth it."

I don't even know what to say. I clutch my glass of champagne, determined to drink every last drop, considering the bottle was nearly half the bill. Naz pours himself a swallow before dumping the rest into mine for me to drink. It's filled to the brim again.

I take a sip. "If I didn't know any better, I'd say you were trying to get me drunk."

"Now why would I do that?"

"I don't know," I say. "Honestly, I don't know much about you."

"I've told you more about me than you've told me about you."

I roll my eyes. "You seem to have me down to a science."

"I don't even know what you're going to school for."

"Well, if you figure it out, let me know, because I'm still in the dark about that myself."

"Ah, well, you're young. You have plenty of time."

"That's what my mother says."

"Your mother." He eyes me curiously. "Are you close with your family?"

"Her I am," I say. "She's really the only family I have... the only family I'll ever have. I'm the lone kid of a single mother."

His brow furrows. "No father?"

"Nope," I say. "He ran out on us before I was born. My mother doesn't like to talk about it, so I don't know why."

"There's only one reason he'd do that."

"Why?"

"Because he's a coward." His voice is stone cold serious. "A real man would never abandon his family."

"Yeah," I say. "You're probably right."

"But you know, they're not the only ones who matter," he continues. "The family we're born into is important, sure, but they're not all we have. They're not all we are. A part of life is making your own family. That's the beauty of it all."

I smile softly. "Do you have a big family?"

"I do," he says, "but most of us aren't blood related."

There's something refreshing about the way he thinks, the way he looks at the world. He doesn't just accept the hand he's dealt.

After a moment, he motions toward my glass. "Drink up."

I slouch back in my chair, sipping my champagne. "Yep, you're definitely trying to get me drunk."

"I am," he admits, leaning over the table, closer to me. "How else am I going to get you to come home with me?"

Those words send tingles down my spine. I'm not sure if it's excitement or apprehension. "You could just ask."

He stares at me, eyes surveying my face as his expression falls serious, his voice dropping low. "Come home with me, Karissa."

My breath hitches. "That's not a question."

"Doesn't matter," he says. "Come home with me, anyway."

Chapter Four

I go home with him.

Everything tells me not to, down to common sense. Even Naz's earlier words about not trusting people should've turned me away.

But still, I go home with him.

What can I say?

The warnings are a shout in the wind, swallowed up in the atmosphere. He's compelling and chivalrous, gorgeous and generous, and I'm intoxicated and in desperate need of something... something that he stirs up, something strong, and primal. He awakens the animal inside of me.

But it's nothing compared to what I see in his eyes. He turns to me as soon as we're alone in his house. The air is heavy, and his eyes are dark, the blue like midnight in the dim lighting. It's like seeing him for the first time all over again, but being greeted by an entirely different creature.

He's a beast. A monster.

And he looks like he wants to devour me.

He steps toward me. His voice is low and husky. "Have you ever been with a man, Karissa?"

My heart hammers hard in my chest as I nod. "I've had sex before."

"That's not what I asked," he says, pausing right in front of me, the tip of his shoes touching mine as he stares down at me. "I don't care about those boys who might've fumbled around between your legs a time or two. I want to know if you've been with a man."

I hesitate before slowly shaking my head. If he is a man, if this is what being with a man is like, I've never been with one. I've messed around with boys at parties, even had a boyfriend for a while back in Watertown that took my virginity in the backseat of a rusty Chevrolet. But whatever is happening right now between us is something I've never felt before.

It's electricity.

He cups my chin with his hand, tilting my face so I have no choice but to look him in the eyes. His thumb sweeps along my bottom lip, and I let out a shuddering breath as he leans closer, tilting his head like he's going to kiss me, but he pauses there instead. His gaze burns through me, seeping down into my soul, seizing me like a prisoner.

I'm a willing captive.

"You don't have to be afraid," he says. "I'm not going to hurt you."

He kisses me then. His lips are soft—so, so soft, like velvet, a stark contrast to the roughness of the rest of him. His kiss is gentle, little more than breaths against my lips that I eagerly inhale, taking him in. I let out a soft moan, hardly catching it as he whispers, "unless you want me to."

A hint of a smile takes over his face when he pulls away. I should be alarmed. I should head right back out that front door and run far, far away, but I can't. I can do nothing but stand there and shiver as he lets go of me, taking a step back. He regards me for a moment, eyes sweeping down my body, as his smile grows.

He's a child with a brand new toy, and I just hope he doesn't break me as soon as I'm out of the package.

He's on me then, his hands seeking me out as his lips once more meet mine. None of the gentleness from a moment ago is in his touch. He seizes me, pulling me into his grasp, taking my breath away with his hard kiss. I gasp as he lifts me up, hands gripping my hips. I cling to him, wrapping my legs around his waist, my arms around his neck, holding on for dear life.

He's strong—Jesus, he's stronger than I expected, holding me like I'm weightless as he carries me upstairs to his bedroom. As soon as we're inside, he kicks the door shut and hauls me over to the bed, his lips still on mine.

He lays me back on the crisp white sheets, him on top, his weight pressing down on me, constricting my chest. My lungs burn, the butterflies in my stomach flapping wildly, ready to take flight.

A strange thrill soars through me when he moves from my mouth, his lips trailing down my jaw line, finding my neck. He kisses and licks, his teeth grazing the skin, as his hands hike up my dress, shoving it to my waist.

I barely have time to think, to agonize over the fact that I'm pretty sure I'm wearing plain white cotton panties that are probably not sexy at all, when his hand slips beneath the flimsy fabric, fingertips grazing my clit. My back arches involuntarily as a gasp escapes my throat, the jolt of pleasure tearing through my insides, the first lightning strike of an oncoming storm.

I'm caught in a whirlwind. There's no other way to describe it, no way to explain it, except that I've been swept up so fast that I can no longer even see the ground. His hands are all over me, tearing off clothes, as his lips seek out every stitch of exposed skin.

The dress is yanked off and flung across the room, barely hitting the floor before he's leaving a searing trail of kisses down my stomach. Slipping his hands beneath me, he makes speedy work of my bra, tearing it off.

He grasps the sides of my panties, and I lift up instinctively when he tugs them down. My knees find one another, drawn together like magnets, as my hands cover my breasts, timidly shielding my naked body from his view as he sits back. He regards me warily, seeming to hesitate for a fraction of a second when he sees how I'm laying there, but it doesn't deter him from pulling his shirt off. His hands make work of his pants, unbuckling the belt and unzipping them, the sound seeming to echo through the quiet room.

It makes my heart race faster than before, so frenzied my vision blurs when he pulls them off along with his boxers, leaving him just as naked as I am.

I can't look.

I can't look.

I can't help it.

I look.

I have to.

He pries my legs apart and moves to the space between them. My eyes are drawn down his broad chest, following the trail of shadowy hair along his toned stomach, straight to his cock. My eyes widened when I catch sight of it.

He plans to fit that thing inside of me?

I only get a brief glimpse, a murky silhouette in the darkness as he grasps ahold of his cock and strokes it, before I feel it pressing against me. My eyes drift closed as he rubs the head of it against my clit, sending those tiny jolts of electricity through me.

"I'll take it easy on you," he says as he pushes inside of me for the first time, moving slowly, covering my body with his.

Don't, a part of me screams, the animal inside trying to claw its way out, but I swallow the word down, almost terrified to verbalize it. I don't know what he means, and I'm already in way, way over my head as it is. I feel like a virgin all over again, except I wasn't nearly as nervous back then. I was just handing over my body then, letting them caress my skin, but I have a feeling this man's planning to go much deeper than that with me.

He pulls out before pushing back in again, moving agonizingly slow, letting my body adjust, but I don't think that's possible. I don't think I can ever get used to him.

"If you want me to stop, just tell me," he says, "and I will."

"Should we..." My voice is a strained whisper. "I mean, should I have a safe word or something?"

I've watched movies, I've read books, and I'm not sure how kinky this man gets.

He stalls mid-thrust, pulling back to look at me, his eyebrow curving. I can see the twinkle in his eyes, amusement, the monster intrigued by my question. "Do you want one?"

"I, uh... do I need one?"

He seems to consider that for a moment, halfway inside of me, before shaking his head and pushing into me, a little harder this time, making my breath hitch.

"Not this time," he says, fighting off a smile. "Just relax, Karissa."

I try.

Dammit, I try.

But as soon as I start to relax, Naz finds his rhythm, hiking my legs up to fill me deeply. I gasp, my hands running through his hair, the slight curls surprisingly soft, as he leans down to kiss me. With his lips on mine, he thrusts hard, so hard he nearly knocks the breath from my lungs. Unnatural noises escape my throat that he greedily swallows with his kiss, increasing his pace, eliciting more of the sounds from me.

Again.

And again.

And again.

I suspected it, from his earlier question, but it isn't until he's inside of me, pounding against me, his arms wrapped around me, holding me so tightly I can hardly breathe, fucking me so hard I can barely think, that I realize just how much I've been missing. Everything before this moment was child's play, but this man is the major league.

He fucks me like he means it, like he needs it, like being inside of me is more important than anything inside of him, and every cell in my body calls out to him, craving more of it. His hands work magic on my skin, slipping between us to stroke my clit. The mere touch sends sparks through me. He rubs circles around it, as my body grows taut. I can feel it, building and building, the pressure filling me up until I'm about to burst.

The pleasure explodes inside of me, unlike anything I've ever experienced before. I squeeze my eyes shut. It's like fireworks all around me when all I've ever seen before were measly sparklers. I cry out, arching my back, my breasts flush against his chest. I can feel myself convulsing around him, squeezing his cock for a second before it's gone. He pulls out, pulls away from me just as I start to come. I'm momentarily stunned by the absence of everything—I feel nothing but coldness, air all around me. No warmth. No him.

No nothing.

My orgasm fades away as soon as it hits, the fireworks a dud that fizzle and fade into the night sky.

Oh, God. No. No. No. Don't do this to me.

My eyes snap open as the bed shifts, and I barely have time to glance over when he pushes my legs apart wider, his tongue softly grazing my clit.

Oh, God. Wait. Yes. Yes. Yes.

He licks and sucks, pumping his fingers inside of me, his head between my thighs. Gasping, I run my hands through his hair, grasping ahold of the locks, as I shudder. It takes a few seconds for the fading pleasure to sweep back through me, somehow even more intense, swaddling my entire body in heat.

Orgasm rocks me, and I let out a shriek, arching my back as I convulse. He doesn't let up, doesn't stop, his tongue running circles around my clit before he sucks on it, his fingers deep inside of me.

I relax back into the bed, panting when the sensation subsides, but I don't have time to catch my breath. He's inside of me again, thrusting deep, as his lips find mine. I don't even think about it, don't hesitate, kissing him deeply as he laughs against my mouth.

"You like that?" he asks, his voice strained, like he can't quite catch his breath. "Can you taste yourself?"

I'm embarrassed for a second, long enough for my face to heat, as he kisses me again, and again. I can taste myself, but I don't have a chance to dwell on it, because he's fucking me just as frenzied as before. His hips slam into mine, noises escaping my throat that he continues to smother with his kiss. I can feel his breath coming out in pants as he thrusts mercilessly, desperately.

And then he's off of me again, pulling out. This time he sits back on his knees and grasps his cock, stroking it as he tilts his head back, eyes closed. I stare at him in the moonlight, stunned by the sight of him coming, a mix of agony and pleasure seeming to twist his features as he grunts. He slows his strokes, stilling his hand, and just sits there, his chest falling and rising as he breathes deeply.

It's beautiful.

I don't know how else to describe it.

Naz is a work of art, confident in every aspect, and it's certainly warranted. I just lay there, my body made of jelly, while he towers above me like fortified steel. I'm suddenly weak and helpless, oh-so-vulnerable and at his mercy, at his *disposal*, and he's not dented even the slightest bit.

I'm fucked.

Literally.

Figuratively.

The man has fucked me in every sense of the word.

I'm no longer a charity case.

I'm a glorified prostitute.

The alcohol is fading from my system. I'm sweaty, and sticky, an ache between my thighs intensifying as clarity seeps in. Every cell in my body yearned for this earlier, yearned for him, except for the ones in my head.

Stupid brain cells.

They'd been lost in a champagne-induced haze, but now they want to come back around and throw a wrench in my moment with their damn common sense.

Anxiety fuels a touch of sickness, sickness that I fight to swallow down, but it burns the back of my throat, the coppery bitter tang on my tongue like I'd stuck it to the end of a battery.

Acid. Pure acid. I want to purge it from my system.

It's late, well after midnight, I assume. I'm not sure. Apart from having no bathroom in here, Naz also has no damn clocks. I feel like I've been lying in his bed for hours, too edgy to sleep, tangled up in his sheets. He's beside me, but not touching me, no more than six inches of space separating our naked bodies, but the man suddenly feels miles away.

I'm agonizing over what to do, what to think, replaying every moment I've spent with Naz, when a peculiar ring echoes through the room. It's muffled, a series of beeps that sounds almost like Morse code. At once, Naz slips away, climbing out of bed and rifling through his pants on the floor. He pulls out his phone, giving a brief glance at the screen before answering with a curt, "Hello."

He heads toward the door as whoever's on the line addresses him, and lets out a deep sigh as he steps into the hallway. "No, I haven't gotten it yet, but I'm on it."

I hear no more, unable to make out his words as he strolls along the hallway in the dark, away from my range of hearing. Not like I'm trying to eavesdrop or anything. But he returns after a moment, slipping back into the bedroom, and haphazardly tosses his phone back down on his pile of clothes.

The bed shifts as he climbs in beside me. His hands seek me out this time, wrapping around me, pulling me back against him. Once again, his strength astounds me as he tugs me into his arms like I'm made of nothing. I feel almost like a rag doll being manhandled.

Sweeping my hair aside, he kisses the side of my neck, something about it easing my nervousness. I feel safe, strangely enough, like a caterpillar wrapping up in a cocoon, waiting to sprout wings.

"I'm surprised you're still awake," he says quietly. "Maybe I shouldn't have taken it so easy on you."

Despite myself, I smile at that. I can't fathom that being Naz when he's subdued. Unrestrained, the man would knock me into next week.

"What time is it?" I ask.

"Two o'clock."

Ugh. "I should probably go."

"Why?"

"Because it's late."

"So?"

"So..." So, I don't know. "I just thought..."

He hums in my ear, his hand slowly sliding down my torso to the ache between my legs. "Less thinking, more feeling."

Sighing, I close my eyes. He takes the words right from me. His hands caress my skin, stroking my clit, as he pins me against him. It only takes a few seconds for my breaths to come out as whimpers.

"That's it," he whispers. "Just feel it."

Feel it, I do... I feel it in all of me, the pressure building until I can't take it anymore. "Please. Don't stop."

"Whatever you want."

"Oh God, yes. Yes. Don't..." My breath hitches, my voice strained as I feel it sweep through me. "Stop."

"Stop?"

He stops.

He fucking *stops*.

"No, no, no," I chant, shifting my hips, desperate for the friction before it fades away. "*Don't* stop. Please."

He chuckles in my ear as his hand moves again, stroking me. His lips find my neck as my body tenses at the release of pleasure. I gasp, incoherent words seeping from my lips. A moment later the pleasure fades away as he stops, for real this time, his hand stilling, cupping the spot between my thighs.

"I like it when my woman knows what she wants," he says, his hand drifting up again, slowly moving along my chest, before reaching my face. I'm stunned by his words, even more shocked when his hand finds my mouth. His fingertips caress my bottom lip before his pointer finger brushes against my tongue. "I like it when she tastes like Heaven, too."

I shiver as he kisses along my neck and down my shoulder, pausing as he presses a kiss on my shoulder blade. His mouth lingers there as he pulls his hand away from my mouth.

"Stay," he says. "I'll take you home in the morning. I have to go that way, anyway."

"Okay," I whisper, but he doesn't wait for my answer. His hands leave my skin, the void sweeping over me as he pulls away, turning over in the bed to go to sleep.

If I'm not a glorified prostitute, I don't know what one is.

⌒⌒

Sleep evades me but I eventually catch it in my grasp. When I awaken, the bedroom is significantly lighter as sunlight streams through the windows. I again have no idea what time it is, but there's one thing I do know.

I'm alone.

Still aching, and yucky, and stark naked.

But alone.

Rubbing my eyes, I climb out of the bed and scrounge up my clothes from last night, still mixed in with his on the floor. I put on my bra and slip on my panties before grabbing the dress. I turn it right side out, trying to situate it, when something on it catches my eye.

It's torn.

It looks like his hands ripped right through it, the weaving fabric loose and pillaging around the hem.

I stare at it, horrified. "Oh God."

"Is there a problem?"

The voice startles me so much I jump, yelping, and nearly drop the dress. Turning to the doorway, I see Naz standing there, his dark hair damp, beads of water running down his bare chest. The sudden urge to lick them strikes me.

Ugh, down, hormones.

He's wearing nothing but a pair of black boxer briefs, fresh out of the shower. I'm momentarily stunned speechless as I survey him, getting my first good look at him out of his suit. He's just as gorgeous now, but there's more to him, noticeable things, things I couldn't see last night. He's covered in old wounds, battle scars, gashes that shine silvery in the light and disappear in the darkness, like whispered secrets.

It's not off-putting, but it is a bit unnerving. I wonder what this man has gone through. He looks like he's been to war.

"Problem?" he asks again when I say nothing, his voice a little louder, drawing my attention from his chest.

"Yeah," I mumble, pulling the dress on, acutely aware thanks to my soberness that my panties are *definitely* not sexy. "My clothes kind of got torn last night."

His eyes scan me, settling on the rip as I point it out to him. "Didn't mean to ruin your dress."

"My roommate's dress, technically," I say, running my fingers through my hair, pulling myself together. "I borrowed it from her closet."

"Ah, well, I'll make it up to her."

"How?"

He shrugs a shoulder, pushing away from the doorway to stroll closer. "Somehow."

Stepping past me, he heads to his closet. It's filled with clothes, a lot more than just black suits, but unsurprisingly that's what he grabs. I watch him, mesmerized by the ease in which he pulls himself together.

Much to my amusement, his hair dries quickly, lying perfectly without him even needing to touch it. Lucky bastard.

He turns to me as he finishes, fiddling with his dark tie, securing the knot. "Why are you wearing your roommate's dress, anyway?"

I glance down at it. "Because it looks good."

"It does," he says, "but what's wrong with your clothes?"

"Nothing, but you were taking me out to dinner, so I needed something to wear for that."

"You don't own anything you can eat in?"

"Nothing I can eat a twelve hundred dollar meal in."

He nods, grabbing his suit coat from the hanger. "But you didn't know I was taking you somewhere like that."

"Maybe I did... maybe I'm good at reading people, too."

"You didn't." He smirks as he shakes his head, as if reacting to a joke only he's in on. He lets out a chuckle, the sound making me feel like maybe I'm the punch line of it. "And you're terrible at reading people, Karissa. *Terrible*."

He puts on his coat, buttoning it, before turning to me again.

"You look beautiful in it, though," he says. "I'm glad you wore it."

"I, uh... thanks." Anarchy reigns inside of me as I swallow thickly. He called me beautiful. I suddenly feel like a young girl, blushing at the compliment. "I just wanted to look nice."

"Why?"

Why? What kind of a question is that?

The words 'because of dinner' are on the tip of my tongue, but they don't taste right. They have the tang of a bitter lie, only slightly

MONSTER IN HIS EYES

seasoned to hide what's beneath. It wasn't dinner I wanted to look nice for.

It was him.

I don't respond, but from the look on his face, it's obvious he knows the answer.

Is there anything this man doesn't know?

He steps toward me, reaching out and gently rubbing my bicep. "Well, like I said, you look beautiful. Pity it's ruined, but I'll replace it."

"You don't have to do that," I say. "I don't even know where she got it, or how long she's had it… or if she even remembers she owns it, honestly."

He struts past, not acknowledging my rebuttal, as he heads for the door. "Come on, I'll take you home now. I'm due in the city soon."

He walks out, leaving me standing there. I slip on my boots, glancing around to make sure I haven't forgotten anything, before heading after him. He already has his keys, the front door hanging wide open with him standing there, waiting.

The drive into Manhattan is awkward. I want to jump out of my own skin. I don't know what to say, or what to think, or what to do about any of this, and he's giving me no indication of where his mind is.

What are we even doing here?

This man bulldozed his way into my world, razing everything I always thought, or felt, or believed, leaving me with wreckage to try to piece back together. It's like I stepped out into the sunlight for the first time, and he is driving me right back into the shadows.

Am I ever going to feel the sunshine again?

I don't want it to be over, but the question remains: what the hell is it?

"Are you okay?" Naz asks when he pulls onto the street leading to my dorm.

"I'm fine," I respond, forcing a smile. "Why?"

"You look upset."

"No, I'm just... thinking."

"Huh."

He says nothing else. Huh. That's it.

What the fuck is 'huh' supposed to mean?

My stomach is in knots when he passes my building and once again pulls into the entrance of the parking garage. I'm reaching for the door before we even come to a complete stop, figuring it's best to just be put out of my misery, when he reaches over and grabs ahold of my wrist. It's not painful, but his grip is firm, locking me there.

"What did I say about thinking so much?"

I stare at him. Less thinking, more feeling. "I know, but I can't help it. I just... I don't know what to think."

Because that makes sense, Karissa.

"Then don't," he says. "Don't think about it. Just enjoy it for what it is."

"What is it?"

He shrugs.

That's it.

He shrugs.

His grip loosens even more, his fingers slipping from my skin as he pulls away, the hand coming to rest on the gearshift again.

I take that as my cue to leave.

Opening the door, I climb out, slamming it behind me. I take a few steps away from the car when I hear the window rolling down, his voice calling out. "Karissa."

My footsteps falter as I close my eyes. He's just fucking with me at this point. He has to be. I turn around, knowing damn well I haven't forgotten my phone this time, considering I hadn't even remembered to bring the damn thing. "Yeah?"

"Dinner tonight?" he asks.

I stare at him. "What?"

"Dinner," he says. "Eight thirty good for you?"

My eyes widen as I say it again. "What?"

Amusement touches his lips, but he doesn't respond, instead putting the car in reverse and backing away. I watch as the car disappears in traffic, dumbfounded.

Is this man serious?

Chapter Five

My mother left half a dozen messages overnight. I call her back, not wanting her to worry, only vaguely listening as she babbles about the flower shop. I hang up as quickly as I can without upsetting her and toss my phone down, glancing at the clock.

It's barely noon.

That means I have eight and a half hours to agonize, to convince myself this is real, that it isn't a figment of my imagination.

Eight and a half hours to gather some courage.

Eight and a half hours to find something to wear.

They're the longest eight and a half hours of my life.

I shower and get ready, having the time today to fix my hair and put on makeup. I stress over clothes again, settling on a pair of pink skinny jeans and a black loose-fitting top. It's not fancy, but it's at least mine this time. Not fit for a twelve hundred dollar meal, but maybe half of that.

Or half of a half.

I continually glance in the mirror as I pace the room, watching the clock and waiting, not wanting to go downstairs too early, but not wanting to be late. By the time eight thirty arrives, I'm little more than a bundle of frazzled nerves, convinced I'm not even fit for a fast food extra value meal.

Pushing back the swell of anxiety, I make sure to remember my phone this time as I head out. My heart hammers hard as I ride the elevator, taking a deep breath when I reach the lobby.

I'm walking with my head down as I turn the corner to the parking garage, expecting to see the Mercedes, but pause when it's not there. Instead, leaning against the painted brick wall in front of me, stands Naz, hands in his pockets, stance relaxed.

I blink a few times, caught off guard. "Uh, hey."

"Hello," he says, pushing away from the wall to stroll toward me.

"Are we still, uh... having dinner?"

"I certainly hope so," he says. "I'm hungry, and I distinctly remember being promised you'd cook for me yesterday."

I laugh as those words strike me, but my amusement dies a harsh death when I notice his serious expression. "You're kidding."

"Do I look like I'm kidding?"

No, he doesn't. I think back, begrudgingly admitting that his words had been he'd be back for dinner, not that he was taking me anywhere. I feel oddly manipulated, but it's my fault for misinterpreting. "Your house then?"

"We went there last night," he says. "Besides, forgive me if I'm wrong, but you have the noodles. So I figure, since we're already here..."

He points toward the dorms.

He wants to go upstairs?

My first instinct is to refuse, but I'm too thrown off to make up any excuses. Besides, I suspect they'll fall on deaf ears. Something tells me he'll talk his way inside eventually.

I motion behind me, stepping aside. "After you."

Somehow I'm more nervous now than I was a moment ago, as I lead Naz into the old dorms. This is my territory, my home... or as close to a home as I get. But yet I feel out of place, a stranger in my own skin, like I'm invading my own privacy by inviting him in.

Naz, on the other hand, looks at ease. There's nothing more intimidating than a man whose feathers aren't ruffled by anything. We step into the elevator and he leans back against the side, watching as I press the number thirteen button.

"Thirteenth floor," he muses. "Good thing you're not superstitious."

"Right? Especially since I stay in the thirteenth room, too."

He says nothing else as we ride upstairs, but he laughs when we reach my room tucked in the corner at the end of the hall: 1313. I pull out my key and unlock the door, pushing it open for him to step inside.

It's a goddamn disaster.

"This is nice," he says, glancing around as he pauses a few feet inside the door. He sounds genuine, but I can't imagine Mr. Fit for a King would find anything nice about a glorified walk-in closet with two little beds.

"It's tiny," I say.

He shakes his head. "It's just cozy."

"What it is is a freaking mess."

"Yeah, I won't argue that one." He glances between my side of the room and Melody's, like he's comparing and contrasting. He doesn't wait for me to tell him which is mine. Within seconds, he steps onto my side, his eyes sweeping along my things.

I just stand by the door, wringing my hands together. I don't have much, but what I have is important to me. We had sex last night, and as nervous as I'd been to have him inside of me, it's nothing compared to this. This is him getting a glimpse of what's beneath my skin.

What if he doesn't find it beautiful?

"You can have a seat or whatever you want," I mumble. "Make yourself at home, I guess."

He cocks an eyebrow. "You guess?"

"Yeah, well, I mean, I don't know what we're doing here or what you really want or..." Or what I'm saying. He has me frazzled. "I repaid you last night, you know... repaid you for everything, like you said about, but..."

"But?"

"But... I don't know."

"You don't know what to think."

I nod.

He lets out a laugh of disbelief as he steps toward me. "Is that all that was to you, Karissa? Compensation? Some sort of thank you gift? Placating me, throwing me a bone, because you thought you owed me? You felt indebted to me?"

I open my mouth to respond—to say what, I don't know—but he doesn't let me speak. He holds his hand up, resting his pointer finger against my lips. He's gentle about it, barely touches me with his fingertip, but the action silences me before I even begin.

"Because if that's all it was to you, I'll go," he continues. "I'll walk out the door right now. I don't fuck women because they owe me... I do it because I want to, because I need to, because they need me. And I don't mean that in an underhanded I bought dinner so you get naked sort of way, bartering favors like this is *Basic Instinct*. I'm not paying to get repaid, to get you in my bed. But if that's all this feels like to you, some sort of twisted business arrangement you're obligated to proceed with, I'll leave."

"Don't," I say quickly as he turns away. "Don't leave. I just, I don't know."

"Don't know what?"

"Why?"

"Why what?"

"Why me?"

He stares at me for a moment. "Why not you?"

His response doesn't answer my question, but it quells some of my anxiety, like maybe he can't see the flaws I see. Maybe what I see in the mirror, the girl my mother raised in little houses, isolated and overprotected, isn't the same woman he's looking at. Maybe one of us isn't seeing me clearly here, and maybe it's him...

Or maybe it's me.

"So you want noodles?" I ask, shifting the subject. "Like, honestly want me to make them?"

"I do," he says.

Sighing, I step over to the cabinet Melody and I share, opening it up to glance at the food. There isn't much. It's been weeks since either of us went shopping. "What flavor?"

"Whatever flavor a noodle is."

"They come in different flavors." I hold up a few packages, showing him. "Beef, chicken, shrimp…"

He grimaces. "Give me whatever your favorite is."

I grab the pink package. Shrimp.

I lead him out of my room and to the small kitchen. My pot from yesterday is still on the stove, still filled with water, the abandoned package of noodles on the counter. I discard it, rinsing out the pot and filling it with fresh water before setting it back on the stove to boil.

There's nothing in here except for an old stove and a sink and a mostly empty refrigerator, a few pots and pans in the cabinets that have been collectively donated. I wait for him to comment on it but he doesn't, instead leaning back against the counter and crossing his arms over his chest.

I can feel him watching as I wait for the water to boil, feel his eyes glued to me as mine are glued to the pot. I know the saying—a watched pot won't boil—but I can't seem to look anywhere except for at it. As soon as it starts bubbling, I toss the noodles in, feeling silly as I clear my throat. Am I seriously doing this? "We just have to boil the noodles for a few minutes."

"Huh." He pushes away from the counter and steps behind me, so close I can feel his breath on my skin, as he peers over my shoulder

73

at the pot. "And where does the flavor come from?"

"This," I say, holding up the square silver packet of seasoning.

He takes it from me. "And why does it look like a condom?"

"Good question," I say, stirring the noodles. "I don't know."

"So what's in this?" he asks, flipping it over, surveying the outside, but it says nothing except 'shrimp flavor'. "Do you at least know that?"

"A hell of a lot of sodium. About as much MSG."

He glances between the package and me. "Now I think *you* might be trying to poison me."

"A little salt won't kill you."

"I'm an old man, Karissa. It might."

"You're not that old," I say, turning to face him, seeing the amusement crinkling his eyes. "I mean, yeah, you're older, but you're not old. It's not like you're entitled to a senior citizen discount. You're barely old enough to be my father."

As soon as I say it, his expression shifts. It's like he's been doused in gasoline, washing away every bit of humor as fire sparks inside of him. I can see it in his eyes, the bright blue hue darkening, as they narrow, turning cloudy and murky, like a storm is waging. My muscles grow taut as he takes a sudden step toward me. I instinctively want to step back, but I can already feel the heat from the stove creeping up my spine.

I don't want to get burned.

"Your father?" he asks, his voice low. "Is that what you see when you look at me?"

"What? No, of course not." I grimace, realizing how that must've sounded. *Gross.* "I'm just saying, you know, you're twice my age... not that it's a bad thing. You're just... a little older."

I stare into those eyes, cursing myself for upsetting him. He says nothing, just staring back, his expression as hard as stone. Seconds pass, seconds that feel like they last a lifetime, before movement in the doorway catches my attention.

74

I look over just as a girl struts in... I vaguely recognize her from encounters in the hallway, brief trips in the elevator, but I don't recall ever talking to her before. She glances up, a can of soup in her hand, and lets out a gasp of surprise when she sees us. "Shit, sorry, I didn't think anyone was here."

My stomach clenches from nerves, my heart hammering hard in my chest. I feel like I've been caught in a compromising position, like this girl has just walked in on something she shouldn't have seen, that she knows things now she shouldn't know about me. It's silly, but after spending my entire life having my mother drill the concept of privacy and propriety into me, I feel exposed, his proximity so intoxicating it's like I've just been caught with a needle in my arm.

He's a drug, an addictive one, and I'm not sure it's a habit I can kick. All it took was one hit. One strong, euphoric hit and I was hooked.

Naz just stands there, in front of me, not reacting for a moment. The fire in his eyes fades, his stance relaxing.

"I'll just come back," the girl says. "Sorry."

She's gone before I can even think to tell her it's okay. What happened to my manners?

I turn away from Naz, glancing back at the stove, and switch off the noodles before they turn to mush. Sighing, I grab the seasoning packet as he holds it out to me.

"Are you mad?" I ask him as I stir the seasoning into the pot. He's being too quiet. I worry I've offended him.

"No," he says quietly. "I'm just wondering if me being here is wrong."

"I'm allowed to have guests," I reply. Granted, I'm supposed to have him show ID in the lobby and sign in, but still... him being here isn't wrong.

"That's not what I meant."

I grab two bowls and divide the noodles before turning to him. All that anger is gone, but he seems genuinely conflicted. "Does it bother you that I'm so young?"

75

He looks at me incredulously. "If it did, I wouldn't be here."

"Okay, then," I say. "There's nothing wrong."

He doesn't look reassured, but he doesn't press the issue. After doing a quick clean up job, we vacate the kitchen and head back to my room, bowls of noodles in hand. I hand him a plastic fork before grabbing one for myself and sitting down on the edge of my bed. I expect him to sit beside me, or at least take a seat at the chair at my small desk, but instead he leans against my dresser, towering above me.

I take a few bites, too starving to ignore my food, while he mostly stirs his noodles around with the fork. I watch him as I eat, smiling to myself when he takes his first bite. It's small, and tentative, his nose scrunching up as he chews and swallows. His eyes are focused in the bowl as he takes another bite, forcing it down.

He doesn't eat anymore.

After stirring his noodles for a few more minutes, giving me time to eat, he sets his bowl on the dresser behind him as his eyes seek me out.

He steps over to me and takes the empty bowl from my hand, setting it on the desk. Grasping my chin, he pulls my face up so I'll look at him. His thumb brushes across my bottom lip, and he's quiet for a minute before whispering, "Only a fool would be bothered by being with you."

Those words make my heart skip a beat. I exhale shakily as he leans down and kisses me, softly and sweetly, over and over again. He pulls back after a moment, still holding me in place, but I'm not ready for the moment to end. Instinctively, my hand moves to his head, fingers running through his hair, as I force him right back to me. He chuckles, not fighting it, and kisses me deeper.

Soft and sweet turns firm and frenzied, the once feather light kisses now brutalizing my lips. I'm not sure which way I prefer it. One way makes my heart flutter; the other sets my chest aflame.

Needing air, I pull away for only a second to take a deep breath, my eyes opening. I look up at him, seeing a smirk touching his lips, when his voice rings out. "Are your neighbors home?"

"Uh, no. Well, except for that girl we saw, but she's on the other side of the hall."

"Good."

"Why?" I ask as he kisses me again.

"Because," he says, "I want to make sure nobody will hear you."

A chill tears down my spine. I'm shivering from it when he pounces, forcing me back onto a pile of discarded clean clothes I left on my bed, his body covering mine. His kisses steal the air from my lungs as his hardness presses against me.

His hands are rough as they tear at my clothes. I'll be lucky if he doesn't rip these, too. He strips me, flinging material around, pulling his own off just as hastily. Grasping me around the waist, he yanks me back onto the small bed, not giving me any time to adjust when he settles between my thighs and pushes inside.

The thrust is so hard, so deep, that pain stabs my stomach. It feels like I've been impaled. I gasp, clawing his back, my nails digging into his skin. He pauses when I cry out but only stills for a few seconds before thrusting again.

And again.

And again.

It doesn't hurt as much as the first, but it isn't gentle, not in the least. His body is heavy, his grip strong, his hands rough as they fondle my flesh. He's smothering me, covering me, as I feel nothing, see nothing, live nothing except for him, existing only in the moment as he buries himself inside of me. I barely even register that the light is on anymore. The man is a wrecking ball, pounding me, and I come to pieces almost instantly.

He pulls out to finish, coming near my navel, just inches from where I yearn for him to stay.

"I'm on the pill." The words are strained as they come from my lips. I'm breathing heavily. My heart is racing. He's sitting back on his knees, and I suddenly feel exposed. "I've been on it for a while."

He stares down at me, nodding once in acknowledgement as he grips his cock, stroking it. My eyes are drawn down to it, and I'm mesmerized, watching him touch himself. My fingertips tingle with the urge to reach out and touch him, to feel him, to give him the pleasure he's giving himself, but I don't get the chance.

In a blink, he's back between my legs, slowly pushing inside of me again. My eyes flutter closed as he once more covers my body with his, picking right back up where he left off moments ago.

He goes longer this time, every few thrusts bordering on ruthless, that agony stabbing me again and again. I let out small yelps, unable to help myself, strangled cries of pleasurable pain echoing through the room. It seems to do something to him, rousing something inside of Naz. Every time I cry out, he lets out a throaty groan, the sound prickling my skin.

He's enjoying it.

He pulls out again when he's done. I don't know if it's intentional, or if it's instinctual, but he comes on my stomach instead of inside of me.

My body is a ball of tingles, my legs weak, like he's knocked the bones right out of me. Naz wraps his arms around me as he shifts us around in the bed, squeezing in behind me. There isn't room for him to move away from me here, not enough space to feel any distance between us. It doesn't seem to bother him, though, as he nuzzles into my neck, his hand resting on my bare stomach.

And just like that, I go to sleep.

∞

The room is dark when I come around much later, the light turned off at some point while I was asleep. I'm still naked, but a blanket covers me... one I rarely use... one that's kept stored in the cabinet.

The bed feels empty, no body beside mine. I instantly feel the void. I sit up, clutching the blanket around me, and jump when I catch sight of the form in the shadows.

Naz is still here.

He's standing in front of my dresser, fully dressed, holding a picture frame he picked up from it. It's a photo of my mother and me the day I graduated high school. It's hard to believe it was less than a year ago.

His head turns my way as he sets the frame back down on the dresser. "You're awake."

"You are, too," I say. "What are you doing?"

"What I shouldn't."

"What's that?"

"Thinking."

I laugh lightly, wrapping the blanket tighter around me as I survey his face in the darkness. "What are you thinking?"

"I'm thinking that I like you, and that's a problem for me."

His serious tone startles me. "Why's it a problem?"

"Because I don't like people," he says bluntly. "I deal with people. That's what I do. But rarely do I particularly like anyone... like them enough to want to deal with them in ways that aren't work to me."

"I don't get why that's a problem."

"Because I wasn't supposed to like you, Karissa."

I'm baffled, unsure what to make of that. "When you say you like me, you mean...?"

"I like you," he says again, as if that answers my question. He pauses for a moment, glancing back at the frame on my dresser. "There's something about you... something I've sought for a very long time. Something I've always wanted. And now that I've found it, I don't know if I can let it go."

"Then don't," I say.

"You don't know what you're asking," he responds. "I'm not a man who just gives up in the middle of something. If I go any further, if I don't walk away now, I won't be able to."

79

"I don't want you to walk away," I say. "I like you, too."

"You don't even know me."

His voice has a hint of anger behind it, a bit of bitterness that makes my stomach knot.

"You don't know me either," I say. "You don't even know my favorite color."

"Pink," he says. "You've had on something pink every time I've seen you... your phone case is pink... so are your sheets."

Maybe that was too easy. "My favorite food."

"You'd probably say Ramen. You accept what you think you deserve, but you deserve so much more, whether you admit it or not. You want to indulge. You like to give in to cravings. That's why your real favorite is chocolate."

"What kind of chocolate?"

"Whatever kind of chocolate you can get your hands on."

Okay, he's right... I do like chocolate. "How about my favorite movie?"

"Peter Pan."

He answers without an ounce of hesitation. I just stare at him, stunned. "How can you possibly know that?"

"Easily. You still see yourself as a child, and not an adult, like you believe you'll never grow up." He pauses, eyeing me peculiarly. "Not to mention you let a strange guy whisk you away with promises of magic, and he had you floating on cloud 9 all night long."

"I, uh..." What the fuck? "How...?"

Before I can get out a coherent thought, he laughs and continues. "You have a copy of the cartoon on your shelf. There's a Tinker Bell poster beside your bed. It wasn't a hard guess."

I feel silly and am immediately grateful the room is so dark so he can't see my blush. "Well what about my—"

"It doesn't matter." He cuts me off as he steps forward, closer to the bed. "We could play this game all night long, Karissa, but those things mean nothing. My favorite color's black, my favorite food is steak, and if I had to pick a movie, it would be *Twelve Angry Men*, but that doesn't tell you who I am."

"Who are you then?"

He takes another step forward, so close that I can see the blue in his eyes now. He stares down at me on the bed, his expression serious. "Someone you should stay far away from."

Those words make me tremble. I believe it—he has a way of making someone believe whatever he says—but still, they don't stop the traitorous feelings inside of me. Maybe I should stay away from him, but I don't want to.

I don't think I can.

Instead of responding, I reach out toward him, running my hand along his thigh. The yearning to touch him still lingers in me. His reflex is startling fast as he snatches ahold of my hand, stilling it on his leg, his grip strong.

"I'm telling you," he says, his voice strained. "I'm warning you. I'm not a good man, Karissa, and I never will be. So don't think you can fix me, or that I'll ever change, because I won't. I can't. You have to know, if this goes any further, if you ask me to stay, I'm not going to be able to let you walk away."

He lets go of my hand. I hesitate. It's only a few seconds— seconds of thinking, something I've spent my whole life doing, before I concede to feeling, the one thing that's brought me more pleasure than before. The seconds feel like an eternity as he stares down at me, our eyes locked, as if he's challenging me. He's waiting for my decision, waiting to hear the outcome, like I'm those twelve angry men with his life in my hands.

My hand, which inches up his thigh again and grazes over his crotch, delivering the final verdict—he's not condemned, but maybe I am.

His eyes drift closed, a soft sigh escaping his parted lips, and I know then, as I feel his cock through the material of his pants, hardening against my palm, that I signed on the dotted line. *I'm in.*

81

It's needless, but I say it anyway. "Stay."

His eyes reopen, a smirk tugging the corner of his lips. "Red."

My eyes widen. "What?"

"If you ever need me to stop, you just say red."

"Red," I whisper, goose bumps coating my arms.

His smile fades at the sound of it. "Don't say it unless you mean it. If you just need me to back off, to slow down, to take it easier on you, say yellow. It works like a stoplight. Understand?"

I nod, my heart in my throat. I'm not scared, but damn if he doesn't have me a bit nervous. He actually gave me safe words. "You're not going to, like, beat me, are you?"

"No," he says right away, his voice sharp. "I'll never hit you. And I'll never hurt you, unless you want me to."

I can't imagine ever wanting that, but the ache between my thighs, the memory of the way he hurt earlier, when he was inside of me, sends a differing chill down my spine.

"They're just in case," he says. "In case I get too rough, in case I lose myself and you've had enough. Better safe than sorry, right?"

"Right," I mumble, reaching for his zipper. I start to tug it down when he grabs my hand again, laughing as he pulls away.

"Not tonight," he says as he holds on to my hand. "I need to go."

My brow furrows. "You're leaving?"

"Yes," he says. "I have work to do."

My gaze shifts to my alarm clock. One o'clock in the morning. "Now?"

"Yes," he says again, lifting my hand and placing a light kiss on the back of it. He follows it up with a quick peck on my lips before letting go and turning away.

He says nothing else.

I stare, watching incredulously as he disappears out the door.

Chapter Six

Days pass.

Days of nothing.

The soreness from our encounter fades from my body as another ache seeps in—the ache of not feeling his touch in days. It's a double-edge sword, a strange sensation I've never dealt with before.

I feel so empty.

It's crazy. I know.

I'm crazy.

He's driving me insane.

Naz steamrolled into my life and then strolled right back out in the middle of the night, offering me nothing more than a sweet goodbye kiss.

I don't know what to do about it.

I don't know what to do with myself.

I spend the days alternating between hiding out in my room and venturing out into the city, slipping back into my world of solitude and cheap food.

And I wallow.

I wallow.

Ugh, I'm pathetic.

This isn't me. I don't fall apart over guys. I don't mope, and stress, and wallow.

So why am I doing it?

After glancing at my phone for probably the hundredth time, waiting for the bastard to ring, I toss it aside with a groan. I could call him; I *should* call him. But I keep waiting for him to call me. I'm becoming one of those girls.

I'm turning into Melody.

Speaking of Melody, she comes back tomorrow, and I haven't heard from her once. I know she's busy, on vacation with the friends she's known for years, so I'm not surprised, but it admittedly hurts to realize I'm so alone.

I don't just mean that because everyone's vacated the premises. I mean it in the 'I could go missing and I'm not sure anyone would notice' kind of way.

A shrill ring echoes through the room. I snatch it up, my heart stilling those few seconds before I glance at the screen. Please be Naz. Please be Naz. Please be Naz.

It's Mom.

Scratch that. Someone would notice.

She would.

Sighing, I drop down onto my bed as I answer it. "Hey, Mom."

"Hey, Kissimmee! How are you?"

"Good. You?"

She sounds good, confirming it when she launches into stories from Watertown, gossiping about the people around town. I only vaguely remember most of them but I listen and occasionally chime in. I worried about leaving her all alone when I moved to the city, but she seems to be doing well.

Dare I say better than even me today?

"Are you sure you're okay, sweetie?" she says after a moment. "You're awfully quiet."

"Yeah, I'm fine. Just... bored."

And lonely.

And kind of hungry.

I'm a mess.

"You should've visited this week," she says. "We could've spent some time together."

"I know... I'll see you soon, though."

"Can't wait," she says. "Anyway, I should get going. I'll call you later, okay?"

We hang up. I toss my phone down, waiting for it to ring again. It doesn't.

I eventually head downstairs, grabbing something to eat from the dining hall while it's open. It's slim pickings, a few scraggly students hanging around from the building. The sun is still shining when I come back upstairs. I crack open my philosophy textbook, trying to get ahead on it, but end up falling asleep with the book on my chest.

I'm awakened much later by a noise. The room is encased in darkness, a soft glow swaddling my desk beside the bed. My phone. Reaching over, I pick it up and glance at the screen as it rings.

Naz.

I answer tentatively. "Hello?"

"You looked beautiful today."

No hello. No greeting at all. I'm stunned. Beautiful? Where did that come from?

My eyes are drawn down to myself. I haven't even changed out of my old ratty pajamas in what I think might be two days. "How do you know?"

"I saw you."

My stomach is in knots. He saw me? "Where?"

"In my dreams."

The moment he says it, a smile lights up my face. "Are you just fucking with me?"

85

"No, but I'd like to be fucking you."

I laugh sharply. My body heats at those words. How does he do that, his responses so slick, so quick?

"I do know you looked beautiful today, though," he says. "I wasn't lying."

"How?"

"Because you always are."

I'm not sure how to respond to that. I start stammering. Thirty seconds on the phone and I've turned into a blubbering fool because of this man.

He laughs, genuinely amused. "Goodnight, Karissa."

Before I can respond, he hangs up. I stare at the phone, biting my bottom lip, as I whisper, "goodnight," into the quiet room.

As silly as it is, I feel a bit better.

At least he hasn't forgotten about me.

⁓❧⁓

Sunday afternoon drags, each minute like an hour, each hour damn near another whole day. The dorm comes alive mid-afternoon as people filter back in. I can hear our suite mates through the thin walls, returning from wherever they headed off to.

I don't know.

Don't really care, either.

I'm a terrible neighbor.

I'm sitting in my bed, knees pulled up, staring down at the book propped up against my legs, when the door flings open. Melody walks in, hauling her bags along, and lets out a groan in lieu of a greeting. I glance up as she discards her things by the door to collapse in her bed.

"Oh God, I'm exhausted!" she says.

"You look refreshed," I point out. In fact, she looks different, a sun kissed glow to her. Her hair is almost platinum blonde, bleached from the sun's rays, while her skin is now a deep tan.

86

It's amazing how much someone can change in a week.

"Refreshed?" She rolls over onto her side to gaze at me. "I feel like I was beaten!"

"Were you?"

Valid question with Melody, one she answers with a sly grin. "A lady never tells."

Laughing, I close my book and set it aside. "Good thing you're not a lady then."

Melody sticks her tongue out before launching into it, relaying details from her trip. I thought I'd feel a twinge of jealousy, hearing all about her adventures, but I'm more amused than anything. Because nothing she says, no matter how exotic, tops my erotic.

You swam with dolphins? You went scuba diving? You sunbathed topless on a gorgeous beach? Well I ate at the finest restaurant in the city, drank thousand dollar champagne, and had my brains fucked out by the man of my dreams.

I should tell her. She's my friend, maybe my best friend, arguably my only friend... I should tell her about him. She's always telling me about her escapades, and rarely do I ever have anything to share in return.

I'm going to tell her.

I am.

I will.

"So what did you do this week?" she asks flippantly

Just not right now.

Maybe later.

"You know, little of this, little of that." A lot of that.

She scrunches her nose at my lame response and launches back into her stories. I'm vaguely listening, her week just short of something out of *Girls Gone Wild*, when she starts talking about someone named Paul.

"Who's Paul?" I ask, interrupting.

"Oh, you know Paul," she says, waving me off.

87

Paul Newman? Paul Bunyan? Peter, Paul, and Mary?

I don't know anybody named Paul.

"Refresh my memory."

Melody rolls her eyes, a slight flush to her cheeks as she rolls over onto her stomach on her bed to stare at me across the room. "He's the guy from Timbers. Remember? Mr. Top Gun?"

"I thought he was a Pat," I say, "or a Pete."

"Yeah, so did I, but no... it's Paul. He's so great. He's just... he's everything. I've never met someone like him before."

My brow furrows. I'm not sure what he has to do with anything. "He didn't stay at your resort or something, did he?"

"What? No, of course not. That would be crazy if a guy just showed up wherever I was. Stalker-y."

Tell me about it.

"He called me, though," she continues. "I told him to after that night at Timbers, but I didn't really expect to hear from him. But he called, and we talked, and he's amazing. We have so much in common."

"That's great." He rubbed me the wrong way, and I don't trust him after the incident with the drink, but my warnings fell on deaf ears to her. She looks happy, and I guess that's what matters. "So you're going to see him again?"

"Abso-freakin'-lutely." Before I can question her anymore, her phone chimes. Melody is up off the bed, all traces of exhaustion gone as she darts for her luggage and rummages through it. She pulls out her phone, glancing at it, and squeals. "He sent me a text! It says: yo, sexy, you settled in? You hear that? He called me sexy!"

She laughs giddily as she throws herself back down on her bed, her attention fixed to her phone as she responds to him. My eyes drift from my roommate to my own phone, silent and still on the desk beside me.

I'll take beautiful over sexy any day.

MONSTER IN HIS EYES

"Happiness."

Santino stands at the front of the classroom, holding his favorite wooden pointer stick. It's long, and thick, arguably bigger than him, with a sharp metal tip like a dagger.

I think he's compensating for something.

He bangs it against the large chalkboard, hitting the word written in all capitals. HAPPINESS. I'm vaguely paying attention, my mind drifting, as Melody slouches in the chair beside me, doodling in the margins of her notebook. I peek her way, rolling my eyes when I see she's drawing hearts around Paul's name.

"Who wants to chime in and tell me what happiness means to them?" Santino asks, scanning the classroom for volunteers.

Hands shoot up, the do-gooders who would offer to shine the man's shoes if he hinted they were dirty, followed by a few other hesitant volunteers. The answers are expected from this bunch, a lot of idealistic bullshit tucked in with some materialism. A guy across the room shouts out something vulgar, making the class snicker, as Santino points his stick at him with disapproval.

"Getting the hell out of this class," Melody says under her breath. "That's my happiness."

"Tell me about it," I mutter. "Longest hour ever."

"Ah, Miss Reed," Santino says, swinging in our direction, his eyes meeting mine through the sea of students, like he has radar that's tuned directly to me. "Was that your voice I heard? Would you like to chime in with your answer?"

"Uh, true happiness is having a deep sense of well-being, and peace, and vitality," I say, remembering reading that in the material. "It's being grateful to be alive."

"That's true," he says, "but that's not what I asked you."

I'm momentarily caught off guard by his sharp response.

"You see, if I wanted the textbook definition, I would've read it," he continues, smacking the book on his desk with the stick. "The question was *your* definition. Pay attention next time instead of gossiping with Miss Carmichael."

"Sorry, sir."

He stares at me, raising his eyebrows. "Well? Your definition?"

"I, uh…" I can feel the gaze of my classmates burning through me, waiting. "I don't know."

"You don't know," he echoes. "You don't know what makes you happy?"

"Well, sure, but happiness isn't really a thing," I say. "It's a state of mind."

He doesn't look the least bit entertained. "A state of mind or a state of being?"

I hesitate before repeating myself. "A state of mind. It's just the way you look at things."

The corner of his lip twitches, but it's not with amusement. He looks like he might have a blood vessel burst if I keep speaking. "Do you pick up all of your philosophical insight from the realm of children's narrative, Miss Reed, or just your views on happiness?"

I blanch, hearing the wave of giggling flow through the room. I start to stammer out a response when he turns away, pointing back to the chalkboard, a sign that says he's done with my shit. "Albert Einstein said a table, a chair, a bowl of fruit, and a violin were happiness for him. Clearly, everyone defines it differently… those of us who can define it, anyway."

I slink down in my chair, embarrassed, as Melody leans toward me, whispering, "Please tell me you weren't quoting Seuss again."

"Walt Disney," I mutter as quietly as can be, but based on the way Santino's gaze darts to me again, I suspect he knew I was talking.

Class is over within minutes after that. I'm out of my seat as Santino shouts, "Two page paper exploring the concept of true happiness due on Thursday! I'll have your mid-terms graded then."

The class groans as we head for the door. Melody falls into step beside me, sighing as she slips her bag on. "You couldn't be normal and say orgasms, could you?"

I laugh, shaking my head. I couldn't say that, but of course, I wouldn't refute it. The mere mention of the word causes a tingle deep inside of me, the memory of the way Naz made my toes curl as I came for him.

That was undoubtedly happiness.

That was Heaven.

I could write the next great American novel about it.

"You know me," I say. "I like to keep things interesting."

"Yeah, well, you ought to be careful," she says. "You know he gets a kick out of torturing students. It's, like, foreplay to him, and if you keep it up, you might end up being the one getting fucked."

Seems to me I'm already on that path, and have been since the first day I stepped into his classroom. He'd gone down the roster, doing his first and only roll call, acknowledging each of us individually. Scare tactic, Melody said... nothing more terrifying than having Satan speak your name. He'd reached my name that day and hesitated, seeking me out. The others he simply nodded at before moving on, but he'd stared at me that afternoon like with one look he knew I didn't belong there.

We make our way to the dorm, strolling along in no rush, the ten-minute trip taking double that. As soon as we make it to our room, Melody flops down on her bed, while my eyes are drawn to the room phone, the little button on it blinking red. We never use it, only ever remembering it's there when the school calls the number to leave a message. I pick up the receiver and press the button to hear the automated message.

"Please come down to the building resource center this afternoon for a pickup. Thank you."

Sighing, I hang up the phone and turn for the door. "I'll be back."

"Where are you going?"

"There's a package or something waiting downstairs."

I head right back down to the lobby, waiting my turn at the resource center window to pickup whatever was left there. As soon as it's my turn, I step up to the woman working the desk and hold my school ID out to her. "I received a message to pick up something."

She punches it into her computer. "Ah, yes, 1313."

I lean back against the wall beside the window, waiting for her to retrieve the package, when she sets a sparkling vase filled with long-stemmed roses on the counter.

"Here you go," she says, smiling sweetly. "Karissa Reed."

My eyes widen as I stare at the flowers. They're in vibrant shades of pink, three dozen of them from what I can see. I'm thinking there has to be some sort of mistake, some sort of mix-up. "Are you sure these are for me?"

"Uh, yes," she says, double-checking. "Positive."

Slowly, I reach out and take the card from where it sticks out in the center of the arrangement. I pull it out of the small envelope and open it, seeing what's undeniably male scribble.

A dozen for every night you've spent with me.
-Naz

I'm stunned. I just stare at the card for a moment before glancing back at the roses. The lady at the desk is eyeing me cautiously, like she's afraid I may pick up the vase and chuck it at her head. I mumble my thanks, grabbing the vase to leave.

It's heavier than I expect.

I carry them upstairs, dazed, just smiling politely when a girl in the elevator comments on them. When I reach the room, Melody is standing in front of her bed, holding up a familiar black sweater dress. "Hey, do you know what happened to my—?"

She doesn't finish her question, but I know what she's asking. I ruined it. Or Naz did. My cheeks flush. Oh shit.

Melody's eyes seek me out, and she tenses as she stares at the ostentatious flowers in my hand. "Shit, it's not your birthday yet, is it? Please tell me I didn't forget your birthday."

"No," I whisper, pushing stuff out of the way to make room to set them on my desk beside my bed. "Just a gift."

Melody watches me incredulously, dropping the dress onto a pile of dirty clothes, forgetting all about it. "The perk of having a Mom who owns a flower shop, huh?"

I shrug noncommittally.

I don't correct her.

I'm a terrible friend.

Her eyes drift back to the flowers on my desk, and she's quiet for a moment. I wait for her to question me more, but she doesn't, a smile lifting her lips. "Lucky bitch."

I laugh. Lucky? Maybe.

Naz certainly makes me feel that way.

Melody flops down on her bed again, cuddling up with her pillow to take a nap after a morning full of classes. I sit down with my philosophy book, hoping to get a start on my paper on happiness, wanting to impress Santino after the disaster class turned out to be.

I try to focus—I try, and try, and try—but my attention keeps drifting to the flowers. The sweet fragrance swirls in the air around me, tickling my nostrils whenever I inhale. My lips keep twitching as I fight off a grin. I feel like the truth is written all over my face, glowing like a neon sign in the flush of my cheeks.

Melody's soft snores fill the quiet room after a while. I glance over at her, making sure she's fast asleep, and contemplate for a moment before grabbing my phone.

My finger hovers over Naz's name in my contacts. I press it, my heart beating wildly as I bring it to my ear.

It rings.

And rings.

And rings.

I'm close to hanging up when the line clicks and he greets me with an exaggerated sigh. "Well hello there."

His voice is rough—grittier than usual.

"I didn't wake you, did I?"

"You did," he confirms.

"I'm so sorry," I say. "I didn't know. I got your flowers and wanted to thank you."

"Ah." I can hear him yawn through the line. "So they made it?"

"Yes." I peek across the room, making sure Melody's still asleep before I continue. "We only really spent two nights together, though."

"You're forgetting about the first night," he says. "Not surprising, though, since you were out of it."

"But we didn't..." My voice drops even lower. "...you know."

He exhales again, loudly, but this time it's not from his exhaustion. It's frustration. "I didn't send them to you for sleeping with me, Karissa. Don't degrade yourself thinking that's your worth. I sent them because I'm grateful."

"Grateful for what?"

"For you."

"Well, thank you," I say. "So how did I give away that I liked flowers? Did I wear a flowery shirt, or smell like roses or something one day?"

He laughs. "No, it was just a guess this time. Most women like flowers."

"I probably like them more than most," I say. "My mother grows flowers for a living."

"Is that right?" He sounds genuinely interested. There's a lot about men that I find attractive, but a man who actually listens is in an entirely different league.

"Yeah, so I sort of have a soft spot for them, I guess. Makes me a little homesick."

"And where's home, anyway? The post office in Syracuse?"

I laugh, pushing my philosophy book aside to lie down. "Close enough. Home is... well, I don't know. We moved around a lot when I was growing up, so it's not really a place to me. It's more the people. Or the person, anyway."

"Your mother," he guesses. "The florist."

"Yes."

"I'll have to keep that in mind," he says. "I'm glad you like the flowers."

"They were a nice surprise." I stare at them on my desk. "I was starting to think maybe you forgot about me."

"Why would you think that?"

"I haven't heard from you," I say. "Haven't seen you."

"That's not from lack of remembering," he says. "I've been busy with work, but you've been on my mind. And you can see me any time you want, Karissa. Anytime. Just say the word and I'm yours."

"Tonight?" I whisper.

"How about right now?" he suggests. "I can be there in an hour."

My eyes dart to Melody, still fast asleep in her bed. "Can you make it two?"

"Whatever you want," he says. "I'll see you then."

He ends the call, and I set my phone back down, unable to fight the smile this time. It's building up inside of me to the point that I feel like I'm going to explode. I let out a silent scream, kicking my legs in my bed and clenching my fists, unable to contain it. I jump up and scan the room anxiously, grabbing my robe before jetting to the bathroom, careful not to wake Melody.

I shower, and scour, and shave, and stress, the giddiness making me edgy. I stay under the hot spray until my fingertips prune. Getting out, I slather on lotion, making every inch of my body silky smooth, coated with a touch of fragrance. Heading back into the room, robe on, towel on my head, I find Melody sitting up in her bed, awake again, searching through her bag.

"Hey," she says without even looking up at me. "Paul called, wants to meet up. Our next classes are side-by-side."

"Really?"

"Yeah, isn't that something?" she says, smiling. "So we're going to walk to class together and then get some dinner afterward."

"Awesome."

"You wanna come with?" She raises her eyebrows as she casts her eyes at me. "Would be nice to get something not out of a can or from the dining hall."

"Yeah, I'll pass this time," I say. "Thanks, though."

"You sure?"

"Positive. You and Paul have fun."

She stands up, grabbing her things and getting them together. "Well, let me know if you change your mind and we'll meet up somewhere, okay?"

"Okay."

I won't change my mind, but I don't tell her that, relieved I won't have to try to explain why I'm getting dressed to leave in the middle of the afternoon. I know I should tell her the truth—I'm breaking every rule my mother ever taught me and violating the friendship code by sneaking out like this. Always make sure someone knows who you're with and what you're doing, how they can find you, and never—ever—go somewhere without a friend knowing. It's an unspoken pact, one I've violated again and again, and I don't even know why.

But I can't say anything.

I'm not ready to tell anyone.

There's something thrilling, something chilling, about having something that's all mine. I've lived a life of secrecy since I was born, a life of uncertainty because of my mother's quirky ways, but this is another level I can't even explain. It's having a different world to step into, a world so much unlike my own—a world where I'm not just another person... I'm a treasure.

He makes me feel like the sun, the world revolving around me, and I'm not ready to invite any others into our universe.

Naz is my very own knight, fearless and chivalrous, although I suspect his shining armor may be concealing a bit of darkness.

Instead of putting me on guard, that thought intrigues me.

I throw on jeans and a soft pink sweater, grabbing a scarf to finish off the outfit, and take time to fix my hair, leaving it down and wavy. I put on makeup, swiping lipstick the same shade as my sweater on my lips. Once I'm ready, I grab my purse, making sure I have my keys and ID and phone on me before heading out.

I keep my head down, not wanting to run into anyone and be delayed. I go outside, walking around the corner to the parking garage just as the black Mercedes pulls in.

Perfect timing.

I don't give him time to get out and open my door for me, climbing in beside him right away. He's dressed as usual, black suit, dark tie, his hair a sexy wave. He hasn't shaved, his facial hair thicker today than I've seen it before. The masculine scent of his cologne fills the car.

"You look nice," he says, cutting his eyes at me as he pulls back into traffic. "Are you hungry?"

"A little," I admit. "You don't have to take me anywhere, though."

"Nonsense. I need to eat, too. What are you hungry for?" Before I can get out a response, he cuts in again. "And don't say 'whatever' or 'anything' or 'it doesn't matter', because those aren't answers."

"Uh, I don't know."

"That's not an answer, either."

"Fine. Pizza."

"Delivery, takeout, or eat in?"

I laugh. "Eat in, I guess."

He nods once, acknowledging me, then drives in silence. I stare out the side window as the city flies by, watching as he takes me straight across the bridge into Brooklyn. He heads deep into the borough to a section I'm only familiar with by reputation, a rough and tumble kind of neighborhood.

Old graffiti covers the outside of some of the buildings as he pulls down a side street and stops about halfway down the block, in front of an old brick building. It looks much like every other place nearby, but people stand outside in front of it and huddle on benches, chatting as they wait around.

Naz parks across the street, right along the curb beneath a tree. I stare at the place, noting the small sign that indicates it's a pizzeria. I didn't expect anything fancy, but this... this doesn't look like somewhere Naz would frequent.

He surprises me, though. He helps me out of the car, pressing his palm to my back as he leads me across the street toward the pizzeria. I realize, as we approach, that the people sitting outside are waiting for tables, but Naz shrugs that off when I point it out to him.

Stepping inside, he pauses and glances around. The place is packed, filled with customers. The inside is a stark difference from the outside, a hidden gem in a seedy neighborhood. Not upscale, but not the dump I imagined from across the street.

It only takes a few seconds for Naz to be acknowledged. A man strutting by just happens to look our way, doing a double take, his footsteps stalling. "Vitale."

Naz nods.

"You need a table?"

Another nod.

"Coming right up, my friend."

I'm flabbergasted. I don't even have a chance to say anything about it before we're led through the restaurant, to a small table that's just now being cleared. We stand there for a second as they rush to clean the area, before Naz pulls out a chair for me. I slip into it, eyeing him peculiarly when he sits down across from me.

He picks up a menu, his gaze wholly focused on it, but the corner of his lip turns up into a smirk, flashing that dimple at me. I've never seen someone look so downright cocky before.

Why is that so hot to me?

"So did you call ahead again?" I ask, picking up my menu. "Cash in another favor?"

He laughs at my question. "No, not this time."

"Then how'd you do that?"

"Do what?"

"You know what," I say. "You didn't even say a word to that man and he seated you right away."

"He knows me."

"I figured that much, Vitale."

He flinches when I say his last name, his expression falling as his gaze abandons the menu to settle on me instead. "Don't call me that."

His tone isn't sharp, but it's most definitely no-nonsense. Not a question, nor is it a request. That's a demand. My skin prickles, that look in his eyes resurfacing as he regards me silently before turning to his menu again. I can tell he isn't reading it. He's staring at it like he's seeing through it.

After a moment, he meets my eyes again, that dark look fading. "They're friends of the family. Nothing more. Having a big family comes with perks. It doesn't just happen at restaurants, either. It's everywhere I go. Get used to it, sweetheart."

"It's just strange," I mumble, picking up my menu. "I don't know that I could ever get used to that."

"You will," he says. "Because it'll start happening to you, too."

I laugh at that. "Yeah, right."

"I'm serious," he says. "Just wait."

Rolling my eyes, I glance down at the menu, scanning through it for something to eat. Unlike the last time he took me to dinner, this I can read.

The waiter stops by while I'm still deciding and Naz greets him briskly, requesting a bottle of 2008 Paolo Bea Santa Chiara. I have no idea what that is, but as the waiter rushes off to retrieve it, I feel a peculiar sense of déjà vu. "Are you trying to get me drunk again?"

"I like to indulge, too, Karissa," he replies. "You getting drunk and loose is just an added bonus."

Laughing, I playfully kick him under the table. He smiles at me, closing his menu as the waiter returns with the bottle of wine. He uncorks it, and Naz takes over, pouring us each a small glass before setting the bottle aside. We order then—a margherita pizza to share. The wine is a strange translucent peach color and has a slight orange tang, going down smoothly.

Naz watches me, his eyes scanning my face as another man approaches our table. He's older, with slicked back black hair and a thick moustache, short and stumpy. He smiles wide, nodding as he greets Naz by name. Last name. "Vitale."

Naz doesn't seem fazed when everyone else does it. "Signore Andretti."

That's the extent of what I understand. The men launch into conversation, the words flowing fluently, but every bit of it is foreign to my ears. Italian, I gather, from the smooth tone and romantic sounding enunciations. They're both smiling, the air around them friendly. Naz laughs after a moment as the other man motions toward me. I'm mid-drink, nearly choking on the wine when their attention shifts.

"*Sì*," Naz says. That I know. Yes. "She is."

The man's expression brightens as he regards me, rattling off something so fast the words all blur together. He reaches over, grasping my hand and pressing a kiss to the back of it. "*Sei incantevole!*"

Eyes wide, I watch him carefully. The man lets go of me and turns to Naz, giving him a thumb's up before scampering away.

"You speak Italian?" I ask, surprised.

Naz picks up his wine. "I have a basic understanding."

"Well, what did he say?"

"He said you're lovely."

I'm taken aback. "And what did you say?"

"A lot," he says. "I thanked him for the table and complimented the wine. He's the owner, you see. He asked me how I was and who you were. I told him I was great and you were someone special."

I stare at him, those words sinking in. "Special?"

"Yes, special," he says. "Don't sound so surprised."

"It's just surreal. I keep waiting for this all to be a dream."

He takes a sip of his wine before setting the glass down and leaning closer, his gaze intense. "When I first laid eyes on you, I thought the same thing. How could I be so lucky as to encounter you, in a city so big? I thought I had to be dreaming."

"Because of me?" I can feel my face flushing. "But I'm just... me."

"You're special, Karissa. I mean that."

Our food comes and I take a bite of the pizza, the crust not too thin, the cheese just rich enough, and the sauce succulent. It's surprisingly delicious for coming from a hole-in-the-wall kind of place, and I now understand why Naz would come here. I devour it as Naz nibbles on a slice, conversation playful, as the wine seems to magically evaporate. *POOF.*

Before dinner is through, my head is fuzzy, my body tingling, the air between us buzzing like an electrical current.

"You ready to get out of here?" he asks as he once again counts out cash to pay the bill. I sneak a peek at it, curious, and am relieved to see it isn't nearly as much as the last time he took me to dinner.

"Sure." I swallow down the rest of my wine before setting the glass aside. He stands up and takes my arm, nodding in greeting to the waiter as we head for the door. People are still lingering outside, gathering in groups, waiting for tables. "Where are we going?"

He cuts his eyes at me as we cross the street toward the Mercedes. The sky is starting to darken, a pinkish hue shining down on everything. "Where do you want to go?"

"Anywhere."

"That's not an answer."

"Anywhere with you."

He smiles. "That's a bit better."

Unsurprisingly, we go to his house. I expect him to take me upstairs, to pull me straight to his room like the last time we were here, but instead he flicks on the light to settle in downstairs. "You want to watch a movie?"

"Uh, sure."

"There are some DVDs in the den," he says, motioning toward a door past the living room. "Go ahead and pick one out."

Stepping the way he points, I head through the living room, my footsteps faltering right in the doorway to the den. It's only dimly lit from the windows, but I have enough light to see everything. The room is massive, possibly even bigger than the entire house I shared with my mother in Waterford. Unlike the rest of his place, which feels so modern and sterilized, the den is well lived in.

He spends all his time in here, I realize.

The furniture is black leather and well worn, the tables wooden matching the paneling of the walls. There seems to be a divider down the middle, a long trailing rug in shades of burgundy and black running from the doorway to the far wall, dividing it into two different spaces.

On one side there's a fireplace with half a dozen bookcases lining the wall, each one packed with books, a desk right in the center surrounded by chairs. It's an office and home library rolled into one. But on the other side of the divider is an entertainment center, one of the most elaborate I've ever seen, with a huge television and what looks like more DVDs than he has books. It's like a movie theater, set up in front of an array of furniture covered in pillows, cozy and welcoming.

My eyes bounce between the sections of the room. I feel like I just got a peek of Naz's soul.

It's a lot more complex than I anticipated.

I make my way over to the entertainment center and scan the movie titles. I recognize some, but most I've never heard of. He has a lot of foreign movies, a lot of black and white flicks, with a few cult classics thrown in. Not the typical action I expect to see, no *Die Hard* or *Lethal Weapon*, no *Terminator* or *Rambo*. On the same token, there aren't any chick flicks, either.

And they're all in alphabetical order. Weird.

I'm instantly curious about his books, wondering what a man like him reads, when I hear his footsteps behind me entering the den. I turn to face him just as he unknots his tie and slips it off, tossing it on the end table beside the black leather couch. His jacket is already gone, his shirt no longer tucked in, his shoes missing. He unbuttons his top two buttons before making work of his cuffs and pushing his sleeves up to his elbows.

Jesus, he looks sexy, still dressy but unshaven and unkempt. Ruffled physically, even if nothing can make him that way mentally.

"Find anything?" he asks as he approaches.

I turn back to the movies, sighing. "No *Pretty Woman?*"

"No." I can hear the smile in his voice. "I'm afraid not."

I scan the titles again as he walks up behind me, snaking an arm around my waist, and pulling me back to him. I relax into his touch, grasping his forearm as he leans down and kisses my neck. My eyes flutter closed, his lips soft and warm against my skin, sending tingles down my spine.

"Just pick something," he whispers. "I don't think we'll be paying it much attention, anyway."

His words prompt me to grab the first movie I see. I don't even look at the name. Naz puts it in and presses play as I settle in on the couch and pull off my shoes. He sits down beside me, relaxing, and wraps his arms around me.

He's right. I don't pay attention to the movie, and I don't know if he does, because I lie there and fall right asleep in his arms.

Darkness cloaks the room when I awaken, except for the soft glow of the television shining on me. It's dead silent, the movie over.

A black blanket covers me, soft and fuzzy, folded in around me like a child tucked into bed. My head is resting on one of the couch pillows, but there's no Naz anywhere to be seen.

Yawning, I sit up and stretch, glancing around, wondering where he disappeared to and how long I've been asleep. There's no clock in here that I've seen. How does this man keep track of time? Reaching for my purse, I sort through it and pull out my phone. Midnight.

I have two text messages from Melody, asking where I am, and a missed call from my mother hours ago. I reply to Melody so she doesn't worry, telling her I'm with an old friend and not to wait up, before putting the phone away and standing up.

I'm nervous as I head for the doorway, hoping he doesn't mind if I go elsewhere in his house. He's not in the living room, not in the kitchen. I ascend the stairs, straining my ears, listening for sounds, but I hear nothing. I creep down the dark hallway, toward the bathroom, past closed doors. There aren't any lights on, no sign of him anywhere up here. Pausing in the hallway, I sigh and start to turn around when movement startles me. I yelp, jumping, when someone grabs me from behind.

Breath fans against my cheek as the soft chuckle rings in my ear. "Did I scare you?"

I can't even answer. I swallow thickly, grasping my chest, as Naz swings me around to him. Through the darkness, I can somewhat make out his face, his body a mere shadow in the hallway. He changed clothes, shirtless and barefoot, wearing nothing more than a pair of dark sweatpants.

"Uh, yeah," I stammer, my eyes drawn to his bare chest. "I woke up and you were gone, and it's getting late, so I thought... uh, I thought..."

Jesus, I can hardly think looking at him. Now that I know

they're there, my eyes are drawn to his sprinkling of scars, only faintly visible, scattered and veiled like stars in an overcast sky.

He grabs my belt loops, hooking his thumbs in them, as he tugs me toward him, pulling me to his bedroom. "You thought we should head to bed?"

"I thought, uh..." I glance at his face, seeing the serious expression. "I thought I should go."

"You should," he says, pulling me flush against him, so close I can feel the heat from his body warming my skin, "but do you want to?"

No.

No, I don't.

His cocky smirk tells me I don't even have to verbalize that answer. I offer no resistance as he pulls me through his bedroom, his hands quickly and smoothly shedding me of my clothes, leaving me even more naked than him by the time he gets me to his bed.

Yelping, I let out a laugh as he picks me up and places me in the center of his bed, wasting no time before settling on top of me. He kisses my mouth, my cheek, my jaw, his lips trailing down my neck and to my chest. I gasp, my hands running through his soft hair when his mouth finds my breasts, his lips wrapping around a nipple and sucking on it. His teeth graze the sensitive flesh as my back arches from the sensation.

His hands grasp my hips, pinning me onto the bed as he makes his way down my stomach, nipping and licking, small stinging jabs ricocheting across my skin when he sucks so hard I'm sure he's going to leave a mark.

I don't mind if he does.

A part of me hopes he will.

Chapter Seven

Happiness is ~~a human condition in which~~...
...~~what happens when people decide~~...
...~~a state of mind if we just~~...
...bullshit.

Happiness is bullshit.

Just like this stupid essay.

Sighing, I scratch out the line and tear the paper from the notebook, crumbling it and tossing it aside. I've been working on the essay for the good part of an hour, trying to get it written since it's due tomorrow afternoon, but that's the best I can come up with.

And I don't even believe it.

It's half past one, and I'm still wearing yesterday's clothes, having just got here sometime around noon. I should shower, and change, but the thought of washing away Naz's scent doesn't appeal to me. I'm exhausted from broken sleep and sore from rough sex, and I want nothing more than to rewind a few hours and go back to the darkness and relive those moments again and again.

That was happiness.

Happiness is being fucked so rough you can hardly breathe, can hardly speak, can do nothing but squeal like a pig as he nails you over and over, pushing inside of you so hard, so deep, that you can feel the man not only with your body, but also with your soul. Happiness is waking up the next morning, barely able to recall your own name, because the only one that mattered in hours was his, screamed so loud your throat is painfully raw, like the name had bled from your lips.

Something tells me Santino won't like that too much.

I rip out that page, too, and toss it in the trashcan, along with the half dozen others I scribbled nonsense on. My eyes drift to the clock, not because I don't know the time, but because I'm wishing it would slow down, each tick leading me closer to Melody coming home from class.

Melody, who texted me all night and all morning, worried despite me telling her not to worry. Melody, who is most definitely going to give me the fifth degree like she is the Gestapo and I'm guilty of treason.

I was worried about it earlier, when Naz drove me home. He asked what was wrong, somehow being able to tell. I said I was worried how I was going to explain myself to Melody, and he merely shrugged and said 'tell her or don't tell her, whatever you want'. I don't have much choice, honestly. He didn't give me much choice.

The love bite on my throat sort of gives it all away.

Happiness is having your very first hickey, put there by a set of soft lips that speak the smoothest words that sound like music to your ears and whispers to your soul.

Yeah, happiness makes you speak in ridiculous riddles and create poetry worse than William McGonagall.

I toss the notebook aside and lay back on the bed, letting out an exaggerated sigh. No sooner do I close my eyes and the door flings open. Melody walks in as I glance that way, her expression full of alarm as she regards me warily. "Jesus, Kissimmee, where the hell have you been?"

"I was… out."

"No shit," she says, dropping her bag before flopping down beside me on my bed. "I figured that much when you weren't here."

"I told you not to worry."

"Yeah, well, you can't disappear all night without me worrying. You didn't even make it back in time for your eight o'clock class!"

"How do you know?" I ask. "Your lazy ass doesn't wake up until I'm back from that one, anyway."

She rolls her eyes, nudging me as I laugh. Her expression shows her amusement for a second before it falls away, her eyes widening. "Is that a hickey on your neck? Oh my God, it is!"

She tries to get a better look but I block her, pushing her prying hands away. "So what if it is?"

"What did you do last night?" she asks. "No, scratch that. *Who* did you do?"

"It's nothing," I say, the words a bitter lie on my tongue. "He's just a guy."

"Just a guy?" She gapes at me. "A guy you didn't tell me about!"

"Actually, I did tell you about him. You remember that guy from that night at Timbers? The one I went home with?"

Her eyes widen. "So you did sleep with him?"

"No." I hesitate. "Well, yes, but not that night."

"But after that night."

"Yes."

She looks torn between hugging me and smacking me, her expression flickering. It eventually gives way and she grins, punching my arm. "You whore!"

I laugh as I move away from her, kicking my leg and hitting her in the side with it. "Reserve the judgment, slut."

Holding her hands up, she laughs. "Fine. So is he a student here or something?"

"He's, uh... he's not a student. He's just a guy."

"Do I at least get a name?"

"Naz." Her brow furrows as I wave it off. "He's older than me, lives in Brooklyn and is an independent contractor. Anything else you need to know?"

"Uh, yeah." She eyes me seriously. "How big is it?"

I kick her again as she laughs and stands up, retreating back to her side of the room. I expect more questions, and I can see she has more she wants to ask, but she keeps them to herself.

I'm instantly grateful to have her as my friend.

"As long as you're safe," she says, "and I know where you are."

"Yes, Mom."

She picks up a pillow and chucks it at me, promptly asking for it back, but I refuse, snuggling with it in my bed instead. Too lazy to retrieve it, she shrugs and lies down, grabbing her phone from her pocket. "Paul and I are going to dinner tonight. You gonna come with this time?"

"Depends," I say. "Where are you going?"

"I don't know," she says. "Somewhere for pizza... maybe over in one of the other boroughs. You know, get out of the city for a bit. You in?"

"Sure," I say, shrugging. "I actually know a place you'd like."

"You know a place?" she asks incredulously.

I laugh. "Yes."

∽

Paul's a lot more attractive when not intentionally dressed like an eighties douchebag, but an air of arrogance surrounds him, a smug smile constantly on his lips. He owns a death trap of a Jeep Wrangler and drives with the top down, my hair blowing all over the place in the backseat as he speeds through the streets, weaving in and out of traffic, on our way to Brooklyn.

I fear for my life, every second of the trip making me wish I'd stayed behind. At least there I'm not racing toward a fiery death.

"I've heard of this place," Paul shouts over the sound of the wind blowing around us all. "They say it's a bitch to get a table."

"Yeah," I respond. "It's totally worth it, though."

We head to the same pizzeria Naz took me to last night, having to park down the street. Paul walks ahead of us as Melody chats my ear off. A few people wait around outside for tables, but it isn't as bad as last time. We step inside, requesting a table from the young hostess. Paul talks to her—flirting with her, right in front of Melody—and she jots us down for a table for three.

"It'll be about thirty, forty minutes," she says. "I'll call for you when your table's ready."

We start to head back outside, to wait on one of the benches. A man opens the door for us, holding it, his gaze meeting mine. I recognize him... the owner... the man Naz spoke to when we were here. I smile politely, stepping by him, as his brow furrows. He rattles off something in Italian, something I don't understand, before he motions for the hostess to come over. He says something to her, something I again don't comprehend, until he reaches the last word. "Vitale."

The hostess looks at me. "He says you're Vitale's special friend, that you were here with him."

I can feel the blush overtaking my face as I nod. "Yes."

The man smiles widely at the confirmation, grabbing my hand and pressing a kiss to the back of it. He rambles for a moment before turning to the hostess, spouting off something else. She nods, and he strides away.

The hostess grabs three menus, motioning for us to follow her. Melody looks at me with surprise, but I just shrug as the three of us are led straight to a table that's just being cleared off. I take a seat across from Melody and Paul as the hostess sets the menus down, smiling at me.

"Mr. Andretti said to send Vitale his regards," she says. "To ensure him he took good care of you."

"Uh, okay," I say. "I will."

Naz isn't here, he's nowhere in the vicinity, and yet his presence can still be felt.

She walks away, and I glance up, catching my friend's eyes. Melody looks dumbfounded. "How did you do that?"

"I didn't," I mumble, shaking my head. "Naz did."

We're catered to all through dinner, waited on fast and showered with extra food. A bottle of wine is brought to the table, despite none of us requesting it, no questions asked about anybody's age. Paul lavishes in the attention, but I can feel Melody's questioning looks cast my way.

When we're finished, Paul asks for a bill as Melody pulls out her wallet. I feel guilty, realizing she's the one paying for all of us. The waiter shakes his head, smiling as he starts clearing our plates. "The bill has already been taken care of."

Melody gapes at him. "By who?"

The waiter says the payer prefers to remain anonymous, but I'm not fooled. A smile tugs my lips as I swirl some of the wine around in my glass, drinking my last few drops. I know exactly who did it.

After we leave, I stall on the sidewalk near the entrance. "You guys go ahead. I have somewhere else to be."

Melody's brow furrows, and she starts to question me, but Paul throws his arm over her shoulder and pulls her away. "Cool. See you later."

Melody looks behind her, shouting she'll see me back at the room, as I pull out my phone and call a cab. It takes it a moment to show up, the ride to Naz's house only a few minutes. It takes every penny in my pocket to afford the fare. I stroll up to the front door, knocking. It's near dusk, his Mercedes parked in the driveway.

The door opens and he appears in front of me, his expression blank. He looks at me, his eyes shifting past me to the street as the cab pulls away, before he meets my eyes again. He's quiet for a moment, just staring at me, before he finally speaks. "You had dinner with another man. I'm hurt."

"Can't be too hurt," I say, "considering you paid the bill."

He smirks, not admitting or denying that, as he steps aside to motion for me to come in.

"I'm going to need a ride back to the city," I mumble, frowning, noting he's already out of his suit, wearing what I'd call pajamas, except I know he doesn't sleep in them... Naz sleeps naked. I hadn't exactly thought this thing out. "You know, whenever you get the chance, if you don't mind... it'll be a long walk otherwise."

"I'll take you in the morning."

"In the morning?"

"Yes," he says, reaching over and cupping my cheek, his voice playful as he adds, "You've got a dinner to pay me back for tonight."

"Disney World."

My footsteps falter on the middle of the sidewalk near Washington Square, about a block from the building housing Santino's classroom. "Seriously?"

Melody stops walking and turns to face me. "Yep."

"You wrote about Disney World?" I ask, needing some clarification.

"Yep," she says. "You know, with Mickey Mouse and Donald Duck and Plato the Dog."

I blink a few times. "Please tell me you didn't call him Plato."

"Of course not." She laughs. "I wrote about the princesses, namely Cinderella, and the whole concept of living happily ever after. I mean, it's kind of your fault, since you quoted Walt Disney last time. It was stuck in my head. And besides, it's the happiest place on earth, right? That's what they say."

"Right," I say, starting to walk again. "That's what they say."

"Why, what did you write about?"

Definitely not Disney World. "I talked about philosophers like Aristotle and their views on happiness."

I can remember exactly how I started it:

Happiness isn't tangible. It's immeasurable, not profitable, often impractical, and some would argue indescribable. You can't see happiness, or smell it, or taste it, or hear it, or feel it... or can you?

I thought it was pretty brilliant, myself, but what do I know?

She blows out an exaggerated breath, making a face. "Where's the fun in that?"

"It's not supposed to be fun," I point out. "It's philosophy."

"Whatever," Melody says. "It ain't no fun if the homies can't have none. Speaking of which, Paul took Santino's class last year and he said that—"

I don't hear anything else that she says, her words falling on deaf ears. I look up as we approach the philosophy building and my heart stalls a beat before kicking into high gear, pounding so ferociously that my vision blurs around the edges, obscuring everything within a frame of blackness.

The butterflies are trying desperately to take flight.

My hands are trembling, my fingers tingling, as I clutch the straps of my backpack around my shoulders. Stepping out of the building, less than a hundred feet in front of me, is the man I left just hours ago, the man I see even when I close my eyes, dressed impeccably as always.

Naz.

He walks a few steps in my direction and pauses, his eyes flickering toward me, but his expression shows none of the recognition I feel inside.

None of the excitement.

None of the giddiness.

My palms start to sweat, my knees weak. I continue walking alongside Melody, trying to listen as she babbles on and on, but his sudden presence is jarring. I keep looking at him; keep waiting for him to see me. His eyes flicker my way a few times, landing straight on my face, but still—he offers no acknowledgment.

Not a wink.

Not a smile.

Not even a cheek twitch.

My stomach coils. I'm not sure what to do, what to say, what to think. In the moment, I'm not sure of anything. He just stands there casually, fifty... forty... thirty feet in front of me, and eventually turns away, his attention going to the building we're walking toward.

I glance that way, seeing Santino near the entrance, looking as uptight as ever, and holding his pointer stick like a cane. I glance between them curiously as I approach, ultimately looking away from Naz, too nervous to meet his gaze.

I'm so close I can smell a whiff of his cologne in the afternoon breeze. I step past him, relishing in the small moment where I inhale the essence of the man, when I'm jerked to a sudden stop. He grabs my arm, swinging me around to face him. I stumble, blinking rapidly, caught off guard as I meet his eyes. A smile lifts his lips. "You're not even going to say hello?"

"I, uh... I..."

I get nothing out but foolish stammering before his hands grasp my head, cradling my face in his palms. He kisses me, suddenly, brutally, his lips hard, the kiss full of passion. I gasp as I kiss him back, stunned by the intensity. It lasts forever but no time at all before he pulls away, still holding my face, his eyes twinkling with amusement.

"Hello," I whisper breathlessly.

He laughs under his breath, his eyes scanning me, and leans over again to press a chaste kiss against my lips. His hands drift down, his thumb rubbing a fresh mark visible on my neck. He seems to admire

115

it for a moment before letting go, turning around to walk away without saying anything more.

"What the fuck?" Melody hisses in my ear as she steps beside me. "What the hell was that?"

"That was him."

"Him? Like, him?"

I watch him cross the street to the Mercedes, parked along the curb, before turning to my friend. "That's Naz."

"Jesus, Kissimmee, you didn't tell me he was sex on legs."

I roll my eyes, unable to stop myself from blushing, as I turn away from her. "Come on, we're going to be late for class."

I look up as we approach the doorway of the building, my stomach dropping when I see Santino still standing there. His gaze is fixed across the street. He shifts his attention to me, nothing but pure disdain in his eyes. "Miss Reed."

"Sir."

He turns to Melody. "Miss Carmichael. I hope you ladies have your essays ready."

"Of course, sir," Melody says sweetly as we stride past.

The man is in rare form today, slamming his stick against his desk and calling on me so many times I lose count. Right before class is over he passes our midterms back to us, pausing in front of my desk for a second. I'm staring down at my book, starting on our next essay, but I can feel his gaze on my face. I chance a peek, meeting his eyes as he slips my paper on top of my book.

"I hope you know what you're doing," he says.

"Me, too," I mutter, flipping my exam over as he moves on. I stare down at it, cringing.

C-

Chapter Eight

Naz's books are just as diverse as his movie collection.

I stand in the den, surveying his vast bookshelves, running my fingertips along the spines as I read the titles. He has everything from Shakespeare to self-help, Edgar Allen Poe to poetry. It's peculiar.

The man even has textbooks on philosophy.

I stall, my fingertips tracing the spine of The Art of War. "Did you read all of these books?"

Naz is sitting at his desk. Not sure why, since he's watching me instead of doing anything. I look his way as he nods. "Most of them."

"Did you go to college?"

His brow furrows at my question. "Yes."

"What did you major in?"

Was independent contracting an option?

"Nothing," he says. "I dropped out before I had to declare one."

"Why did you drop out?"

"I had to."

"Why?"

"Because things happened that made it so." I regard him curiously, wondering what things happened, but he motions for me to come close before I can pry anymore. I step toward him as he turns in his chair, tugging me between his legs, his hands on my hips as he squeezes me between him and the desk. "Are you writing a book about my life, Karissa?"

"No." I place my hands on his shoulders as I gaze at him, my fingertips trailing up his neck, twirling a curl near his ear. "I'm curious."

"Be careful what you ask," he says quietly, his hands drifting along my jeans to cup my ass. "The answers aren't always pretty."

Leaning down, I kiss him softly and whisper against his mouth, "I just want to know you."

He pulls away, leaning back in his chair to gaze at me. He's so quiet I start to get self-conscious, my face flushing at the intensity of his stare, when he lets out an exaggerated sigh. I watch as he unknots his tie, pulling it off and tossing it on the desk beside me.

His jacket was discarded the moment we stepped in his house an hour ago.

Slowly, he unbuttons his shirt, his eyes fixed on mine as he pulls it open. I try not to look, try to keep eye contact, but I can't help it. My eyes are drawn down to his chest as he tugs on the neck of his undershirt, pulling it down as far as it will go. I take in the sight of his tanned skin peppered with old scars, my right hand drifting from his hair down his neck.

I hesitate before running my fingertips along the marred skin, connecting the dots of his old wounds like maybe they can tell me the story. He remains quiet as I draw on his skin before he clutches my wrist, stilling my movements. I meet his eyes then, startled by his strong grasp, and see that look.

That look.

It sends a chill down my spine.

He says nothing as he stares at me. Nothing about what he just did really explains it, but somehow I understand. Whatever happened to him was bad... bad enough to stop life in its tracks and send him on a different path.

"What would you have majored in," I ask, "if that hadn't happened?"

"I don't know." He lets go of my wrist. I press my palm flat against his chest, faintly feeling his steady heartbeat as he speaks again. "That's not who I am now. I hardly remember that man anymore."

He pushes his chair back, my hand dropping from his chest. I take it as my cue to move away when he starts buttoning his shirt again. I stroll back over to the bookshelf, surveying his collection of textbooks. "Did you like philosophy in college or something? You have a lot of books about it."

He scoffs. "Hated it. Failed it."

"Funny, me, too. Probably wouldn't be if my professor wasn't such an asshole, though."

"Ah, Daniel Santino." Naz laughs to himself. "He's always been a bit of a dick."

I turn to Naz curiously, wondering how much I can question him before he shuts down again. "How do you know him?"

"He knew my—" He pauses for a beat. "My family."

I don't know what answer I expect, but that's not it. "So you're friends?"

That thought creeps me out.

"Hardly," he says. "I only see him in a professional capacity."

"Thank God," I mutter. "I don't know how I'd feel about you being friends with the devil."

"The devil?"

"Santino... I'm pretty sure he's Satan."

"Nonsense," he says. "The man is little more than a pesky cockroach."

"Yeah, well, in that case, I wish someone would squash him."

Naz laughs. "Be careful what you wish for, sweetheart."

He stands up and grabs his tie, laying it around his neck, not bothering to fix it. "You hungry?"

"Uh, yeah, but I really should get going," I say, pulling out my phone to glance at the time. "I can just grab something back at the dorms."

"I'll drive you."

"You don't have to."

"Nonsense."

Nonsense. I think that might be his favorite word. "But—"

"But what?" He cuts me off before I can answer. "You don't want to inconvenience me? Waste my time? Waste my gas? Don't want me to have to go out of my way? You don't want to be a bother?"

"Well... yes."

"What did I tell you that night in your room? I said there was no turning back. So don't start getting cold feet on me now. I'm yours, Karissa, anytime, day or night."

"I'm not getting cold feet."

"But you're thinking and not feeling. You're overthinking."

I can't really argue with that.

Guilty.

"Let me drive you to the dorm," he says. "It's the least I can do."

He drives me back to Manhattan.

Despite my earlier words, he buys me dinner on the way. Nothing fancy, nothing he would even eat, but it's definitely more my speed.

I'm still sipping on a chocolate milkshake when he pulls the car into the parking garage beside my dorm to drop me off. I thank him, leaning over and kissing his cheek. I'm about to get out when he says my name, drawing my attention to him.

"I have a party to go to this weekend," he says. "Come with me."

My eyes widen. "A party? Like, with people and dancing?"

"It's more of a dinner party, but yes, there may be some dancing."

"A dinner party," I echo. "Like with... dinner?"

I have no idea what a dinner party is really like, but I watch TV.

I watch Real Housewives of wherever the fuck they are these days. I've seen what they call dinner parties.

"Yes, with dinner," he says with a laugh. "They're not usually my thing, but it's business, and I'd rather not go alone, if I have someone to go with me."

"Uh... I don't really have anything to wear to a dinner party."

"Don't worry about that. I'll have something dropped off. You're, what, a size two?"

I bark with laughter, still sipping my milkshake. "Maybe one of my ass cheeks."

He smirks. "Just say you'll go with me and I'll handle the rest."

I consider it for a moment, wanting to say no because of my nerves, but I can't get the word to come out. How can I deny him when he's been so great to me? "Yeah, okay, sure."

"Great," he says. "I'll be in touch."

I get another C- on my paper on happiness. It's all marked up, more red marring the pristine white paper than black ink from my words. Santino has critiqued every line to the point that I can practically hear his ridiculing voice when I read his comments. On the very top, in all capitals, underlined half a dozen times, is the word PRETENTIOUS.

Pretentious. *Me.*

The man with a flashy pointer and a stick up his ass called me pretentious. I'm stunned. I'm pissed. I'm upset on the trek home from class, so furious that Melody doesn't even try to speak to me as she clutches her paper on Disney World.

She got a B+.

I caught a peek at it when he handed them back, seeing very little red scribbled on hers, so little, in fact, that it made what was written up top stand out even more.

J.M. DARHOWER

REFRESHING.

I quote Walt Disney in class and am mocked. She writes an entire paper on the subject and he calls it refreshing.

As if I couldn't be any more dismayed.

I stride right into the building, swiping my student ID for entrance. Melody's right behind me, treading lightly. We walk to the elevator and cram inside when my phone starts to ring. I consider not even looking at it, in no mood to talk to my mother, but I pull it out to silence it. I just happen to catch sight of the screen right before I hit the button and stall, seeing Naz's name.

"Hello?" I answer hesitantly.

"Are you busy?"

"No."

"Good, because there's a car waiting downstairs to take you to Fifth Avenue."

"Right now?"

"Yes, right now," he says. "You need a dress, don't you?"

"Uh, yeah."

"And take your roommate," he says. "I seem to remember owing her a dress, too."

I don't know what to say, but it doesn't matter, because he doesn't wait for me to respond, anyway. I lean against the side of the elevator, waiting, as we seem to stop on every floor on the way up. By the time we reach thirteen, Melody and I are the only ones left. It dings and Melody starts to step out, but I grab ahold of her and pull her back in, pressing the lobby button.

Her brow furrows as she looks at me. "Where are we going?"

"I don't know," I admit. "Fifth Avenue somewhere."

"Why?"

"I guess we're going shopping."

She looks torn between confusion and excitement, like she wants to jump up and down but she has no clue how the hell we can be going shopping when we've been living off of noodles all week. I don't explain, still stewing on my grade, as she crams her paper in her bag. She cuts her eyes at me, frowning as I watch. "I don't know why that man has a hard-on for you. You're a lot better at that crap than me. You should be getting all A's."

I just shrug, having no idea how to respond, as we stride out of the elevator and make our way outside. I notice it then, parked along the curb right in front of the dorm: a sleek black town car with a man leaning against the side of it, waiting. He glances up, pushing away from the car when he sees us. "Miss Reed?"

"Yes."

He smiles politely, opening the door for us to get in. I hesitate, but Melody pushes right past me, climbing in the back seat. I join her, sighing as the driver shuts the door and climbs in up front. Melody is chatting non-stop on the drive, excited, even though she has no idea where we're going or what we're doing.

Hell, I don't know myself.

All I know is I need a dress.

The driver takes us to Fifth Avenue in Midtown West and drops us off in front of an upscale boutique. I stand there along the curb, staring through the glass doors, as the town car pulls away, disappearing into traffic and leaving us there. Melody's wide eyes regard the store with much the same excitement as in the car, but even she seems a little hesitant.

"What now?" she asks.

"I guess we go in."

She shrugs, grabbing my arm and pulling me into the boutique. It's swathed in a soft glow, faint classical music playing. The store is arranged by color and scheme, with sections of different designers, the clothes along the walls while the middle section is sprinkled with furniture like we're in someone's home.

It's not like the stores I'm used to, with racks upon racks crammed together of every size imaginable, mass-produced and distributed to anyone who wants it. These are one-of-a-kinds, where you hold your breath and pick a dress and hope like hell you can squeeze into it.

I pause right inside the door, glancing around, as the saleswoman appears. She struts, poised, eyebrows raised like she's potentially approaching feral animals and she thinks we might bite. I'm about to blurt out that this is a mistake, that I'm most definitely in the wrong place, when she says my name. "Karissa Reed?"

I gape at her. "Yes."

"Mr. Vitale said he would be sending you by this afternoon," she says, giving me what I surmise is her warmest smile, although it still looks quite frigid. "He left instructions, evening attire for you and a dress for your friend... to replace one that was damaged?"

"A damaged dress?" Melody glances at me. "You mean my sweater dress? The black one?"

I nod slowly. "Yeah, we kind of... I mean, he kind of..."

She holds her hands up to stop me. "Enough said."

I laugh nervously, glancing back at the saleswoman as she eyes us, her gaze even icier than just a moment ago. She clears her throat dramatically, waving around the store. "Well, help yourselves to anything in the store. The dressing rooms are through there." She points toward the back. "I'm here to help if you need it."

"Thanks," I mumble as she walks away. I turn to Melody, about to say something—anything—when she lets out a squeal and drops her school bag in the middle of the store, grabbing my hand and yanking me over to a rack of clothes.

She's thrown into fast-forward as she descends upon the store, picking up dresses and holding them up to herself, running to the closest mirror and twirling around. The girl is a shopping machine. I scan some racks, noticing not a single piece has a price tag. "How am I supposed to know how much they cost?"

That icy voice clears nearby. "Mr. Vitale said you're to pick out what you like, not what you think you can have."

"That sounds like him," I mutter, picking up a sleek black dress and surveying it before sticking it back on the rack. I doubt I could squeeze a thigh into the thing.

Melody accumulates a dozen dresses she wants to try on, forcing a few on me along the way. I humor her, trying them on before pushing them aside. They're flashy and revealing, nothing I would be caught dead in. I find a simple black dress in my size and pick it up, heading toward the dressing rooms with it when another catches my eye. It's on a rack of pink and purple dresses, but the color falls somewhere in between, like raspberry.

I walk over to it, running my hand along the material. The gown is soft with an embroidered see-through overlay, giving the illusion of it being strapless but with three-quarter length sleeves. I don't know much about fashion besides that—don't recognize the designer's name or know what it's made of—but it's utterly beautiful.

And it's my size.

I take it into the dressing room, forgetting all about the black dress, and set to work putting on the gown. I struggle zipping it the whole way up in the back and step out of the dressing room wearing it, finding Melody admiring herself in a full-length mirror. She's wearing a black dress that seems to be made of leather and lace, low cut and skin tight. Her gaze catches mine in the mirror and she freezes.

"Can you zip this?" I ask, turning around so my back is to her. As soon as I do, I catch sight of a familiar set of eyes along the street. Naz.

He steps into the boutique. The saleswoman greets him warmly—a hell of a lot warmer than she greeted us—but his eyes are fixed solely on me as Melody zips me up. The dress is snug, tight around my chest, but it's bearable.

And damn, it's beautiful.

Naz walks toward us, ignoring the saleswoman as she attempts to strike up conversation. His eyes scan me as he approaches, but as soon as he's right up on us he focuses on Melody instead. He holds his hand out. "I haven't had the pleasure of actually meeting you yet. Melody Carmichael, I presume?"

My brow furrows. I most definitely didn't tell him her full name, but for some reason I'm not surprised he knows it.

Melody's flustered, blinking a few times as she takes his hand.

"Ignazio Vitale," he says, pressing a kiss to the back of her hand. "I've heard a lot about you, Miss Carmichael."

"I, uh... you, too."

He laughs, letting go as he turns to me. "I doubt that."

His eyes scan me, lingering on my breasts before trailing down my stomach, following the curve of my hips and the whole way down to my feet. A slight smirk touches his lips, just enough to flash a dimple. "Nice dress."

"You think so?" I ask, glancing down.

"Yes," he says. "It looks great on you."

Melody's gaze shifts between the two of us as she waves our way. "Isn't this like, against the rules? You're not supposed to see the dress beforehand."

"That's only when you get married," I mutter, grasping the dress where it starts to flare beneath my hips and twirl it a bit.

"We're not quite at that point," Naz says, pausing before offering a quiet "yet" that hits me so hard I blanch. He's not looking at me, though, as he seeks out the saleswoman. He waves her over, and she plasters a smile to her face as she approaches. Naz motions toward the dress I'm wearing. "How much is this one going to run me?"

The woman looks it over. "The Monique Lhuillier is eleven."

I gasp. "Eleven hundred bucks?"

The woman's eyes burn through me. "Eleven thousand."

The moment she says it, I feel like I can't breath, the dress suddenly too tight, constricting my airflow. I'm on the verge of panicking as Naz motions towards Melody's. "And for Miss Carmichael's?"

"The Stella McCartney is on sale for eight-fifty."

"Eight-fifty *what?*" I demand.

"Dollars," the woman says.

"Oh." I glance at Melody's dress. Still expensive, but that's a hell of a lot better. "Can I have one of those instead?"

Before the woman can speak, Naz interjects, telling her he'll take both dresses. He turns to me, a hint of amusement in his expression. "Pick out some shoes to go with it."

I start to say I don't need shoes, just like I don't need an eleven thousand dollar dress, but Melody grabs my arm to drag me away before I can argue. I stumble, nearly tripping over the bottom of the dress.

"I don't know how the hell you snagged that man, Kissimmee, but you keep him. You hear me? Any man that offers to buy you new shoes to go with your new dress needs to be kept. You don't let him go for anything."

I laugh incredulously. I feel like I'm caught in a whirlwind as I plop down on one of the comfortable chairs, slipping my feet into shoes Melody thrusts at me. She picks out a pair of metallic beige pumps she says look perfect with my dress, and I don't contradict her, or ask how much they cost.

I'm afraid to know.

Naz pays with an American Express card. It's the first time I've ever seen him use anything other than cash. I quietly mention it, not sure if he's even paying me any attention, but his soft laugh tells me he heard. After signing the receipt, everything paid, he turns to me. His eyes flit around the shop, seeing Melody as she checks out the mannequins by the front door, before he speaks. "It's not often I spend so much I don't have the cash on hand to cover it."

"Why do you carry so much cash?" I ask, trying not to dwell on the fact that he spent that much on me. "Aren't you afraid of someone robbing you?"

He lets out a sharp bark of laughter like that's the most absurd thing he's ever heard. "Who's going to rob me, Karissa?"

"Someone," I say, shrugging. "This city's dangerous. There are bad people everywhere here. I mean, maybe it's safe in other places, but not New York City. It's safe for nobody here."

He reaches out and grasps my arm when I try to take a step away, keeping me locked in place. His expression is serious, his eyes once more surveying our surroundings before settling on me again. "Who told you that? Your mother?"

"Yes. She's terrified I'm going to get robbed or raped or killed. She thinks it's bound to happen the longer I stay here."

"Nonsense," he says right away. "This is the safest big city in the country. I'm not saying there aren't bad people out there, because there are. I know there are. But it's nobody I'm afraid of, and I don't want you to be afraid of anyone out there, either."

I don't know what to say, so I merely nod. He grabs our things, the dresses and my shoes, and lugs them to the door with me beside him. Melody begrudgingly follows us out after grabbing our school bags, frowning as she stares back at the windows longingly. "I could live in that place."

"Not me," I say. "One dress and a pair of shoes later, and I already feel like Vivian in Pretty Woman."

"There's no comparison," Naz interjects. "Besides, you haven't seen your necklace yet."

Chapter Nine

I thought he'd been joking.

I was hoping he was joking.

He'd done enough for me already.

But as I stand in his living room and stare at the large black velvet box in his hand, I realize he meant it. The man bought me jewelry.

I don't know how to react, standing there in the long raspberry colored dress, my knees weak as I try to balance in the pair of the highest high heels. They make me nearly as tall as him, the two of us eye-level for the first time. And in his eyes I see that darkness, the murkiness I discover whenever his mask slips.

It should probably terrify me, but I feel only a slight chill.

At first glance I thought he was dressed normally, but closer inspection tells me differently. He's wearing a three-piece suit, the vest making him look sturdier than ever, the tie just as dark as the rest of it. Glittery cuff links accent his white shirt—diamonds, I think. Something tells me the man wouldn't wear anything fake. His shoes are shined, his suit fitted, and a handkerchief in the breast pocket of his jacket is the same pristine white as his shirt.

He looks like he just stepped off the end of a runway and strutted right toward me. His age shows in the crinkle around his eyes, the shadow of hair on his face that he never seems to fully shave, but he carries it well. He doesn't make me feel as young as I am, or as young as he probably should make me feel. When he looks at me, I don't feel like an eighteen-year-old girl, freshman at NYU, still trying to find her way.

When he looks at me, I feel like a woman, a woman worthy of the look he gives, worthy of his admiration, worthy of a designer gown, and a dinner party, and whatever the hell is in the box in his hand.

He opens it without saying a word. My eyes leave his to look at it. It's simple, relatively speaking, nothing like the one Edward gave to Vivian, but that was a movie and this is real life, and I'm starting to wonder if I will ever deserve any of this.

The necklace is beautiful, the gold chain sparkling under the soft lights. There's a small pendant on the end of it, completely round, a crystal stone surrounded by gold. Something is written along the shiny metal but I can't make it out from where I stand, and I want to step closer, to see what it is, but I can't move.

I'm afraid I'll bust my ass in these heels.

He pulls the necklace out and sets the box aside as he walks around behind me. My hair is already pulled up and pinned—Melody's handiwork—so it's easy for him to slip it on and fasten it. He leans down, kissing the back of my neck, as I grasp the pendant to gaze at it.

Carpe Diem. Seize the Day.

"Why me?" I whisper as he steps back around to pause right in front of me. It's a question I've asked before, but one I just can't understand. Out of all the women in the world, why would he choose me?

He answers the exact same way he did the other time. "Why not you?"

Smiling, I let go of the pendant and meet his eyes. "You spoil me, you know."

"No, I don't. Not nearly enough, anyway." He reaches out and cups my chin, making it so I can't look away. "It could be like this all the time, Karissa, every moment of every day. I can give you the best of everything. You just have to let me."

"Why would you?" I ask. "What do you get out of this?"

He leans forward and lightly kisses my lips. "I get you."

"You act like I'm a treasure."

"Aren't you?" he asks. "The way I see it, I hit the jackpot."

I laugh. "I'm more like a five dollar scratch-off than the mega-millions lottery."

"You just don't know your own worth."

His phone rings, shattering the moment. Pulling it from his pocket, he glances at the screen. "Time to go. The car's here."

"You're not driving?" I ask.

"No," he says. "Drunk driving is reckless and stupid."

"You've driven before after you drank."

"I didn't drink enough to get drunk then."

I scoff. "We shared a whole bottle."

"Did we?" he asks. "Because I remember you drinking three quarters of it on your own both times."

My face flushes. "No way."

He nods.

"Ugh." I make a face. "So, what, you're going to drink your fair share tonight?"

"I'm going to drink more than my fair share," he says. "As much as I paid for these tickets, I intend to drink every drop of alcohol they have in the place."

My eyes narrow at those words. "Tickets? What kind of dinner party is this?"

"It's more of a fundraiser, but I figured calling it a party would make it more appealing for you."

"Fundraiser? What kind?"

"The political kind."

I'm stunned, and stammer a bit, but have no idea what to say. He's taking me to a political fundraiser? I'm imagining formal speeches and tuxedos and uptight old men with bitter young wives wanting to bomb other countries and trample civil liberties. Are those the kind of people Naz hangs around? Are those the kind of people we're supposed to be?

But that's not me, and it never will be, and I'm not so sure that could ever be him. I'm imagining a room full of Santinos, judging, deriding, and pointing their sticks at people who they think don't belong. "I don't think I can do this."

"I think you can," Naz says, taking my hand as he leads me outside. There, parked in front of his house, is a stretch limo. The driver opens the back door and Naz ushers me inside. The leather seats are cool, the air temperate, a bottle of champagne in a bucket of ice in front of me.

"This is absurd."

Naz merely laughs as he pours a glass of champagne and hands it to me. "Drink. Relax."

I take the glass and sip it as he pours himself one. "I'm only eighteen, you know, in case you don't remember."

"I haven't forgotten."

"I can't be drinking." Contrary to my words, I guzzle my champagne, downing it so fast that he pours me a second one before he takes his first sip. "I'm not old enough."

"Don't worry about it," he says, relaxing back and putting his arm around me like it's nothing. "It's fine."

"It's illegal."

"Does that bother you?"

"What?"

"Breaking the law," he says. "Do you feel remorse? Do you want to do penance? Ask for forgiveness? Turn yourself in? Beg for leniency? Swear you'll never do it again, that you'll be a good girl forever, that you'll never so much as litter or speed or steal Wi-Fi or jaywalk or pee outside again?"

I laugh. "I've never peed outside."

"But you've done the rest?"

"Yes."

"All illegal," he says. "No big deal."

"That's easy for you to say."

"It is," he admits, clinking his glass with mine. "I'm practically aiding and abetting a criminal right now."

"But—"

He cuts me off. "I don't live my life by someone else's rules. I'm my own boss, my own judge and jury, my own authority. The government calls you an adult, and expects you to pay taxes, but they can't let you enjoy a glass of wine to unwind? I don't agree. I don't care what they say."

"Yet you won't drink and drive."

"That's not because it's illegal," he says. "It's because I'd like to live to see tomorrow so I can take full advantage of another day. I have purely selfish motives. I'm a selfish man."

"You don't seem very selfish to me."

"Ah, but I am. I'm selfish, and possessive, and I have a tendency to be a little controlling... and impatient... and I'm a bit of a neat freak."

"I've noticed—the latter, anyway. I don't know about the rest, but you definitely are a neat freak. Your house is spotless. How often do you have someone clean it?"

"Never," he says. "I clean it myself."

That surprises me, and I think he has to be joking, but his expression is serious. I just can't imagine him on his hands and knees, scrubbing the kitchen floor once a week. "Why?"

"I don't like people coming into my house. I don't trust them."

The drive into Manhattan flies by, as the champagne once again seems to evaporate right before my eyes. By the time we make it to the party, I'm a little lightheaded, and his hands are already doing crazy things to me. Just a simple stroke of my arm, his thumb caressing the clothed skin, seems to set my entire body on fire.

The fundraiser is at a swanky hotel on Park Avenue. The limo drops us off and Naz puts his arm around me, pulling me close to him. I feel him press a kiss to my hair before he whispers, "You're going to do great."

I hope he's speaking the truth.

He hands over our tickets and the second we're through the door, Naz's face lights up, his dimples out in full force, as he greets people by name. He introduces me as simply 'Karissa' as we make our way through a sea of large round tables to one toward the center of the room. Name cards are placed at every seat, and I spot his easily. Ignazio Vitale. Beside it, the card also bears his name with the word 'guest' beneath it.

He pulls the chair out for me, and I sit down, eyeing the other cards at our table but not recognizing any of the names. The seats fill with people Naz seems to know. He introduces me to them, but they pay me no mind, too engrossed in striking up conversation with my date.

My date.

It sounds so weird.

A waiter fills my glass with champagne when he reaches our table, not asking my age, not even hesitating as he looks at me. I pick up my glass and sip it right away, earning a chuckle from Naz. He puts his arm around me, and leans closer, nuzzling into my neck, kissing the shell of my ear as he whispers, "my beautiful little jailbird."

Although it surprises me, nobody bats an eyelash at his playful display of affection. I wonder if it's because he does this often, if he brings women around and shows them off to these people, until I realize nobody's looking. Nobody's watching, their eyes everywhere but on the two of us, like they're purposely giving him privacy.

A political fundraiser is everything I thought it would be, yet nothing like I expected. There are tuxedos, and speeches, and a few snooty people I peg as politicians, but most of the crowd is relaxed. The food is fancy, the champagne expensive, and the people engrossing. The atmosphere seems to flow in waves: the first course prim and proper, the second a little more lax, the third casual, and by the forth everyone's chatting and laughing like old friends.

Or maybe everyone's just drunk by then.

"Dance with me," Naz says, throwing his napkin down on the table as he stands. A band is playing some sort of slow melody on a stage across the room, the floor in front of them clear of tables as couples dance the night away. I shake my head, but he doesn't notice, or else he doesn't care, as he pulls me to my feet and leads me that way.

"I don't think this is a good idea," I say as soon as we're on the dance floor.

"Come on." He pulls me into his arms. "Don't tell me you can't dance."

"Oh, I can dance," I say. "I just can't dance to this."

It sounds like elevator music.

He chuckles, placing his hands on my hips to draw me even closer to him. "Just follow my lead."

I wrap my arms around his neck as my fingers tinker with the wayward curls at his nape. It's easy, mindless, as we really just stand there and sway. It lasts a good minute before I let out a deep sigh. "Okay, this is boring."

As soon as I say it, the song changes, the tempo picking up. Naz swings me around, twirling me, and I nearly fall on my ass without a warning. Every step he takes makes me stumble, but he doesn't seem to mind, and I'm just too drunk to care what anybody thinks... anybody except for him.

He's all that matters.

I'm swaying and twirling, staggering and laughing, tripping over his feet and he just laughs along with me. He dips me once, dips me so low my feet come out from beneath me and I land flat on my back. He bends down, smirking as he yanks me to my feet again, as a male voice cuts through the music behind me. "Mind if I cut in?"

The voice is rough, not gritty in the sexy way, but more like grating sandpaper against sensitive skin. I turn quickly, seeing a vaguely familiar man, a man I've never met before, but I've seen him in pictures and on the television.

The news, mainly.

The front page of the newspaper.

Tucked in the crime section day after day.

His name is a written warning, his face synonymous with 'dangerous'. Growing up, my mother never talked about the boogeyman in the closet or the creature hiding under the bed. She told me about real monsters, and that includes the one standing in front of me.

Raymond Angelo.

The man's question is clearly meant for Naz, although his cold eyes are on me. He's mid-sixties and graying, tall and stocky. He looks like leather and smells like cigars.

I'm grateful Naz said he was possessive, because I think there's no way in hell he'd turn me over to a man like Raymond. My heart pounds hard as Naz hesitates for a moment before he scoffs. "You wouldn't know what to do with her if you had her, old man."

Raymond cocks an eyebrow. "Maybe not, but I'd sure try."

Both men laugh.

They *laugh*.

My heart somehow pounds even harder at that.

Naz waves toward Raymond, introducing us as Ray and Karissa. The man regards me strangely before his eyes flicker to Naz, holding his gaze, like they're having a silent conversation than ends in a nod.

Raymond looks at me again. "It's a pleasure to meet you,

Karissa. I'm sorry to interrupt, but I just need to borrow Vitale here for a moment."

"Uh, okay." I don't know what else to say. Naz kisses my cheek, whispering he'll be right back, as he follows Raymond to the edge of the dance floor. They chat quietly before embracing and going their separate ways.

Naz strolls back over to me, his eyes scanning my face. He pulls me back into his arms, acting as if we weren't interrupted.

"Do you know who that man is?" I ask, unable to help myself. I keep my voice low, not wanting anyone to hear me, especially not Raymond Angelo. He's notorious. He's dangerous.

How could Naz not know?

He pulls back to look at me. "The better question would be do *you* know who he is."

"Of course," I whisper. "He's a gangster."

Naz makes a face at my choice of word. "He's an opportunist. A businessman."

"He's a criminal."

"Says the little jailbird."

"I'm nothing like him. I drink, sure, okay, but he…"

"He what?" Naz asks. "What does he do?"

"He hurts people."

"He does," Naz admits. "But he's also family."

I stop moving. "You're related to him?"

"Not all family is blood, Karissa. Remember?"

I gape at him as those words sink in. I guess there's a reason he fears no one in the city. The ones most people are terrified of are the same ones he calls family.

"Are you okay?" he asks, that chilling look back in his eyes as he regards me. "Tell me if you're not."

Am I okay? Jesus, I don't know. I probably shouldn't be, knowing what I know, remembering what my mother told me, but I'm more surprised than anything. After a moment I nod, and he pulls me closer to him for a kiss. The feel of his lips relaxes me, tingles creeping down my spine. It's a kiss of reassurance, a kiss telling me I'll be fine.

I choose to believe it.

I don't want to think otherwise.

He smirks when he pulls back, running his pointer finger across my bottom lip. "I reserved us a room upstairs. How about we make the most of tonight?"

⌒⌒

The room is modest, the furniture outdated and antique, but it has a certain charm to it, like I've stepped back half a century. Naz switches the bedside lamp on to the lowest setting, a soft glow swaddling the room. It adds a golden hue to the already golden fixtures, illuminating the tan carpet and matching bedspread.

I stroll through the room, over to the vast window. We're high up, giving me a wide view of the city, the lights twinkling in the night. I feel like I'm in another place, living another existence, breathing some other sort of air as I stand here, looking at the world from a different point of view.

It's hard to believe, three miles away, my life waits for me to return to it come morning. I'm Cinderella, wondering if I'm destined for a happy ending after this.

Naz pulls his jacket off and sets it aside as he strolls over to stand behind me. My gaze shifts from the skyline to his distorted reflection in the glass as he reaches for the zipper of my dress and tugs on it. The sound seems magnified in the silence as he pulls it the whole way down, his rough knuckles grazing my spine.

It sends a chill through me.

He pushes the dress forward, off my shoulders and down my arms, letting it drop to the floor like it's nothing. I stand there wearing only a lacy thong, almost the exact shade as my skin tone.

The woman reflected back at me in the cold glass looks stark naked, completely exposed and bared for him. It's peculiar, seeing myself that way. I don't make a habit of checking myself out, but as I watch him stroke my bare arms and kiss my shoulder blade, I actually find what's in front of me beautiful.

Turning to face him, I step away from the dress and kick off the heels, regretting losing those extra inches when I have to push up on my tiptoes to reach his lips. I kiss him softly, wrapping my arms around his neck.

It's a sweet kiss, slow and gentle. My fingertips tremble against his skin.

He pulls back, surveying me. "You sure you're okay?"

I nod slowly. "Why wouldn't I be?"

He offers a slight shrug as his gaze leaves my face and trails down my body. "You want to play around a bit?"

"Yes."

I answer instantly, not even stopping to think what that might mean until he smirks at me. There's a slight sinister pull to it, like a predator spotting prey in the distance. I kiss the corner of his mouth, and try to squelch my flare of anxiety, as he pulls me away from the window and over to the bed. I run my hands down his chest, reaching for the buttons on his vest, but he grasps my wrists. "Uh-uh, did I tell you to do that?"

"You didn't tell me not to."

He pulls my hands away as he leans down, whispering, "Don't."

The lone word is little more than warm breath against my skin, fanning the flames of my desire, kindling the fire deep inside of me. I exhale shakily, but before I can speak, he shoves me away from him and spins me around. I gasp as he picks me up and throws me on the bed on my stomach, straddling my legs and pinning me there.

"Wait," I say, my heart racing. His weight presses on me as he pulls on my panties, tearing them off. "Wait just a second, Naz."

"I don't have a pause button, sweetheart." His voice is chilling, a sense of detachment to it. "If you don't want to play, you know how to stop me. All you have to do is say the word."

"Stop."

"That's not it."

He doesn't stop, and I'm not at all surprised. I knew that wasn't the right word, but I can't say it. I can't use a safe word. Not now, not for this. I can't shout "red" or even "yellow" when all I want is green. When all I want is to feel him inside of me, to have him consume me, to be the air he breathes and the only thing he needs.

My head is foggy and his body is constricting, his weight welcoming as it presses upon me, one hand heavily on the center of my back as I hear him fumble with his belt buckle with the other.

I try to look, try to see, my cheek flat against the bed as I crane my neck to get just a peek, but it's barely a glimpse, a flash of dark suit in the dim lighting. He doesn't undress, doesn't even take off his shoes, merely unbuckling his pants enough to free himself from his restraints.

He's between my legs, forcing them apart and shoving against me, pushing roughly inside of me. I cry out as he fills me, stretching me to form around him. It doesn't hurt, my body reacting the second he laid a finger on me.

"Fuck, you're so wet," he says, laying down on me, his heavy suit rubbing against my bare skin. The buttons are cold against my back. "You like it like this, don't you?"

He thrusts a few times, hard, and I bite down on my bottom lip to keep from crying out, but he doesn't accept my silence.

"I asked you a question," he growls.

"Yes," I gasp, closing my eyes. "I love it."

"I know you do." His voice is a lust-fueled murmur in my ear as his hand snakes around my stomach, slipping below, his fingertips seeking out my clit as his strong arm forces me back against him tighter, angling my ass so he can pound into me deeper. "You're a little ragdoll, aren't you? You want to be tossed around; you want me to use you any way I see fit. Because you know... you fucking know..." He thrusts so hard pain stabs my stomach. "You're my favorite toy."

I shouldn't find his words as hot as I do, but they spark something inside of me, tingles engulfing my entire body, from the top of my head to the tips of my toes. It's emotional, an overwhelming honesty, that I can't restrain from tumbling from my lips. "I want to be."

"You are," he says, stroking my clit as he fucks me harder... and harder... and harder with each thrust of his hips. "I knew it the first time I saw that timid smile and those wide, innocent eyes. It was wrong... fuck, it was so wrong of me to want it, to want you, but I couldn't resist."

His voice is strained, the words coming out like breathless panting.

"I thought I could play with you a bit, and let you go, but once I had you, Karissa, I had to keep you. I couldn't walk away."

"Then don't," I whisper, not sure if it's loud enough for him to even hear, but he squeezes me tighter to him, stroking my clit faster, fucking me deeper, as he whispers back in my ear.

"I won't," he says. "I can't. You're mine now."

His fingers work their magic. I come apart in his arms, locked in his embrace, captive beneath him, but I've never felt so free before as I do in that moment, when the pleasure sweeps through me, taking every speck of anxiety, every worry and insecurity I've ever had, and wiping them away. He bottoms me out and then makes me whole, filling me up with everything he says, and does, making me feel what he believes.

I'm beautiful.

I'm special.

I'm his.

He says nothing else, slowing his movements, letting the orgasm wash over me and fade away before the switch in him flips again.

All at once he turns from man to beast, pawing me, clawing me, ravaging every inch of my body that he can reach. He fucks me mercilessly, to the point I can't think. I can do nothing but take it, absorb the impact, my voice nothing but incoherent noises conjured up from his animalistic feats.

The words are there the entire time; "yellow" is on the tip of my tongue, so close to springing forward whenever he gets so rough I can't breathe, but I swallow it back again and again with a gasp of air. I don't want him to stop; I don't want him to slow down. I don't want him to restrain himself with me. I want everything he'll give me. His hands are strong, his body like steel, but as he pounds into me, I think maybe it's what's inside that's heaviest.

He's purging his soul, and as scary as I think the deepest parts of him might be, I want it all.

I want to see it.

He pulls out to finish and sits there on his knees, catching his breath, before moving off of me. I can't move, can do nothing but lay there. I think I'm now a part of the bed, nothing more than thread that has started to unravel. He's quiet as he sits there, and despite my eyes being closed, I know he's watching me. I can sense his gaze.

After a moment, he reaches over, his touch feather-light as he runs his fingertips along my back. Freckles dot my skin, an inheritance from my father... the only thing that man ever gave me.

Naz traces them, much like I once did the scars on his chest, like he's connecting the dots to form a picture. My eyes open, but I don't move, not wanting to disrupt what he's doing.

It's soothing.

"What are you drawing?" I ask quietly.

"The future."

I smile to myself. "What does it look like?"

"I'm not sure yet," he says. "It's still coming together for me."

He looks passive, relaxed, still fully dressed and now tucked away, not at all like someone who just fucked me ruthlessly. He's a gentle giant, harmless and soft, like a teddy bear.

Except deep down, I know he's not.

And when his eyes cut my way, and I see the darkness on the surface, I'm reminded that this man hangs out with monsters.

And one might even exist inside of him.

Chapter Ten

I'm pouting.

Full on puppy dog eyes, lips puckered and pulled down into a frown kind of pout.

Ugh, pathetic.

So much for the strong woman I felt like last night, owning her sexuality and taking what she wants from the world. I've reverted about a decade, to the pouty, moody pre-teen who gave her mother a fit for refusing to let her to stay out past dark so she could go to a school dance.

"So unfair," I mutter, slouching in the cool leather seat. The gaudy evening gown feels absurd this morning, big and showy and heavy against my skin.

Naz chuckles beside me. He's got his feet kicked up with his suit half fixed, the tie knotted loosely, the jacket and vest resting beside him on the seat. His eyes are on his phone, doing whatever it is he does. I don't know.

"You have nobody to blame but yourself," he says. "I told you, you're welcome to come home with me."

"But you have stuff to do, and I'm still wearing this dress, and I really need to shower, and I have class in the morning anyway, so I should just head back to the dorm, you know, because of all that."

"So I've heard."

It's the third time I've ran through all of my excuses on why I need to go, but I don't sound any more certain than I did the first time. Every bit of it is true, sure, but I'm dreading saying goodbye to this man.

So I pout some more.

"You know I have hot water," he says, "and clean clothes."

"Women's clothes?"

He laughs again. "I'm afraid not, but I'm sure I have something you can fit."

"I bet I'd look great in one of your suits."

That draws his attention. His eyes scan me for a second as he raises an eyebrow, a look of curiosity on his face. "Huh."

Huh. That's all he says before turning right back to his phone.

"I still have school tomorrow," I point out.

"I can drop you off in the morning," he says.

"But don't you have stuff to do?" I ask. "I wouldn't want to bother you."

"Yes, but you wouldn't be bothering me."

He has an answer for everything, but still, I just sit in the back of the car and pout as the driver heads through Greenwich Village, straight toward NYU. The car pulls up to the curb when we arrive, the driver getting out. Naz puts his phone down, his hand covering my cheek as he leans over to kiss me.

I don't know what to say, figuring I've said it all already when I thanked him half a dozen times for the great night, so I say nothing, getting out when the driver opens the door for me. I make the trek inside barefoot, carrying my shoes, and dig my ID out of my purse to scan myself inside.

I can feel eyes on me as I stroll through the lobby, feel them on me while I wait for the elevator, feel them on me during the trip upstairs, acutely aware that I'm doing the most obvious walk of shame of all time.

But I'm not ashamed, not in the least.

I stroll down the hallway when I reach the thirteenth floor, straight to my room in the corner. Loud rap music pours from it, rattling the walls. My hand grasps the knob and turns as soon as I get there, grateful Melody never locks the damn door because I don't think I have my key. As soon as I start to open it, I hear her voice.

"Oh God, oh yes!" she cries. "Just like that!"

The thump-thump-thumping of her bed hitting the wall sounds like a jackhammer. I stall instantly, not wanting to see what's going on in there. My hand is off the knob again, the door clicking closed, neither of them even hearing it from the way she cries out.

"Oh, Paul, baby, you feel so good!"

Cringing, I walk away, shaking my head. *Awkward*. On my way back to the elevator, I pull out my phone, letting out a resigned sigh as I dial the number. I press the down arrow just as he answers.

Naz foregoes any sort of greeting, merely saying, "I'm waiting downstairs."

He is. The car is still parked there, exactly where it was when I got out, the driver waiting by the curb. He opens the door for me, and I slide in, seeing Naz still focused on his phone, looking just as casual.

His eyes cut to me when the door closes. "Huh."

"Huh," I echo. "What does 'huh' mean?"

It's his second favorite thing to say, besides 'nonsense'.

"It means it didn't take you as long as I thought it would to change your mind. I expected you to at least change before you started regretting it."

"And what, you were just going to sit down here?" I ask. "How long would you have waited?"

"As long as it took."

"And if I didn't change my mind?"

"You would've," he says, matter-of-fact. "You like me."

"I like you?"

"Yes."

I laugh but don't dispute it because yes, I like him. I like him a lot, so much that I'm terrified to admit to what degree I like this man. And from the way his eyes flit to me, and the smirk that touches his lips, I suspect he might know my dilemma, might know just how bad I have it.

"It's okay, though," he says, "because I like you, too."

His house is ice cold when we get there. I can see my breath whenever I exhale, a cloud of fog in the air around me. I shiver, wrapping my arms around myself, but the chill doesn't seem to bother Naz. He sets his coat and vest down on the living room couch as he watches me.

"You know where the bathroom is," he says. "Go ahead and take a hot shower. I'll warm the place up while you do that."

I hesitate. "Am I supposed to put the dress back on?"

"No, I'll leave something on my bed for you to wear."

I make my way upstairs on my own. It's dark up here, despite the sun shining brightly outside, like the top half of his house is always in shadows. I head straight to the bathroom and lock myself inside, turning on the hot water to try to warm the air.

I reach behind me, struggling to unzip the dress on my own, and step out of it, unsure what to do with the thing so I just leave it in the corner. I step under the water, flinching at the heat, but I don't dare turn the temperature down. The room is way too cold.

I stand under the spray until my skin turns pink and wrinkled, soaking up as much of the warmth as I can, relishing the sensation of the water beating against me. The pressure feels like hands kneading my taut muscles, soothing the soreness away. Faint bruises blemish my skin in places, remnants of his strong grip, reminders of the way he owned my body, like it belonged only to him.

I swipe some soap and even some of his shampoo, stepping out smelling like Irish Spring and men's Frizz-Ease. Goose bumps spring up along my flesh as soon as the air hits me. I dry off, wrapping a thick white towel around me as I scamper from the bathroom.

Just like Naz said, clothes are laying on the bed, a pair of black sweatpants and a plain white undershirt. I drop the towel and pull them on, scowling at my lack of underwear and bra. It takes me rolling down the pants a few times at the waist for them to stay up, still dragging at my feet.

I stroll back downstairs, arms crossed over my chest as I seek out Naz, wondering where he went. I head for the den when I find him nowhere else, and hear his voice as I approach the doorway.

"Yeah, you're right, it's more complicated than I expected."

I stall a few feet from the door, realizing he's on the phone and not wanting to interrupt. I know I should walk back away, to give him some privacy, but I just stand in place.

Call it curiosity.

"I haven't changed my mind," he says, "and I'm not going to. You know better than to think I'll walk away in the middle of anything, especially something like this. I've been waiting for this moment for a long time, Ray. Just as long as you."

I shiver. I'm not sure if it's the cold or the name that causes it.

"Santino's been stalling," he says. "I'll pay him another visit this week and light a fire under his ass to get the file."

A file? That's what he wants?

"No, I don't want to do that if I don't have to. I told you, it's changed... it's complicated. Santino will come through. He's just afraid of sticking his neck out, you know, and getting his head chopped off. He thought he wouldn't have to see me again after he paid you, but he should know not all debts can be forgiven with just cash."

He pauses for a moment, the silence deafening. My heart is pounding so hard I'm afraid he can hear it, that he'll know I'm standing here. But after a moment, he lets out a laugh. "Ah, come on,

Ray, you know me. You know I like playing with fire. It's one of my specialties."

More words are exchanged, but I don't hear them. I back away from the door, jetting back upstairs whenever it's safe and I don't think he'll hear my footsteps. I walk back to the bathroom and grab my dress, taking it to his room, where the towel still lays on the floor. I pick it up, too, and glance around, looking for a hamper, but there isn't one in here.

Turning around, I'm about to head out in search of one when I nearly run straight into the body blocking the doorway. It startles me so much I scream, a high-pitch shriek, as my knees nearly give out. Naz is standing there, eyeing me warily, as I clutch the dress tightly to my chest.

I didn't hear him come upstairs.

"You scare easily," he says. "I was just coming to check on you. You've been gone a while."

"Yeah, I, uh… I mean, I took a long shower, and I didn't want to get out because, you know, it felt good, and it's cold… and why is it cold?"

I'm a terrible liar. I know.

He's looking at me like he knows it, too.

"I forgot to turn the heat up yesterday before we left," he says. "Temperature dropped overnight. I lit a fire in the fireplace in the den, so it's warm down there."

"Oh, great," I say, holding out the bundle in my arms. "I was just going to put these somewhere… wherever they go."

He takes them from me, and motions with his head for me to head out. I step past him, walking back downstairs with him on my heels. He veers right to a room I've never been in—the laundry room. He drops the stuff off and follows me to the den.

It is warm in here, and I relish the sensation as I head straight for the source, feeling the flames from a few feet away, wiping the chill away, but it doesn't nothing to rid my skin of the goose bumps.

"How about a movie?" he suggests.

"Sure," I say. "You pick this time."

"You ever see *Twelve Angry Men*?" His favorite movie, I remember. I shake my head, having never even heard of it, and a look of disturbance crosses his face. "Huh. We're going to have to rectify that."

He puts the movie in as I sit on the couch. An old black-and-white flick, it turns out. Naz settles in beside me, putting his arm over my shoulder and pulling me to him.

Sighing, I tuck in at his side.

He's quiet, engrossed in the movie, his hand absently stroking my arm, tickling my skin and distracting me from the movie. After awhile he leans down, pressing a kiss to the top of my head. "You smell like me."

"I used your shampoo," I say. "And your soap. Hope you don't mind. I probably should've asked first."

"I told you to make yourself at home," he says. "I don't want you to feel like you have to tiptoe around, afraid of doing something wrong or hearing something you shouldn't, like phone conversations."

My blood runs cold at those words. I can feel his eyes on me and not the screen. "I, uh..." I don't know what to say.

"It's okay," he says, those words silencing me. He kisses the top of my head again, subject closed as he goes back to watching the movie. A few minutes pass before Naz lets out a light laugh. "So, tell me something... did you at least google me?"

I tense. "What?"

"Come on," he says, shifting around in his seat as I sit up. "Don't tell me you didn't do your research."

I scoff. Of course I googled him. I did it after waking up in his bed that first morning, right after learning his name. I'm not an idiot. What woman wouldn't? "So, yeah, okay... I did. But can you blame me?"

"Of course not," he says. "Did you find anything?"

"No," I grumble. "Nothing."

"Disappointing," he says playfully. "But if it's any consolation, I had about as much luck with you."

"You googled me?"

"Of course," he says. "You can never be too careful. Had to make sure you were who you said you were."

Chapter Eleven

Change doesn't happen overnight. There's no button that's pushed to magically alter everything.

Change happens little by little.

Day by day.

Hour by hour.

It's the ticking of a secondhand, moving painstakingly, as it makes its way around the clock. You don't realize it until it's already over, the minute gone forever, as you're thrust right into the next one, the time still ticking away, whether you want it to or not.

Before long you have a hard time remembering the world as it once was, the person you were then, too focused on the world around you instead.

A world full of promise.

A world full of excitement.

A world full of Naz.

I can't fathom a world any other way.

I'm not sure when it happened, which minute it was that drove me to the brink, pushing me over the edge and making me feel like I can fly without wings. Time consuming turned all-consuming as the man became the beat of my heart and the blood in my veins, stealing the little piece of my soul I always kept tucked away. He crashed through my defenses and knocked down my walls, and all it took was ticking seconds, one after another, slowly altering it all.

"You've changed."

I glance across the room at Melody when she says that, the television remote in my hand. I've been channel surfing for the past ten minutes, flipping so fast it's starting to look like a strobe light flashing. She's huddled on her bed, philosophy book open on her lap. "What?"

"You've changed," she repeats.

I just stare at her.

"We have a fucking test in like an hour on Confucius, and I don't think you've cracked open your book all morning. Usually you're the one cramming until the last second, yet you look like you don't give two shits about anything. You're all chillaxing and relax-y. Confucius says your ass has changed."

I let out a laugh. "It's pointless. I could get every answer right on the test and the bastard would just deduct points because I didn't dot an 'i' or something."

"So, what, you're giving up?"

"Real knowledge is to know the extent of one's ignorance."

Her brow furrows. "Are you on drugs?"

"No," I laugh. "It's Confucius. It means it doesn't matter if I open my book or not, Melody. I'll never know everything, I'll never get it all right anyway, and whatever... I'm cool with that."

She looks stunned. "You've changed more than Biggie Smalls."

My brow furrows. "He changed?"

"He went from ashy to nasty to classy, didn't he?"

I laugh as she recites one of his songs and lean back against the wall, spreading my legs out on my bed. "Yeah, well, you've changed, too. I don't think I've ever seen you study so much for something before. What gives?"

"I just want to try to do good," she says, slamming her book closed. "Paul got a B in Santino's class last year, so I really want to get one, too, so he doesn't think I'm an idiot or something."

"You shouldn't change who you are for a guy."

"Ha, look who's talking! You went from rocking Payless boots to nine hundred dollar Jimmy Choos."

"Is that from a rapper?"

"No, that was all me. Pretty good, huh?"

Okay, maybe she hasn't changed *that* much.

"Regardless, I'm still me," I say. "Just me with more stuff."

A lot more stuff.

My eyes scan the room at the mention of it. My side is starting to look like Melody's, our living space entirely too small to cram everything in it anymore. One thing I learned quickly is that Naz is a giver, never hesitating to lavish me with the best of everything. Shoes. Clothes. Flowers. Orgasms.

So many fucking orgasms.

The material things I can do without, and I tell him that, again and again, but only a fool would turn down an orgasm from him.

"The point is," I say, turning back to Melody, "you shouldn't feel like you have to work to impress Paul. If he's not already impressed, if he doesn't already think you're brilliant, then screw him."

She scowls at me but doesn't respond because she knows I'm right. Tossing her book aside, she gets up, stretching, as she steps over to the mirror to put on lip-gloss. I start flipping through channels again. I'm as ready as I'm going to be, wearing jeans and a sweater and my favorite scarf. All I have to do is put on my aforementioned Payless boots.

"Have you told your mom yet?" Melody asks.

"Told her what?"

"About your sugar daddy."

I roll my eyes and cringe, unsure which response that warrants. "First of all, he's not my sugar daddy, he's my..."

"Your what?"

Fuck if I know. Boyfriend sounds so silly. It doesn't begin to cover the force of nature that is Naz. He's too much to cram into a box with a pretty little label. "He's just... mine."

"Well, have you told your mother about your whatever he is?"

I scoff. "Of course not. She'll lose her mind."

"You think so?"

"I know so. This is a woman who tried to keep me from going to prom because she was terrified. I tried to explain that there would be chaperones, but it just freaked her out more. She all but cried when I insisted on going, telling me it wasn't safe, that I had to promise her I wouldn't leave the dance, that I wouldn't go anywhere alone with anyone without her knowing. I'm surprised she didn't sit out in the parking lot and watch the whole time." I pause. "Actually, she might've done just that. But the point is she's liable to have a stroke when I tell her about Naz."

"You'll have to tell her eventually."

"I will," I say. "But I have to spend next weekend with her, and I'd rather it not be one long freak out where I try to explain something to her that I can barely understand myself, you know?"

"I do not envy you," Melody mutters, her focus on her reflection. "Actually, I'm lying. I do. I envy those new black Louboutin pumps you got. They would look great with the dress I'm wearing tonight."

"You can borrow them," I say.

She swings around to face me. "Really?"

"Yeah, why not? You let me borrow your clothes all the time."

More like she forces me into them but close enough.

She squeals, running over to attack me with a hug, but I shoo her away so I can pull on my boots. After gathering my things, I sling my bag on my back.

"You're going in that?" Melody asks. "All sweater-y and scarf-y?"

I roll my eyes. "It's just a test. I have to come back here to shower for tonight, anyway. Who cares what I look like?"

Melody shrugs, grabbing her things and following me out the door. The trek to the philosophy building takes about fifteen minutes today, the sidewalks congested as people rush around. Melody's yammering away as usual, still talking up a storm when we walk into the classroom.

Santino is sitting at his desk, hands folded in front of him, eyes scanning the crowd as we take our seats. We sit in our usual spots in the back, but even from here I can tell he looks like hell, glasses askew and hair unkempt.

"Looks like Satan hasn't slept," Melody says. "Too busy torturing poor souls for a moment of rest."

He wastes no time, passing out the tests before everyone has even sat down. I skim through it as soon as I get mine, assessing the potential damage. Mostly multiple-choice, but even the few fill in the blank and paragraph answers feel easy enough.

If I don't pass this one, we have a problem.

I can hear Melody huffing beside me as I breeze through the test. I'm done in fifteen minutes, the rest of the class following suit not far after. Melody is the last, with twenty minutes to go. Santino collects the tests but instead of dismissing us early, he picks up a piece of chalk and writes a single word in all capitals across the chalkboard.

MURDER.

There's a flow of murmurs through the classroom that he silences when he picks up that godforsaken stick and whacks it against his desk so hard I'm surprised it doesn't break.

"Show of hands," he says. "Who thinks murder is wrong?"

All at once, every hand in the classroom goes up.

His eyes scan us. "Why?"

Just as fast, nearly every hand drops back down. Santino scans who's left, pointing at a boy in the front row.

"Because it's illegal."

Santino stares at him like he's an idiot before moving on, pointing at a girl along the side.

"It's immoral," she says. "It's wrong to take someone's life."

He moves right along, calling on others, who give much the same answers. After everyone who volunteered has spoken, he scans our faces again and shakes his head. "Why is it you all know murder is wrong but you can't say why it's wrong, except that it just is? It's wrong because it's illegal; it's illegal because it's wrong; it's wrong because it's immoral; it's immoral because it's wrong. But why?"

The silence is deafening.

"Show of hands," he says again. "Who believes in the death penalty?"

The majority of the class raises their hands, Melody included. I waver but eventually put mine up, not so much a cynic as not wanting him to call on me for this conversation. He smirks, all crazy-eyed, as he surveys our hands. "Ah, so you guys don't think murder is wrong?"

Hands slowly drop down.

"If we define murder as the premeditated killing of another human being, is putting someone to death not murder? What makes one situation right and the other so wrong?"

"Because people on death row are murderers," the same guy from earlier says, not bothering to raise his hand this time.

"So it's okay to murder somebody if they've also murdered?" Santino asks. "Equal justice? An eye for an eye?"

"Yes," the boy says. "But that's not murder. Murder is killing someone innocent."

"Did you know," Santino says, tapping his stick against the floor, "that since the death penalty was reinstated, 139 people slated for death have been exonerated and set free? In that same time, we've executed over twelve hundred. How many of them do you think were innocent? Maybe none, but if it's even one, doesn't that make it murder? After all, you've killed an innocent man."

Nobody knows what to say... except for the same damn boy. "It's unfortunate that they had to die, but it's for the greater good."

"And that's precisely what a lot of murderers would say about their victims," Santino says. "So again, show of hands. Who believes in the death penalty?"

Only a few brave souls raise their hand this time.

"Two page paper on the topic of murder," he says, turning away from us with a wave of the hand, dismissing class. "Due Tuesday."

A collective groan echoes through the room. It's a holiday weekend—Easter. I get up and grab my bag, heading for the door with Melody beside me. We stroll through the building and I glance up just as we step outside, my footsteps stalling when I come face to face with Naz. He's parked out front, leaning against the side of his Mercedes, his eyes zeroing in on me.

"Uh, hey," I say when he steps toward me, suddenly wishing I had done a little more to get ready, after all.

"Hey." He kisses the corner of my mouth before turning to Melody. "Hello again."

"Hey there," she says, smiling warmly at him, before her eyes turn to me. "I'll meet you back at the room, Kissimmee."

Naz's brow furrows as Melody walks away. "Kissimmee?"

"It's what my mother calls me," I say, shrugging. "Play on my name or something, I guess."

"Kissimmee," he says again. "Like the city in Florida?"

"Yep," I say. "So what are you doing here? I thought we were meeting up later?"

"We are," he says. "I'm actually here on business."

"Ah." I eye him peculiarly. "I guess I'll let you get to that, then. See you later?"

"Wouldn't miss it for the world."

He kisses me again before strolling away, heading inside now that almost everyone has cleared from the building. I stare at the door for a moment, and I'd be lying if I said I wasn't tempted to follow him inside, to watch him, to see what he's doing, but I don't. He's caught me every other time, and I know if I follow, he'll catch me again.

Sighing, I turn away and make the walk back to the dorm.

When I see Naz again, hours later, he seems to be in a peculiar mood. He doesn't even look at me when I slip into the passenger seat of the Mercedes, doesn't even attempt to get out to open my door. I don't expect it, or need it, but when he's usually chivalrous, it stands out to me.

As soon as I snap my seatbelt into place, he swings the car around and merges into traffic, not saying a word. His eyes are focused on the road, darting between the windshield and the rearview mirror, never once turning my way. I settle into the seat, leaving him to his silence as we drive through Manhattan toward the bridge.

We were supposed to go to dinner. I'm not sure where, but I dressed up for it, even putting on a pair of the new heels he bought me. But it becomes clear when he heads toward his neighborhood that we're going straight to his house instead.

I turn to him, confused, and start to speak, when his eyes meet mine finally. The look he gives me makes me swallow back my question, the darkness telling me that his bad mood is deeper than just on the surface.

I think I prefer the silence to what might come from his lips.

Instead, I turn back away, staring out the side window as the houses rush past, familiar now from coming here so often. He still doesn't speak when we arrive, getting out and standing beside the car, waiting for me to walk ahead of him.

He unlocks the door, ushering me inside. The click of the deadbolt behind me is magnified in the icy silence as he relocks the door right away. I flinch involuntarily at the sound, watching him.

"Is everything okay?" I ask, unable to contain the question any longer. It's been a while since I've felt this nervous around him. I've grown used to him, but it feels different now. He feels different. I'm used to my relaxed, smug playboy, charming and intense, and not this wound tight, unnerving man in front of me.

He nods, pulling off his jacket before turning to me. "Why?"

"You just seem... edgy."

"It's been a long day," he says. "You okay with ordering in for dinner?"

"Sure."

He strolls to the kitchen, flicking on the light as he goes. I follow behind, stalling in the doorway to glance around. I haven't spent any time in here, and he doesn't seem to, either, although it's immaculate, everything polished and shiny and appearing still brand-new.

Naz grabs a takeout menu from a drawer beside the refrigerator and pulls out his phone, dialing the number on it. An Italian place, it turns out. He orders a large pepperoni pizza and hesitates, turning to me while he's still on the phone. "Do you have anything chocolate? Yeah, chocolate, some kind of dessert." He's quiet for a second before he cuts in, raising his voice. "I said chocolate. I don't know what universe you live in, but panna cotti with berries isn't chocolate. You want to treat me like a jamook, like I don't know what fucking panna cotti is, and I'll show you a jamook."

I tense, staring at him with shock as his anger surfaces. He tosses the menu back in the drawer and shuts it before interjecting again. "Give me both of those. Yeah. And hurry it up."

He hangs up, tossing his phone down on the counter with no regard, and brushes right by me without speaking. I stare at his discarded phone, my stomach clenching, as he heads upstairs.

I don't follow.

Instead, I make my way to the den, not turning on the light or touching anything. I sit down on the couch and pull out my own phone, tinkering around with it to distract myself. I'd text Melody but she's on her way to meet Paul's parents to spend Easter with them, and I don't want to burden her.

It takes Naz a while to return. I don't hear him, never do, but he pops up in the den, switching on the light when he walks in. My eyes remain glued to my phone as I flick little colorful birdies across the screen, but I can feel his eyes.

Now he's looking at me.

His voice is quiet, calmer, when he asks, "What are you doing?"

"Killing pigs."

He lets out dry laugh. "My favorite pastime."

I cut my eyes at him. "You play Angry Birds?"

I can't imagine him playing games like this.

"Sure, whatever." He sits down on the arm of the couch beside me and offers a small smile. The sight of it, although strained, lightens the air. He might be mad, but he's not mad at *me*. "You look beautiful tonight. I feel bad not taking you out. I should be showing you off."

"It's okay." I set my phone aside and shift my body to face him. "I don't mind staying in. I like being here."

"Good, because I like you being here." He reaches out and cups my chin, running his thumb across my bottom lip. I think he's going to kiss me, and my breath hitches in anticipation, but he switches focus instead. "So, how's school going?"

"Uh, okay." We've mentioned school before, but it's the first time he's outwardly asked me about it like this. "Most of my classes are going well."

"How's philosophy?"

"Terrible."

"Huh." He pulls his hand away from my face. "If it gets too bad, let me know and I'll take care of it."

"You going to take my tests for me? Do my homework?"

"Whatever you want me to do."

A loud chime echoes through the house, and suddenly he's tense again, his back stiffening and shoulders squaring. He sits freakishly still, like he's been turned to stone by Medusa's stare, as the chime rings yet again.

"Pretty sure that's probably the pizza dude at the door," I say.

He cuts his eyes at me as he stands up, mumbling "stay here" before stalking out. I stay where I am, twiddling my thumbs, until he returns with the food. He sets the pizza box on the table with two smaller containers on top of it. Nosey, I pop them open, seeing it's chocolate mousse and tiramisu.

"You like chocolate," he says, waving toward it as if to explain. He got them for me. "Eat up. I need to make a few calls and handle some things."

"You're not going to eat?"

"Not right now."

"Afraid it's poisoned? Because the way you talked to the guy on the phone, I might be a little worried, too."

He laughs as he turns on the TV, turning the volume up, before dropping the remote on the couch cushion beside me. "It's safe. I'll be back in a bit."

He walks out, leaving me in the den alone again.

I eat and flip through channels, eat some more and flip some more, going again and again until I'm stuffed and I've been through every show a few times, settling on some reality program I'm not really paying attention to. I tinker with my phone some more before getting up and strolling around the den, once more migrating to his bookshelves.

I don't know how much time passes—fifteen minutes, maybe thirty—before he strolls in, catching me as I pull an old, worn book off the shelf. *Crime & Punishment.*

"Good book," he says, sitting down in his chair behind his desk, setting his phone in front of him. "Ever read it?"

"No."

I'm suddenly regretting everything I said to Melody earlier this afternoon. I want to read the damn book just so I don't look like an idiot to him. "Huh."

I return the book to the shelf, my fingertips skimming the spines

163

of those near it. "You have enough philosophy books I think you probably could do my work for me."

"It's an interesting subject," he says. "When you don't overthink it, anyway."

I turn to him curiously. "Do you believe in the death penalty?"

"Yes."

He doesn't even have to think about it.

"Do you think murder is wrong?"

I expect another emphatic answer, an outright yes, but this time he hesitates. "That's too broad of a question. Are you excluding justifiable homicide?"

"Is killing ever justifiable?"

"Of course it is." He gazes at me, and he looks like he wants to say more, but he hesitates again. "Have you heard of the Plank of Carneades? Santino teach you it?"

"No."

"Let's say we're shipwrecked, and we both see a plank floating in the water, but it's only big enough to hold one of us."

"This sounds eerily like the end of Titanic."

He laughs and continues. "You get to the plank first, but knowing I'm going to drown if I don't do something, I shove you off and steal it for myself. Because of that, you die. Was that murder?"

"Yes."

"Are you sure?"

His question makes me pause. "You killed me for the plank."

"Or did I just defend my own life?" he asks. "It's kill or be killed, so yes, Karissa, sometimes killing is justifiable."

"But I wasn't threatening you."

"Maybe not, but you were still a threat."

He stares at me pointedly. I don't know what to say to that. I don't know what to think.

"It's irrelevant in this case, though," he says. "I'd give you the plank."

"Because you couldn't kill?"

"Because I couldn't kill you."

Those words should freak me out, and I do feel a tingle creep down my spine, but I get a strange thrill at the protectiveness in his voice. Every girl wants her very own Jack Dawson.

Slowly, I stroll over to him and climb onto his lap, straddling him in the chair. I wrap my arms around his neck, gazing into his eyes, drinking in the hint of emotion I find.

He's a whirlpool of darkness, and I feel myself getting sucked deeper and deeper into the depths of his abyss.

I'm drowning in him.

His hands run up my back as he pulls me to him for a kiss. I can feel him hardening, straining the crotch of his pants, heat rushing through me at the sensation. To know I have the same effect on him that he has on me is intoxicating. My fingertips tingle with the urge to touch him.

My hands drift down between us. I reach for his belt, fumbling with the buckle for a second before he restrains me. I pull back and start to pout when he undoes his belt, making work of his button and zipper, before pulling me back to him for another kiss.

I don't waste my chance. The second he lets go, my hand slips into his pants and wraps around his cock. I pull it out between us, stroking it as I kiss him back with everything in me.

He's warm, so damn warm. I can feel him growing in my palm, hardening like concrete. My thumb grazes the head, feeling the bead of wetness. I suddenly want to taste it, run my tongue along the slit and take him in my mouth, but he doesn't give me the chance.

He grasps my hips, pulling me toward him, grinding himself against me. "Let me inside of you."

The words make me shiver.

I don't undress, slipping the skimpy fabric of my thong aside, grateful I wore this damn dress, after all. I lift up and sink down onto him, my eyes rolling in the back of my head.

I shift my hips, kissing him deeply, savoring every second he's inside of me. It's unlike any other time, a stolen moment of passion, no rushing for the finish line or desperately jumping hurdles, merely enjoying being in the race. My hands seek out his, our fingers entwining, as he presses them against his chest.

It's the most intimate thing I've ever experienced. Fully clothed, I somehow feel completely exposed, sliced open and vulnerable, yet so, so valuable. The man could snap me like a twig, but he holds onto me like I'm the strong plank, like I'm that lifeline in the water, his means of survival, his only chance of rescue. He holds my hands so tightly my fingers ache, but his face looks relaxed, like he's not worried at all about drifting away.

He breaks the kiss as he tilts his head back, his eyes closed, his lips parted as he lets out a shaky breath. I kiss his mouth, his cheek, his scruffy chin, my lips traveling all over his face, exploring his skin. He doesn't move, doesn't do anything but squeeze my hands tighter, pressing them against him harder. It's like he's pulling me inside of him, and I can feel his pulse, his strong heartbeat, pounding in his chest.

He's a tornado of emotion I can't begin to understand, but I love it. I love *him*. And I know it when I look at him, seeing such serenity in his expression. I want every cell of him in every cell of me, because when he's inside of me, I feel beautiful. I feel strong. I feel like I know what love means.

Love means seeing the beauty in the ugly, the light in the dark, and accepting that even if the lights are off, and I can't see what's in front of me, there will be something there to guide my way. Love means turning yourself inside out, handing yourself over to somebody else, and trusting them... trusting them to touch you, to handle you, to bend you, but never, ever break what you give them.

And I love him.

Fuck, I love him.

"I love you." The words tumble from my lips as a strained

whisper, a shuddering breath forced from me as the butterflies take flight in my stomach, constricting my chest until I can't fucking breathe.

His eyes slowly open to meet my gaze. He doesn't move—doesn't react—stares at me so hard it feels like he's eye-fucking my soul, like maybe he thought he heard me, but it couldn't have possibly been so.

So I say it again. "I love you."

The second time gets a reaction, his expression strained like he's fighting off a flinch. Before I can do anything else, he speaks quietly. "Don't say it unless you mean it."

"I love you," I say for the third time. "I lo—"

I'm cut off mid-word. Naz is up out of the seat with me clinging to him in shock. He roughly drops me on his desk, things digging into my back. Stepping between my legs, one hand clutches my hip to keep me in place as his other hand settles on my neck. He thrusts inside of me hard, and I gasp, the noise cut off when the hand around my throat squeezes.

My chest viciously burns when I try to inhale, pressure mounting inside of me. He fiercely thrusts into me again and again, not letting go of my neck. My vision blurs, time standing still, as his calloused fingers press against my jugular.

I can't breathe.

I can't breathe.

I can't breathe.

The pressure builds, and builds, and builds, until I feel like I'm going to burst. Both hands clutch his arm, grasping it as tightly as he's pressing against my neck, terror like I've never known overwhelming me. I claw at the skin of his arm, trying to pull him off, but he's strong.

So strong.

Too strong.

Seconds feel like hours. It's only a few, no more than ten. Ten seconds that last an eternity as he chokes me. The pressure builds until it has nowhere else to go, blackness speckling my vision as I explode.

It's terrifying, the way my body seems to have caught fire, the bomb going off inside of me, obliterating me at the core. I inhale sharply, my lungs hungrily swelling as the weight on my neck lessens when he loosens his hold.

My body convulses, a shrill sound escaping me, primal, inhuman. I'm a fucking animal.

Orgasm rocks me, tingling my scalp and curling my toes. I desperately try to catch my breath but every muscle spasm knocks it right back out of me as I gasp... and gasp... and gasp for more air. It feels like it goes on forever, the pleasure so intense, and the high so high, that before it even dissipates I feel like I've slammed into the ground.

"Yellow," I cry out, the word strangled. All at once Naz's hand leaves my neck entirely as he slows his movements. He doesn't stop, doesn't pull out, leaning further over the desk to look down at me. His eyes meet mine, worried. Tears obscure my vision, one slipping down my cheek that he wipes away.

He pulls me up, shifting me to the edge of the desk, his arms wrapping around me. His movements are measured, his hands gentle. A strange sort of elation settles through me as my body relaxes, a lingering tingle in my limbs as he holds me against his chest. Never in my life have I felt such force. Never before have I been so grateful just to breathe.

I've never felt so alive.

It's sick. Maybe I'm sick. But I'm almost tempted to ask him to do it again.

I don't, though. I do nothing.

I say nothing.

He finishes not long after. He doesn't pull out this time. I can feel him coming inside of me, convulsing, filling all of me with all of him for the first time.

He stops then, his breathing haggard, as he whispers into my hair, "I love you, too."

⌒⌒

I'm alone.

I sense it as soon as I open my eyes.

The bedroom is pitch black. It's the middle of the night, though I'm not sure of the time or how long I've been asleep. I'm stark naked but wrapped up in Naz's sheets, the scent of him clinging to me.

I roll over onto my side, blinking away the sleep. Reaching over, I run my hand along the crisp white sheets. Naz's side of the bed is bitter cold. He's been gone for a while.

I contemplate closing my eyes again, figuring he'll be back eventually, but curiosity gets the best of me.

Where could he be?

Climbing out of bed, I grab Naz's button down shirt from the floor and pull it on, fastening a few of the buttons on my way out the door. I head downstairs, hearing a faint swishing sound when I reach the bottom of the stairs.

A light shines from the laundry room. Stepping that way, I grasp the knob and open the door, cringing from the brightness when I look inside. The room is empty, completely still, except for the swishing of the washing machine.

He's doing laundry? Now?

It has to be at least three in the morning, maybe four. We didn't go to bed until midnight, making love yet again before I fell asleep. The second time had been nothing but gentle, none of that aggression present, like it had been purged from him down in the den. The memory of it makes the hair on my nape prickle. He made no apologies for it.

I'm not sure I want him to be sorry, anyway.

Turning away from the laundry room, I stroll through the rest of the house, not finding him in any of the usual places. Everything is dark and cold, goose bumps coating my skin as I wrap my arms around my chest.

I go from the kitchen to the den to the living room, my footsteps tentative as I glance toward the front door. I stare at it in the darkness, noticing right away that it's ajar. The deadbolt is facing up, the chain lock dangling.

Walking over to it, I grasp the knob and pull it open, shivering at the blast of cool air. My eyes scan the pitch-black neighborhood as I peek out, making sure nobody is around, before stepping half-clothed into the doorway and tensing.

The Mercedes isn't where he parked it earlier.

I stare at the vacant driveway and step onto the porch, my eyes scanning the surrounding street, but it's nowhere to be seen.

"What are you doing?"

The low voice behind me makes me jump as I spin around, clutching my chest. My heart is pounding like a bass drum, echoing in my ears when I see Naz standing inside the house, near the door. "You scared me!"

He's wearing a pair of dark sweat pants, barefoot, bare chested, partially encased in shadows that fade away when he steps forward. He raises an eyebrow, his expression serious when he asks again, "What are you doing?"

"I woke up and you were gone," I say, wrapping my arms tighter around me as another gust of cold air wafts by, making me shiver. Before I can say anything else, Naz grabs my arm, pulling me back inside the house.

He shuts the door, making a point to lock it again, before he speaks. "I couldn't sleep."

"Where'd you go?"

"Nowhere."

"But your car's gone."

"It's in the garage."

"Why?"

"Because that's where I put it."

His answers spark more questions, ones I don't get to ask. He reaches toward me, pressing his palm flat against my cheek, before his hand drifts down my neck. I tilt my head back, expecting him to keep going, but he pauses like that, his fingertips pressing against the pulse point. "Your heart's racing."

"It usually is around you."

His hand moves lower, his thumb grazing the dip in my throat as I swallow harshly. "Did I scare you?"

"I just said you did."

"That's not what I meant," he says, his eyes leaving mine to look at his hand wrapped around my throat.

Oh. That.

Slowly, I nod when he meets my eyes again.

"Did you like it?"

I hesitate before nodding again.

The corner of his lip twitches as his hand drifts lower, down my chest, before he pulls away. "The car's in the garage because I cleaned it out. Like I said, I couldn't sleep."

"What was there to clean?" I ask. "Your car is always pristine."

"You haven't seen the trunk."

I laugh. "What's in the trunk?"

"Nothing now."

He takes a step toward me, wrapping an arm around me, as he kisses the top of my head. "I have work to do. You should go upstairs."

He starts to walk away, but I catch his arm to stop him, not wanting to go upstairs without him. He stalls, glancing down at where I'm touching him. My eyes drift that way, and I tense, seeing the claw marks on his arm. "Did I do that to you?"

He doesn't respond, merely leaning toward me, pressing a soft kiss on my lips before pulling from my grasp. "Go get some sleep, Karissa. I'll be up in a bit."

Naz walks out of the room, leaving me standing there alone as he heads for a door beyond the kitchen, one that leads into the garage, I gather, when I hear the engine of the Mercedes roar to life seconds later. Sighing, I turn away and go back upstairs, not bothering to take off his shirt when I climb back into bed.

Naz is awake before me the next morning... if he even slept at all.

When I climb out of bed and venture downstairs, he's already showered and dressed, standing in the kitchen washing dishes.

It's a peculiar sight, one that makes me pause to appreciate.

His jacket lies on the counter behind him, his sleeves rolled up to the elbows, his hands submerged in the hot, soapy suds. He scrubs a glass with an intensity that is almost unparalleled, like someone ridding a brick wall of graffiti.

I'm surprised it doesn't shatter in his hands.

The smell of chemicals clings to the kitchen, a strange mixture of bleach and noxious lemon. The floor glistens, everything within eyesight scoured.

I haven't ventured any further in the house, but something tells me the other rooms are just as spotless.

Seeing how Naz doesn't do much cooking, he doesn't have many dishes to wash. He finishes up the glasses before moving on to a knife, washing it so hard with a rag I worry he's going to cut himself. He tosses them all into a dishwasher when he finishes, turning it on to wash them yet again, before turning to me. "Good afternoon."

My expression falls. "Afternoon?"

"Yes," he says, glancing on the counter beside him at where his watch lay. "It's a quarter after twelve."

My eyes widen. "I need to hurry or I'm going to miss my bus!"

"Your bus?"

172

"My bus home! You know, for Easter? I told you I was going home for the weekend. I'm supposed to catch the bus at 1:30."

He pulls the plug on the water in the sink as he turns to me. "I forgot or I would've woken you."

"I should've reminded you," I say, frowning. It slipped my mind last night to ask him to make sure I was awake.

"I can just drive you," he says as he grabs a towel to dry his hands. "No need to worry about any bus."

"That's crazy," I say, shaking my head. "It would take you all day to get there and back."

"It's only four hours to Syracuse."

"We don't live in Syracuse," I say. "We live about an hour outside of it."

"Not a problem," he says.

"But I just... I can't ask you to do that," I say. "And my mother, she wouldn't like it. She doesn't really like being around people, and I haven't exactly told her... I mean, she doesn't know..."

"She doesn't know you're seeing someone," he guesses, fixing his sleeves.

"Yes," I say. "I'm going to tell her, I am. It's just that..."

"She won't understand," he guesses again.

"Yes," I say. "I appreciate the offer, though. Really. And I'll tell her, but just not right now. If I get back to the city soon, I can make it to the bus."

He grabs his coat and slips it on, fixing the collar. "Get dressed, then, and I'll get you there."

Just as he says, he gets me back to Manhattan on time, even having a spare minute to grab a coffee on the way through. I kiss him, offering a timid smile before kissing him again.

And again.

And again.

"I'll miss you this weekend," I admit, whispering the words against his lips.

"I'll be here when you get back," he says. "Go, before you miss your chance."

I kiss him once more before begrudgingly climbing out of the car, watching as he drives away, heaviness in my chest that I can't explain.

He's my breath of fresh air, and I feel like I can't breathe anymore when he's not around.

Chapter Twelve

My mother is a crazy cat lady, just without all of the cats.

She has a dog instead.

Killer is small mutt she picked up from the side of the road when I was sixteen, the day we moved to Watertown. I don't know what he's mixed with, his fur a tangled mix of gold and dingy white, his ears floppy and eyes unnaturally big. He's as passive as a dog gets—slobbery and loving, downright lazy when it comes down to it. His name is ironic, considering he wouldn't hurt a fly.

Literally. Won't even hurt flies.

Despite the lack of cats, my mother shows all the classic symptoms of a slightly neurotic woman, lacking friends and drowning in paranoia, a quirky hermit pulled right off the pages of something Tim Burton dreamed up. Her hair is a tangled, untamed wave that she lets hang loose, her brown eyes shielded by a pair of glasses with thick black frames.

Her flower shop is not far from the bus station in Watertown, about a mile trek near sundown. I drag my bag behind me as I walk, wanting to surprise her. The shop is a little white barn shaped building with a hand painted sign above it simply reading 'flowers'.

She never even gave the place a name.

I don't know how she gets any business. It astounds me that she makes enough money to pay the bills.

A bell above the door chimes when I step inside, everything brightly lit and sweet smelling. Arrangements of flowers are set up all around, the old cash register on the counter right in front of me with nobody manning it. Killer is curled up on the floor with a chewed up tennis ball. He lifts his head the same time a pair of eyes peeks out from the back room.

"Kissimmee!" My mother bounds out, sprinting right for me, and damn near trips over the dog. She wraps her arms around me as Killer jumps up and down around us, barking excitedly.

"Hey, Mom," I say, hugging her back, before leaning down and rubbing Killer's head. "Hey, buddy."

Killer licks my hand in greeting.

"Did you walk here?" Mom asks, prying my bag from my hand and setting it aside as she assesses me, smoothing my hair and fixing my clothes and downright fussing over me until I push her hands away. "You should've told me. I would've picked you up!"

"It's fine," I say. "It's not that far."

"Still, honey, it's getting late, so you shouldn't be walking alone. You never know what—"

"Mom," I say pointedly, cutting her off before she can launch into her usual lecture on safety. "I'm fine. Really. I've still got all my fingers and toes, my head's still on my shoulders, and I've got no broken bones. No harm done."

She gazes at me skeptically, her expression softening as she smiles. She pulls me back into a hug. "I've missed you. How long are you here for?"

"Just the weekend," I say. "I have to be back for class on Tuesday, but I'm all yours until then."

"Great, great." She pulls away and starts flitting around the shop, putting things away. "As soon as I clean up, we'll get out of here."

Killer runs over and grabs his ball, bringing it to me. He nudges my hand, staring up at me. I yank the ball from his mouth as I back up to the door. "We'll wait outside."

She starts to object but I ignore her, opening the door for the dog to run outside. Patches of grass surround the shop, so I lead Killer around the side of the building, tossing the ball toward the back of the lot for him to retrieve. He barks enthusiastically, bringing it back to me over and over again.

It only takes my mother a few minutes to step out, locking the door as she lugs my bag with her. "Come on, guys!"

She drives a beat up Jeep Grand Wagoneer, the only car I've ever known her to own. It's older than me, large and rumbly, a beast of a vehicle filled to the brim with memories. My things have been boxed up and crammed into the back at least a dozen times, routinely taking me to a new life, a fresh start, in another city, so much I'm surprised I even know who I am.

Mom tosses my bag in the backseat, and Killer jumps in with it, as we climb up front. She lives ten minutes from Watertown, outside the city limits, in a small place called Dexter. The house is tucked in among some trees in the middle of nowhere, along a river, the land overrun with flowers and plants.

I was just here a few months ago for Christmas, but it feels different now—smaller, more secluded, not as cheerful as I remember it being. The paint is chipping, white flakes coating the front porch.

She has more locks on the front door now, so many it takes her a good minute of fumbling to get it unlocked. Concern stirs up inside of me as I wait for her to open the door, but I don't say anything.

I think it, though. She's getting bad again. The signs are there, signs I remember from when I was younger. Heavily locked doors and barred windows, nights with no sleep as she paces around, listening to the howl of the wind and thinking it's out to get her. She'd be fine for weeks or months, sometimes even a year, before she started acting like the walls were closing in on her, the world pressing upon her.

I hoped she finally found a place where she felt at peace, where she felt at home, but all of those locks make me uneasy. Locks are supposed to keep you safe. Locks, with her, are a sign of vulnerability.

My old room is just how I left it, smaller than even the dorm. It's suffocating. I drop my bag right inside the room before venturing into the kitchen as my mother starts making dinner. I pause by the window and gaze out into the vast overgrown backyard, watching as Killer runs through the trees in the distance.

He won't go far. He never does. I think that's why my mother treasures him so much. He never leaves her, never wanders from her side for too long.

When he plops down in the yard, my gaze shifts from the pane of glass down to the windowsill, noting the thick nails sticking out of the old wood, indiscriminately hammered in.

She nailed the windows shut recently.

"Everything going okay here, Mom?"

"Sure," she says. "Same as ever."

She doesn't sound very convincing.

The night flies by as we catch up. She seems relaxed, happy even. It eases my worries a bit.

Maybe I'm just overreacting.

Murder is ~~premeditated killing of innocent...~~
~~...wrong because it's just not right to kill...~~
~~...considered immoral by society because...~~
...what I seem to be doing to this fucking essay.

I'm murdering it.

Sighing, I scribble out the words on the paper. I lean back in the old wooden chair, my feet propped up on the counter as I sit behind the register at the flower shop. My mother is scanning through the plants, smelling the bouquets and fixing the arrangements. She's had a total of two customers all day, making a whopping thirty bucks.

I don't know how long she can keep this up.

She doesn't seem bothered or worried at all. Killer lies on the floor near my feet, watching her. It's late afternoon on Saturday, and as much as I love my mother, and am grateful to get the chance to spend some time with her, I'm already bored shitless in this place.

I wonder how Naz is doing. I want to call him, to hear his voice, to see what he's up to, but I resist the urge. My hand absently drifts up to the necklace around my neck, and I tinker with the small pendant he gave me. I wonder if he's thinking about me, too. I wonder if he misses me yet.

"Is that new?"

My mother's voice draws my attention back to her. She's watching me. "Uh, yeah."

"It's pretty," she says, stepping closer. She grasps the necklace, eyeing it. "Where'd you get it?"

"It was a gift from a friend."

Her eyes narrow as she reads the inscription. "Carpe Diem."

"Yeah, it's a Latin saying." Standing up, I switch the subject. "I'm hungry. Is that hot dog place still around the corner? I can grab us some lunch."

"Yeah," she mumbles. "How about I come with you? I'll close up a little early today."

I wait for her to finish what she's doing, crumbling up my pathetic start of an essay and toss it in her trashcan. We head out, strolling down the sidewalk, Killer wandering along right behind us. My mother seems on edge now, eyes darting around nervously. Halfway there she stops abruptly, shoulders squaring, body tensing as she scans the traffic flowing by on Main Street.

"Mom?" I grab her arm. "Are you okay?"

She blinks a few times, turning to me, and forces a smile. "Yeah,

I've just been thinking... this town is getting so big lately. So many new people. Nothing like it used to be."

"It seems the same to me."

Even smaller, maybe.

"I don't know," she says hesitantly. "I think it might be time to move on now."

"But you love it here," I say. "And you have the shop."

"I can open a shop anywhere," she says. "Maybe out west. Finally get away from New York for good. You've always wanted to see California."

"Yeah, but..."

I don't know what to say.

"We can get a little house near the water," she says. "Killer will love the beach. It's perfect. It'll be just like old times, you and me on the open road, starting over brand new somewhere. What do you say, Kissimmee?"

"Mom, I can't move to California."

"Why not?"

"Because I have school," I say. "I have a life in the city."

"You can have a life anywhere."

Her blasé attitude about it frustrates to the point that it almost hurts. Will she ever understand my need for stability? My need for somewhere to finally call home?

"I like my life here," I say. "For the first time, I have friends, friends that really know me, friends I want to keep. I don't want to leave them."

She shakes her head, appearing distraught, like she hadn't anticipated me resisting. It was different when I was younger. When she said go, I had to go. But now I'm grown. Now I'm off on my own.

"You don't understand," she says. "The city is just so dangerous."

"It's not... no more dangerous than anywhere else. It's my home. I can't just move again. I'm happy where I am."

She says nothing else about it.

MONSTER IN HIS EYES

She says nothing at all, to be frank.

She walks with me to get lunch, walks with me back to the shop, and drives us to the house in Dexter without uttering a single word to me. The night is strained. I go to bed early, lying in the small room and staring at the ceiling.

Guilt is eating away at me.

I hear her pacing the house, mumbling, words I can barely make out and am frightened to hear. The words 'Carpe Diem' come from her lips like she's a broken, skipping record, and I clutch the pendant of my necklace tightly, fighting back tears. Because I know she's talking to *him*, appealing to an invisible man named John, the one who walked out on her when I was born.

I know it's not my fault. Not my fault she's this way. Not my fault he left her. But fuck if I don't feel guilty anyway.

My door creeps open as I lay there. The latch on it never worked, making it easy for Killer to come in. He jumps up on the bed, taking up residence near my feet, curling up close to me.

Service is shoddy out here, the signal on my phone wavering between one and two bars, barely enough strength for me to make a call. I dial Naz's number, holding the phone to my ear, and drape my other arm over my eyes as I listen to it ring.

I don't know why I'm calling him, and I feel silly when his voicemail picks up. It's an automated message. I don't even get to hear his voice.

Sighing, I hang up without leaving a message and set my phone aside as I close my eyes, trying to get some sleep.

I wake up early Sunday morning, sunlight streaming through the windows. I start to climb out of bed, hearing my mother moving around the house, when my phone beeps at me. I pick it up, glancing at the screen. One missed call. Naz.

He didn't leave a message, either.

Sunday's better, as my mother immerses herself in all things Easter, fresh lilies on the table and a vast array of food to eat. We

181

watch movies and talk about good memories, neither of us mentioning any of the bad.

But Monday morning, when I wake up and pack my things to leave, the shame hits me like a freight train to the chest. We've reverted a few months, back to last August, like I'm leaving her for the first time all over again.

She has tears in her eyes when she drives me to the bus station. "Promise me you're being careful. Promise me you're staying safe."

"I promise, Mom."

For a second I wonder if I just lied to her, wondering what she'd think if I told her about Naz right now.

She'd probably kidnap me.

"I love you, Kissimmee," she says. "I'll call you, okay?"

I give her a quick hug, petting Killer as he pokes his head up from the backseat, and get out of the car before I make this any worse. I don't want to dwell. I can't dwell. My guilt will make me want to stay.

But every other part of me needs to go.

Chapter Thirteen

My paper on murder is only half written, scribbled on notebook paper on the bus on my way back to the city. I was too exhausted when I made it to the dorms to finish, too distracted to worry about typing it up all day.

My mother isn't answering her phone. Either I've upset her and she's avoiding me, or she's deep in the middle of moving already. Either way, it makes my guilt flare, and I spend all morning leaving messages, wishing she'd call me back.

Karma.

Before I know it, Melody is rushing me out the door, shouting we're going to be late for class if we don't hurry.

Where did the time go?

I'm quiet as we make our way to the building, lost in thought, until Melody laughs under her breath. "Well, look at that..."

I look, out of sheer curiosity, and my footsteps falter. The familiar black Mercedes is parked in front of the philosophy building. Naz leans against the side of it, one hand in his pocket, the other holding a single blood red rose, twirling the flower as he stares down at it.

My breath hitches at the sight of him, my stomach flipping and flopping, as I'm suddenly lightheaded. Hesitantly, I step toward him as Melody makes her way inside the building, not wanting to be late. Santino makes a spectacle of tardy students.

"Got a hot date with a philosophy professor?" I ask, pausing in front of him.

He smirks, his eyes shifting from the flower to me. "I'm actually hoping to nail one of his students."

I laugh as he pushes away from the car, stepping up on the sidewalk, but my humor dies when he walks past me, right in the path of a petite blonde girl. I don't know her, but her face is recognizable. She's in philosophy with me.

"For you," he says, holding the rose out. "A pretty flower for a pretty girl."

She takes it, blushing, as she rushes into the building, nearly running right into the door. Naz laughs to himself, like it's the most amusing thing ever, a young girl flustered by his charm, but I feel only molten lava brewing in my gut.

It burns.

"Why did you do that?"

"She looked like she could use a cheering up," he says, turning back to me, raising his eyebrows at my expression. "You're not jealous, are you?"

It's ridiculous, I guess... maybe I'm silly, or stupid, or naive, but it's the first time I've stopped to consider I might not be the only one. Sure, I see him a lot, but there are hours, sometimes days, when we're not together and I don't know what he's doing during that time. He works, of course... he says he works a lot... but he doesn't keep the usual type of schedule.

There could be others when I'm not around.

I hate being insecure.

"You are, aren't you?" The humor is gone from his voice. "You're actually jealous."

"Are there others?" I ask quietly. "There aren't, right?"

"Other what?"

"Other girls."

He stares at me, no amusement in his expression as he leans closer. "There are no girls. I don't mess around with girls. They have nothing to offer me. I need a woman. And if you're asking me if I'm seeing anybody else, if I'm fucking another woman, the answer is no. I'm not interested in anybody else, Karissa."

His response relieves me, while also knocking me off kilter, startled by the passion in his voice.

"I told you I loved you," he says. "What am I going to have to do to make you believe it?"

"I, uh..." I stammer, hoping it's a rhetorical question, but his expression tells me he actually wants to know. "I don't know."

"Don't I show you enough?" he asks. "If you need something from me, if you need something more, tell me and I'll give it to you. I'll give you the world. I just need to know what you need."

"I don't need anything," I say.

He hesitates, his voice dropping even lower. "Have I given you reason not to trust me?"

"No."

"Then trust me," he says. "I'm asking for your trust now. If you want me to walk in that room and take that flower back from that girl, if that's what it'll take, I will. I'll rip it right out of her hands and give it to you."

"No, I don't want you to do that," I say. "I just... I didn't know."

"Well, now you do," he says, pressing his palm against my cheek. He leans forward, pressing the lightest kiss to my lips. "I love you."

Those words make me melt. If it weren't for the fact that he's touching me, kissing me, holding me, I'd swear I was nothing but a puddle at his feet. He kisses my lips and then my forehead, wrapping his arms tightly around me in a hug, before finally—hesitantly— pulling away. "You should get to class. You're late now."

"Ugh, I am," I say, scowling as I turn to the building.

"I'll walk you in," he offers, pressing his hand to the small of my back to get me to move. I head inside with him beside me, in no hurry as we stroll toward the classroom door. I can hear Santino talking, already in the middle of a lecture.

I begrudgingly walk inside and try to slip into the empty desk beside Melody undetected, but it's pointless. The second Santino turns my way, he catches my eyes, and stalls mid-sentence. Strained silence chokes the room, everyone waiting for him to continue, but he seems to have forgotten he was even talking.

"Ah, Miss Reed, how kind of you to grace us with your presence," he says, causing over a hundred sets of eyes to turn to me. "Please, have a seat, get comfortable. Make yourself at home. I'll wait."

He does. The bastard waits.

Everyone watches as I sit down, putting my bag beside me on the floor. "Sorry I'm late, sir."

"Oh, no, I'm sorry," he says. "I do so hope coming to class hasn't been any trouble. I'd hate to be an inconvenience or take up too much of your precious time. I know you have much better things to do than philosophy. Your grades certainly reflect that notion."

Ouch. Awkward murmurs flow through the room. They die down when Santino launches right back into his lecture, still dwelling on the topic of murder. Sighing, I glance around, noting a few sets of eyes still lingering my way, while my gaze drifts back to the door. A blast of humiliation rushes through me, making my cheeks flush. Naz is still standing in the hallway, right in front of the doorway.

He heard every word.

He doesn't look at me, his gaze following Santino at the front of the room. He lurks there for a moment before taking a step back, shaking his head as he walks away.

I turn back around and pull out my notebook and pencil, determined to pay attention and take notes, but I'm already two steps behind and before I can seem to catch up, class is over. I'm up out of the seat, stuffing everything into my bag, when Santino's voice carries through the classroom. "Miss Reed, if you can spare a minute, I need a word with you."

Melody shoots me a sympathetic look, mouthing 'good luck' as she heads for the door without me. I don't blame her. I wouldn't stick around either. I take my time, waiting for most of my classmates to clear out, before moving to the front of the room. Santino's erasing the chalkboard and doesn't acknowledge me for a moment, even after glancing behind him and seeing me standing here.

"Sir?" I say. "Is there a problem?"

He sets the eraser down and turns around, staring at me through his thick glasses. He doesn't look angry or hostile, like I expect. He looks disappointed. Without speaking, he reaches into his briefcase and pulls out a paper, holding it out to me. I see the red scribble all over it, my name written along the top. My test on Confucius, complete with a big, fat D in the top corner.

I take it from him. "I don't understand. I knew this stuff."

"It's not a matter of knowing it," he says, pulling out his chair and sitting down at his desk. "It's a matter of applying it. You can tell me what the man said, but you can't seem to connect it to the real world. It brings me to your essays... same problem. You can define happiness, but you can't apply it. You tell me what Aristotle and Socrates thought about happiness, but never, in the entire paper, did you tell me what made you happy."

I stare at the test in my hand, dumbfounded. "Not making D's."

"There you go," he says. "I would've given you at least a B for that had you applied it to yourself."

Frowning, I unzip my bag and shove the test inside, on the verge of tears from frustration. There's no way I can turn it around at this point, no way I can pull this grade up unless I completely ace the final exam, and the rate I'm going? Impossible.

"You had an essay due today," he says. "Do you have it for me?"

I begrudgingly pull the paper from my bag, tempted to not turn it in at all. He stares at it when I hold it out and takes it from me, the disappointed look deepening. He sets it down on top of a stack of others as he shakes his head. "See you on Thursday, Miss Reed. And don't be late this time."

"I won't, sir."

Slinging my bag on my back, I head from the classroom, feeling like a weight is pressing upon me. I stroll outside and glance up, pausing when I see the Mercedes still parked there by the curb. A quick look around tells me Naz isn't anywhere in sight, so I pull out my phone and call him, getting his voicemail.

Shrugging it off, figuring he walked somewhere, or is working in the neighborhood, I start toward the dorm, in no rush to get there.

It takes me the entire walk to shrug off my solemn mood, trying to force a smile on my face, to act like it isn't bothering me before facing my friend. When I get there and push open the door, I'm immediately greeted by Paul's face.

Melody's boyfriend is stretched out on her small bed, remote in his hand, watching ESPN, while Melody sits at her desk, digging through her backpack. She glances up, giving me the look I expected. Pity. "What did he say?"

"He said I'm not cut out for philosophy." I drop my bag on the floor and plop down on my bed. "He said I say a lot of shit but I don't know what any of it means."

"He said that?"

"In so many words, yeah," I mutter, closing my eyes. "And to top it all off, after he says it I hand over an unfinished assignment, proving exactly what he said—I'm not cut out for it."

"I don't believe that," she says. "That's crazy."

"You're failing Santino's class?" Paul chimes in with disbelief. "I didn't think that was possible."

"I'm not failing," I say defensively. "I'm just not passing."

Paul laughs. "What's the difference?"

"The difference is I'm surviving by the skin of my teeth but that's not good enough to keep my GPA where I need it to be."

"Tough break," Paul says. "Seriously, though, Santino's class is a breeze. I bullshitted my way through it and still got a B."

His words don't make me feel any better. In fact, they piss me off even more.

My phone rings as I'm lying there. I pull it out, glancing at the screen to see Naz's name. Sighing, I answer it, muttering a quiet, "Yeah?"

He's silent for a moment. "You okay, sweetheart?"

"Yeah, why?"

"You called me."

"Oh, yeah… I just saw your car was still there, so I called to see what you were up to."

"Ah, I was just handling some business. You back at your dorm?"

"Yeah, just got here."

"You want to grab some dinner?"

"I'm not really hungry."

"You want to come to my place?"

"I really shouldn't. I have class early in the morning, and I still have some homework to do for it. It's probably going to be a long night as it is."

"That's not what I asked. I want to know how you feel, not what you think. It doesn't matter if you should come over. I asked if you wanted to."

I hesitate. "I do."

"Then I'll pick you up in five minutes. Bring your homework. I'll help you with it."

I start to argue, but he hangs up on me. Standing up, I grab my bag, waving to Melody as I head for the door. "You crazy kids have fun. I'm going to Naz's."

"Will you be back for class in the morning?"

"Yes," I say. "Just don't expect me any sooner."

She laughs, wishing me a goodnight. Paul says nothing. I don't think he much likes me either, and that's okay. He watches my television and throws his dirty socks on my floor and eats my Ramen noodles and the cherry on top of the icing is he makes a better philosophy grade than me.

I'm beginning to like him less and less.

Naz is double-parked right in front of the dorm, not seeming to give a shit as people honk, annoyed that he's blocking traffic. I laugh as I climb in the passenger seat, seeing he's staring down at his phone, paying no mind to what's going on outside of the car.

He lives in his own little world, where he's the king, and I'm more than happy to be his minion... although, when he looks at me, flashing that dimple, I feel like nothing less than his queen.

He pulls into traffic and drives straight to Brooklyn. He takes off his coat and loosens his tie when we get to his house, tossing his keys down on the living room table.

"You sure you're not hungry?" he asks. "I can make you something."

"You? Make something?"

He laughs. "I probably have something you can make yourself."

"Thanks, but I'm okay. I just wanna get this work done so I can try to relax."

I settle into the den, cracking open my math book to finish some problems. Naz distracts me more than anything, sitting beside me on the couch. He sucks at math, fucking up basic multiplication when he tries to help.

I even catch him counting on his fingers a few times.

I merely smile, having to do some of the problems over again, but I don't mind much, even if it does take twice as long. It doesn't feel like work with Naz involved.

I'm finishing up the last problem as he twirls a piece of my hair around his finger. It's the typical word problem bullshit, two trains going too damn fast and eventually intersecting, but nobody gives a shit where. Naz watches me as I try to work it out, his mere gaze distracting.

"I have a word problem for you," he says.

"I'm listening."

"If Naz forgoes sleep, and Karissa gets naked, how many orgasms can he give her before sun up?"

"Hmm, I'm not sure," I say, trying not to smile, but one cracks my face. "I'm not sure you have enough fingers to count that high."

"Oh, I know I don't," he says. "Besides, my fingers will be busy doing other things tonight."

Chapter Fourteen

I'm dumbfounded.

Santino stands at the front of the classroom, droning on and on about something. I don't know. His voice is little more than a dull murmur as I stare at the paper on my desk.

I expected an F on this essay. It's incomplete, and impersonal, and everything Santino didn't want.

So why is there an A written at the top?

There's no other red. No comments, no corrections. No explanation. It's the first time it has ever happened to me. I don't know what to think. My eyes shift from my desk to Melody's, wondering if he took it easy on everyone this time around, but she got her coveted B, her essay marked up.

It makes no sense.

I stay quiet through the lecture, not raising my hand, not uttering a peep. When he dismisses us for the day, I stand up and put my bag on, clutching my paper.

"I'll meet you back at the room," I tell Melody. "I have to ask Santino a question."

She looks at me like I've sprouted a second head, like I've just said the world was going to end. She looks at me like I'm certifiably insane. Hell, maybe I am. But I have to ask him.

I don't understand.

I wait until most of my classmates are gone again before approaching his desk. He looks up at me, his expression blank, and doesn't speak. He looks like I'm the last person he wants to talk to.

"Sir, I just had a question about my paper."

He raises an eyebrow.

"Well, it's just that, I didn't get a chance to complete it, or type it like I was supposed to. It wasn't finished when I turned it in."

"I noticed," he says.

"Yeah, so I'm just curious... why the A?"

He stares at me. Hard. Like if he stares any harder, he might telepathically blow me up, obliterate me right in front of his eyes. When he speaks, his voice is icy. "Not good enough for you?"

"No, it's not that," I say quickly. "I just didn't expect..."

He lets out a sharp bark of laughter, not sounding amused in the least. "I'm sure you didn't."

My brow furrows.

"Look, Miss Reed, I don't know what you want me to say. If you'd rather have the F that paper deserves, I'll happily give it to you. But I'm quite certain, on the topic, you're well versed, even if you didn't put forth the effort to show it."

I feel like a fool. The man gives me an A and I'm questioning why instead of taking it and running. Whether it's deserved or not, he threw me a lifeline, giving me a fighting chance of scraping by this semester.

"Thank you," I say, clutching the paper as I back up a few steps.

"Don't mention it," he responds, looking away from me. "Ever again."

I nod, turning around and quickly getting out of there. The air is warm when I step outside, spring well upon us. It's so warm that even I feel the heat, and push the sleeves of my long-sleeved shirt up to my elbows as I pull off my scarf. It's the last week of April, and in a mere two weeks classes will be over for the semester. I have a lot of work to do between now and then, but I feel calm, like maybe I won't screw it all up, after all.

Just two more weeks, and I can say goodbye to the professor known as Satan, never having to step foot in that godforsaken classroom again.

Two weeks. I can do two weeks.

I'm in Hell.

It's dressed up pretty to look like a renowned private university, but don't be fooled—it's Hell. I've been trapped in the deepest pit for going on fourteen days, the world pressing down upon me until I'm barely able to breathe. The toxic cloud of smoke from the raging inferno swept out from the gates of Santino's classroom and blanketed everything, suffocating everyone in its path. Judgment day is coming, and it's coming fast.

Finals.

I'm being dramatic, but it's hard to see the world clearly when you haven't had a full night sleep in two weeks. Everything's drowning in a haze of notes and practice tests.

"Okay, what about this one?" Melody says, holding up an index card with something in Latin written on it: *modus tollens*.

"*Modus tollens*," I say out loud, not sure if I even pronounced that right. "It's, uh, one of Voldemort's people in Harry Potter."

She laughs, spouting off a definition that makes just as little sense to me as the words themselves. I wave her away, motioning for her to show me the next one.

Probability.

"Oh, this one's easy," I say. "It's if something's, like, probable."

Another laugh.

Another flashcard.

Another wrong answer.

"I'm done," I say, falling back on the bed and draping my arm over my eyes, getting a whiff of something rancid as soon as I do. "Ugh, what stinks?"

"That would be you," Melody says, tossing the flashcards down.

"Gross." I grimace, begrudgingly rolling out of bed and seeking out a clean towel. "I'm going to go shower."

"Please do," she says. "Soak the stench away."

I flip her my middle finger as I trudge to the bathroom. I turn the water on hot, hoping the steam and heat will loosen some of the tension from my muscles. I stand under the spray and close my eyes as the water pelts me until I damn near fall asleep.

Swaying, nearly slipping, I blink a few times as I reach for the knobs to change the temperature. The moment the cold water hits me, I'm jolted awake, a shiver ripping through me. I wash up quickly before getting out, not having the energy to stand there.

I half-ass dry off and wrap the old pink towel around me as I trudge back into the room. As soon as I open the door and step inside, I come face-to-face with Paul. He stands in the middle of the room, half on my side, half on Melody's, tossing one of her balled-up dirty shirts into the air. He turns to me as I freeze, and I expect him to look away, seeing as how I'm damn near naked, but his eyes rake down my body instead. *Gross.*

Melody groans when he finally looks away, but he just lets out a laugh as he tosses her shirt in the vicinity of her overflowing hamper, like it's a basketball. He retreats back to his girlfriend's side, flopping down on her bed, laying his head on her lap. Melody covers his eyes with her hands, shooting me an apologetic look.

I ignore it, grabbing some clothes from my closet and heading back to the bathroom to change in peace. When I step back into the room, the two of them are kissing. She makes no apologies for that.

Melody's a great friend, and she's always willing to listen, but when it comes to sharing a living space, I've decided she's a terrible roommate.

I block them out the best I can as I fix my hair and try to pull myself together, not bothering with makeup or much more than a ponytail. My eyes flicker to the clock. It's nearly noon. We have about two hours until exam time.

Gathering up my things and snatching the notecards from the floor beside Melody's bed, I head for the door. Melody pulls away from Paul when she notices. "You're leaving already?"

"Yeah, I'm going to go downstairs and grab a cup of coffee." I pause. "Or a whole pot."

"Oh, well I'll meet you down there when it's time to go."

I walk out, shutting the door behind me, and head downstairs to the attached dining hall in the back of the building. It's busy, surprisingly, given that a lot of finals have already finished, some students already leaving for the summer. I'm on my last day, my last exam, before the break. The rest have gone smoothly, but philosophy will be my make or break.

I use the last little bit of money on my meal card to purchase the largest coffee they have, drowning the bitter liquid with copious amounts of sugar, enough to leave me bouncing off the walls for hours. I find a small table in the corner and sit down, scattering the flashcards out around me. I scan the terms on the front before flipping them over, trying to memorize the definitions on the back, but it all seems to be floating around in my head and not sinking in.

I know better than to cram at the last second.

It never helps.

But I do it anyway.

I go over them again and again, refilling my coffee twice. By the time Melody surfaces, sliding into the chair across from me, I'm jittery and frantic and ready to get it the hell over with.

"You look like a crackhead needing a fix," Melody says, grabbing my coffee and taking a sip. "Ugh, how much sugar is in this thing?"

"Enough," I say as I glance across the table. Her hair is tousled, but not in the intentional way. "You look like you've been fucked six ways to Sunday."

She takes another drink, grinning, her expression telling me yep, that's precisely what she's been. I grimace when she holds the coffee out, offering the rest to me. "Yeah, no, I'll pass. I know where those lips have been."

Rolling her eyes, she downs the rest of it before tossing it in the nearest trashcan. "Well, come on, fellow sinner. Satan awaits, and you know how he feels about people being late."

We get there early today, the first ones in the classroom. Santino's sitting in his chair, rolling his pointer stick around on his desk. He glances up, hearing us, his eyes meeting mine as I take my usual seat. He looks like he wants to say something but remains silent as the rest of the students filter in.

At exactly two o'clock, when every seat is filled, he stands up and grabs a stack of papers.

Wordlessly, he passes them out, waiting until everybody has one before clearing his throat. "I only know one thing, and that is that I know nothing. Let's hope you all know just a little bit more than Socrates today, ladies and gentlemen. There's no time limit. Turn it in when you finish."

He retakes his seat, going right back to tinkering with his pointer stick. I watch him for a moment before taking a deep breath and glancing down at my test, reading the first question.

Explain the equation of universal modus tollens using examples from real-life situations.

I'm fucked.

It takes me well over an hour to get through all five pages of the exam. My hand is cramping, my head is throbbing, and an irrational surge of anger flows through my sleep-deprived, caffeinated body whenever someone else gets up to turn in their finished test.

How dare they be done already?

I turn the page to the back, ready for this to be over with, and read the last question.

**Thales said 'the most difficult thing in life is to know yourself.'
Who are you?**

I try to contain it, to swallow it down, but a bitter laugh escapes that disturbs those around me. I can feel their eyes but I don't look up, my gaze glued to the paper. What kind of fucking question is this? I glare at it, and glare at it, and glare at it some more, before turning my head to subtly peek at Melody's. She's also on the last question, the entire back of the paper filled, like she just wrote her autobiography for him. She sets down her pencil while I'm looking, a smile touching her lips as she stands up to turn it in.

I almost trip her.

I think about it.

I consider it.

My leg bounces in anticipation of darting out in her path, stopping her from walking up there. It's childish, and irrational, but she looks so damn confident while I'm struggling to finish.

Sighing, I turn back to my paper and glare at the question some more. Melody returns and gathers her things, mouthing that she'll see me back at the room.

I merely nod, tapping my pencil against the side of the desk as I listen to others move around. The room is clearing out quickly. I don't like it.

Who am I?

Someone who doesn't like philosophy anymore.

I consider the question for another moment before finally writing my answer.

I don't know.

Standing up, I march to the front of the room, test in hand. Santino looks up at me as I approach. I hand my paper to him, face up, but he turns it over when he takes it. His eyes flicker from my pathetic three- word answer to me, and for the first time all semester, his lips curve.

He's smiling.

At *me*.

Creepy.

I say nothing, nor do I return his smile, merely walking away. I grab my things and jet out the door, feeling a sense of relief on the walk back to the dorm. Never again am I trusting Melody when she tells me to take a class, when she says it's easy.

I want to go straight to the room, but I have a meeting with my advisor that I'm already late for. I consider skipping it, saying fuck it, but she'll reschedule and I'll be forced to come back out this way.

Sighing, I make my way across the street to another building and head straight inside, plopping down in a chair outside her office. She spots me from the open doorway and waves me inside, launching into small talk.

In one ear and out the other.

The sound of her acrylic fingernails clicking against computer keys echoes through the small office. The woman is hen pecking at the letters, taking way too long to punch my information into the system. She pauses every few seconds to hmm and huh and huff, the sounds grating on my nerves.

Can we just get this over with?

I've registered for all my classes for next semester, a full course-load, and turned in all my paperwork. The counselor is just making sure I'm not missing anything, a process that should've taken thirty seconds, but we're going on five minutes at this point.

"Looks like everything's in order," she says finally. "Most of your final grades have already posted... we're just waiting on philosophy. As long as you graze by with at least a low B in that, your GPA will be high enough to maintain your scholarship, no problem."

She makes it sound so simple. All I need is a B. I'll be lucky as hell if I even get close to that. But I need a 3.5 GPA if I want my tuition paid next year, so a B it has to be.

Dear God, please let me have gotten a B.

"Great," I say. "Is that it?"

"Yes, that's it."

I'm up out of the chair, mumbling my thanks as I bolt for the door. I probably look rude, but I'm too exhausted to care. My thoughts are a flurry of math equations and percentages as I stroll along on my way back to the dorm. I come to the conclusion that to get my B, I need to make an 89 on the final exam.

When I get to the room, Paul's not around. *Thank God.* Melody is putting on lipstick, babbling something about going out with him to celebrate, but I barely listen. I drop my bag on the floor and take off my pants, not even bothering to put any more on as I fall straight into my bed.

Chapter Fifteen

Something startles me awake.

I sit straight up in bed, disoriented, like I've been ripped from a dream I can't quite recall. The room is a pitch-black haze of confusion. It's late.

Really late.

A glance at the clock tells me it's one o'clock in the morning. A glance at Melody's empty bed tells me she still isn't home. Rubbing my eyes, I stand up and stagger to the bathroom. As I'm washing my hands, I hear the door in my room and quiet footsteps along the floor.

Sighing, I turn off the water and dry my hands. Guess I'm not alone anymore. I just hope she didn't bring Paul home with her. The last thing I want to find is a guy in there.

I turn off the bathroom light and step back into the room, blinking, attempting to adjust to the darkness, surprised she didn't turn on the light. I glance toward Melody's bed and pause, brow furrowing.

It's still empty.

I hear a noise to the right of me, a footstep in my direction. My heart stalls, rendering me immobile, before frantically pounding so hard it's like a machine gun going off in my chest. I start to turn that way when arms roughly grab me, yanking me toward them in the shadows.

A scream bubbles up inside of me, barely bursting out, when a large glove-clad hand clamps down over my mouth, silencing it right away. I'm pinned.

Oh fuck.

Oh fuck.

Oh fuck.

My knees are giving out on me, my vision is blurred with tears, and if I hadn't just gone to the bathroom I'd be pissing myself right now. I try to remember everything I've learned about self-defense, but my mind is scrambled.

I'm fucked.

I struggle against the arms, screaming into the palm, when I hear a soft chuckle. "Relax, sweetheart."

I nearly hit the floor when I sag with relief. Naz. He loosens his hold enough for me to swing around to face him, meeting his eyes in the darkness. My heart is still pounding, my stomach churning from the rush of adrenaline and fear. I need to purge it from my system before I throw up.

I lash out, my fists hitting his chest, punching him hard. He laughs, still amused as he snatches ahold of my hands. He's wearing a pair of black leather gloves. "Or don't."

I try to shove away from him, but he wraps his arms around me, laughing even harder.

"You scared me!" I growl. "Jesus, Naz, you can't do that to me!"

"I'd apologize," he whispers, "but I'm not sorry. I like it when you fight back."

"I just... my God!" I pry out of his arms and grasp my chest, willing my heart to calm down. "How the hell did you get in here?"

"I just walked right in. Your security around here isn't very secure, Karissa. The girl in the lobby looked right at me and didn't say a word. And not to mention the fact that you left your door unlocked. The place practically has a sign on it that says 'come inside' so I thought I'd come inside, and maybe..." He reaches out, brushing his hand along my cheek before swiping his thumb along my bottom lip. "...come inside."

Rolling my eyes, I smack his hand away. He laughs yet again, whispering, "feisty".

I want to be mad. I want to be furious. He just broke into my room and scared the daylights out of me. But I can't make myself be angry when all I feel is elation at the sound of his laughter, the sound of his happiness.

"You're an ass," I mutter. "I can't believe you just did that to me."

He shrugs, stepping by me to stroll through the room as he pulls off his gloves. I watch incredulously when he sits down on my bed. "What can I say? You've been busy, and I've missed you."

I have been. I haven't seen him much the past two weeks, and damn if I haven't missed him, too.

I step toward him, pausing in front of him. A sliver of moonlight streams through the nearby window, illuminating where I stand. I'm suddenly acutely aware of the fact that I'm not wearing any pants. Why does he always catch me when I'm wearing the unsexiest panties? I tug on the hem of my shirt, trying to cover them.

His expression shifts, the amusement fading when he grabs my hand. "Come on, don't be like that. Don't hide from me."

He scoots back onto the bed and tugs me to him as he kicks off his shoes. I hear the clunk as they hit the floor. He pulls me onto his lap, and I straddle him, my arms around his neck as he slowly starts unbuttoning his shirt.

My heart is racing again, thumping in my chest, but this time it's not fear that does me in. I watch in the dim lighting as he sheds himself of his shirt before meeting my gaze.

I can see the want in his eyes; the same yearn brewing in my gut. I kiss his mouth, his cheek, his chin, before working my way further down. He leans back as I reach his chest. I can feel the ridges of his scars as I kiss the old wounds, caressing the skin with my lips. "What happened to you, Naz?"

I place a last kiss on the biggest scar, not far from his heart, before meeting his eyes again.

"I lost my life," he says quietly. "And then I almost died."

I want to ask him what the difference is, if his heart is still beating how was his life taken from him, but the look he gives stalls me, silencing my words before I can say too much. I've never seen him so vulnerable. Those eyes are dark, so fucking dark, it's like a hurricane brewing inside of him.

I wonder how he survives such turmoil.

I don't ask. I don't think he has an answer. I just wrap my arms around him as he kisses me. Naz pulls me down onto the bed, shifting around so I'm lying beside him. It's sweet, his hands gentle as they remove my clothes, exploring my bare flesh with his fingertips. A subtle sadness seems to coat every movement. The sudden urge to make him feel good overwhelms me.

I want that laughter back.

I want to make him happy.

I want him to be happy *with me*.

"Tell me how you like it," I whisper, trying to keep my nerves from showing in my voice. "You can be rough. I'll fight back."

He cracks a smile at that as he rids himself of the rest of his clothes, shifting our bodies again so he's on top of me.

"Next time," he says. "Tonight isn't for playing.

"What's it for?"

"Loving."

He pushes inside of me slowly, his lips meeting mine again as his body weight presses upon me. It's slow and sweet. It's all pleasure and not a stitch of pain.

He's making love to me.

My legs wrap around his waist as he thrusts, filling me deeply before pulling back out, over and over. He holds me to him, sweaty skin gliding together as he gives me all of him, gritting his teeth and groaning against my neck as he comes inside of me.

We lay there afterward, me in his arms, my head on his chest. He holds me against him like I'm delicate, one hand splayed out on my back, the other resting on my head as he strokes my hair. I haven't said a word. I'm not sure there are any words to say. I'm afraid talking about it will cheapen it, rationalize something that should just be felt instead.

Less thinking, more feeling.

I'm starting to get it now.

He's just as quiet. If not for the way he's touching me, I'd think he was asleep. I lay there, starting to doze off, when his soft voice carries through the silence. "It was a 12-gage shotgun. They spent hours pulling all the buckshot from my chest, but it didn't matter, because my heart was shattered."

"Literally?" I ask quietly. I can't fathom it. A shotgun blast to the chest. Who would do such a thing to him?

He sighs, holding me tighter, his voice barely a whisper. "Might as well have been."

Melody's home.

I see her—or rather, hear her—as soon as I open my eyes. Snores rattle her chest, drawn out and obnoxious, so loud I'm startled awake for the second time.

The arm around me is heavy, the body pressed tightly against mine warm. I don't know why I'm so surprised he's still here. I almost expected last night to be a figment of my imagination. His hand gently strokes the skin on my lower stomach, around my navel, dipping slightly lower toward my sensitive bits when I stir. "Good morning."

"Morning," I whisper, my voice thick with sleep. "How long have you been awake?"

"All night," he says.

I think he's joking, but when I shift around, so I can turn my head and see his face, the first thing I notice is the exhaustion. He looks like I did at a few points the past two weeks. I reach back, wanting to smooth away the bags under his eyes. "Couldn't sleep?"

"I often can't," he says. "And if you're wondering, Darth Vader over there staggered in about an hour ago and went straight to sleep."

Shame stirs up inside of me. "Oh God, we're naked."

"She didn't notice," he says. "She didn't even look over here."

"She could've."

"So?" He removes his hand from my stomach to brush my tousled hair aside. I feel his lips against my neck, soft and warm, tingles flowing down my spine at the sensation. "You can't tell me the thought doesn't turn you on."

"What thought?"

"The thought of being seen," he says. "The thrill of maybe being caught. Of someone watching you as you get pleasured, wishing they were you, or that they were the one fucking you, drowning in jealousy because they know they'll never be that lucky. Never. They'll never have you, Karissa... never be you. Because you're mine—mine and mine alone."

His arm snakes around me again, pulling me back tighter against him. I shiver when I feel his erection pressing against me from behind, his hand traveling to the spot between my thighs. My eyes drift closed as he strokes my clit, his lips still on my neck, sucking and nipping his way to my shoulder. Heat engulfs me, my body flushing as I grind against his cock. He groans, stroking faster, rubbing harder, as soft whimpers escape my throat.

It's wrong.

It's wrong.

Oh God, it's so wrong.

So why the hell does it feel so right?

Melody's snores are barely loud enough to conceal my moans. I should stop him, should pull away as my hands grip his arm, but I can't. I won't. I don't want him to ever stop touching me.

I can feel the tension building, the sensation sharpening, and rushing toward where he's rubbing. My breath hitches in anticipation, and I'm close... so close... so fucking close. My toes curl, my entire body wound like a tight coil ready to spring loose, when a faint set of beeps rings through the room. All at once Naz stops when he's doing.

My eyes snap open, the sensation fading as he pulls away and sits up. "No, no, no," I chant, rubbing my thighs together, desperate for friction. I flip over onto my back, my gaze seeking him out. "Please."

It's torture, the ache spreading through me. Naz glances at me as he brings his phone to his ear, answering the call with a quiet, "Hello."

I start to pout when he tucks his phone in the crook of his neck, listening to whoevers on the line. He presses a single finger to his lips, shushing me, as his other hand slips beneath the blanket only partially covering me. My breasts are exposed, but I don't care. I can't care. Not when he touches me again, his free hand rubbing circles around my achy clit. My eyes roll in the back of my head, and it doesn't take long for my body to tense again, the feeling returning.

"Yeah, I'm handling it," he says, his voice quiet, and stone cold serious, the gritty, callous tone pushing me further toward the edge. I can feel it creeping up on me and fist the sheets, toes curling again. "I'll be there this weekend."

Oh God.

Oh God.

Oh my fucking God.

My lips part, my breath hitching, a silent scream burning my chest as I struggle to keep from making any noise. Pleasure sweeps through me, my body convulsing.

"I don't think I'll be alone," he says. "I'm sure she'll be more than happy to, uh... come."

He tries to hide the amusement in his voice but he laughs lightly. I peek over at him as the tension recedes, my body relaxing against the bed. He stares down at me, the look in his eyes nearly making me come again.

His hand leaves that spot, drifting up my stomach to my chest. He palms a breast, sweeping his thumb across the erect nipple.

"Yeah, I know," he says. "I'll see you then."

He hangs up, tossing the phone down on the bed, and leans down to kiss me. His lips are hard against mine, frenzied. I reach for him, my hand snaking beneath the blanket, wrapping around his cock. I stroke it once, twice, before he pulls away and snatches ahold of my wrist, stopping me. His eyes regard me peculiarly, a smirk slowly turning his lips. "Huh."

"Huh what?"

"You're good at being quiet."

"I didn't want to interrupt your call," I whisper. "Or, you know, wake Melody."

He curves an eyebrow. "Huh."

Huh. Again. Him and that fucking word that's not even a real word. "What?"

"We might have to test that out some more," he says, kissing me again, softly this time, before climbing out of the bed. I stare at him incredulously as he stands in the middle of the room, completely naked. His movements are unhurried as he gathers up his clothes. "Not now, though. I'd love to stay, but you know..."

I pull the blanket up around me, covering my body, as I sit up and watch him dress. He pulls himself together with ease, running his hands through his hair to tame the locks, before sitting down on the edge of the bed beside me.

Monster in his Eyes

"Come with me this weekend," he says, slipping on his shoes. It's not a question. It's a request. I've noticed that about him. He asks things of me without ever really asking. It's cool, and confident, like he already knows my answers so he doesn't bother bullshitting.

"Where?"

"Away," he says.

Another thing I've noticed. He doesn't ever seem to answer my questions, either.

I shake my head. "I shouldn't."

"But you want to."

Of course I do. "Why?"

"Why not?"

I laugh as he stands back up and fixes his shirt collar. "I don't know."

"Your classes are over, aren't they?"

"Yes. I took my last exam yesterday."

"Did you pass?"

I shrug. "I hope."

"I'm sure you will," he says. "So why can't you go with me?"

"Well, Melody and I talked about going out on Saturday to celebrate."

"To celebrate classes being over?"

"No," I say quietly, drawing my knees up to my chest as I wrap my arms around them. "To celebrate my birthday."

He freezes as he stares down at me, a look of surprise passing across his face. It's the first time I've ever caught him off guard, the first time he didn't seem steps ahead of me. He shakes his head after a second, stepping closer, and leans down like he's going to kiss me again. I stare into his eyes as he pauses there.

"Come away with me this weekend," he says again. "I'll show you the time of your life."

"You already have," I whisper. "A few times."

"Sweetheart, you haven't seen anything yet."

His kiss, when it finally reaches my lips, is nothing more than a peck, a soft touch before he stands up. He says nothing else, and doesn't wait around to hear my response.

The cocky bastard just walks out.

I sit there for a moment, clutching the blanket around me, before I start laughing. I just laugh, shaking my head, as I stare at the door. He turns me upside down, making all the blood rush to my head, and then he just leaves me sitting there, lightheaded and inebriated by the essence of him.

Standing up, I grab a towel and some clothes, dragging the blanket with me to the bathroom to take a shower, hoping to wash away the lingering guilt I feel as I stride right by my sleeping roommate, snoring and clueless.

Have I mentioned I'm a terrible friend?

I wash up and pull myself together, getting ready for a day where I have nothing planned. I'll do some packing, maybe, some sleeping, definitely, and probably just drown myself in mindless television all afternoon. I should really find a job, find somewhere else to go, seeing as how I have to be out of the dorm in seven days.

Summer break. I was looking forward to it months ago, counting down the hours until the semester was over, but now I dread even thinking about it. I anticipated going back to Watertown to spend the summer with my mother, but after the visit a few weeks ago I'm not sure how plausible that is.

I'm not even sure how long she'll be there, to be honest, or if she's already gone.

I try not to think about it, try to clear my head as I stand under the warm water, but it lurks in the back of my mind, an ominous rain shower in the distance. My future is as hazy as a storm cloud.

I wonder if Naz drew another picture of the future, if it would be clear for him yet.

I haven't told Naz. I'm not sure how he's going to take a long distance relationship, even if it is only two months.

I'm not sure how I'm going to take it.

He's been gone twenty minutes now, and I already miss his touch so much.

I head back into the room after I'm clean, and changed, feeling wide-awake but I don't want to disturb Melody. So I grab the remote, turning the television on low, and stare at it in the morning light.

Talk shows.

Baby daddy drama.

Cheating boyfriends.

Celebrities in rehab.

I lose myself in everyone else's drama, momentarily forgetting my own issues. Melody stirs in bed a few hours later, as the clock starts to approach noon, and rubs her eyes. "Oh God, I feel like ass."

"Long night?" I ask, flipping the channel to find more mindless entertainment. *Court shows.*

"And morning," she mutters, sitting up. She's still wearing the same clothes from yesterday, old makeup streaking her tired face. "I didn't wake you when I got home, did I? I tried to be quiet, but I was drunk as shit."

"No," I say. "Didn't bother me at all."

She climbs to her feet and trudges toward the bathroom. I flip through channels again, not paying it much attention, finding something less dramatic.

Game shows.

"Wake up, wake up, wake up!"

The voice shrieks right beside my ear, rousing me from a deep sleep. I yelp, holding my hands up defensively as someone shakes me. Disoriented, I open my eyes to see Melody's blurry face right in front of me, grinning like a maniac. "What?"

"Wake up!" she says again, physically yanking me to a sit.

Groaning, I push her away and blink rapidly. "I'm up, I'm up... ugh, why am I up?"

"I did it," she says, jumping up and down in front of me. "I got my B in Philosophy!"

It takes a moment for her words to sink in. Suddenly wide-awake, I stare at her, anxiety brewing in my stomach. "Wait, grades are posted?"

"Yes!" she says excitedly. "Can you believe it?"

"Uh, that's wonderful," I say, rubbing my eyes. I'm trying to play it cool, but it's senseless. The anxiety makes me want to puke. Standing up, I push past her to boot up my laptop, logging into my school account to check my grades. My heart pounds rapidly in anticipation, but as soon as the page loads, everything in me comes to a stop. My stomach lurches, my heart nearly stalling.

Philosophy: C

"No, no, no," I chant, scrolling through the page, going back to look up my grade on the final. 88.

Eighty-eight.

Eighty-fucking-eight.

"This can't be happening," I say, shaking my head. Bile burns my throat that I try to swallow back. "I missed it by one point."

I'm dumbfounded. I don't know what to think, or feel, half asleep and out of it as I scroll back to my final grades. Melody babbles behind me, but her words go over my head. I don't hear it, nor do I hear my phone ringing. The sound evades me until Melody thrusts the shrieking object right in my face.

My eyes shift to the screen as I swallow thickly, pushing my feelings down. *Don't panic*, I tell myself. *You'll figure something out.*

I close the browser on the laptop before answering the phone. "Hey."

My voice sounds meek. I clear my throat and repeat myself, but Naz chimes in before I can finish the word. "What are you up to?"

"Nothing. I, uh... nothing."

A moment of silence. "What's wrong?" I start to say 'nothing' when he continues. "And don't say *nothing*."

I let out a deep sigh. "I got a C in Philosophy."

"You passed!" He sounds genuinely enthused. "That's great."

"No, it's not. I needed a B to keep my scholarship. I don't understand why I didn't get it! I studied my ass off for that final. I missed the mark by one point... just one point. That's it."

The words pour out of me, tears stinging my eyes. One fucking point. It's unbelievable.

I'm kicking myself for not answering the question on the back of the final seriously. I would've written my entire life story had I known I'd need just one more damn point.

"Ah," he says. "I see."

The nonchalance of his voice twists me up in knots, anger simmering inside of me. It's not Naz's fault—it's nobody's fault but my own—but I'm too upset to be calm about it. I let out a deep groan, shoving my chair back to stand up. "You know what? Fuck this. I'm going to go talk to Santino to see if there's anything I can do to change it."

I hear Melody inhale sharply, not a fan of my plan.

"You want me to handle it?" Naz asks.

"No, I'll do it," I say. "It's my problem."

He bids me good luck, telling me to let him know how I make out. Hanging up, I throw on some clothes and slide my feet in a pair of shoes before heading for the door. I walk to the philosophy classroom, my nerves a frazzled mess, as I silently plead to whatever God is listening for a break.

Just give me this, please.

The classroom is open, the lights on. I expect to find him in his small office in the back of the building but instead he's sitting there, papers and books splayed out in front of him. His glasses are low on his nose as he studies a textbook, taking notes from it.

Carefully, I step in the classroom, knocking on the doorframe to garner his attention. "Professor Santino?"

He glances at me over top his glasses before turning back to his book. "Miss Reed, what can I do for you?"

"I, uh... I wanted to talk to you about my grade."

"What about it?"

"Why did I get a C?"

"You should be asking yourself that, not me."

"But I did everything I could."

"Did you?"

"Yes. I needed a B. I was only one point away."

He finishes writing whatever he's writing and puts his pen down, leaning back in his chair. He eyes me peculiarly for a moment, grabbing his pointer stick to tinker with it. He uses it to motion toward the front row of desks, wordlessly telling me to take a seat. I nervously oblige, sitting right in front of him.

His expression is hard, no compassion, or understanding, before his eyes flit around the room. "This classroom has two exits. Why do you think that is?"

Ugh. I thought I was done with him calling me out to answer absurd questions. Is it extra credit for my extra point?

"Because the classroom is so big, and it holds so many students, that it's logical to have more than one exit in case of an emergency," I say. "There's probably something in the fire code about it, about having a certain number of exits per however many people occupy the room, so whoever designed it had to include them. It holds 100 students so I'm guessing 50 people per exit?"

He raises his eyebrows. "Is that your final answer?"

I hesitate. "Yes."

"It's because it's safer, Miss Reed."

My brow furrows. "That's what I said."

"No, it's not. You referenced hypothetical fire codes and mathematical equations. You said it was logical, not that it was safer.

And that, Miss Reed, is the difference between a B and a C. You always complicate things and miss the entire point."

"But that's what I meant," I say.

"Maybe so, but let this be a lesson to choose your words carefully, because people will take you at face value and hold you to what you say and not what you mean."

"But I—"

Before I can get anything else out, he picks up his pen and goes back to his work, cutting me off. "Good day, Miss Reed."

Shoving my chair back, I stand up. I should've known coming here was pointless. I storm out of the room, tears stinging my eyes again, this time stubbornly falling down my cheeks. I wipe them away with the back of my hand as I pull out my phone, dialing Naz's number.

It rings twice before he answers.

"I fucking hate him," I say right away, stepping outside. "He's such a dick."

"I take it appealing to his compassion didn't work."

"No, it didn't, because he's heartless. He treats me like I'm ignorant... like I'm just this stupid little girl who doesn't understand anything."

My voice cracks as I try to hold back tears. The line is stone cold silent for a second before his quiet voice carries through. "You're crying."

"No, I'm not."

"Don't lie to me."

It's stupid to cry. I feel ridiculous. I wipe away more wayward tears, trying to pull myself together. "I'm fine. I just... ugh, he makes me so mad. He's so smug and acts like he knows everything and I just wish someone would knock him down a peg."

He lets out a sigh. "Don't worry about it, Karissa."

"But I don't know what to do about it all."

"It'll work out," he says. "What you need is some time away, some time to clear your head and not think of everything. Come away with me this weekend."

I roll my eyes. He sounds so damn relaxed, nothing bothering him. I wish I had his confidence. "You know I will."

Chapter Sixteen

The town car is idling along the curb in front of the dorm, the driver standing beside it, waiting for me. I pause a few feet away, my bag dragging the sidewalk, a new red dress still in plastic and on the hanger, draped over my arm.

I'm a mess, sweaty and tired, wearing a pair of black leggings and an oversize white shirt, the outfit complete with a pair of flip flops.

I couldn't put on my shoes. My toenails are wet, painted red to match my dress. I was in the middle of doing it when Naz called, informing me the car was waiting downstairs. He hadn't given me much notice. I had to rush around at the last second getting all of my stuff.

The driver takes my things and puts them in the trunk. I don't wait for him to open the door for me, opening it myself. Naz is sitting there, phone to his ear, dressed as usual. He casts a look at me as I climb in beside him, talking to whoever's on the line.

"We're leaving Greenwich now," he says. "We should be to Jersey in about half an hour."

My brow furrows. He's taking me to New Jersey?

He hangs up without saying goodbye, slipping the phone away, as he leans toward me and quickly kisses my lips. The driver gets in and pulls away from the curb, merging into traffic.

"So what's in New Jersey?" I ask curiously.

"A lot," he says. "Full-service gas stations, saltwater taffy, the Jersey Devils, Palisades Park... Atlantic City, the Jersey shore... and Snooki, of course."

"Snooki?"

"Oh, and the Sopranos." He raises his eyebrows. "You watch it?"

"Uh, I caught a few episodes."

"Great show," he says. "Purely fictional, of course."

I laugh, shaking my head. "So that's why we're going to Jersey? Because of TV shows and gas stations?"

"Of course not."

"Then why are we going?"

"You'll see."

Not long after we cross the state line, the car heads toward a small airport. As soon as I see the sign for it, I cut my eyes at Naz. "We're not really going to New Jersey, are we?"

"Of course not," he says. "There's nothing in Jersey."

Rolling my eyes, I watch out of the window as we approach a private jet parked off to the side, the car pulling right up to it. A group of people hangs out beside it, chatting as other cars unload luggage, their belongings being loaded onto the aircraft.

Most of the faces on the tarmac are foreign to me, middle aged men and a few women, maybe a dozen in total. But dead center in the crowd, I recognize Raymond Angelo.

He's smiling cheerfully, his arm around a blonde woman not much older than me.

Everyone is dressed impeccably—suits and dresses, not a single hair out of place. They fit in with Naz, in his expensive black suit, but not me. I don't belong here. I'm not like these people. They're lobster and caviar, thousand dollar bottles of wine.

I'm more like something you can order in a drive-through.

I reach over and grab Naz's arm when the car stops. He hesitates, shooting me a peculiar look, as the driver opens the door.

"Give us a moment," Naz says. "Go ahead and load our things."

"Yes, sir."

Once we're alone, Naz shifts around in the seat to face me. "What's wrong, sweetheart?"

"I can't do this."

"Why?" he asks. "Afraid of flying?"

"No," I whisper, although now that he mentions it I feel the anxiety bubbling in my stomach. "I mean, I've never flown before, but that's not it. I just... I don't fit in."

"I know you don't."

I guess I expected him to contradict me, because his agreeing catches me off guard. "What?"

"I know you don't fit in, Karissa, but that's one of my favorite things about you. You stand out."

"What if they don't think so?"

"Then it's a good thing I don't care what they think."

He says it so matter of fact, like any differing opinion is just plain wrong.

"Trust me on this," he says, reaching over and cupping my cheek. "It's going to be the best weekend of your life. And if anyone here ruins it for you in any way, I'll make certain they pay for it."

He gets out of the car without awaiting a response, and my chest tightens. Something tells me them paying for it won't be monetarily.

I take a deep breath as Naz opens my door, and before I can talk myself out of this, I step out to join him.

Eyes shift our way. I can feel them on me, meeting curious gazes as I scan the crowd. The looks aren't so much hostile as they are puzzled taking in the sight of me. The women especially regard me with skepticism. They're painted up pretty, Picasso masterpieces, while I feel more like one of his rough sketches.

Raymond breaks from the pack, stepping toward us. "Ah, Vitale, perfect timing."

Naz nods to acknowledge that, but Raymond isn't looking at him. No, Raymond is looking at me.

He takes my hand, kissing the back of it. "I'm honored you'd join us, Karissa."

I want to say it's not intentional, that I had no idea I was joining the likes of him, but I keep my mouth shut, merely smiling tersely to keep from saying anything. My mother taught me enough to know he isn't the kind of man that takes kindly to being offended.

Naz doesn't dawdle. Pressing his hand to the small of my back, he leads me past the crowd onto the plane. The inside looks bigger than it does on the outside, all cream-colored and wood-paneled, with more than enough seats to accommodate everyone.

Naz stops dead center of the plane and plops down on the end of a long couch, a small two-cushion portion segregated from the rest. I sit down beside him nervously, but he eases some of my anxiety by draping his arm over my shoulder and pulling me closer. He presses a kiss to my hair, his cologne swarming my senses, making me lightheaded, as everyone else boards the plane.

Raymond decides to sit beside me, nothing more than a cushioned armrest separating me from the infamous man. The blonde sits with him as the others file in. I peek at her, unable to fathom what she sees in him.

I know Naz is older than me, and maybe people see our age difference as extreme, but he's still quite youthful, and regal, and so goddamn sexy. There's an attraction with him I can't deny—don't want to deny. But Raymond is much older, maybe old enough to be that woman's grandfather, and has not a smidgen of the sex appeal.

In fact, he looks a little like Shrek to me.

I sit quietly, tucked in at Naz's side, my heart beating frantically in my chest, each thump echoing in my ears, an anxious rhythm I fear everyone around me can hear. They all settle into their seats, chatting, but none of the conversation means anything to me.

I feel invisible, and for that I'm grateful.

The plane takes off after everyone is buckled in. My heart is in my throat as we ascend into the air, my fist clenching Naz's suit coat. My ears pop, my stomach clenching from the altitude.

Nobody else seems bothered by it. In fact, nobody else seems bothered by anything. As soon as we're in the air they return to where they were, picking up conversation right where they left off, like this is nothing to them. My hand loosens the fabric of Naz's jacket, but I don't let go.

I won't let go of him.

His presence is the only thing keeping me from freaking out.

Beside me, Raymond is telling a story, laughing at his own jokes, as everyone around us listens attentively. He's clearly the center of their little world, the sun these men orbit around.

Everyone, that is, except for Naz. He appears to not be paying attention. He tilts his face toward me, his breath fanning against my cheek as he whispers, "You okay?"

I nod.

"You recognize everyone here?"

Brow furrowing, I shake my head. How would I? I only know Raymond, but I don't dare say that out loud. He's sitting close enough that he'd hear me speak his name.

"Huh."

I glance at Naz, his face a few inches away. "What?"

"I'm just surprised."

"You? Surprised?"

He smiles. "It happens every now and then. I just figured you'd know these faces since you recognized Ray."

Just as I suspected, Raymond perks up at the sound of his name. He stops mid-story, diverting his attention. "She recognized me?"

"She did," Naz confirms.

"Nice to know my reputation still precedes me," he says.

"Always will, boss," the guy across from us says. Boss. The word sticks out like a flashing neon sign in the darkness. "As long as Vitale's around to make sure of it, anyway."

I feel Naz tense, his body turning to stone, his arm around me suddenly boulder heavy. I glance at him again, seeing he's glaring at the man who just spoke. Everyone else seems to notice it, too. A few cleared throats and some awkward silent seconds later, the conversation veers back away from us.

Naz still glares, though.

He doesn't relax.

I don't know what the man meant by what he said, how Naz effects Raymond's reputation, but it's clear that Naz didn't like it a bit.

It's a five-hour flight—five long, stuffy hours, as I obsessively look at Naz's watch, counting the minutes. It isn't until we land that I even find out where we're going. I ask Naz a few times but he merely shrugs, leaving me in the dark, until the wheels of the plane touch down again. Naz's arm is still around me, still just as heavy... he hasn't spoken in a while. The others excitedly chatter about this and that, as Naz pulls me tighter to him. "Welcome to Las Vegas."

I turn my head to face him, raising my eyebrows with surprise. "Vegas?"

He nods.

"What are we doing here?"

"What else do you do in Sin City?" he asks. Before I can respond, his hand comes up and grasps my chin, holding me there as he leans down. The tip of his nose brushes against mine before he tilts his head and kisses me—softly, sweetly, barely touching my lips, as he whispers, "sin."

I'm blushing from his public display of affection, but no one notices. They're intentionally not noticing, from the way everyone avoids even making eye contact with Naz now. It reminds me of the fundraiser, how even when crammed in with so many others, Naz has a bubble surrounding him.

He's his own universe.

There are limos anticipating our arrival. I step off of the plane and stand on the tarmac, my body stiff and head foggy from being up in the air all afternoon. The sun is just now going down here, bathing the sky in an orange glow, casting everything around us in shadows. It's warm, almost stiflingly so, but still I shiver when Naz pauses behind me, his hand resting on my hip. People flow around us like we're rocks in a rushing river, unloading bags and taking them to the awaiting cars.

I'm not surprised when Raymond pauses beside us. He seems to be drawn in our direction, his body language nonchalant, but his voice is serious when he speaks. "Don't do it."

My brow furrows. I glance at him, seeing he's staring straight ahead, like he hadn't spoken at all.

Naz's hand on my hip tightens. "I won't... for now."

"That's all I ask," Raymond says.

Their conversation makes no sense to me, over just as quickly as it started, as Raymond strolls away to where the blonde he's with waits. I watch as my bag and dress are placed in the last car in line, along with Naz's luggage. As soon as the trunk is closed, everything situated, the driver opens the back door to the limo.

Naz gently pushes me. "Come on, sweetheart."

I don't resist, walking over and getting in. It's just as pristine as the last one we rode in, impeccably clean, the smell of leather fresh, like no one has ever stepped foot inside of it before, like no one has breathed this air or sat on these seats. Naz slides in beside me and the driver shuts the door, climbing in up front to drive away once the others clear out.

I turn to Naz curiously. "Don't do what?"

He raises his eyebrows. "What?"

"Raymond told you not to do something."

"What?"

"That's what I'm asking you."

He stares at me for a moment as we start to drive, like he's contemplating an answer. Shrugging, he looks away. "It doesn't matter. I'm not going to do it."

"For now?"

His lips curve into an involuntary smile. "For now."

"Will you tell me if you do it?"

"Do you want me to?"

I hesitate. His question is matter-of-fact, and I'm not sure what to say. My instinct is to say yes, of course, but do I really? Something tells me some things are probably better left unknown. "I'm not sure."

His nod is the only response I get.

I've never been to Vegas before, never even thought I'd have the chance. It's surreal, as I stare out the window, watching as the lights of the city come into view. The sky is darkening, the sun fading more and more every second, but the streets show no sign of slowing down. If anything it seems like the world is just now coming to life, lights flashing as people swarm the streets.

The limo drives past hotels, names I recognize—Venetian, Caesar's Palace, Flamingo, and the Bellagio—before pulling straight up to the MGM Grand. I stare up at the hotel with wide eyes, the vast building glowing green, the name burning bright yellow in the darkness. I gape at it as I climb out of the limo. I feel like I've stepped into another world.

Naz gets out, pausing beside me. He looks less than impressed, like this is just another place on the map, a stop along the road of life, but to me it's life altering. Someone carries our bags as we're ushered straight through a remote entrance, Naz's hand pressed to my back again, leading me, but not letting me fall behind. The private lobby we're taken to is elegant, secluded away from the main entrance, the sort of place I expect Naz to stay—cool on the surface, relaxed, while a world of turmoil exists just a few steps away.

It moves like the speed of light around me. We're led away from the lobby, to the elevators, where the man carrying our luggage presses the button for the very top floor.

The penthouses.

A man—a butler, it turns out—accompanies us upstairs and opens the door to our suite. As soon as I go inside, my eyes widen. The vast space in front of me is unlike anything I've ever seen before. I look around in shock as Naz converses with the man by the door.

The suite rivals even Naz's house in style. There's a dining room, a little kitchen, a living room, and even a space with a pool table. The black and white checkered floor stands out against the dim brown and yellowish tones of everything else as I trudge along, footsteps faltering when I come upon the wall of glass. I peer out, stunned to see there's a pool up here.

The butler departs when Naz refuses a guided tour, leaving us alone. I turn to Naz, leaning back against the cool glass and peering at him as he strolls forward, taking off his coat. "Like it?"

"Like it? It's amazing."

"It's nice," he agrees, hanging his coat on the back of a chair. "The upstairs is even nicer."

I gape at him. "Upstairs?"

"Of course," he says, motioning toward a set of stairs off the side. "Where do you think the bedroom is?"

I don't wait for him to say anything else, flying right by him and up the two sets of stairs. I pause when I reach the top, gasping so loud Naz hears me downstairs, based on the sound of his laughter.

"Told you," he calls out.

The upstairs is elegant, with two bedrooms and the largest bathroom I've ever seen. I could drown in the massive tub, the shower an immense glass box that's damn near as big as the dorm room back at NYU. I step inside of it, spinning in circles, completely baffled. I can see the lights of the city through the windows from the shower, can see down to the landing leading to the first floor.

When I emerge from the bathroom, Naz is in the master bedroom, shifting through his things. I pause in the doorway, shaking my head. "Who else is staying here?"

"Nobody," he says. "Just us."

"There are three freaking beds. Why do we need three beds?"

"We don't," he says, cutting his eyes at me. "We might try them all out before the weekend's through, though."

I smile. I like that plan.

He's pulling clothes out and hanging them up in the closet, putting things where they go like he's moving in. I leave everything in my bags, not even sure what I packed, but I'm certain it's not worthy of hanging in a closet of that caliber. He glances at me as I pick up a little binder from the bedside stand and flip through it. Room service.

"Are you hungry?" he asks.

"Uh, yeah, a little." I can't remember the last time I ate. "Can we order something?"

"We can," he says, "but how about we go out somewhere instead?"

"Where?"

"Wherever you want to go." He finishes what he's doing as his phone starts ringing. He pulls it out, barely glancing at the screen before answering stoically, the conversation short and full of nothing more than 'yes' and 'no's. Hanging up, he slips it back away and turns to me. "I need to run an errand... won't take more than a few minutes. Why don't you shower and change, and we'll hit the city?"

"Okay," I say, glancing around the room, my eyes falling on the garment bag. "Should I wear the dress?"

"No, save that for tomorrow."

"What's tomorrow?"

My question prompts him to smile as he steps toward me, cupping my cheek, brushing his thumb across my lips. "Why don't we focus on tonight before you start worrying about tomorrow? We waste too much time looking for the next thing and not appreciating what we have right now... and right now, what we have, is endless opportunities. The sky isn't the limit in my world, Karissa. There is no limit. You want it? You got it. Whatever it is."

"Anything?"

"Anything," he swears. "Just name it."

"A bacon cheeseburger."

He laughs. "A bacon cheeseburger?"

"Yes."

"Okay then." Leaning forward, he kisses me before turning away. "Shower, and we'll hit the town for bacon cheeseburgers."

Naz leaves, and I scour through my bag, cringing. Had I known we were going to Vegas, I would've borrowed some of Melody's clothes. I end up settling for black pants and a pink top, nothing unusual for me, but at least it isn't jeans.

I head into the bathroom and strip out of my clothes, turning the shower on warm. I step into the glass box, letting out a deep sigh of contentment. Water blasts me from all angles, the pulsing spray feeling like a massage.

I lather up from head-to-toe with the sweetest smelling soap. Closing my eyes, I stand there, letting the water cascade around me as it rinses away the bubbles, steam building up and fogging the glass. After a minute I reopen my eyes and glance around, freezing when I catch sight of something down on the landing.

Naz is standing there, staring up at me.

A shiver ripples down my spine. I can feel his gaze. I probably should be unnerved by the fact that he's watching me, but I feel a tinge of excitement. Maybe I do like the idea of being caught.

Hesitating, contemplating, I step closer to the glass wall and peer down at him as I run my hands up my stomach and to my chest, palming my breasts. A smile slowly spreads across Naz's face as he shakes his head and walks away.

I turn back to the water and finish my shower, stepping out when I'm squeaky clean. I get ready, putting on my clothes and adding a dash of makeup, doing my best to fix my hair, when I hear movement on the floor below again. Naz returns, stepping into the bathroom as I apply lip-gloss in the mirror. He strolls over, pausing behind me, his hand on my hip as he leans down and kisses my neck. "You're a vixen."

"And you're a voyeur."

He laughs. "Guilty."

He's already ready, of course, not needing to change, looking and smelling just as fresh as he had when he picked me up from the dorms. I don't know how the man does it, always looking as put together as a work of art. I slip on my shoes and take his hand as he leads me from the suite.

A man stands outside our door. Naz nods as we stride by but says nothing. I glance at him curiously, even more surprised to have another waiting by the elevators for us. The man presses the button and the door automatically opens. Without having to utter a word, the man steps onto the elevator with us and presses the button for the ground floor. As soon as we reach it, Naz nods again.

We start to walk away, heading into the bustling casino, when I turn to Naz. "It's kind of weird how they cater to you."

He looks amused by my assessment. "Their service is top-notch. Anything you ask for, they'll make it happen."

"Anything?"

"Yes, anything," he says. "Even bacon cheeseburgers."

He takes me straight to a restaurant... an upscale world-renowned sort of place with a name I can't pronounce run by a man with an accent I assume to be French. All it takes is Naz saying his last name, Vitale, and we're taken right inside, led straight to a small empty table in the back, just as a waiter descends upon it, carrying plates of food. My brow furrows as I slide into the seat Naz pulls out, stunned when a burger is set in front of me.

I gape at Naz when he settles into his seat, a plate identical to my own in front of him. "You called ahead?"

"I mentioned to the concierge that you wanted a bacon cheeseburger," he replies, "so he made it happen."

It's unfathomable to me, being waited on hand-and-foot, but I say nothing as the waiter brings us drinks—the non-alcoholic kind.

I pick up the burger to take a bite. It's got a peculiar flavor to it, bitter like balsamic vinegar, and is topped with some kind of green that reminds me of spinach. I chew the bite slowly as I pull off the top bun and scrape off all the leafy shit. My gaze shifts around the table as I frown.

"What's wrong?" Naz asks. I meet his gaze, seeing he's watching me as he takes a bite. He seems to like it, considering he takes a second bite right away.

"There's no ketchup on the table."

"There usually isn't in a place like this."

"This is why I like places *not* like this," I mutter, "because they have ketchup on the table."

He motions for the waiter, who makes his way over to us. Naz tells him to bring us some ketchup and the man nods, scurrying off to return a moment later with a little dipping bowl filled with what I guess they assume to be ketchup, but it looks a hell of a lot like stewed tomatoes with how chunky it is. I dip my finger in to taste it, cringing. There's that balsamic vinegar flavor again.

"What's wrong?" Naz asks again. His voice has a slight impatient tone to it. I shake my head, pushing the ketchup aside, and put the bun back on to take another bite. I can feel Naz's eyes, his question lingering over the table, my brushing it off not good enough for him. "Karissa, what's wrong?"

"Nothing," I say, offering a tentative smile. "It's fine."

"You're not using your ketchup."

"Yeah, uh… if you can call it that."

He reaches over and picks up the bowl, doing just what I did—dipping his finger in to taste it. He makes no face, no sound, but as the waiter walks by our table he reaches out and thrusts it at him.

The waiter stalls, wide-eyed, and takes the bowl. "Problem, sir?"

"Ketchup," Naz says, his voice even. "I asked for ketchup."

"Yeah, this is—"

"Not ketchup," Naz says, finishing his sentence. "Heinz 57 is ketchup. That's not ketchup. I don't know what the hell it is, but I asked for ketchup, so I expect to receive ketchup."

The waiter scurries off once more as I gape at Naz. He continues to eat, unaffected, as the waiter returns within moments with a new bowl of what is undoubtedly ketchup this time. I thank him, staring at the bowl, hesitating, as Naz lets out an exasperated sigh. "Now what's wrong?"

"It's just that, if ever someone were to poison your food, this might be the moment," I say, staring at the ketchup.

"You think it's poisoned?"

"Or at the very least spit in."

I'm worried I'm aggravating him, not trying to be difficult. I pick up my burger to take another bite, resigned to just forcing it down because I'm too hungry for this shit, when Naz lets out a laugh—loud and genuine. He pushes his chair back to stand up, holding his hand out to me. "Come on."

I glance at his hand before meeting his eyes. "Where are we going?"

"To get you what you really want."

I put my burger down and take his hand, following him out of the restaurant, past our confused-looking waiter by the door. We stroll around, passing dozens of restaurants, some bearing the name of celebrity chefs, before Naz pulls me into a busy sports bar.

This place is a world of difference from the other, like night and day. The bar is barely confined chaos, loud and bright, with people wearing jeans and ball caps, drinking beer and yelling at the TV. The smell of greasy food wafts through the air, making my stomach growl.

Naz grabs a table dead center of the room, where a waitress

appears with menus. I order a Coke, practically bouncing in my seat, as Naz hands the menus right back. "A beer. I don't care what, just make it in a bottle and keep the top on. And two bacon cheeseburgers."

The woman scribbles it down and departs with a smile.

When our drinks arrive, I sip on my Coke as he pulls out his keys, using a bottle opener to pop the top on his beer. He takes a swallow. His face contorts with disgust, his expression making me laugh. "Not good?"

"Beer never is," he says, holding his bottle out to me, offering some.

I hesitate. "Are you sure?"

"It's your birthday."

"Tomorrow."

"Close enough."

"I still won't be twenty-one."

His lips curve with amusement as he holds it closer to me. "I feel like we've had this conversation before. Is my little jailbird having second thoughts about sinning in Sin City with me?"

"Of course not."

"Then take it."

I take the beer from him and drink, grimacing. It's disgusting, but I take a second swallow and push it back across the table to him before anyone catches me.

The food comes out quickly—a juicy burger on a fresh roll, grease dripping when I bite into it. It's so good I moan, dramatically rolling my eyes in the back of my head. "Now *that's* a bacon cheeseburger."

Conversation is playful as I stuff myself, whereas he only eats half of his burger, instead filling up on alcohol. I sip enough from his bottles to catch a buzz, my head a little fuzzy and my body light like somehow I've learned to defy gravity and float into the sky.

He's sipping on his fourth beer as I lounge back in my chair, watching him quietly. He's beautiful, in a dark sort of way, the kind of beauty that's natural. He doesn't try, and I think that's what I love most about him—he just is. Naz, with his rough edges and slightly sinister smile, is pure passion and genuine grit, the kind that makes the hair on my arms stand on end while my spine simultaneously tingles. He can be frightening, but he's downright fascinating. I've never been around someone who wields so much influence.

How can someone surrounded by an air of danger make me feel so downright safe?

"You're quiet," he says, raising an eyebrow as he stares back at me. "What are you thinking?"

"I'm just thinking about how beautiful you are," I admit.

He laughs as he sets his beer down, pushing it across the table to me, offering the last little bit. I pick it up, chugging it, grimacing at the warm bitter taste. Naz pulls out his wallet and throws down a wad of cash, not bothering to wait on the bill—our waitress is backed up, so busy we haven't seen her in a while—but it's more than enough to cover what we owe.

He stands up, fixing his tie. I follow his lead, slipping my arm around his as we start for the exit, strolling out onto the casino floor.

"You know how to play blackjack?" he asks.

"No."

"It's pretty basic," he says. "You add up the value of the cards. Closest to twenty-one without going over wins. Got it?"

"Uh, sure," I say, eyeing him peculiarly. I really don't. "Why?"

"Because we're about to go blow a lot of money playing it."

I gape at him, and start to argue that I'm not legally old enough to gamble in Vegas, but yet again it's pointless. He bypasses all the tables around the main floor, taking me to an entire other part of the hotel—a casino within a casino. This place is upscale and exclusive, so much so we have to be escorted in. We're taken to a back room, to some private blackjack tables. As soon as we step inside I recognize a voice, looking around and seeing vaguely familiar faces. Everyone from the plane is here, laughing and carrying on, gambling the night away.

Naz takes a seat at a table beside Raymond. As soon as he sits down, a man working approaches, hesitant, a twinge of fear in his eyes as he stammers. "Mister, uh, Vitale, sir... your friend..."

"Girlfriend," Naz says. The word makes me stall, heart thumping so hard I grow dizzy. Girlfriend. It's the first time he's ever called me anything like that. A strange sort of silence falls over the room, voices hushing. I glance around at the men, seeing their curious gazes. They seem as affected by the word as me. "I'm well aware she's not old enough to place bets, but she's my good luck charm, so if you're going to deny me her presence, then I'll be forced to take my money elsewhere."

"No problem," the man says, backing off at the threat. "We're happy to accommodate you."

I pause behind Naz, nervously following the lead of the others. A few women linger in the room, off to the side. Raymond's blonde stands behind him, rubbing his shoulders attentively, while he seems to barely remember she's there. Naz grabs my arm, though, tugging me to him. I blink a few times, startled, when he pulls me onto his lap. I settle onto the chair with him, leaning back against him, trying to shift around so I don't block him from seeing what he's doing. A few of the guys cast him peculiar looks, but nobody says anything as he's dealt in.

Despite him telling me the rules of the game, I have a hard time keeping up with what's happening. These men are obviously big time, everything moving swiftly, white, yellow, and brown chips tossed around worth thousands of dollars, very little spoken in the way of game playing. They chatter about nonsense, using their hands to signal how they want to play. I watch Naz, trying to count up his cards, but he distracts me, his breath fanning against my cheek, his lips finding my neck periodically between bets.

I don't know how the hell he can concentrate.

Drinks flow to the men. Naz offers me sips of his, and nobody says a word. They play and play, joking around, throwing away thousands of dollars that none of them seem to bat an eyelash at. The night wears on as he whispers to me, asking me what he should do a few times. I know he knows better than me, but I play along, giving him my opinion. He listens every time, laughing when I cost him damn near everything, like that amuses him.

The alcohol gets to me after a while, my ass numb from sitting in this chair. I have to be heavy on Naz's lap, so I stand up. Naz stalls mid-game to look at me questioningly.

"I need to stretch my legs," I say, glancing around. "Where are the restrooms?"

"Ah, just down the hall," Naz says, motioning toward a door.

"I'll show her," the blonde chimes in, eyes seeking out mine as she smiles. "I'll show you."

Naz turns back to his game. "She'll show you."

I follow the woman out of the room and to a bathroom just down the hall like Naz said. I could've easily found it myself. The woman lingers in the bathroom, checking her makeup and fluffing her hair. I'm trying to pee in peace as she tries to hold a conversation through the stall door. "So you and Vitale, huh? That's interesting."

"Yeah... why's it interesting?"

"I don't know, it just is," she says. "He doesn't bring women around... never has. I've been with Ray for five years now and I've never seen Vitale with one."

I like to think I'm above gossiping, but my interest is piqued. I stroll to the sink to wash my hands. "Naz is just a private person."

Her eyes widen. "Naz?"

"Yeah, Naz," I say. "Isn't that what everyone calls him?"

She shakes her head, regarding me like I'm unstable. "It's always Vitale... or Ignazio, if they're close. Never Naz."

My brow furrows. "Are you sure?"

"Positive," she says. "Ray sometimes calls him that in private, old habit, you know? But not to Vitale's face. It's sort of a raw wound, I guess, so they tread lightly. I wasn't around back then when it happened..."

Her words only confuse me more. "When what happened?"

"When he lost his family." I just stare at her, having no idea what she's talking about, and that seems to dawn on her. She blanches, taking a step away from the sink as she forces a smile on her cherry red lips. "We probably should get back."

I want to ask her more, ask her what the hell she means by that, why it's such a raw wound and what happened to his family—a family he never talks about—but I know she's right. We should get back. And Naz wouldn't like her talking about this, whatever it is...

We're strolling back to the room when she offers me another smile. "I'm Brandy, by the way."

"Karissa," I say. "So you and Raymond have been married for five years?"

She laughs. "Oh, we're not married. We've been together that long, though."

"Oh... I figured he was married."

She pauses at the entrance to the room as we are welcomed back inside, casting me a peculiar look. "He is. I'm just his girlfriend."

Brandy takes her place back at Raymond's chair, her hands on his shoulders. She leans down, placing a soft kiss on his cheek, but he brushes it off, too focused on the card game to pay any attention to her.

I hesitate for a moment, watching them, my stomach in knots when it strikes me that this girl is his mistress. She seems nice, and it's not my place to judge, but it worries me.

A lot.

My gaze shifts to Naz.

I wonder what being *his* girlfriend means.

As if he can sense my gaze, his head turns my direction. His brow furrows as he stares at me, questions in his eyes. I smile and start toward him, pushing back my worry, but he's already noticed my mood shifted.

Tossing his cards down, he stands up. "I'm out."

"Already?" Raymond asks, surprised.

"I'm down over thirty grand," Naz says. "That's probably a sign."

"A sign your good luck charm isn't as good as you thought?" a guy jokingly calls out, a guy I recognize from the plane, the same one who upset him on the way here. Naz doesn't humor that with a response as he's cashed out. He slips his money away, not bothering with any goodbyes.

Naz is halfway to me when Raymond laughs dryly. "Strike two."

That makes Naz's expression soften a bit.

He reaches me, taking my hand, and pulling me with him toward the exit. He says nothing until we're out in the hallway alone, away from prying eyes. He stops, turning to me, raising his eyebrows. His expression is so serious I balk. "What did she say to you?"

"What?"

"You're looking at me like you think maybe you don't know me," he says. "What did that girl say to you?"

It stuns me how easily he reads me.

I stammer for a moment until he reaches out with both hands, cupping my cheeks and forcing me to look at him. "Tell me."

"Nothing really. She just said nobody calls you Naz, not since... you lost your family."

I expect anger—toward her, or me, or somebody. Instead, what I see is hurt, a slight flinch before his eyes close, like what I said stings him so much he can't even look at me.

He stays that way for a moment, but it fades when he opens his eyes again. He lets go of my face and grabs my hand, bringing it up to press it against his chest. "I told you what happened."

The scars.

My chest aches at his words. Guilt nags at me for bringing it up.

MONSTER IN HIS EYES

I start to apologize, start to change the subject, but he silences my words by leaning down and kissing my lips. It's soft and sweet, unhurried, as his tongue sweeps along my bottom lip before meeting mine. I moan into his mouth, earning a soft chuckle when he finally pulls away.

Chapter Seventeen

Naz is quiet as we head upstairs, so close I can smell his cologne, yet he feels a thousand miles away. He's lost in his mind, consumed by thoughts I can't begin to understand.

When we make it up to the suite, there are chocolate covered strawberries waiting on the table and a bottle of champagne chilling in a fresh bucket of ice. He obviously planned something, but it's disregarded as he strides right by and heads upstairs.

Wordlessly, I follow him, keeping my distance to give him some space, but we eventually meet in the master bedroom. He steps toward me, quiet as he speaks. "Do you love me?"

"You know I do."

"Say it," he says, his voice dropping lower. "Tell me you love me."

"I love you."

He cups my cheek. "Say it again."

"I love you."

His hand drifts lower, wrapping around my throat. "Again."

"I love you."

He squeezes lightly, not painfully, just enough to make me gasp. "Again."

My voice is barely a whisper as the words pour out of me. "I love you, Ignazio."

His expression hardens when I say his name, his eyes darkening. The monster is peeking through, peering at me from behind his mask. He wants to come out. He wants me to play with him.

He says nothing, though, letting go of my neck. His hand drifts lower, down my chest and across my breasts. He gropes them through the fabric before reaching down and grabbing the bottom of my shirt, pulling up on it. I raise my hands in the air, letting him pull it off. He unbuttons my pants, tugging down the zipper, and I step out of them when he pulls them off of me.

Slowly, his eyes scan me then, from the top of my head to the tips of my toes before trailing back up again. He meets my gaze as he takes another step forward, standing right up against me. I can feel the heat emanating off of him, his cologne intoxicating.

It makes me dizzy.

"If you could read my mind..." He pauses, laughing darkly. "You'd be trembling."

I nearly tremble from the insinuation. "What are you thinking?"

He steps around me, stopping behind me, and sweeps my hair out of the way. A hand grasps my hip, pulling me back to him as he leans down to kiss my neck.

"I'm thinking the only way you could possibly be any more perfect right now," he says against my skin, "would be if I were fucking you so hard the people in the lobby could hear your screams."

That does it.

I shiver, but he isn't finished yet.

"I want to push you to your limits, Karissa. Push you so hard, so far, that you hate me for it."

"I could never hate you."

As soon as I say it, his hand is around my neck again, pulling my head up, forcing me to look back at him. "Don't say that unless you mean it."

"I mean it," I whisper. "I love you."

He stares down at me for a moment before leaning over to kiss my lips, tugging me back so far it's almost painful so he can reach my mouth. "I love you, too. Promise me you'll remember that."

"I promise."

"Good," he says. "Because I'm about to fuck you like I don't."

My voice is little more than a shaky breath. "Okay."

"Remember your safe words."

"I will."

He lets go of my throat, lets go of me, as he takes a step back. I stand still, trying not to shake, and peek over my shoulder to see him unfastening his dark tie.

"And if you really love me," he says, pulling off the tie before looking at me again. He looks furious. The sight of his anger, the icy tone of his voice, makes my knees weak. I'm definitely trembling now. "If you mean it, you'll fight back."

My lips part, the response on the tip of my tongue knocked right out of me. I gasp, alarmed, when Naz roughly grabs a hold of me and drags me to the bed, pushing me onto my stomach.

There's nothing gentle about his hold, nothing loving, or nice, about the man touching me. He forces my arms behind my back, wrapping the tie tightly around my wrists, knotting them together. I struggle as he restrains me, but he's too strong, too fast for me to physically stop him. The moment my arms are secure, I hear him fumble with his belt, my heart racing at the clank of the buckle.

He won't hurt me.

I know it.

He loves me.

I remember it.

But it's hard to think, hard to submit, when you've got a man double your size, a beast, a fucking *monster*, pinning you down.

So I don't think.

I feel.

And I feel like I need to fight him.

I kick my legs, resisting and yelling for him to get off of me. It doesn't work. Of course it doesn't. In one ear and out the other. His hold gets stronger, his grasp rougher. I'm his favorite toy, I know it, and he's about to see what it takes for me to break.

I won't let him, though.

I can't.

He won't break me.

I manage to roll over onto my back, my hands beneath me, and push up into a sit before he can think to stop me. I'm about to stand up when he tears off his belt, making me tense.

Making me flinch.

My reaction forces him to pause for a fraction of a second, just long enough for me to notice, before he comes at me again. He doesn't swing, doesn't strike me, instead forcing me back onto my stomach, the belt thrown aside, discarded. He pins me there with his body weight, overpowering me.

"What the fuck is wrong with you?" I ask, a growl in my voice that surprises even me. He doesn't answer. He doesn't speak. Short of an icy gaze, he doesn't even acknowledge me.

His body is heavy as I buck my hips, struggling against him. He yanks my panties down, not bothering to take them off, the fabric around my knees making it harder to kick. An arm slips around my waist, roughly pulling my hips off the bed, forcing me onto my knees with my ass up in the air.

"Get off of me," I snarl, struggling in his arms and damn near escaping, but he tightens his hold.

He fumbles with his clothes, not undressing, just pulling himself from the confinement of his pants. "Make me."

"Fuck you."

The words are barely from my lips when he thrusts inside of me—so hard, so deep, so abrupt, that I cry out because of it. My face is forced into the mattress again and again, muffling my shrieks, as he pounds into me. One arm stays firmly around me to lock me in place, his other hand pressed flat on my back, between my shoulder blades. I'm pinned but I wiggle around, shifting my hips, fighting him, until he thrusts deeply and pulls back too far, slipping out of me.

I regret it as soon as it happens, feeling the void, the ache already growing, but I react instinctively. It's fight or flight, and fighting isn't working. His hold loosens, his hand leaving my back as he grasps himself to thrust back in.

Before he can do it, I'm gone.

I slide out from beneath him, panting, and force myself up, but I didn't think it through. Fuck.

I'm fucked.

I can't run. I can barely shuffle, making it only a few steps before I nearly fall. I cry out as I trip, but Naz grabs ahold of me, tossing me right back onto the bed before I can hit the floor, face-first.

He laughs, forcing me back into position. "Did you really think you could get away from me that easily?"

He's mocking me, like my attempts to escape are feeble, like I'm weak, like I hadn't just exerted damn near all of my energy doing what I just did.

He might not hurt me physically, but fuck if that didn't sting.

Adrenaline surges inside of me, my anger and embarrassment overwhelming. He wants a fight? I'll give him one. I struggle with everything in me, his tie burning as it rubs my wrists, the knots not loosening even the slightest bit.

"Untie me," I demand as he pushes inside of me again. I want to say more, but the sensation renders me momentarily speechless. Fuck, he feels good...

"Untie yourself."

"I'm trying." I wiggle against the restraint some more. "Please? Just loosen the knots."

He laughs again. Laughs. As good as he feels inside of me, he's starting to piss me off.

"You know, fine, whatever," I growl. "You think you're so tough? You can't even fight fair. You're the weak one here. Fucking coward. Pathetic."

I don't know where the outburst comes from, but it works. Naz grabs my arms roughly, pulling on the restraint as he unknots my wrists. As soon as my hands are free, he flips me around so I'm on my back and he's on top of me.

I meet his eyes. Anxiety brews inside of me, mixing with a tinge of excitement. His expression is terrifying. He says nothing, but it's written all over his face.

He's going to make me eat my words.

My legs are hauled over his broad shoulders as he ruthlessly hammers my insides, pounding and pounding. His hand is on my throat, pressing against my jugular, making me lightheaded as he brutally fucks me.

And fucks me.

And fucks me.

His grip is so strong I think I'll still feel it tomorrow, handprints embedded in my flesh in deep shades of black and blue, as he ravishes my body, obliterating my insides. I fight him, trying to drop my legs, each thrust painfully deep. I claw at his hand, pushing against his body, struggling in his grasp. My nails dig into his skin, leaving marks on his armor, drawing blood that doesn't faze him a bit.

I seem to be more unnerved by it than him.

No matter what I do he subdues me, so much stronger, so much tougher. I can't overpower him. I can't win. My frustration mounts at that realization until I ball my hands into fists and punch his chest with everything in me.

I hit him so hard I hear it, hit him so hard my knuckles hurt. As soon as my fist connects, the force seems to ricochet through both of our bodies, tensing my muscles.

Oh shit.

He snatches my hand as he leans down to me, so close our noses touch. My heart races. I'm expecting venom. Instead, he startles me with a kiss.

"That's it, sweetheart," he says against my lips. "Fight me before I fuck you to death."

I think he might be capable of it, but I've gone too far to admit that out loud. I'm worked up, on emotional overload. "You're not man enough."

He groans, kissing me again, his lips just as brutal as the rest of him. Jesus, he likes this. It unnerves me for a second. Sex with him is always passionate, but this? This is intense. He's in complete control of my body, but I can tell he's lost control of himself. This isn't Naz. This is the monster, fully unsheathed.

This is Ignazio Vitale.

He loves me. Still, I try to remember. I don't ever want to forget. But this man battering my body, the one clutching my throat, fucks me like he hates me, like my life is in his hands alone.

Like he has no qualms ending me if he sees fit.

It's treacherous.

It's terrifying.

So why am I enjoying it so much?

"Oh God," I whisper, my voice strained, my vision blurring. I can feel the tears building and the pressure mounting... I feel like I'm about to explode beneath him. I'm a live wire, sparking everywhere he touches. It's electrifying. My hands find their way into his hair, gripping the locks, yanking on it. I don't know whether to push or pull, beg him to get away from me or give me even more.

Closing my eyes, my back arches, thrusting my breasts against his chest as the convulsions violently rip through me. My voice escapes me in a shrill scream, strangled by his hand on my throat, but loud enough to make my ears ring. He's unaffected, though—doesn't slow down, doesn't take it easy.

The orgasm tears it all away from me, taking my apprehension, my anxiety, and my will to fight. I drift away in a cloud of ecstasy, my mind gone, my body finally succumbing to him. I don't struggle anymore, even though he's still rough, even though he's physically asking for it.

Oh God, he broke me.

He broke me.

But I had no idea broken could feel so good.

Tears leak from the corner of my eyes, ones he kisses away as he whispers the word, "remember." I know I could get him to stop with a simple word, and maybe that's why I don't say it. I don't want him to stop. I want to be his. I want to be his everything. I want him to take me, and make me, and use me, and abuse me, because he thinks he has control and I know now that's what he craves. I want to play his game with him, because I know one mere syllable from my lips will stop him dead in his tracks, and if that's not real power, I don't know what is.

Hours, or days. Minutes, or seconds. I don't know how long he keeps it up, how long he plays this game of his. I just remember existing in the moment until the world fades around me, sleep pulling me away.

And then I'm roused awake.

The room is eerily dark, bathed in a sort of neon glow, as the lights from the strip shine in through the window, the curtains drawn open. I sit up, wincing at the stab of pain. My body is sore and achy; I'm naked and grimy. I feel like I ran a marathon and collapsed straight into bed.

I'm not even sure I can walk anymore.

My fucking legs are numb.

Across the room, bathed in green and gold light from the glow of the building, stands Naz, staring out the window, fully dressed.

Did he even undress?

He stands completely still, like he's a fixture of the room. The only sign of life is the rise and fall of his chest, subtle breathing, innate. He's not doing it. It's just happening.

In fact, he's not doing anything.

I thought he broke me in the moment, but I was wrong. I think he woke me up instead, like my life so far has been nothing but a monotone dream and he showed me what it's really like to open your eyes. I've never felt so alive. But broken is what I see when I look at him. It's like a thread was cut, something severed, and disconnecting the man I know from the body in front of me.

The monster came out. I saw him. I played with him. I welcomed him inside of me, and I didn't push him away.

I think, looking at Naz, that the monster decided to stay.

"Naz?" I call out, but he doesn't react, like he didn't hear me. My voice drops lower, a concerned whisper. "Ignazio?"

He moves.

His head turns, his eyes regarding me from across the room. After one quick glance back out of the window, he strolls toward the bed. He doesn't speak, slowly unbuttoning his shirt as he approaches. I see it when he gets closer, the tear in the fabric, the hints of blood streaked on the sleeves. I gape at it as he pulls his shirt off, seeing the deep gashes and claw marks raking down his strong arms.

I'm alarmed. I think I might've hurt him more than he hurt me.

He undresses in silence before climbing in bed beside me, shifting his body so he's on top of me. He nuzzles into my neck, settling between my thighs. Not a word spoken, he eases inside of me.

The first few strokes are gentle, followed up by an uncomfortable deep one. I gasp, my voice strained as I cling to him and croak, "yellow."

He slows his thrusts until he's barely moving, covering my body with his, making love to me. I feel him in every cell in my body, listening as he pants and moans into my neck, his warm breath fanning against my skin. He's usually quiet during sex, unless he's teasing me, but I hear him now... hear his shaky breaths and strained moans. I wrap my arms around him tightly, twirling the soft curls at his nape around my fingers. It's sweet, sweet... so fucking sweet... as he trails kisses along my jawline before pulling back enough to look down at me.

He still says nothing, but the curve of his lips, the soft smile he offers in the darkness, brightens the air between us. It's beautiful. So beautiful.

It's everything.

He's everything.

He finishes inside of me, still staring down at me, a look of ecstasy passing across his face that I marvel in. His lips part, eyelids drooping, as the softest whisper of a moan escapes in the form of my name. "Karissa."

Afterward we lay there, me on my stomach beside him on the bed, the blanket draped around me. I'm half asleep, exhausted and content, when I feel his feather light touch on my back, his fingertips tickling as he caresses my skin. My eyes close, the sensation causing my toes to curl as I bite down on my bottom lip, forcing back a giggle.

He's drawing something, or writing on me... what, I don't know. I try to follow the pattern, make sense of his movements, as he coats my flesh with goose bumps.

"What are you doing?" I whisper, not at all surprised when he doesn't answer my question. He keeps drawing patterns for a few minutes, nearly lulling me to sleep, before leaning over and pressing a soft kiss between my shoulder blades. He wraps his arms around me, pulling me onto my side toward him, my back flat against his warm chest.

"I was connecting the dots," he says quietly. "Your freckles are like stars. They tell a story, depending on how you connect them."

I smile to myself as he takes my hand, linking our fingers together. "What did they tell you?"

"They told me you're beautiful," he says. "And I'm a lucky son of a bitch to have you all to myself."

Chapter Eighteen

I stand in front of the long mirror, tugging on my dress, trying to situate it on my body. It feels tighter than I remember, showing more skin than I usually show. I'm all put together, my hair pinned up and makeup on, my lips the same blood red shade as my clothing.

In this light, it makes my skin look as pale as porcelain.

Picking up my powder compact, I brush some more light makeup on around my neck, nervously covering the faint black and blue hue. It doesn't hurt, and it doesn't much bother me, but I worry about others.

I know how it looks.

I know what everyone else will think.

I'm lost in my thoughts, my mind drifting back to last night, when I catch glimpse of the form appearing in the doorway behind me. My attention is drawn to Naz's reflection in the mirror, and I'm momentarily staggered.

I've never seen him so casual before.

Dark, loose-fitting jeans and a belt, white shirt and a midnight blue blazer clad his toned body. He hasn't shaved, and maybe it's my imagination, but his hair looks more out of place than usual. As that thought passes through my mind, he runs a hand through the locks, confirming my suspicions.

He's disheveled.

It's sexy.

So fucking sexy.

But it's not what I'm used to. He always carries himself with an air of perfection, everything in order and under control. This man in front of me is organized chaos, what seeped through the cracks when his armor fractured.

I stare at him for a moment, my nerves flaring. He was gone most of the day, leaving me to entertain myself. Not sure where he went, or why, but I was glad when he returned. Things feel so much colder when he's not around. "Ignazio."

He strolls into the bathroom, gaze fixed on mine in the mirror. "Is there a reason you're calling me that?"

"It's your name," I say as I put on my earrings. "It's what everyone else calls you."

"They usually call me Vitale." He pauses behind me. "And you're not everyone else."

He reaches around me, his hand coming to rest at the base of my throat as he gently brushes his thumb across the bruising on my neck. He says nothing, but the words are written in his deep dark eyes and the frown on his lips. I've never seen it from him before, but he looks almost remorseful.

He doesn't apologize, though. He lets out a sigh, pressing his cheek to my hair as I relax back against him. I watch his reflection as he closes his eyes, holding me.

It's peculiarly intimate.

He looks so vulnerable.

I stand still, just staring at him, falling more in love each passing second.

"Come on, birthday girl," he says eventually. "The night awaits."

Nineteen feels no different to me than eighteen. Not that I

expected it to, but it's strange. It doesn't feel like my birthday. I guess every day is a special occasion when I'm with this man.

Naz leads me down into the casino, holding my hand as we stroll along. I can't keep my eyes off of him, and he notices, laughing after a few minutes and nudging me. "What's up with you tonight?"

"Nothing, I'm just... surprised."

"By what?"

"You," I say. "I'm used to the fancy suits."

"Yeah, well, suits are for business."

"And jeans are for what... pleasure?"

He smiles. "Something like that, although clothing tends to be optional in that case."

We're led back to the same area he gambled at the night before, to a vast courtyard surrounding an elaborate mansion. It looks like an Italian villa, like we were ripped straight out of Vegas and thrust into *Under the Tuscan Sun*. The scent of flowers with a hint of lemon clings to the air in the glass enclosed property. It's breathtaking.

The evening sunshine feels nice on my face as we're seated out on the patio. It'll be dark soon, the lights already glowing on the building, but I'm enjoying what's left of the warmth while I can.

Naz sits across from me, ordering for the both of us, requesting a bottle of wine. No one here questions it.

Maybe nineteen is different.

Maybe I look old enough to drink tonight.

Or maybe he's just too intimidating to ever second-guess when he asks for something.

We drink and eat, talk and laugh, the air surrounding the table relaxed. There are other people around, I'm sure, but I can't see any, nor do I hear them. We're tucked away into a secluded space, where nothing else seems to exist.

"I've always dreamed about going to Italy," I say, leaning back in my chair as I glance around. I can feel the alcohol simmering in my bloodstream, relaxing my body and setting me at ease.

His voice is quiet as he distractedly whispers, "I know."

I almost ask how he could possibly know that, but it's pointless. What does this man not know? "Have you ever been?"

He nods, taking a sip of his drink. "They did a decent job of recreating it, but nothing quite matches the real thing."

"I bet it's like heaven."

"It is," he says. "I'll take you someday."

"To heaven?"

He smiles. "Wherever you want to go."

I can tell he means it, his voice genuine. "I couldn't ask you to do that."

"I know," he says. "That's why I offered instead."

Naz motions for the waiter when the man steps outside and tells him to bring us whatever's chocolate on the dessert menu. A few minutes later some kind of chocolaty something is placed on the table in front of me. I have no idea what it is, but it's creamy and rich, one of the greatest things I've ever tasted. I'm shoveling it into my mouth when Naz speaks quietly. "I'm in love with you, Karissa."

I freeze with the spoon halfway to my mouth and peer across the table at him. "I love you, too."

"No, I don't just love you," he says. "I'm *in* love with you."

His voice is so earnest it paints my flesh with goose bumps. "Is there a difference?"

"There is," he says. "When you love somebody, you want what's best for them... but when you're in love with them, you want them for yourself. And they're not always the same thing. Just because I want you, doesn't mean I'm the best thing for you... because I'm not. I know I'm not. It isn't easy to reconcile. Because I know I should let you go, should let you walk away from me right now, but I can't do it. I can't. I'm selfish, and I'm in love with you, and I want nothing more than to keep you for myself."

"I don't want to walk away from you. I'm never going to."

"Don't say that unless you mean it."

"I swear it," I say. "I meant it when I asked you to stay that night, and I mean it now. I'm in love with you, too."

"Do you ever think about the future?" he asks.

"All the time."

"What do you see?"

"I'm not sure," I admit, swirling my spoon around in the chocolate whatever-it-is. "I'm not even sure what waits for me back in New York. If I don't have my scholarship, I don't even have school anymore."

"Don't worry about that."

"How can I not?" I ask. "I'm not sure about anything anymore… anything except for you, anyway. You're the only thing in my life that I'm sure about. I know I want you… need you. I know I love you. Nothing else really makes any sense anymore."

"Don't say that unless—"

"Unless I mean it," I mumble, cutting him off. "Believe me, I mean it."

"Do you want to know what future I see? What I see for you?"

I meet his eyes. "What?"

"I see you having everything you've ever wanted," he says. "Everything you've ever dreamed of. Clothes, shoes, houses, cars… boats."

I laugh. "Boats?"

He shrugs. "You might want a boat, you know, take one down the canal in Venice when you visit Italy someday."

"Okay, I'll give you that one," I say. "I don't really need all of that, though."

"But you can still have it," he says. "Anything you want out of life. You can finish school and build a life however you want it to be. A family, children… whatever you want. I see it for you."

I smile. "It sounds wonderful."

"It can be," he says quietly. "God willing, it will be."

"Does this life include you?"

"Do you want it to?"

"Of course. I'd give all that other stuff up if it meant I could just keep you."

He stares at me in silence for a moment, not responding to what I've said, before slowly reaching into his coat. He pulls out a small velvet box, and every muscle inside of me seizes up at the sight of it. My heart stalls a beat before kick starting again, like its been shocked into action, frantically pounding against my rib cage.

Oh shit.

Oh shit.

Oh shit.

He wordlessly flips the box open, the last tiny bit of sunlight hitting the oval-shaped diamond dead center of the ring. I gape at it as it sparkles in the light. I don't know anything about jewelry, couldn't guess the carat to save my life, but I know enough to tell it's extravagant.

He says nothing.

I say nothing.

He glances down at the box in his hand, pulling the ring from it after a moment, holding it up in front of him.

There's no way he's doing what I think he's doing.

There's just no way.

His eyes lift to meet mine again, and I see the truth there, lurking in the darkness. "You really mean it?"

I slowly nod. "I wouldn't say it if I didn't."

This has to be a dream. It's a dream. I'm asleep, or in a coma. Maybe he choked me last night until I fell unconscious, or maybe I'm dead, or maybe he's just fucking with me. Maybe I'm mistaken.

Maybe someone's playing a cruel joke.

Something, anything… but there's just no way this is real. There's no way this means what I think it means, that he means what I think he means. There's no way he's about to say—

"Marry me."

Those two words suck the oxygen from the courtyard. My chest burns, my eyes blurring. I inhale sharply. I can't fucking breathe.

Blinking rapidly, my gaze bounces between him and the ring. My brain is screaming in protest, shouting out everything that is wrong about this entire thing. The list is a mile long. I've known him only months. There's so much about him that's a mystery to me. I'm young, and maybe I'm naïve, and he's dark, and maybe he's a bit dangerous. I only vaguely know his history, and my mother doesn't even know he exists.

So many things wrong, so why do those words feel so right?

Marry me.

He didn't ask.

It's not a question.

He knows.

He fucking knows me.

My voice betrays me when I try to speak. My lips part, but nothing comes out besides a shaky exhale. Naz stares at me, a smile slowly spreading across his face, flashing those deep dimples. He holds the ring out, cocking an eyebrow.

I extend my hand across the table, trembling as he slips it on my finger.

I let out a squeak before stammering incoherently, but my words are cut off when he stands and leans across the table, silencing me with a kiss. I kiss him back as he lets go of my hands, and I reach up, wrapping my arms around his neck. It's a fiery kiss, full of all of Naz's passion. It vibrates through my body, throttling my soul, his lips, and skin, and words forever altering me.

How could I ever deny something so all consuming? How could I say no to someone who means so much to me? It's crazy, and stupid, and utterly overwhelming, but how will I ever fly if I'm too terrified to take the first leap?

"I will," I whisper against his mouth. "I'll marry you."

Chapter Nineteen

The air is electric.

I can feel it buzzing along my skin, the hair on my arms sticking straight up as the current flows through my body. Every centimeter of me tingles.

The arena is loud... so loud I can hardly hear myself think. Thousands upon thousands of people cram the vast room, packed together in seats, screaming and stomping. The noise seems to pound through my skull, fueling the electricity. It's pandemonium.

Naz leads me straight to the front row, surrounding a large boxing ring. As soon as we get there, I spot the two empty seats in the middle, most of the row filled with familiar faces. Naz ushers me to one, and I nervously sit down beside the girl I'd met last night—Brandy. She's leaning against Raymond, his arm draped around her, as he eyes us curiously, gaze shifting from me to Naz. "Vitale."

"Ray."

Raymond's eyes drift back to me once more, meeting mine, before scanning me. His gaze settles straight on the ring on my finger, like he knew to look for it. A laugh bursts from him as he shakes his head. "You did it."

"Yes," Naz says. "Just a bit ago."

"Did what?" Brandy asks. "What happened?"

Raymond motions toward my hand, and I slip it onto the seat beside me, out of view, but I'm not fast enough. Brandy's eyes widen as she snatches ahold of my hand, holding it up. "No fucking way! You got engaged?"

I can feel the heat rushing to my face. The entire row seems to silence as a dozen sets of eyes strain to look our way.

"We did," Naz says.

The silence is broken by quiet murmurs, a few congratulations, but even more shock. Brandy clutches my hand tightly, admiring the ring in the light, as male laughter cuts through the air. Naz tenses at the sound as it echoes from the guy who rubbed him the wrong way last night.

"Never thought I'd see the day," the guy says. "Vitale tying the knot again."

My expression falls at those words.

Vitale tying the knot again.

Again.

The others fall silent once more, looking away. I turn to Naz, confused, and see he's staring straight ahead at the ring, not a hint of emotion on his face. He's a stone cold statue. It's like he hadn't heard... he's here, but he's gone.

"Strike three," Raymond mutters, the words barely audible over the roar of the crowd. "You're out."

Naz slouches back in his seat after a moment, throwing his arm over my shoulder and pulling me toward him. I have a million questions (like what the fuck did he mean by *again*?) but I know now's not the time to ask that. Naz presses a kiss to the top of my head and says not a word as the arena erupts in chaos.

I don't know what's going on—who's who or what's what—but everyone around us is immersed in our surroundings. Two men make their way to the ring, music blaring as people scream. One's in blue shorts, the other in red, with names I can't pronounce and faces I don't recognize.

The brutality right from the ding of the bell is alarming. I sit still in my seat, in Naz's arms, as the men in the ring ferociously pound on each other, round after round, very little letting up. We're so close I can see the blood, sweat, and tears, hear the sickening blows, the grunts and pants and cries. It's barbaric.

I'm appalled.

A quick glance at Naz tells me he's enthralled.

He watches the fight with gross fascination. The others around us cheer and jeer, screaming and jumping up out of their seats, but Naz just sits there, watching attentively, his thumb absently stroking my arm.

The fighters seem to be equally matched as they go toe-to-toe. Naz squeezes me tighter to him after a few rounds. "Who are you pulling for?"

"Blue shorts guy."

"Blue shorts guy," he echoes with a laugh. "Is there a reason?"

There is, but I'm not going to admit it. The guy with the blue shorts has a design shaved into his hair on the side of his head. It's fascinating.

Instead, I shrug. I don't really care who wins.

The fight goes on and on. Every punch sends the crowd reeling. I hear their frenzied yells, feel it vibrating the floor beneath my feet, rocking the air around me. Naz doesn't say anything else, watching, his expression darkening as he stares into the ring. During the last round, the room erupts in commotion when red shorts hits blue so hard I hear the crack and feel the thump as he hits the ground.

He's out cold.

It's over. Half the arena cheers, while a low thrum of boos seems to underlay the celebration. Naz finally pulls his eyes away from the ring as I frown. "Guess red shorts won."

"Guess so," he says. "Good thing, too."

"Why?"

"Because I had a quarter of a million riding on him."

I gape at him as he stands up. He offers me his hand, and I take it. We don't say goodbye, don't hang around to celebrate, don't even wait for the official announcement of the winner. We leave the arena, heading back into the casino, and make our way back up to the penthouses.

I let him dwell in silence during the journey, but once we're back in the suite, I can't take it anymore. My head is a frantic jumble of thoughts, puzzle pieces I can't quite fit together.

He turns to me right inside the door, his expression serious. It's dark, the light so dim he looks like little more than an eerie shadowy form. I can barely make out his eyes. I want to ask him questions, but the words are intimidated.

He knows me, though.

I know he does.

"I was married once," he says quietly, unprompted, answering what I long to ask. "It was a long time ago—a long, long time ago. Feels like forever, like another lifetime. I was a different person then, a different man. I didn't have much, but I had her… and then I didn't have her anymore."

My feelings are at odds with each other. I'm not sure what to say. "What happened?"

"I told you what happened," he says, and as soon as I hear those words, I know. He lost his family. "She was only eighteen. She didn't deserve what happened to her. She should've survived… they should've survived."

"They?"

He hesitates for a moment, as if maybe he's not going to answer, but the response finally leaves his lips in a whisper. "She was pregnant."

I can't breathe again, and it's not from a hand around my throat. It's the lump of emotion that I can't swallow down that blocks the air from entering my lungs. A baby.

He lets out an exaggerated sigh. "They died, and I survived. I was younger than you are right now... young and dumb, didn't think these things could ever happen to me. But I'm not naïve anymore, Karissa. I'm not going to lose another. I'm not going to make those mistakes again."

"Who could do such a thing?"

"A coward," he says. "A fool. He deserved to be punished, but the authorities let him walk away. They let him go. So I vowed someday I'd make him pay."

"Have you?" I ask quietly.

"No," he says, taking a step toward me. "Not yet."

I can see him better now that he's closer, can see the sadness lurking in his eyes. I don't think twice before reaching out and cupping his cheek, feeling the coarse, bristly hair against my palm. Naz doesn't like to be touched much... he prefers to do the touching, to be the one in control, even if it's only for show. I may not know everything about his history, but that is something I do know. It's something I've learned being with him.

So I expect him to pull away, to grasp ahold of my hand, to move from my reach or divert my attention, but instead he just stands there, staring down at me, letting my fingertips trail along his jawline and explore his face.

"I won't let it happen again," he repeats. "You're special to me, Karissa. I didn't expect you to be."

"What did you expect?"

"I don't know what I expected," he says, "but I didn't expect your innocence."

"I'm not that innocent."

His expression softens. "You're a cute little kitten."

I roll my eyes. "I am not."

"You are," he says. "You may growl, and hiss, and meow, and maybe sometimes you bring out those claws, but I know how to make you purr. I'm the king of the jungle. I'm the predator."

"Does that make me your prey?"

He shakes his head. "That makes you my queen."

I caress his face before threading my fingers through his hair. "You make me feel like one."

He says nothing in response, and I say nothing else, as he finally pulls my hands away from him, linking his fingers with mine to pull me toward the stairs. He takes me up to the second floor, to the master bedroom, where he slowly, and carefully, strips me out of my clothes. I nervously stand in front of him naked as his eyes scan my body.

After a moment, he turns and strides away.

My brow furrows. I hear him in the closet, and he returns holding one of his neckties. I stand still as he walks around behind me. I'm waiting for him to try to tie my wrists together again, thinking maybe he'll go for the ankles, even preparing for him to wrap it around my neck, but I let out a soft gasp when he slips it around my eyes instead. The room is cloaked in darkness as he blindfolds me, tying it securely in place.

A yelp escapes my throat when I'm suddenly jolted, lifted up in the air. Naz picks me up, cradling me in his arms, and I blindly reach for him, clinging to him. He lays me down on the bed, whispering for me to relax.

My instinct is to fight it, to tense up. It's alarming being in the dark. I try to relax, but my body is coiled like a spring. Every touch is like a jolt, the sensations heightened from the anticipation.

Closing my eyes, succumbing to the blackness, I lay there as he has his way with me. He kisses and caresses every inch of skin, bringing me to the brink again and again. He's slow and gentle, sweet and genuine, as he whispers how much he loves me when he makes love to me.

I paw at him, clinging to him, kissing and nipping at whatever skin my mouth can reach. I have no idea if it's his chest, his chin, or his cheek. It doesn't matter, though. It's him, and he's everything.

Every part of him.

It goes on and on until we're both sweaty and satiated. Naz pulls the blindfold from my eyes as he hovers on top of me, still deep inside of me. I blink away the darkness, adjusting to the dim lighting of the room, and watch as his lips curve. "You're mine forever," he whispers.

I return his smile. "I'm yours."

"Never forget it."

"I won't."

He pulls out of me, pulling me to him in the bed. It doesn't take long for sleep to pull me away from him.

I sleep deeply, waking up in the middle of the night to find myself alone in the bed. I call out his name but get no answer. His clothes are gone from the bedroom floor, his shoes aren't here, and neither is his wallet.

He's not in the suite anymore.

I wander between rooms for a bit before making my way back to the bedroom. I wrap myself up in the sheets, snatching Naz's pillow from his side of the bed. It's cool to the touch, smelling a lot like him.

I drift off again. Something jolts me awake much later, sunshine streaming through the window, bathing the bed in a warm glow. Opening my eyes, I see Naz when he steps into the bedroom. Yesterday's clothes hang from his frame, slightly disheveled.

He looks exhausted.

"Hey," I mumble, sitting up in bed and clutching the sheet around me.

He pulls off his shirt. "Good morning."

Naz strips right in front of me and says nothing else before disappearing from the room. The faint sound of water running reaches my ears after a moment, the shower starting up in the bathroom. Curious, I slip out of bed and join him.

Naz stands under the spray in the shower, head tilted back and eyes closed as the water pelts him from all angles. I stop just outside the reach of the spray, taking a moment to admire him. Water runs down his strong frame as steam surrounds him like a fog. His chiseled jawline accents a stern expression. Despite his exhaustion, his arousal is obvious, his cock hard and twitching like he could easily go twelve rounds with me, right here, right now.

Something tells me, from the look in his eyes when he looks over at me, that a bout with him today would be as ruthless as the brutality we witnessed in the boxing ring.

He shifts position, motioning with his head for me to come closer. I step under the spray, flinching from the scalding water, as he wraps his arms around me.

"Where'd you go last night?" I ask quietly.

"Work," he says. "Had something to take care of."

He reaches past me to grab some shampoo. It's the little bottle provided by the hotel, but I can tell it's not the cheap shit I've been subjected to at the hole-in-the-wall places I stayed in over the years in between houses with my mother.

He squeezes some onto his palm before setting it aside. I start to step away from him, not wanting to get in his way of showering, when he runs his hands through my hair. I freeze, stalled in place by the sensation, as he lathers the shampoo up in my hair. His touch is firm, sending tingles down my spine, as he massages my scalp. My eyes drift closed, a soft moan escaping my lips.

He doesn't stop there. I can do nothing but stand there as the man washes me from head to toe, lathering soap on every inch of my body before rinsing it away. He says not a word, doesn't even look me in the eyes again until he's finished. His eyes trail along my skin once I'm clean, lingering on the fading bruises along my neck. Reaching up, he brushes his fingertips along them, but he still makes no comment.

Instead, he turns away.

"Our plane leaves in two hours," he says. "We'll have to head out soon."

It feels oddly like a brusque dismissal, his stance doing nothing to warm his words. I mumble, "okay," under my breath as I head out of the shower, grabbing a towel on my way. I dry off, wrapping it around me, as I go back into the bedroom.

My eyes are drawn to his clothes on the floor, but I leave them there, focusing my attention on my own things. I dress quickly and pack, throwing my hair into a ponytail before making my way down to the first floor of the suite.

I can hear the shower turn off, hear Naz going about his business upstairs, as I walk to the vast windows and gaze out. We've been here for two days, yet it feels like we just arrived hours ago. There's so much I haven't done, so much I haven't seen, parts of the suite I haven't even ventured to yet.

Naz comes down, dressed back in a black suit. He's distracted as we check out, distracted on the drive to the airport in the limo. The others are already there, on the tarmac, belongings being loaded onto the plane when we make it that far. Naz bypasses them all, guiding me straight onto the plane.

We sit in the same seats as before.

The others take their same seats, too.

They're more subdued today, nobody saying much of anything as we settle in for the trip home. I glance around at their faces, my gaze settling on the seat across from me.

Empty.

We're coming home with one less person than we went to Vegas with.

Chapter Twenty

You cannot step in the same river twice.

The first day of philosophy class, Professor Santino stood at the front of the classroom and uttered those words, quoting the philosopher Heraclitus. He said it with such conviction, and it made so much sense in theory, until he asked us to explain what it meant.

I didn't raise my hand.

There were a few responses, but they always went along two lines—either it's because you've changed, or it's because the river has. The debate lasted nearly the entire hour. At the end of the class, someone asked Santino to tell us which side was right.

The man shrugged a shoulder, absently tapping his pointer stick against the hard floor. "Nobody knows. Maybe it's both."

Standing in my dorm room so many months later, surrounded by all of my things, jet-legged and feeling out of place, I think I finally understand it. I'm not the same person who left here forty-eight hours ago.

And when Melody bursts in, wide-eyed and frantic, I seem to instinctively know: this place isn't the same, either. Minutes, hours, days passed... time that changed me, time I can never get back or experience here. Time I wasn't around for.

Lost time.

It changes everything.

Melody's breathing hard, staring at me like a mad woman. I freeze in front of my closet, a stack of hangers in my hand as I prepare to pack them in a cardboard box. Her eyes hold secrets she's desperate to spill, but I can tell from her expression they might not be ones I want to hear.

"Have you heard?" she asks, her eyes flickering toward my desk, where Naz quietly stacks up my books, his back to us.

"What?"

"Satan," she says, shutting the door. "He's dead!"

I blink rapidly. "Huh?"

"Satan," she says again. "Santino! He's dead!"

My stomach sinks, everything inside of me coiling, barely holding the swell of nausea down. I have a million questions, but all that sputters out are mere syllables. "What? When? How?"

"It happened Thursday... or Friday. I don't know. But somebody killed him! They stabbed him or something... impaled him." Her voice drops low, cracking as she steps toward me. "They said it was his pointer thingy, that the stick was like, stuck, in his chest! Can you believe it?"

I can't. Her words hit me, bouncing off the surface, refusing to sink in. How can he be dead? "Who did it? Who killed him?"

"Don't know," she says. "The police are investigating, but I don't think they've arrested anyone. It's just... wow. Someone killed him."

"Who would do such a thing?" I look at Naz, who is packing up my books in silence. "Naz?"

He turns at the sound of his name, raising his eyebrows. "Yes?"

"Professor Santino... he's dead!"

His expression is stoic. "I heard."

"Can you believe it?"

"Yes," he says, his curt answer catching me off guard. "I'm only amazed it didn't happen sooner."

"What? What do you mean?"

"Daniel didn't have a lot of friends, Karissa," he says. "It was only a matter of time before he pushed the wrong button."

I stare at him. How can he be so unaffected? Sure, Santino wasn't nice, but Naz knew the man.

Melody clears her throat, drawing my attention back to her. She launches into conspiracy theories, who could've done what and why and how, like this is a game of Clue and she can riddle it out with the right game pieces. I listen to her, my attention consistently shifting to Naz. He steadily packs, but I can tell he's listening.

"It's just so crazy," Melody says after a moment. "Thank God we're moving out this week. I don't know if I feel safe here right now, you know? It's creepy."

"I know," I whisper. "My mom always said New York was too dangerous."

A loud whack echoes through the room. I flinch as Melody gasps. My eyes dart to Naz in shock as he reaches down and picks up a textbook from the floor that he dropped. Wordlessly, he places it in the box, continuing on with the others, as if he hadn't interrupted.

"So you're packing now," Melody says. "Are you going home for the summer?"

Before I can respond, Naz interjects. "Forever."

"What?" Melody asks.

"She's going home forever," Naz clarifies.

Melody's gaze shifts between us. "Wait, what? You're moving back in with your mother?"

"No," I say quietly. "I'm moving in with Naz."

These were things I hadn't given much thought to last night. In fact, it didn't really hit me until we landed in New Jersey and Naz told me he'd help me gather my things to move in.

I told him that was crazy; I couldn't live with him.

271

He told me it would be crazy not to, considering we were engaged.

Melody stares at me with shock, and I almost feel guilty. The girl doesn't know the half of it yet.

"You're moving in together?" she gasps. "Already?"

"Uh, yeah."

"Are you ready for all that?"

Such a loaded question, one I'm not even sure the answer to. Before I can conjure up a response, Naz chimes in, laying it all out on the table. "I certainly hope she's ready, considering she agreed to marry me."

Melody looks like she's been slapped, her eyes so wide I'm surprised they haven't popped out of their sockets. She just stares at me, and I smile sheepishly, holding out my hand to show her the ring.

I expect her to be confused.

Maybe even angry.

But I don't anticipate her excitement.

She lets out the loudest shriek as she grabs my hand, jumping up and down with delight, yelling at me to spill every last detail. I explain what I can, what I remember. It's not much of a story, but the dreamy look she gets in her eyes tells me it's enough to make her swoon.

Naz remains quiet throughout my story.

He's still packing like it's the only thing that matters.

Melody is rambling too fast for me to keep up when a series of familiar beeps rings out in the room, interrupting her train of thought. Naz pulls out his phone, glancing at it, and turns to me. "I have to get going. Have something to handle for work."

"Okay."

"I'll be back to pick you."

"I, uh... I'd rather stay here tonight."

A look of hurt passes across his face, wounded pride, like I've rejected him. "You want to sleep here?"

"Yes. I mean, if you don't mind. I have to finish packing, and it'll give me a chance to catch up with Melody."

Naz looks like he's going to argue, but his phone ringing again stops him. Sighing, he kisses the side of my head and strides toward the door. "I'll be back tomorrow morning."

He walks out without waiting for me to escort him down, and I shrug it off. What are they going to do? Evict me? Certainly isn't the first time he's wandered these halls alone.

I turn to Melody as she flops down on her bed, staring off into space, shell-shocked. "You're engaged."

"I am."

Her skeptical gaze turns to me. "Have you told your mother?"

"No," I whisper. "Not yet."

Loud laughter bursts from Melody, like it's the funniest thing she's ever heard. I smile at the absurdity, although my insides are knotted tightly, so much I can hardly breathe.

My mother's not going to take this in stride.

She's going to think the city corrupted me.

And maybe it has, but I'm happy that way. I can't step in the same river twice, but that's okay, because there are more rivers out there, unchartered water, that I'll get to explore with the man of my dreams.

The sky is still dark. It's so early it barely constitutes 'tomorrow' or 'morning' when Naz reappears at the dorm. He once more makes it up to my room without anyone signing him in, slipping right past the flimsy security of the dorm, reminding me how unsafe a place like this can be. Santino's death lingers on the back of my mind, knowing there's a killer roaming around putting me on edge.

Maybe moving in with Naz is the best idea. At least with him, I'm safe. Nobody is stupid enough to mess with him.

He knocks on the door of the dorm room before dawn, rousing both Melody and me from sleep. We locked the door last night for probably the first time all semester. Melody merely rolls over, throwing her blanket over her head with a groan as I flick on the light and open the door. Naz strolls in, dressed as usual, a pair of black gloves on his hands.

Groggily, I rub my eyes as I survey him. "Is it cold out or something?"

He raises an eyebrow in question. "Why?"

"You're wearing gloves," I point out.

"No," he says, glancing down at his hands, before turning away from me and surveying my things. I finished packing last night, everything shoved into boxes except for my pillow and blanket. "This should all fit in the car, but if not, we can come back for it later."

"Okay."

I flop back down on my bed, yawning, and watch as he stacks boxes and picks them up, heading out the door.

It takes him less than ten minutes on his own to take everything downstairs to the Mercedes, parked in a coveted spot right along the curb. He has it all crammed in and loaded before I even get around to sliding on my shoes. I tell him I'll meet him at the car as I snatch the blanket off of Melody's head and shove her over to sit down.

"What?" she groans, half-asleep. She elbows me as she tries to grab her blanket.

"I'm leaving," I say. "Wanted to say goodbye."

"Later, hooker," she says. "See you later, not goodbye."

"See you later," I say, throwing the blanket back over her head. I stand back up and head for the door.

"So just chill," she calls out. "'Till the next episode."

Rolling my eyes, I head out, finding Naz waiting downstairs with the passenger door open for me. I get in, some anxiety brewing in my stomach when he climbs in beside me.

"You ready to go home?" he asks as he starts the car.

Home. Such a simple word, but the connotation of it makes something inside of me soar. I've never really felt like I was standing on stable ground, like there was somewhere I could call home permanently. My life has always been a series of temporaries: new towns, new people, new schools, and new houses. New everything. The world around me fluctuated, so many variables in my word problem of life to ever figure out the answer of who I am.

But Naz is my new constant.

My permanent.

He makes it easier to find my answer, to find my place.

My home.

"Yeah," I say, offering him a small smile. "I'm ready."

I'm quiet on the drive to Brooklyn, quiet when we pull up to the house, quiet as we head inside. We unload my things, taking them up to his room... our room... for me to unpack.

"Should I...?" I hesitate, looking at the massive dresser. "Can I...?"

"Whatever you want," he says, answering my unasked questions. "What's mine is yours, Karissa."

There's an extra closet in here, half of the drawers in his dresser empty, like it was all waiting for me to move in all along. Naz lingers in the room while I unpack before excusing himself when his phone rings. He comes back a few minutes later, pausing in the doorway. "I have some work to take care of... I'll be back around noon. Settle in, get comfortable..."

"I will."

He strolls over, kissing me, a smile tugging his lips. "I'm happy you're here."

"I'm happy to be here," I whisper, but he's already gone before the words are from my lips.

I finish unpacking, almost everything I own belonging in the bedroom, before I head downstairs to the den. I take the few DVDs and books I own and put them on his shelves, mixed in with his.

When I'm finished, I glance at the time. Barely ten o'clock in the morning. I have at least two hours until Naz gets back, so I do what any self-respecting woman would do when left all alone with her guy's belongings for the first time.

I snoop.

I've seen what Naz has on the surface, but I dig deeper, wanting to see more of the man, the parts of him that are tucked away. I rifle through shelves and cabinets, even searching his junk drawer in the kitchen, before heading back to the bedroom and turning to his things.

You can tell a lot about a person by what they keep hidden in their underwear drawer. It's their private spot, the one place they don't expect anyone to touch out of decency. It's where I always hid my love letters, my birth control when I got it at sixteen without my mother's consent, the vibrator I bought on my eighteenth birthday... but Naz's drawer is a ghost town.

What a letdown.

I shut the drawer, glancing in the others to find nothing out of the ordinary, before heading to his closet. I count a dozen black suits, not including the one he's wearing and whatever's dirty, but he has a good bit of other clothes. I wish he'd wear the others more often. I'm checking out his tie collection, most solid colors, when my eyes drift to the shelf on the top of the closet.

A silver metal case, no bigger than a shoebox, sits in the corner. Curious, I reach up on my tiptoes and pull it down, nearly dropping it as soon as I get my hands on it. It's heavy. I can hear stuff jingling around inside. There's a lock on the box, but I haven't found any keys during my search that would open it.

Scowling, I shake the box, trying to figure out what's inside, before straining my muscles to shove it back up on the shelf.

Another letdown.

Giving up, I head out of the bedroom, looking in closets and scarcely furnished guest rooms, before heading back downstairs.

Every other room is exactly as expected... nothing but laundry stuff in the laundry room, a spare room full of exercise equipment, and the massive garage is full of tools, old faded stains on the concrete.

I find a door leading down into what I assume is the basement, a musky, dank odor wafting out of it. There's no light switch, and the stairs are flimsy, the little bit of light filtering down from behind me illuminating tons of cobwebs, so I don't dare go down there.

No thanks.

It's twelve o'clock on the dot when I hear the front door open. I'm sitting on the couch in the den, my feet tucked beneath me as I flip through channels on the television. Naz walks in, letting out a deep sigh as he flops down beside me. He looks older than when he left just hours ago, the bags beneath his eyes heavier, a weariness in his face that hints at exhaustion.

"You look tired," I say, settling on some cooking show.

"I am," he says. "I feel like I could sleep for a week."

"Take a nap."

"I'm not a toddler."

I shrug. "I take naps."

"Yeah, well, it's beauty sleep for the beautiful," he says, looking at me, "but there's no rest for the wicked."

I roll my eyes. "I wouldn't call myself beautiful."

"I would."

"I wouldn't call you wicked, either."

"I would."

"Regardless," I say, "if you're tired, you should go to sleep."

"Yeah, I should," he admits, although he makes no move to go upstairs, settling in on the couch as he kicks his shoes off. "You find anything interesting today?"

My brow furrows. "When?"

"When you went through my stuff."

My heart seems to stop for a second as I turn to him. "Why do you think I went through your stuff?"

"Because you're human," he says. "It's normal to be curious, and you're a smart woman... I'd expect no less."

I'm not sure what to say. He doesn't sound upset in the least, but his matter-of-fact tone, pegging my actions from the start like he knows me better than I know myself, still unnerves me. "No, I didn't find anything."

"Figured you wouldn't," he said. "Nowhere near as interesting as what I found in your drawers in the dorm."

Now my heart does stop. My eyes widen. "You went through my stuff?"

"Of course. I'm human, too."

"What...? When...?"

"When you were sleeping that first night. You woke up and caught me."

I know when he's referring to... he'd been looking at the picture frame on my dresser when I woke up. "So that's what you were doing."

"Yes," he says. "Although, I have to say, I was surprised you only had one vibrator. That's at odds with the vixen you turn into when I get you naked."

Blood rushes straight to my face. I can feel my cheeks flame with embarrassment. I look away from him, covering my face with my hands, as he lets out a loud laugh. Before I can think of something to say he grabs ahold of me, laying down on the couch and pulling me into his arms. I tuck in against him, my head on his chest. "Ugh, I'm so embarrassed."

"Don't be." He kisses the top of my head. "Do you use it often?"

"Oh God," I groan, closing my eyes. "You're not helping me not be embarrassed, Naz."

"There's nothing to be ashamed of... I'm just curious."

"No," I whisper. "Not anymore, anyway. Not since you."

Ugh, are we really talking about this?

"Good." I can hear the sleep in his voice. "I'm glad."

"You are?"

"Yeah," he says. "I like to know I can keep you satisfied."

Chapter Twenty-One

They say what goes around, comes around. Do unto others, as you would have them do unto you. It's the Golden Rule. I've always tried to follow it, to be a good person, but karma has caught up to me.

Dozens of calls. Just as many messages.

I haven't heard from my mother in weeks.

I'm regretting all those times I sent her to my voicemail, regretting the missed calls and days where I didn't respond to her messages. Every time her answering machine clicks on, I grow a little more worried, leaving yet another message she won't respond to.

"Mom, it's me... call me."

"I'm worried, Mom... where are you?"

"Why aren't you calling me?"

"Please, just let me know everything's okay."

I'm in the den, where Naz spends most of his time when he's home, sprawled out on the couch in my pajamas. I've been here for seven days now, and it still feels surreal, like I'm just visiting, although Naz acts like I've lived here all along. His guard dropped easily, quickly, the façade of perfection he always carried melted away now that I've moved in.

Today he's sitting at his desk, still wearing a black suit, but he didn't bother putting on a tie and his feet are still bare. The top few buttons of his shirt are undone, his sleeves shoved up to his elbows, the bottom not tucked in. His laptop is open in front of him as he types away. He's doing whatever it is he does, I'm not entirely sure. I asked and he said 'dealing with people'.

For someone who deals with people every day, I rarely see another living soul come around him.

He works odd hours, leaving occasionally on a whim, slipping away in the middle of the night and returning before I'm awake. I have my suspicions about what kind of dealing he does, but I don't bring them up to him.

Maybe because I don't think he'll admit it.

Or maybe because I'm afraid he will.

Sighing, I open up the contacts on my phone and find my mother's name, hitting the button to call her. Bringing the phone to my ear, I listen as it rings twice. I wait for her machine, the monotone 'leave a message' voice, but instead a series of beeps greets me before the line dies.

I call her back again right away, hoping it's a fluke, once more getting the beeps. My stomach drops. The tape is full. I don't know what to do, what to think, but sickness brews inside of me at the realization.

She hasn't been listening to my messages.

"Do you think I should call the police?"

The typing instantly ceases as Naz's eyes dart over top of the computer, meeting my gaze. "Excuse me?"

"I can't get my mother on the phone," I say. "I haven't heard from her in weeks, so I'm wondering if I should call the police, you know, to have them go check on her."

He stares at me for a moment. "People go weeks without talking to their parents. That's nothing out of the norm. I haven't spoken to mine in months."

His words distract me from the worry. "You have parents?"

"Of course," he says. "I didn't create myself."

I roll my eyes. "I know that. I just didn't realize they were still around. You don't ever talk about them."

"We're not close," he says. "Ray's more of a father to me than my own father ever was."

My curiosity is piqued. He opened the door, so I stick my foot in, seeing how far into the room I can get. "Have you known Raymond long?"

"Since I was your age," he says as he shakes his head. "Younger, actually. I was sixteen."

"How'd you meet him?"

He's quiet, and I think he's about to shut down, to change the subject, when he lets out a deep sigh and closes his laptop, sitting back in his chair. "I stole from him."

That was not the answer I expected. "You stole from him?"

"I did," he admits. "He owned this store back then... this little corner store, but it was a front for this gambling ring. I used to walk by it on my way home from school. I went in one day, grabbed a soda, and paid for it with a five-dollar bill. As soon as the guy opened the register, someone from the back called for him. When he wasn't looking, I reached over the counter, swiped the money from the register, and walked out."

"Did you get caught?"

"Of course," he says, laughing to himself. "Barely made it a block. I was about to cross the street when a car cut me off. Ray stepped out, said he wanted his money back. I gave it to him, of course. I knew who he was. He counted it out as I stood there, asked me why I did it. I gave some smart-ass response about how it was his fault for employing idiots who leave money out like that. Figured if he was going to hurt me, I may as well get my digs in while I could."

"Did he hurt you?" I ask hesitantly.

"Yes, but not as bad as he could've," he says. "I took the beating like a man, licked my wounds and went home. My pride was hurt more than anything. I wasn't mad he caught me, or that he beat me... I was mad he robbed me. You see, before he left, he took *my* five dollars."

I can see where this is going. "I'm guessing you did something about that."

He smiles. "I went to the store and demanded my money back."

"Did he give it to you?"

"No," he says. "He gave me something else instead."

"What?"

"A job."

I hesitate as those words sink in. "And you've worked for him ever since?"

He stares at me, and I can see the door closing, shutting me out. He doesn't answer, but his lack of denial is all I really need. His silence rings as confirmation. He looks away after a moment, standing up. "If you're worried about your mother, Karissa, go check on her."

"I can't really afford—"

He cuts me off with a sharp laugh of disbelief. "You're mistaken, sweetheart. What's mine is yours."

He always makes everything sound so easy, so cut and dry, black and white, when the world is too messy to be categorized so simply.

"Besides, you don't need any money to go check on your mother," he says. "I'll drive you."

My eyes widen. "You will?"

"Yes," he says. "Put on some clothes and we'll go."

⌒⌒

Night has fallen by the time we make it to Watertown. I'm half asleep in the passenger seat after the five-and-a-half hour ride, the only thing keeping me awake my worry.

And the fact that Naz really has no idea where we're going.

I didn't realize it, until he set out on the road north, that all I ever told him was that it was an hour outside of Syracuse.

Watertown seems dead at even such an early hour, only a few cars out and about, most places closed for the night. I give Naz directions to the flower shop, not surprised when we pull up in front of it and the place is dark. I know she's not there, her car nowhere around. It's too dark for me to see anything, to tell if she's even been here recently.

I sigh, fidgeting with my seatbelt. "The house is in Dexter. It's a few miles outside of town."

I give him directions, and he sets out on the road with no complaint, quiet as he follows the road out of town. We navigate the back roads in the darkness, my stomach dropping when we pull down the path leading to the house.

Her car isn't here, either.

The house is dark.

He parks the Mercedes out front near the shabby porch and cuts the engine. I make no move to get out. She isn't anywhere around. I'm no closer to answers than I was hours ago in Brooklyn. "She's not here."

"You're sure?"

"Positive."

"Come on," Naz says. "Let's have a look anyway."

I don't argue, getting out of the car and following him onto the porch. He pauses and knocks on the door, and although it's silly, because I've already told him she wasn't here, I'm touched by the respect that shows.

He waits, knocking until I grow impatient, pushing past him and reaching for the knob. I think it's senseless, considering she keeps a dozen locks on her door, so I'm astonished when the knob turns smoothly.

The door creaks as it opens, the sound running through me,

turning my worry into fear. She wouldn't leave her door unlocked like this, not intentionally, not unless she had no other choice. My heart is pounding hard, thumping painfully in my chest, and blurring my vision. Bile burns my throat that I swallow back as I whisper, "Something's not right."

In fact, it's terribly, terribly wrong.

Naz says nothing, stepping past me into the house. He strolls down the hallway in front of me, his footsteps heavy against the old wood. I follow him, flicking on lights as I go to get a better look. Everything seems in place, exactly as I recall it last time I was here. There's no sign of a struggle, no sign of any sort of foul play, and although that should ease my concern, it does little to help me.

It's like she vanished into thin air.

"Killer?" I call out, wondering if he's around anywhere. "Killer!"

Naz's footsteps stop abruptly as he turns to me. "Kill who?"

"It's our dog... Killer."

"Ah." He glances around. "Looks like the dog's gone, too."

I check the other rooms, eventually making it to my mother's bedroom, tensing when I open the door and finding the first sign of disarray. Things are strewn around, drawers left open and clothing torn from hangers. Her suitcases—suitcases I've seen stuffed with belongings over a dozen times in my life—aren't on the bottom of her closet, where she always kept them stored.

She's gone.

And she left in a hurry.

"She ran."

I turn to Naz in the doorway when he speaks. "What?"

"It looks like she ran out of here," he says. "Like she was running from something."

"Or someone," I say, shaking my head.

"Why do you say that?"

"She's been running my entire life, from someone, or *to* someone... I don't know. It's like she's chasing a ghost."

"Or a ghost is chasing her."

"Yeah," I whisper. "Guess it caught up to her again."

I stroll through the room, looking through drawers, rifling through the things she left behind as Naz walks out. Down the hallway, I hear the answering machine click on as Naz presses the button to listen to the messages. My voice echoes through the house, message after message, growing more worried with each one.

I pull open the top drawer of her dresser. It's mostly empty, but some stray things remain. I sort through it, finding a Polaroid picture, and pick it up. It's old and faded, a much younger version of my mother that looks startlingly like the woman I see when I look in a mirror.

It's strange, seeing her look this way, so used to the stressed woman who raised me, age showing on her face, hair prematurely gray. I clearly got my looks from her, though. She's with another woman in the picture, a stunning brunette with olive skin. The words 'best friends forever' are scribbled on the bottom in a foreign handwriting.

I don't know the woman, never saw her picture before. It surprises me, seeing my mother so normal. She had a best friend.

"Did you find something?"

Naz is back in the doorway, startling me when he speaks. I shake my head, tossing the Polaroid down on the dresser. "Just an old picture."

I plop down on her cold unmade bed. I wonder how long it has been since it was slept in. Days? Weeks? Since the last time I was here?

Naz strolls over, pausing in front of the dresser, as he looks down at the picture. He gazes at it for a minute in silence.

"I'm sorry," I say quietly.

He doesn't turn around, his shoulders tensing at my apology. "For what?"

"For wasting your time," I say. "For having you drive the whole way up here for nothing."

"It wasn't for nothing," he says, turning around. "At least we know now."

I leave Naz in there to go to my room, scrounging up some of my belongings. I don't know when, or if, my mother will ever come back here, and I don't want to just abandon everything. Naz surfaces, loading my things into the car. I give one last look around the house, locking the door as I leave, feeling bad for leaving so much behind but I can't take it all with me.

Naz is quiet on the drive home. It feels so much longer than the drive there. He said at least we know now, but he's wrong. I feel like I understand less than I did hours ago.

"She'll come for you."

My brow furrows as I glance at Naz, barely making out his face in the darkness. We're nearing Brooklyn again. Neither of us has said a word in hours. "What?"

"Your mother," he says. "She'll come for you."

"How do you know?"

"Because I told you—only a coward leaves their family."

Chapter Twenty-Two

The cafe is quiet with school out, the students that frequent the area day after day all gone for the summer. I sit in the usual seat I planted myself in weekly for studying, sipping my warm chocolate mint tea. It tastes like a liquid peppermint patty, rich and creamy, something that always made Melody cringe.

At the thought of my friend, I glance at the nearby clock and sigh. She's late, unsurprisingly. I'm not even sure if she's still coming. I haven't heard from her all day. Naz is working, so I came into the city on my own, making plans to spend some time with my friend. He left me some cash, *a whole lot of cash*, and my own house keys so I can come and go.

I guess that officially makes it my place now, too. *Weird.*

I take another drink, savoring it, when I hear Melody's voice behind me. "Well, I guess some things never change."

I turn around, eyes widening as I look at her. Her usual blonde hair is now bright platinum, stark red and black streaks running through it.

"Do you like?" she asks, fluffing up her hair. "Switching up on you ordinary bitches."

I laugh, shaking my head. "It's very you."

"Right? I thought so, too." She orders a coffee and plops down across from me, sipping on it before she launches into her usual rambling, going on and on about what she's done already this summer (way too much) and how things with Paul are (better than she hoped but man, he needs to get a job), before she flips the script right back to me. "So how's engaged life?"

"Fine," I say, shrugging.

"Fine," she echoes. "That's it? Fine?"

I shrug. "Yeah, fine."

She rolls her eyes at my response, launching into a dozen questions: When's the wedding? Where? Do you have a dress? Who's all invited? Can I see the ring again? I humor her, although I haven't given much of it any thought.

"So what are you going to do next year?" she asks. "You know, since your GPA wasn't high enough to keep your scholarship."

I think I preferred wedding talk to this. I let out a sigh, shrugging. I've tried not to think about it, but it's been lingering there, in the back of my mind. I've got a tuition bill coming that I could never pay. I know Naz says what's his is mine, but how can I ask for thousands to pay for my classes? "I'll figure it out."

"You better," she says. "We totally need to take this class together—Ethics & Society."

"Hell no," I say. "Fuck no. Shit no. No more philosophy classes."

She laughs. "Come on, it'll be easy."

I ball up a napkin and throw it at her. "Negative."

She shrugs, finishing off her coffee. "Your loss."

She can't stay long, having to meet her parents for lunch across town. I bid her goodbye, making plans to meet here again next week, and she starts to walk away but pauses after a few steps. "Oh, I almost forgot! This came for you the other day... it was sent to the dorm room."

She tosses an envelope down on the table. I glance at it, seeing no return address, but the handwriting strikes me as familiar… my mother's.

I finish off my drink and throw it away before heading for the door. I tear open the envelope, yanking out the single sheet of notebook paper, and unfold it. It was scribbled hastily, no sweet greeting or small talk, straight to the point.

Sorry if I've worried you. I can be reached at the number below. Call me as soon as you can. I love you.

I stare at the number, the area code 201 striking me.

She's in New Jersey?

I reread the words a few times, going over the numbers in my mind. I push my confusion aside, grateful to have something. I don't have any answers, but at least she's okay. She's out there, and I have a way to reach her.

I fold the letter up and stick it back in the envelope, shoving it in my pocket. I make the trip back to Brooklyn and am approaching the front door of the house when someone speaks. "Karissa Reed?"

I stall and turn around, eyes widening at the sound of my name on this stranger's lips. He's nobody I've ever seen before, an older man with graying hair, wearing an ill-fitting blue suit. Another younger man lingers on the sidewalk, trying to act casual, his hands on his hips, pushing his coat out of the way and exposing a shiny gold badge clipped to his belt.

Police.

"Uh, yes," I say hesitantly, staring at the badge for a moment before turning to the one who addressed me. "Can I help you?"

"We're hoping so," he says. "We wanted to ask you a few questions."

"About?"

"About Daniel Santino."

My brow furrows. Professor Santino? "What about him?"

"Would you mind coming down to the station with us?" he asks, smiling tersely. It doesn't escape my notice that he avoids answering my question. "It'll only take a few minutes."

I glance between the two men and the car parked near them—clearly an unmarked police cruiser. "I don't know."

The second officer struts toward me, his expression hard. I watch enough mindless television to know the good cop/bad cop act, and this one obviously is the latter. "You can come with us now voluntarily or we can pick you up later and take you downtown, whether you like it or not."

Frowning, I oblige, climbing into the backseat when the older officer opens the door for me. He's kinder, trying to be friendly and chatting as he drives toward the police station. Detective Jameson with the Homicide Unit.

His partner, Detective Andrews, is clearly naturally an asshole. He sits in the passenger seat, silent, scowling.

When we arrive, I'm taken to a small drab room with nothing but a table and some chairs, the walls slate gray, a sign on the door that says 'Interrogation'. I nervously sit down in a chair with the men across from me. They offer me something to drink, but I'm too anxious to accept it.

Their questions seem simple on the surface: When's the last time you spoke to Daniel Santino? What did you talk about? Why were you there? They ask me again and again, the same tedious questions in a loop just worded a little differently each time, as if they expect to trip me up and get another response eventually.

I was the last person seen with him.

His estimated time of death coincided with my visit.

"Wait, you don't think... I mean, you seriously don't think I had something to do with this, right?"

Both men just stare at me.

"He was alive when I left him," I say, in utter shock that they're insinuating I could be involved. "I would never hurt someone, much less kill them. I wouldn't... I couldn't. Check the security cameras. You'll see!"

"The cameras in that building weren't recording," Detective Andrews says. "They recycle on a 24 hour loop. By the time he was discovered, the footage was erased."

"Well, I swear he was alive. He was! I would never do something like that. I'm not that kind of person!"

"I believe you," Detective Jameson says. "We're just trying to lock down a timeline of that afternoon."

He sounds genuine, but his words are at odds with Detective Andrews's attitude. He's treating me like a flat out criminal. His expression is hardened, his voice icy when he chimes in. "How long have you been involved with Ignazio Vitale?"

Naz's name catches me off guard. "Excuse me?"

"Ignazio Vitale," he says. "How long have the two of you—?"

"I don't see how that's any of your business," I say, slipping my hands from the table onto my lap when the man's attention shifts to the ring on my finger.

"You're aware of his reputation, I presume? It's not a far stretch to think—"

"Naz is a good man," I say defensively, cutting him off. "He has nothing to do with any of this."

"Are you sure about that?"

"Of course," I say. "I don't care what reputation you think he has. He's done nothing wrong, and neither have I... I didn't do anything. I just went to talk to him about my grade, and then I left, and he was still alive."

"And where was Ignazio at that time?"

My brow furrows. Before I can respond, the door to the interrogation room opens, another man poking his head in. Clearly their superior, based upon the way both men straighten their backs, giving him their undivided attention. He struts in, eyes skimming me, as he shakes his head. "You're free to go, Miss Reed."

Detective Andrews shakes his head in disagreement. "We still have a few more questions."

"Tough," the man says. "She's lawyered up."

My eyes widen. I did what?

Detective Andrews is just as surprised, turning to me. "I didn't hear you ask for a lawyer."

I didn't know I needed one.

Detective Jameson, on the other hand, stands and gathers his things. He pulls out a business card, slipping it across the table with a smile. "If you ever want to talk, my door is always open."

He walks out, past his superior. I stand, rubbing my sweaty palms on the legs of my jeans and slip the business card in my pocket with my mother's letter as I look between the men. "So I can go?"

"Of course," the man says, nodding tersely. "Thank you for coming in."

"Sure," I mumble, my head down as I bolt out of the interrogation room. I hear the officers whispering behind me, their conversation heated, as I head into the lobby. Looking up, my footsteps stall when I come face-to-face with the last person I expected to be standing here. "Naz."

The corner of his lip twitches. "You okay, jailbird?"

I nod.

"Good." All humor fades from his expression, eyes darkening with rage as he turns his focus to the officers gathering behind me. His gaze shifts between them, taking them in, the pure hostility wafting from him enough to make the hairs on my arm stand on end. "If you gentlemen have anything else, my attorney will be more than happy to field your requests, which you're well aware of. It's why I pay him, after all."

"We had no questions for you," Detective Jameson says. "We just had a few for Miss Reed."

"Who is my fiancée, which you're also now aware of," Naz says. "Bullying a young woman is quite unbecoming of you, Jameson. I thought your mother would've taught you better than that."

Naz doesn't wait for the officer to respond. He motions with his head for me to come with him. I step past, and he presses his hand to my back, leading me out of the police station. His car waits by the curb for us. I slide in nervously, sickness brewing in the pit of my stomach.

Naz pulls into traffic, heading toward Brooklyn, before he relaxes. He slouches somewhat in the seat, letting out a deep sigh. I'm not sure if it's relief I hear or if it's exasperation.

"How did you know I was there?" I ask quietly.

"An associate gave me a courtesy call when he saw you brought in. I got there as soon as I could."

"Thank you," I say. "I'm glad you showed up."

He looks at me. Reaching his hand out, he cups my cheek, stroking the skin with his thumb. "I'll always show up."

"You promise?"

"I swear it."

∽∾

I'm sitting on the bed, the note from my mother sprawled out on my lap. My gaze shifts through the numbers over and over, reciting them to memory. I'm stalling, I know it, and maybe it's senseless, but I'm almost afraid to call her.

She'll have questions.

Much the same ones I have for her.

What are you doing?

Where are you staying?

Why?

My answers are probably more scandalous than hers.

Sighing, I pull out my phone and dial the number, bringing it to my ear as it rings. I wait, almost expecting some sort of answering machine to greet me, when the line picks up. "Hello?"

295

This is not my mother. This voice is male, gruff with a thick sort of accent. I sit in silence for a moment, unsure of what to say or how to react, when he says it again, impatiently. "Hello?"

"I, uh… can I speak with Carrie?"

"Who?"

My stomach drops as I glance down at the paper. I know I got the numbers right. "Carrie," I say. "Carrie Reed?"

"Ah, yeah, hold on." I hear shuffling, then his muffled voice rings out in the background. "Carmela! I think it's her!"

My brow furrows. Carmela?

There's another rustling before a breathy voice picks up. "Kissimmee? Is it you?"

"Uh, yeah. What's going on, Mom? Who's that guy? Why'd he call you Carmela?"

"Never mind that now," she says dismissively. "I'm glad you're okay."

"Me? I'm fine. Where have you been? I've been worried!"

"I needed to move on, sweetheart. I told you that when you visited. It was time."

"You said you were thinking about it," I say. "I didn't expect you to pick up and leave everything behind. I went to check on you and—"

"You've been to the house? Was it ransacked?"

"Uh, no… why would it be?"

"No reason," she says. "Look, I can't really get into it on the phone. I'll explain everything, I will… I just need you to come see me. Can you do that, Kissimmee? It's important."

"I guess."

"Come alone," she says. "Okay? It's important nobody else know where I am. Understand?"

I understand, all right. She's snapped. All those years of running from memories and chasing phantoms has caught up to her, and she's lost what little sanity she had left. There's a difference between being crazy and being insane, and I'm terrified she's tiptoed over that line these past few weeks. "I'll come alone. Just tell me where you are."

She spouts off an address, and I scour through the drawers until I find a pen to scribble it down. She once more reiterates my need to come alone before hanging up, not once asking me how I am or where I've been or what I've been doing.

I toss my phone down on the bed beside me as I stare at the address. New Jersey. It wouldn't take me too long, half a day to get there, get my answers, and get back here to Brooklyn. Maybe I can convince her to come back with me, get some sort of help, because whatever she's doing isn't normal.

"What do you have there?"

I glance up as Naz walks in the room.

"It's, uh… a note Melody gave me," I say, shrugging as I fold it up and shove it back in my pocket. "I had coffee with her today, you know, before the whole interrogation thing."

I would tell him if he asked, tell him the truth about the letter, about talking to my mother, but he doesn't raise the subject any further. He pauses in front of me, grasping my chin and pulling my face up to look at him. He leans down to kiss me, his lips soft and sweet.

All it takes is a simple touch from this man and I melt. His presence always makes the bad seem not so bad, the good just so much better, the world around me so beautiful and brand new. He makes me feel special, and safe, like the universe could be crumbling but he'd keep the ground beneath my feet secure.

He wipes my worries away.

I'll deal with my mother tomorrow.

Tonight, I only want him.

With trembling hands, I reach out and start unbuttoning his shirt. He lets me, never breaking the kiss, his hands cradling my head. He pulls away when he has to, letting his clothes drop to the floor, leaving him naked in front of me.

Light filters in from outside, enough so I can make out every contour of his body. I want to trace every line, caress every crevice, taste his flesh with my tongue, and show him how much I love him with my lips. He sits down on the bed and reaches for me again, but I slip from his grasp and drop to my knees on the floor instead.

His expression is strained as he stares down at me. I wrap my hand around the hard shaft and stroke a few times, watching him, before lowering my head into his lap. I flick my tongue out, tasting the tip of him.

An unnatural groan vibrates his chest.

His hands stroke my hair as I take him into my mouth. I can't take all of him—can barely take half of him. I've never tried to satisfy a man like Naz, so I just go at it and hope for the best.

It doesn't last long before he stops me. Grabbing a hold of my arms, he pulls me up onto the bed with him, whispering, "That's enough, Karissa."

"Was it not good?" I ask nervously.

"It was great," he says quietly. "But you shouldn't ever kneel in front of me."

I'm not sure whether to be flattered or offended, but he gives me little chance to be either. He takes over, stripping me as he pulls me deeper onto the bed with him.

He lies back, letting me climb on top of him. I sink down on him, taking him inside of me, a chill running down my spine when I hear him groan again. The sound is so primal, unrestrained.

I ride him, grinding against him, arching my back and taking him in as far as he can go. His hands are on my hips, but he doesn't guide me, for the first time since we've been together he's letting me do the work.

I can tell when he's getting close. My hands are on his chest, covering his scars, feeling his heartbeat against my palm. It's racing, although he looks relaxed, his stomach muscles clenching as his eyes close.

I can feel it as he comes, filling me with all of him. He groans again, this time louder, his grip on my hips tighter. When he relaxes, I stop moving, and he opens his eyes to look at me. I offer him a tentative smile, but he doesn't return it, knocking mine off my face when he yanks me off of him, onto the bed, and settles on top of me.

I yelp, caught off guard, as he nuzzles into my neck, nipping at the skin. "That wasn't easy for me."

He pushes inside of me, the thrust deep, making me gasp. He's harder now than he was before he even came. "I know."

He's a machine, going on and on as night falls, not stopping until my body is tired, both of us covered in sweat from head to toe. I lay in his arms, my head on his chest. We're both quiet as we catch our breath, his heartbeat settling back into a steady, normal rhythm.

I don't think my heart will ever beat the same.

"Are you okay?" he asks quietly after a while.

"Yes," I whisper. "Why wouldn't I be?"

"You were hauled into the police station today. That has to be upsetting."

"It was," I admit. "They think I... I mean, they thought I had something to do with what happened to Santino."

"No, they didn't," he says. "They don't think that."

"But they said—"

"Just because they say it, doesn't meant they believe it," he says. "They don't think you killed Santino."

"Then why did they say it?"

"Because they think I did."

I tense. "That's just crazy."

I expect him to agree, to laugh it off, but he says nothing. He makes no noise at all. The silence that smothers the room is deafening, chilling, and I'm not sure what to say after that. I lay there, staring into the darkness, as Naz's hand strokes my bare side, holding me tightly like he'll never let me go.

I take the train to Manhattan, and then another train to New Jersey, hailing a cab outside of the train station in Newark. The driver looks at me peculiarly when I read off the address, making no move to pull away.

"You sure that address is right?" he asks, looking at me in the rearview mirror.

"Uh..." I glance at the paper. "Yes."

"Okay, then."

He starts on the road. Newark reminds me of a smaller New York City, with the skyscrapers and busy streets. I'm admiring it as we drive through the city, tensing a little when he starts weaving away. He passes through neighborhoods, each one growing rougher, until we start to approach what looks like the slums. Windows are smashed and boarded up, graffiti covering the sides of crumbling buildings, trash scattering the sidewalks.

Please keep going.

Please keep going.

He stops.

The cab pulls up in front of an old brick house. The one attached to it is abandoned, completely gutted, but the other looks inhabitable. Barely. My mother's car is nowhere to be seen. I see no signs of life around it, no lights on inside and no furniture on the small porch. I'm about to tell the driver to keep going, to take me back, because there has to be some mistake, when the curtain in the front room shifts around.

Someone's inside.

I pay the driver and get out, starting toward the house. I step up on the porch and knock, my heart hammering in my chest as I wait. My mother can't stay here, in this house, in this neighborhood. It's not safe.

The door yanks open, a pair of deep brown eyes meeting mine.

They belong to a man with jet-black hair, parted to the side and styled back, shiny from the amount of product in it. He has a moustache, but the rest of his face is freshly shaved. He's wearing dark gray slacks and a vest, with a light button down shirt. An unlit cigar is between his lips.

He doesn't look like someone who would live in the slums.

"I'm looking for Carrie," I say.

"I know," he responds, the thick accent striking me. The same guy from the call. He steps aside, motioning for me to come in. Hesitantly, I step inside, seeing the house is mostly empty. He stands at the door for a moment longer, his gaze sweeping along the street. "You come alone?"

"Of course."

Satisfied, he shuts the door. He strolls past me, a peculiar sway to his walk, a strange limp like he can't quite bend one of his knees. "Your mother's not here."

I stare at him, tensing as he heads into the living room and sits down on the shabby old couch—the only stitch of furniture in the room. "Where is she?"

"Have a seat," he says casually, motioning toward the torn, filthy cushion beside him.

"Where is she?" I ask again, making no move to come any closer. My eyes shift to the door, making sure it's unlocked in case I need to make a hasty exit, before I glance back at him. He's watching me, his lips curving with amusement as he strikes a match and lights his cigar. He tosses the match down on the wooden floor, stomping it out with his shiny black dress shoes.

"I'm not going to harm you, girl."

I try for the third time. "Where is she?"

He slouches on the couch, resting his arm along the back of it as he stretches out, his gaze still firmly on me. "She stepped out."

"Why? Where did she go?"

"She thought it was best if she wasn't here, if I explain it to you."

"Explain what?"

He takes a drag from his cigar and is quiet for a moment, flicking his ashes straight onto the floor. "Why I left you."

I stare at him, as every ounce of strength I tried to build, putting me on guard, fades away in a wave of shock. No way. I stare in disbelief, those words sinking in, my eyes roaming his face. Even from this distance, the freckles dotting his skin stand out like tiny beacons, displaying the truth before he even has to say it.

I haven't been able to get ahold of my mother in weeks because she's been with *my father*, the man who abandoned us, who walked out on us. It's his fault she is the way she is, his fault she was constantly chasing ghosts, chasing him... and she found him. She fucking found him.

And she's obviously even worse off for having done so.

"I know why you left," I say, taking a step back. There are a few feet between us, but it suddenly feels way too close. "You left because you're a fucking coward."

"Kissimmee..."

"No," I say, shaking my head, the sound of that nickname coming from him stirring up anger. "Don't dare call me that! What gives you the right?"

"Considering I gave you the nickname, I say I have plenty of right," he says. "I called you that when she was pregnant, my little Kissimmee baby. You were made there, you know, down in Kissimmee. So that's what gives me the right."

"You have no right to even talk to me. You're nobody to me. Nothing. You lost all rights when you walked away. I didn't need you. I *don't* need you. But she loved you."

"I loved her, too. I still love her. She knows that, she always has."

"You're wrong," I say. "She was a mess, could never settle down or trust, always running because of you."

He stands up. His presence feels imposing, intimidating. I take another step back as he starts toward me.

"It wasn't me that had her running."

"Whatever helps you sleep at night, buddy," I say. "You weren't there. You didn't see it. You didn't live it. I don't care what bullshit excuse you make up... running out on us is unforgivable, and if she thought you explaining it to me would make it any better, she's sorely mistaken."

"Don't act that way," he says. "I deserve to be heard out. I'm your father."

"You're nothing," I say. "John Reed is nobody to me."

I spit the words with as much hostility as I can conjure up, meaning them with everything in me, but instead of flinching, instead of being hurt, he laughs. His laughter is loud and amused, striking me harder than fists.

"John Reed," he says, shaking his head. "You're right—he is nobody. He's nothing. He doesn't even exist. But I'm your father, Johnny Rita, and you're my daughter, and your mother... your mother's my wife. Carmela Rita."

"Her name is Carrie Reed."

He shakes his head, his tone mocking as he says, "Whatever helps you sleep at night, girl."

"I'm not a girl—I'm a woman. And I don't care what you have to say. I'm done talking to you."

I storm outside, slamming the door behind me. I half-expect him to come after me, but he doesn't. *Of course.* My eyes sting as I walk away from the rundown house, trying to put space between that man and me.

It isn't until I'm a few blocks away with tears streaking my cheeks that I realize the predicament I'm in. Frustrated, exhausted, I sit down on the curb by the street sign on a corner and pull out my phone to call a cab.

It takes them twenty insufferable minutes to get to me. It drops me off at the train station in Newark, and I buy a ticket back home.

It's nearing dark when I make it back to the house in Brooklyn.

The sun is setting, everything looking as I left it, the driveway vacant of Naz's car. I'm in a daze, my stomach in knots. I feel like I've been drained, and I'm not sure which way is up.

John Reed. Johnny Rita.

Carrie Reed. Carmela Rita.

Who are they?

Who am I?

I thought I knew, but now I'm not sure. I'm drowning in a river of secrets, living in a world built upon lies. Does Karissa Reed even exist? Or am I Karissa Rita?

Who the fuck is that?

Tears swim in my eyes again as I unlock the door and step inside the dark house. Things make even less sense now. What was real? What was a lie? I shut the door and lock it again, turning to head straight for the stairs, when a sharp voice in the darkness stops me dead in my tracks.

"Where'd you go?"

Jumping, I turn around and come face-to-face with Naz in the living room. I grab my chest, startled. "You scared me. I didn't realize you were home. Your car isn't in the driveway."

"It's in the garage," he says, stepping toward me, his hands in his pockets. "Where'd you go?"

"I, uh... I went to see my mother."

"You found her?"

"More like she found me," I mumble, reaching into my pocket and pulling out the crinkled note. "Melody gave me this yesterday... I called the number, and my mom gave me an address, told me to come see her."

He steps closer, reaching his hand out, silently asking to see the note. I hand it over to him and he reads it, cringing. "You went to this place *alone*?"

"She told me to. Said it was important."

He folds up the note and hands it back to me as he meets my

MONSTER IN HIS EYES

eyes. He stares hard as he reaches over and cups my cheek. "You've been crying."

"It's been a long day."

"Did you see her?" he asks. "Did you talk to her?"

"No, she wasn't there."

His eyes narrow suspiciously. "Was somebody else?"

I nod. "My father, if you can believe it."

I can hardly believe it myself.

Naz's expression hardens. He's so still I'm not sure he's breathing. "What did he say to you?"

"A lot," I mutter. "But nothing really. All lies, or maybe it's all the truth. I don't know. I figured out who he was and left."

"What did he want?"

"To explain why he left."

"And did he?"

"No, I didn't give him the chance."

Naz's thumb strokes my cheek as he lets out a deep sigh. "Maybe you should."

My brow furrows. "You think so?"

"Yeah," he says. "I'm interested to hear what he has to say."

The trip to Jersey is quicker with Naz driving. I feel better now having him with me, like instead of being on defense maybe I'm on the offense this time. He holds my hand on the center console, his thumb soothingly stroking my skin.

He has no issue finding the house, navigating the streets of Newark like he's well versed on the dilapidated neighborhood. My mother's car is there now, parked out front. Naz pulls the Mercedes to a stop behind it, cutting the engine and getting out without a word.

He opens my door for me and I get out, taking a few steps

305

toward the house when Naz grabs my wrist, pulling me to a stop. I look at him peculiarly, and he shakes his head. "Wait here."

My brow furrows. "Why?"

"Just trust me."

I shrug it off, walking back toward Naz and pausing right in front of him, my eyes on the house. It's completely dark, illuminated only by the streetlight out front. It's nine at night, maybe a little later. "Maybe they're asleep."

"They don't sleep here."

My brow furrows. "How do you know?"

"I just know," he says. "I can tell by looking at it."

Before I can ask him any more, the curtain in the living room moves. The door yanks open, my mother appearing, eyes wide.

She looks frantic.

"Karissa," she shouts, her voice high-pitched, full of panic. "Oh God. Get away from him, sweetie."

I blink a few times, caught off guard, as Naz slips his arms around me, pulling me flush against him. One arm encircles my waist as his other settles along my chest, his hand drifting up, resting at the base of my throat. He's holding me protectively, my armor against the brutal outside world, but my mother sees it differently.

She lets out a panicked noise as she rushes forward, descending the small porch steps and wavering in the yard.

"It's okay," I say. "It's fine, Mom."

"Please let her go," she pleads, ignoring me, her focus on Naz. "I'm begging you. Let her go, Vitale."

My blood runs cold when she says his name... his last name... the name *those* people use for him. This isn't right. She doesn't know him. They don't know each other. They can't.

"I'm not going to hurt her, Carmela, but I'm not letting her go."

My knees nearly give out on me. He called her Carmela. If not for Naz's strong hold, I would hit the ground. I turn my head, seeing Naz's serious expression, his eyes as dark as the night around us.

"Naz," I whisper. "What's going on?"

"What's going on is your mother isn't happy to see you near me."

"Why?" I ask, my voice trembling. "Who are you?"

"You know who I am," he says. "The question you should be asking is who are they."

"Mom," I call out. "Mom, what's happening? How do you know Naz?"

She doesn't look at me, but I know she hears my words. Her alarm grows when I call him Naz. She pleads with him more. "Please, she's my daughter... my little girl. She's been through enough. Don't do this to her."

"I've done nothing to her," Naz says, his hand shifting higher, tightening around my throat. I gasp as he leans down, kissing my temple. "Nothing she hasn't wanted me to do."

My mother's on the verge of hyperventilating. "Just let her go and let's talk about this. I'll give you whatever you want, whatever it is. Take me, but leave her alone. Please, I'm begging you. I'll do anything."

Naz loosens his hold, and I breathe deeply, disoriented. "Johnny here?"

"No."

"Bet he went out the back door when he saw me, didn't he?" My mother doesn't respond to that question, which seems answer enough for Naz. He laughs bitterly. "Once a coward, always a coward."

"Tell me what I can do," she says. "Just... whatever it is. Just tell me."

"You know what I want. You stay out of my way, and I won't hurt you, Carmela. It's as simple as that. I don't want to hurt you—for her sake, I hope I don't have to. But nothing's going to stop me from getting what I want."

"I understand," she says, taking another step toward us. "Just let Karissa go. Please."

"I can't do that," Naz says. My mother makes an unnatural noise at his refusal. I'm too stunned to react. One of Naz's arms lets go of me as he reaches for the car door. "Get in."

My eyes widen as I look at him. "What?"

His eyes meet mine. "Get in the car."

The voice in the back of my head screams for me to pull away from him, to run to my mother, but his troubled expression is enough to make my feet move toward the car.

I slide into the passenger seat, and he slams the door, standing there for a moment longer.

He loves me, I remind myself. There's no reason to be afraid.

But this isn't *my* Naz, the Naz I fell in love with, and Ignazio Vitale scares the hell out of me.

Through the window, I can hear my mother pleading with him some more, his voice casual as he shrugs off her concerns.

My heart is in my throat, my stomach queasy when Naz gets in. He says nothing, starting the car and speeding away. He never looks at me, never addresses me during the drive. His hand no longer tries to hold mine. Things are so tense I think I might explode. It all keeps playing in my mind in a loop, their words, and his actions, everything that happened today playing over and over again.

I'm not sure what to think about any of it.

We get to the house, and I wrap my arms around my chest as I stand in the living room, trying to combat the swell of nausea as reality slams into me. "I don't understand."

Naz loosens his tie. "What don't you understand, Karissa?"

"Any of it."

He's quiet for a moment as he takes off his coat. "I told you one day get him."

"What? Who?"

"The man who stole my life from me."

My eyes widen as that sinks in. "It was *him*? My father?"

"Johnny Rita and I were practically family. He was my best

friend. And that meant nothing to him. He murdered my wife and kid right in front of me."

"Did you know?" I whisper. "Did you know it was me all along?"

His expression offers no apologies. I think I'm going to be sick. I shove past him, running for the kitchen, and fall to my knees in front of the trashcan, losing whatever's in my stomach. Naz follows, pausing in the doorway behind me.

"You knew," I say, my vision blurred. "You used me all along just to try to find my father... just so you can kill him!"

"That's not true," he says. "I knew who you were, Karissa, but I didn't use you so I could kill him. It was never my intention to kill Johnny. I said I wanted to make him pay."

"How?"

"He killed my family," Naz says. "So I was going to kill his."

Oh God.

I lose it again, heaving until my body has nothing else to give. I hear Naz approach, feel his hand pressing against my back. Trembling, I cower away, scurrying across the floor and pressing my back against the cabinets as I pull my knees up to my chest, trying to slink away. I stare at him, horrified.

He was planning to kill me.

Oh God, he's going to kill me.

"You promised," I cry. "You promised you wouldn't hurt me."

He crouches down in front of me. "And I'm not going to. I can't lie to you, Karissa. I've never lied to you."

I scoff.

His expression hardens. "Name one time I lied to you."

"You lied about everything!"

"No, everything I've told you was true. Just because I didn't tell you all of it doesn't mean I lied. Everyone has secrets."

"I don't."

"You did," he says. "I was your secret. We keep the darkest parts of us to ourselves until we think others are ready to see them.

Sometimes that never happens, but I knew it tonight... knew it was time for you to see me."

"See you? You're a monster!"

"I am," he admits, "but don't pretend to be surprised. You knew that about me all along."

"I didn't."

"Ah, I don't lie to you, so at least give me the same respect in return," he says. "The pieces were all there from the beginning, every single one of them. Just because you refused to put them together, to look at the big picture, doesn't mean you didn't know what it was. I told you I wasn't a good man. I told you I never would be. That's reality, sweetheart, and you still asked me to stay." He reaches for me, grazing the back of his hand along my cheek and down my neck, across my chest. "You handed over your body so willingly, like it already belonged to me."

I smack his hand away, the loud crack echoing through the silent kitchen as I try to move further away from him. "There's something wrong with you."

"There's a lot wrong with me," he says. "Has been ever since your father aimed a shotgun at my chest and pulled the trigger."

"Why?" The word is barely audible as tears spill over from the corner of my eyes. "Why did he do it? Why would he?"

"Revenge."

"Why?" I ask again. "What did you do to him?"

"Nothing," he says. "It wasn't me he wanted vengeance against. He did it to get back at my wife's father."

"Her father?"

He nods. "Ray."

I blink rapidly. I can only stare at him in shock.

His wife was Raymond Angelo's daughter?

"I was caught in the middle, condemned to die at the hands of someone close to me, someone who was supposed to love me. God spared me, but you see, nobody would've spared you, not when I was done with you, so you're lucky... you're fucking *lucky*... I fell in love with you."

My voice is weak when I whisper, "You don't love me."

"Oh, but I do," he says. "Because if I didn't? You'd be dead already."

I let out an involuntary whimper at the sound of his voice, so matter of fact, with no sign of regret in his words. He would've killed me... he so easily could have, so many times. If it's love that kept me alive, what does it mean for now? What does it mean for my future?

"Nothing's changed," he says, as if he can read my mind. "I'm still the man I was two hours ago, the same man I was two weeks ago, two months ago... two years ago. I'm the same man you gave yourself to, the same man you fell in love with. Nothing's changed."

He says it like he means it, like he really believes it, but looking at him, I don't see that man anymore. I see a man who not only could end my life, but a man who I think someday might.

"I'm not going to hurt you," he says quietly, and I close my eyes, unable to take the expression on his face, the look that wants me to believe it, that almost makes me believe it.

I sit still, my breath hitching when I feel him touch my face, caressing my cheek, fingertips grazing my lips as I exhale shakily. I can tell he leans closer, his cologne stronger, his body heat wafting across my skin, warming me on the outside, but I'm so, so cold inside. He's turned my blood to ice, stopped my heart from pumping it from fear that if it does, it might still beat for him.

"Tell me what you're thinking," he says, his lips near mine. He kisses the corner of my mouth. "Say something."

His lips meet mine softly. I don't kiss him back, instead whispering a lone word. "Red."

Red.

His lips leave mine in the next breath, his hand dropping from my face. I open my eyes in enough time to see him stand up. He stares down at me for a moment in silence. He has the audacity to look upset, like I've wounded him, like the word hurt him more than he could ever possibly hurt me. It feels like an eternity passes around me as I stare up at him with watery eyes, trying to keep my tears from falling, before he looks away, turning his back to walk out of the room.

I sit there for a while, not having the energy to move, before forcing myself to my feet. My knees are weak, wanting to give out as I leave the kitchen. My gaze darts to the front door, and for a brief second I think about running out of it, but where can I go? Who can I turn to?

Who will believe me?

What would he do?

Instead, I head upstairs.

I climb into bed with my clothes on, not even bothering to take off my shoes. I'm on the verge of tears, but the shock of it all is keeping them at bay.

The city is dangerous, my mother repeatedly told me. There are people who will prey upon me, who will corrupt me, who will use me and abuse me. I have to be on guard, alert, always keeping my eyes open to the dangers of the world, because they're real, and they'll destroy me.

I heard it over and over.

So many times.

Who would've expected I'd fall in blindly with the biggest threat of all?

Chapter Twenty-Three

The world keeps turning.

I keep moving.

Life around me continues to go on.

Naz acts like nothing changed. He meant it when he said it, truly believed it, but it's different for me now. It's all different. The truth seeped into my bones, infused in my muscles, as much a part of me now as the blood in my veins.

Blood that still feels too heavy in my chest, making each beat of my heart painful.

The den is quiet. The television is on, but muted, reruns of Real Housewives playing on the screen. Naz isn't watching it, instead sitting at his desk with a book. He's reading. *Reading.* I don't think anything Raymond Angelo pays him to do requires him to look in a book.

I stand just outside the doorway, looking in. I know the TV is on for me. He does it every day, turns on something he's seen me watch before, like he's trying to coax me into the room with him.

I haven't gone in yet.

It's been a week.

He hasn't left the house. Every day the same thing, the same routine. He lies beside me at night, but I don't think either of us gets any sleep, staring into the darkness, lost in the bitter silence. He hasn't touched me... hasn't tried to touch me... since I spoke the safe word in the kitchen. Not so much as a brush of his arm against mine in seven days.

I'm grateful. I'm relieved.

But I ache.

I mourn the loss of his touch.

What's wrong with me?

He tore me in two—half of me still clinging to who I thought he was, while the other half is shattered by the man he turned out to be. I love him. I hate him.

If I never saw his face again, I would be better off.

But yet I stand in the doorway, not looking at the silent television, instead looking at him. I wonder what he's thinking, what he's reading, what he'd say to me if I talked to him. I wonder if he knows how I feel about him right now, if this is how he's felt about me all along.

He set out to destroy me, but he fell in love with me instead.

I fell in love with him, and that's what destroyed me in the end.

He says he would never hurt me, but he doesn't realize he already has.

He hurt me by loving me.

By being who he is.

Because I am who I am.

I stare at him like I used to stare at my philosophy book, like maybe all the answers will magically transfer into my brain so I know what I'm supposed to know, so I understand what so far has evaded me. My stomach knots, constricting the flight of the butterflies he gives me, until his gaze shifts my way. He doesn't move anything except his eyes as he regards me carefully. I feel like a child being watched, but he still looks at me like I'm a woman.

Monster in his Eyes

He looks at me like he needs me more than the air he breathes. My lungs can't seem to work when he looks at me that way. My chest burns, my stomach churns, my vision goes hazy and my knees go weak, all the while the two halves of me scream at the top of their lungs. I love him. I hate him. He's everything that's good. He's the worst of everything. He gives my life meaning. He'll take my life away someday.

My Prince Charming turned out to be the villain of my fairy tale, and part of me thinks that's okay, because eventually, it'll all disappear, anyway.

Nothing lasts forever.

Happily ever after, I think, doesn't exist.

Naz curves an eyebrow in question but remains silent. I hesitate for a moment before turning around and walking away.

There's nothing to do.

I mindlessly walk laps around the house, sitting in one room for a bit before moving on to the next, never going into the den. I consider calling the number my mother gave me, but it feels like a betrayal to Naz, and I'm not sure what to say to her, either. The fact that she hasn't called me sticks out like a sore thumb.

I text Melody and act like nothing is wrong.

I flick little birdies across the screen and annihilate pigs to occupy my time.

I even go outside and walk around the back yard. There's nothing out here, except for trees and grass, a lawnmower that desperately needs used and some rose bushes that seem like they've died a long time ago. I find the outside entrance to what I assume is the basement, and I consider going down there out of boredom, until I catch Naz watching me from the window in the den.

His gaze burns through me, so I go back inside, just to escape it, going upstairs and falling into bed, succumbing to exhaustion and taking a nap. When I awaken, the room is dark. It's well after nightfall.

My throat is dry.

My stomach growls ferociously.

Rubbing it, I head downstairs again. The light in the den is the only one that's on. I head into the kitchen, my footsteps faltering when I find a carton of Chinese food sitting on the counter beside the fridge. It's still warm when I pick it up, and I pop the top open, seeing it's beef Lo Mein with no vegetables.

He ordered it for me.

It's what I ask for when he orders Chinese.

I grab a fork and start eating, curiosity fueling me as I stroll toward the den. Once again, I pause near the doorway and look in.

The television is still on, the channel changed to some cooking competition. Naz is sitting at his desk, his feet kicked up now. He's changed, wearing a pair of sweat pants, which means he came upstairs while I was asleep.

His eyes drift my way. I haven't made any noise, but he seems to always know when I'm there. He stares at me, his gaze shifting to the food in my hand, before he turns back to his book.

It feels like an hour passes.

It might've been only a minute.

The silence is getting to me.

I haven't used my voice all week, so I'm surprised it still works when I open my mouth. "What are you reading?"

He doesn't react. He doesn't seem surprised that I've spoken. His eyes stay glued to the book until he flips the page. "The Prince."

"What's that?"

"It's Machiavelli."

"Machiavelli." I lean against the doorframe. "Like Tupac?"

Laughter escapes his lips—real laughter—the sound lightening the air in the room. I know who Machiavelli is, but I wasn't sure what else to say. He looks away from the book, those deep dimples out in full force. "Have you read it?"

Slowly, I shake my head.

"Everyone sees what you appear to be," he says, "few experience what you really are."

I take a bite of the food. I know he's quoting *The Prince*, but damn if it doesn't feel like he's talking directly to me with that. "Does he have any advice for what someone's supposed to do when they see what you really are and it scares them?"

He's quiet for a moment, his eyes narrowed as if in thought, before he responds. "Never was anything great achieved without danger."

I don't say anything to that. I stand there for a while eating as he goes back to reading. My feet grow tired eventually, and without even thinking, I walk into the den and sit down on the edge of the couch.

Chapter Twenty-Four

Naz is fast asleep.

He's on his side, facing away from me, hugging a pillow as he snores softly. It's the first time in a week I've been up in the morning before him.

I move soundlessly around the bedroom, pulling on clothes and putting on shoes, my eyes periodically shifting to him to make sure he's still asleep. I grab my phone, tossing it in my purse, and head toward the door when I hear his voice. "Going somewhere?"

I turn to him, seeing his eyes are open now, regarding me suspiciously.

"I'm meeting Melody for coffee."

"Is that right?"

"Yes," I say. "Or actually, it's tea... chocolate mint tea, from the cafe we always went to."

"In Manhattan."

"Yes."

He sits up. "I'll drive you into the city."

"No," I say, holding my hand up to stop him before he can climb out of bed. "I can take the train there, no problem. I've done it before."

Truth is, I need some space to breathe, to think, without the smell of his cologne surrounding me, without his presence looming in the next room.

He stares at me. Hard. It's as if he's trying to decide whether or not to trust me, as if I've given him some reason not to. I haven't, though, and he seems to accept that after a moment. "Be careful, Karissa."

"I will," I say, hesitating, staring at him as he just sits there and watches me. After a moment I turn away, striding out the door.

I get to the city a few minutes early and step into the cafe, surprised to find Paul behind the counter. He looks at me, smirking. It gives me the creeps.

"I didn't know you worked here," I say.

"Just started," he says. "What can I get for you?"

I order and take my usual seat, but I don't touch my drink. It freaks me out a bit that Paul made it. Last time I drank something his hands touched, I ended up collapsing on the sidewalk in the middle of the night, drugged.

Melody strolls in at ten o'clock on the dot, taking a few minutes to flirt with her boyfriend before joining me. She plops down with a coffee, and before I can even say hello, she reaches into her purse and pulls out an envelope. "Oh, before I forget, you got another one of these letters."

I look at it with surprise, taking it from her. "When did it come?"

"Yesterday."

I tear it open as Melody starts rambling. I pull out the single piece of paper and unfold it, seeing the scribbled writing just like the last one.

Friday night. Midnight. Meet at the entrance to Washington Square Park. You have to get away from him. Leave everything behind. I love you.

"Well?" Melody says, snapping her fingers in my face. "Are you listening?"

I glance up, shoving the letter back into the envelope. Friday night. Midnight. I'm not sure how I could get away at that time. "No, sorry, what did you say?"

She repeats herself, something about Paul. I don't know. I still don't listen. My mind is stuck on the note, my stomach in knots. I still don't know what to do, what to think.

We've been here for going on an hour when Paul takes a break and squeezes himself in at our table. Sighing, I look away from them when they start getting touchy-feely, my gaze shifting to the window. My expression falls, my muscles tensing, when I see the familiar Mercedes parked across the street.

The motherfucker followed me.

I should've known. I'm more exasperated than shocked by it. Now that I know his secret, he's not going to let me out of his sight. He's not going to risk it.

He's not even breathing the same air as me, but I suddenly feel like I'm suffocating. I can feel his hands around my throat, little by little squeezing the life out of me.

Melody excuses herself to use the restroom. As soon as she walks away, I turn to Paul. I have a chance to slip away, and I need to find some way to do it... to at least hear them out, hear their side of the story.

It's my mother, after all.

I owe her that much.

Maybe my life was built upon lies, but there's no denying she raised me for eighteen years on her own. The side of me that's fractured is frantic for this opportunity, while the other half is already grieving the loss of the man waiting outside.

"I need something," I tell Paul, my voice barely a whisper. "Something to make someone sleep for a while."

His eyes widen. "Like Ambien?"

"Stronger."

He stares at me. "I can't get anything like that."

I make a quick glance around before focusing on him again. "The first night Melody met you, you bought her a drink... a drink I drank... a drink that knocked me out for half a day. I want whatever you put in it."

"I don't know what—"

"Cut the shit, Paul. I don't have time for it. Can you get it?"

He nods slowly.

"When?"

"Tonight," he says. "I can get it from a friend of mine."

"I'll be back this week for it."

He starts to babble about how he doesn't usually do those sorts of things, how he knows he made a mistake, how he loves Melody and doesn't want anything to ruin it. I don't respond, and he silences himself when she returns from the restroom and retakes her seat.

I stand up to throw my drink away. Hesitating, I pull out the letter and rip it up into a bunch of tiny pieces and throw it away, too. I tell Melody and Paul goodbye, but they don't hear me, too busy sucking face.

I consider pretending I don't see Naz's car, but it's pointless. Instead, I cross the street, walking around and climbing right into the passenger seat. He glances at me. There's no apology in his expression.

"I told you I didn't need a ride into the city."

"I know," he says. "But you said nothing about not needing one back home."

Semantics.

Night is falling, casting most of the house in shadows. It's dreary outside, cold and wet, a light rain falling, the weather matching the feelings simmering inside of me.

I've been back and forth all day, on edge as I roam the house. I can't sit still. I can't do much of anything.

It's Friday.

It felt like it took forever getting here, but yet it came too soon. I'm not ready.

I don't know if I'll ever be.

"Are you hungry?" Naz asks, stepping into the doorway of the kitchen as I stand in front of the sink, looking out into the back yard. He still hasn't let me out of his sight, but he's attempting conversation now, a semblance of normalcy. "I can order something."

"Actually," I say, turning to him, "I think I'd rather cook."

He's caught off guard. I get a strange thrill at surprising him. "You? Cook?"

"Hey, now," I say defensively. "I can cook."

"Since when?"

"Just because I don't do it doesn't mean I can't. My mother taught me a little bit."

It isn't until the words are already out that I realize what I've said. My eyes widen, regretting the fact that I brought up my mother, like me not speaking about her might make Naz forget she exists. Like the absence of her name on my lips might somehow save lives. He regards me peculiarly as he strolls further into the kitchen, hands in his pockets.

"I remember Carmela's cooking," he says casually. "She was good... much better than Maria. Maria could burn a pot of water with nothing else in it."

Maria...

His wife?

I'm surprised at the ease in his words. I'm not sure how to respond, how to react, merely whispering, "Oh?"

"We had dinner with them that night, you know," he says. "Your mother made lasagna."

I always loved her lasagna. It was my favorite thing she made. I smile at that, but it fades at the recognition of how Naz's story will end.

"We went home afterward, and your mother didn't send any leftovers. I think about that a lot these days. She always sent leftovers when we had dinner there. But she didn't that night." He pauses a few feet in front of me, eyes fixed to mine. "Makes you wonder if she didn't bother because she figured we'd be dead by morning, anyway."

His words send a chill down my spine. I don't want to think that, don't want to believe it. It's so at odds with the woman who raised me to be kind, and loving, and compassionate.

"So yeah," he says, "you can cook if you want, but if it's Ramen noodles, I can't promise I'll eat it."

He offers me a playful smile before walking out. If I hadn't been confused before, I sure am now.

I don't make Ramen. Instead, I make spaghetti and meatballs. It's nothing fancy, not even homemade, everything prepackaged.

Okay, I'm not *that* good of a cook.

I make up two plates when it's finished, carefully looking around to make sure I won't be caught, before I pull the small vial of white powder from my purse that Paul gave me. I sprinkle it over one of the plates and dispose of the evidence before mixing it in with the sauce. It dissolves easily.

It's invisible, tasteless, and undetectable until it's too late.

I know that from experience.

Taking the plates to the table, I set the tainted one down in front of my seat.

I know Naz. I've figured out his quirks. He pours his own drinks and he rarely trusts food. It's a gamble, trying to predict what he'll do, because if I'm wrong, I'm completely screwed.

Naz joins me at the table, taking his seat, as I take a small bite of the contaminated spaghetti, not enough to knock me out. He watches me before glancing down at his own plate warily. He doesn't say it, but I know what he's thinking.

It might be poisoned.

His eyes meet mine again, suspicious, and I know I got him. He reaches across the table and grabs my plate, switching ours, just in case. He saw me take a bite of that one, so he knows it's safe.

As usual, he offers no apologies. I don't expect one.

Weeks ago, I would've laughed at it, thinking it was a joke, that he was paranoid, but I understand now. I'm the daughter of the man who murdered his family, the daughter of the man who nearly killed him. He may love me, but I don't think he could ever truly trust me one hundred percent.

Can't say I blame him.

I don't deserve it.

Each bite he takes proves it more and more. It's not enough to harm him. Just enough to make him sleep so I can leave.

We drink wine at my suggestion. I need the liquid courage, and I hope intoxication will mask the onset of the drug in his system. I make sure he has his fair share. I need to be coherent enough to walk away.

He's feeling it, whether he realizes it or not.

The man who smiles at me across the table, who speaks playfully, who calls me his little jailbird, reminds me startlingly of the man I fell in love with. Like when we strip away all pretenses, and block all the pain, and anger, he's who exists deep inside.

The monster just overshadows him.

When he's finished, I take our plates to the kitchen. Guilt is nagging at my chest. It's already after ten o'clock. Time is ticking away too fast.

I'm not ready.

I'm not ready.

I'm not ready.

I wipe my sweaty palms and absently fix my dress. I wore one of Naz's favorites—the red dress from Vegas. I fill up the sink with soap and water to do dishes to pass the time when Naz enters the kitchen.

He walks up behind me, stopping flush against me, his hand settling on my hip as he pulls me back toward him. It's the most he's touched me in a while, since the day I safe worded him right here where I stand. His other hand sweeps my hair out of the way, and I shiver when I feel his breath on my neck. He kisses the skin as his hand on my hip drifts forward, beneath the dress, slipping inside my panties.

I can't help myself.

I whimper at his touch.

I nearly lose it at the first graze of his fingertips. So gentle, so natural, his caress so attentive. It's like none of the past two weeks has happened, and he's forgotten I ever hated him.

Closing my eyes, I try to forget, too.

I feel the onset of an orgasm, my knees going weak, my breathing labored as I grip the edge of the sink. He rubs, and rubs, and rubs some more, fumbling with his belt behind me, unbuckling his pants. The voice in my head is telling me to stop this, to stop him, but I can't.

I won't.

Maybe I need this just as much as him.

Maybe I need it more.

Maybe, the other half of me screams, I just need *him*.

He shoves my dress up, pushing my panties aside. As soon as the orgasm rocks me, pleasure bursting beneath my skin, he bends me over just enough to push into me from behind.

I cry out as he fills me.

It's been so long.

Too long.

He's not brutal, he isn't playing a game, but there's urgency to his thrusts as he pounds into me from behind. An arm encircles my waist, the other hand finding home at the base of my throat, the same way he held me in the street in New Jersey. The hold says 'you're mine; you belong to me; you always will.' It says I can try to forget, but my body will forever remember this touch.

It hurts.

It hurts.

Oh God, it fucking hurts.

Not physically. The wound is deeper, an emotional scar I think won't ever heal, no matter how much time I give it. He touches my body but he tears at my soul, ripping pieces out of me that are now his and his alone.

He doesn't take long before I feel his muscles tense. The last few thrusts are deep, agonizing, as he groans into my hair and lets loose inside of me. When he finally stills his movements, his body sags against mine, heavy and satiated, his breathing labored.

I'm quivering, my body trembling from head to toe. Tears sting my eyes when he pulls out. I hope he thinks it's from pleasure, and not because I'm trying desperately not to cry in front of him.

"Are you okay?" he asks, fixing his pants as I lay against the counter by the sink, shielding my face. Confident Naz sounds almost unsure these days.

I don't look back at him as I nod. I'm okay, or I will be, I think. He leans over me, kissing my neck once more as he tugs my dress back down, before he steps back.

The tears fall as soon as he leaves the kitchen. It takes me a good twenty minutes to pull myself together. I wipe my eyes and fix my clothes, careful as I head toward the den. He's sitting at his desk, his head down on top of his book.

He's still reading *The Prince*.

Slowly, I step toward him. He's fast asleep already. I stare down at him, my fingertips grazing his jawline, feeling the scruff, before I run my fingers through his hair. He doesn't even stir.

I hope he's dreaming, that he's happy, and at peace, if only for the moment, because when he wakes up, I know there will be hell to pay for somebody.

"I love you," I whisper, although I know he can't hear me. "I shouldn't... but goddamn it if I don't love you, anyway."

Pulling the engagement ring off my finger, I set it on the desk beside him before turning around and walking out.

Twelve o'clock on the dot.

I stand at the entrance of the park, near the massive arch, shivering in the damp night air. I'm kicking myself for not changing clothes, for not putting on pants. But Naz's scent clings to these, the memory of his touch infused in the fabric, and I'm not ready to let go of that yet.

My eyes studiously scan the neighborhood, on alert, waiting.

A minute passes.

Then another.

And another.

Ten minutes come and go, then fifteen. I start to panic. What if all this was for nothing? Nearly twenty minutes pass before a car comes up the street, creeping to a stop right in front of me. It's a black BMW, expensive, and new. The passenger window rolls down as my heart races.

I see his face. John Reed. Johnny Rita.

"Get in," he says.

I hesitate, wondering if I've made a mistake, but I can't know that, not until I hear what they have to say. Sighing, I climb in the car, refusing to look at him. "You're late."

"Yeah, well, I had to make sure you were alone," he says, pulling away. "Can't trust people these days."

"Tell me about it," I mutter, trying to quell the anger flowing through me. This man might be my father, but that doesn't make him my family. He's a stranger, and I don't trust him. "Where's my mother?"

"Waiting," he says. "She was afraid you wouldn't come."

"Because my entire life was a lie? Because I don't trust you?"

He looks at me. "Because she didn't think you'd be able to escape."

He makes it sound like I was a prisoner, like I was held against my will, like I hadn't welcomed Naz into my world. "You know nothing about what I have with him. Neither of you do."

"I know more than you do. You're nothing but a means to an end to him, something for him to play with. He ain't stupid. He's biding his time, and you make it easier for him. That's all that is."

Anger brews inside of me. I want to demand he stop the car, that he let me out, that he never look or speak to me again, but where does that leave me? Cold, and alone, with nowhere to go, and no more answers than I showed up with. So I just glare at him for a moment before turning away.

"I know what you're thinking," he says.

I scoff. "You know nothing."

"Maybe I don't know the person you are, but I know the one you were born to be," he says. "I know your blood, girl. It's in my veins, too. And I know you're thinking maybe he's a good man, that maybe you can help him."

I'm not a good man, Karissa, and I never will be. So don't think you can fix me, or that I'll ever change, because I won't. I can't

"You're wrong," I say quietly. "He can't be fixed."

"Then why were you with him?"

"Because I thought maybe he didn't need to be."

"He's fucked up, Karissa. His head doesn't work right."

"Yeah, well, why do you think that is? Huh? Could it have been the bullet he took to the chest?"

He grips the steering wheel tightly. He doesn't like that I talk back to him. "There are two sides to every story."

"Then please, by all means, tell me yours. I'm dying to hear what compelled you to murder a pregnant woman and almost kill your best friend, because I'm sure there's a perfectly reasonable explanation for that."

He slams the brakes harder than necessary, the car jolting to a stop at a red light. His eyes zero in on me. He's got a temper, one I can feel building in the car. It makes my skin crawl, sending up red flags that beg me to zip my lips. It's not smart to piss off the driver of the car you're in.

"Nobody's innocent," he says. "Nobody. Not me, not him, not her, not your mother... not even you. I did what I had to do to survive the game, and then afterward, I did what I had to for you and your mother to live."

"You left us."

"I had a target on my back, girl. What the hell did you expect me to do?"

"Not put a target on your back in the first place."

He laughs bitterly but doesn't respond to that. I say nothing else, watching out the window. It's the longest drive of my life, even longer than the trip to Waterford with Naz, over an hour trapped in this car with this man as he takes us somewhere in New Jersey.

Somewhere I've never been before.

The house is modest, but a far cry from the slums they were in last time. It's a home—somebody's home, complete with trimmed hedges and a white picket fence. I follow John inside nervously, finding my mother sitting on a plush burgundy couch in the living room, Killer asleep on the floor near her. The television is on, some movie playing in the background, but all I hear is my mother's frantic voice as she rushes toward me. Her hands paw at me, her eyes wild. "Are you okay, Kissimmee? Please tell me you are. Please tell me he didn't hurt you."

She's on the verge of tears.

I shake my head, in a daze, trying to adjust to my surroundings. "No, of course not. He didn't hurt me. He wouldn't."

John laughs bitterly again.

"You're sure?" she asks. "You can tell me if he did."

"I'm fine, Mom. I just..." I look past her, around the room. It's well lived-in, the scent of flowers clinging to the air from a lit candle. "Who lives here?"

"I do," John says.

I turn to him, brow furrowing. "How long have you lived here?"

He seems to consider that for a moment, startling me when he reaches into his coat and pulls out a gun. Every muscle in my body seizes up at the sight of it, but he turns around and slips it on top of the mantle over his unlit fireplace before turning to me. "How old are you these days?"

"Nineteen."

"About nineteen years, then."

I blink rapidly. "You've lived here the whole time? The whole time we've been moving around, running, you've been here?"

"Yes."

"Do you not see how fucked up that is?"

He shrugs.

Before I can completely lose it, my mother grabs my arm and pulls me down onto the couch with her. "I know it's hard to understand..."

"No, it's quite easy, actually," I tell her, raising my voice so loud that Killer perks up, lifting his head to look at me. "You've spent years on the run because of something he did, and it hasn't affected him at all. He has a house, a home, something I've wanted my entire life, but I couldn't have... he had it. He *has* it."

She casts her eyes toward John as he lingers in the room, relaying some silent message to him that I don't understand. None of the hate I want to see from her is present when she regards him. No, I see something else instead. Compassion.

It fuels my hate more.

He excuses himself then, giving us some privacy. As soon as he's gone, she turns back to me again. "Just because he's been in one place doesn't mean he hasn't been affected. He lost his family."

"Him?" I ask incredulously. "*He* lost his family? He killed Naz's!"

"I know," she says, her words striking me hard. I never doubted it, but the confirmation is a hard pill to swallow. "He did."

"Did you know?" My voice is tentative. I'm afraid of her answer. "Did you know he was going to do it, that he was planning to...?"

"Of course not," she says, those tears in her eyes breaking forth and running down her cheeks. "Maria was my best friend. Had I known... had he told me... I would've stopped him. I would've done whatever I had to in order to stop him. But I didn't know until it was too late, until it was over, until he came home..."

She closes her eyes as she flinches at the memory.

"So why are you here now?" I ask, my voice low and accusing. I'm trying to stay calm, but I don't understand how she can sit in this room, in this house with him. How she can run to him after what he did. "Why are you even near him?"

"He had no choice," she says. "He had to... he had to do something."

"So he killed a woman," I say with disbelief. "That was his solution? He shot his best friend. Naz told me all about it, how he smiled in his face, acted like nothing was wrong, and then tried to kill him that night."

"Vitale told you that?" She raises her eyebrows in question. "Did he tell you he was planning to kill John the whole time that was happening?"

"You don't know what you're talking about."

"No, you don't," she says pointedly. "Vitale can play victim in the whole thing, and he was a victim... he was... but he wasn't the only one."

"That excuses nothing," I say.

"You're right—it doesn't. It happened, and there's nothing anybody can do to change it. But there's been enough death. Too much death. Instead of gunning for John after that, they came for his family. So he left us, so we could go into hiding, because maybe if they thought he didn't care about us they wouldn't bother killing us. But it didn't work. Clearly, it didn't work. Because he found us." She pauses, looking at me. "He found *you*."

I just stare at her. I always thought my mother was unbalanced, that she was needlessly paranoid, but she'd merely been trying to stay two steps ahead of the monster... a monster I unknowingly ran straight to the moment I was away from her.

Despite her warnings, I walked straight into the lion's den, serving myself up on a platter, the meal he was always looking for.

There's something about you... something I've sought for a very long time. Something I've always wanted. And now that I've found it, I don't know if I can let it go.

Closing my eyes, I drop my head, covering my face with my hands. The truth was right there from the beginning. It's all too much to come to terms with. My head is ferociously pounding. My chest feels like it might burst.

Killer appears at my legs then, nudging me with his nose as he whines. I wrap my arms around him, laying my head against the top of his.

He never lied to me.

He never thought to kill me.

At the moment, he's the only one I don't seem to hate.

"I need some time to think," I say. "Some time to process."

She rubs my back gently. "There's a spare bedroom upstairs. We're going to ride out this weekend here and then we'll go."

"Go where?"

"As far away from here as we can go."

Those words do nothing to make me feel better. Going, I think, might kill me more than staying.

I'm not a man who just gives up in the middle of something. If I go any further, if I don't walk away now, I won't be able to.

The bedroom is decently sized, the furniture light oak and appears unused. No dents, no nicks, no scuffs on the wood, and if I had enough energy to look, I'd bet all the drawers in the dresser are empty, the stiff sheets most definitely never slept on before.

I couldn't make out much of it in the dark, my head hurting too much to turn on the light when I climbed into the bed. Despite my exhaustion, I couldn't fall asleep, wide-awake as Naz's words repeatedly roll through my frazzled mind.

I know I should let you go, should let you walk away from me right now, but I can't do it. I can't.

The sun rose a few hours ago, although it doesn't shine, a thick cloud covering blanketing the sky. Rain beats against the window. I lay in the bed, staring at the ceiling, listening to the subtle noises of someone moving around downstairs.

My stomach is growling.

My chest is aching.

I can't get his voice out of my fucking head.

I've lost enough, Karissa. I won't lose you, too.

It has been twelve hours since I walked out of the house. He'd be awake now, the effects of the drug long out of his system.

I wonder what he thought when he woke up.

I wonder how he's feeling.

I wonder what he's going to do to me.

I hear a faint buzzing as I lay there. I ignore it at first until it strikes me that it's my phone. Sighing, I reach for my purse on the floor, rifling through it. Glancing at the screen, my blood runs cold.

Naz.

He's calling me.

I look at his name until it stops ringing. I'm about to toss the phone back into my purse when it vibrates again.

Voicemail.

I feel sick as I stare at the alert. My teeth gnaw at my lip nervously until I can't take it any more.

Monster in his Eyes

As much as it frightens me, I have to listen.

I'm a glutton for punishment and crave the sound of his voice. I have to know how angry he is, how much he hates me right now...

I have to know he's okay.

Pressing the button, I bring the phone to my ear. Silence greets me, strained silence, before he exhales loudly and the line goes dead.

He offers me no words, only a single breath.

Sighing, I toss the phone aside. I can still hear noise downstairs. I'm no closer to figuring out how I feel about them than I was last night, but I can't stay in this room anymore. I creep down there, hearing someone move around the kitchen, the scent of bacon wafting my way.

My mother's cooking.

John, on the other hand, sits on his couch, toying with his gun. He doesn't look away from it as he greets me. "Good morning."

There's nothing good about this morning. The sky is crying and something inside of me is dying.

Wordlessly, I sit down in a chair, not looking at John.

"Nothing to say, girl?"

I've got nothing to say to him.

My mother, hearing his voice, steps out of the kitchen. "Oh, good morning, sweetie."

"Morning."

There's still nothing good about it.

The day is a daze. I eat breakfast, eat lunch, humor my mother's attention, answer some of her questions, and try to pretend John is nowhere around.

I think about Naz.

And think about him.

And think about him some more.

I think about him until my head starts pounding again, and my heart feels like it's been crushed.

"I'm going to bed," I mutter, standing up. My mother's cooking dinner now and tries to stop me, but I say I'm not hungry as I head for the stairs.

She's making lasagna. John requested it. I wonder if either of them remember that's what they ate that fateful night. They act like nothing is wrong, like we're some happy family that has regular dinners and normal conversations.

The universe is fucking with me.

I climb into the bed and squeeze my eyes shut, hoping sleep takes me away from reality for a while.

Hoping, while I'm unconscious, the answers come to me.

Tap

Something pulls me out of a deep sleep so abruptly I'm disoriented. For a second, I forget where I am, the darkness thick and heavy in the room, smothering everything.

Tap

I blink a few times, trying to adjust to the void, as the hair on my arm stands on end at the noise. I lay completely still, straining my ears. I think it might be Killer, or am I hearing things?

Tap

I hear it again. It doesn't sound like the dog. My muscles tense up. It's getting louder, growing closer, restrained and methodic.

Tap

It hits me like a crack across the face. Footsteps.

Tap

I sit upright, heart racing. I'm on guard, eyes darting frantically around the darkness, as I inhale sharply. I barely have time to blink when the form is right in front of me, like a menacing black shadow hovering by the bed.

A scream bubbles up in my chest, just breaking free, when the darkness shifts. The cry barely pierces the silence when the form shoves against me, climbing on top of me to hold me down, a glove-clad hand roughly covering my mouth.

Trembling, I blink my tear-filled eyes, my chest burning as I inhale. A blurry face appears right in front of me, dark eyes piercing like daggers, the expression terrifying.

Naz.

Ignazio.

My heart is pounding so hard I'm sure he can feel it as he pins me to the bed. I'm on the verge of hyperventilating, terrified, tears streaming down my cheeks. He just lies there, restraining me, staring so hard I don't even think he blinks. Something marks his skin, a small streak on his jawline, with tiny flecks around his neck.

When he inches closer, I see that it's blood.

Blood.

There's fucking *blood* on his face.

I sob into his palm as the tip of his nose grazes mine. He's here. He found me.

Oh God, how did he find me?

"If I let go, you can't scream," he says, his voice gritty and emotionless. "Do you understand?"

I try to nod.

"I mean it," he warns. "The last thing you want to do is wake your mother."

My mother... is asleep.

Not dead.

Not bleeding.

He slowly pulls his hand away, his hold on me loosening. I don't move. I don't so much as breathe too loud. My Naz is long gone. The monster woke up from the drug-fueled nap.

"You're going to get up, and as quiet as possible, you're going to follow me outside," he says, matter of fact. "As long as your mother stays asleep, I'll leave her alone, but if she wakes up..."

He doesn't finish that thought. He doesn't have to.

Her blood will be the next spilled.

I can't let that happen.

He lets go of me when he decides I get the point. I'm surprised my legs work when I climb to my feet. My body shakes as I fumble around in the dark, trying to grab my things, all knobby-kneed and tongue-tied.

I'm fucking terrified.

He loves you, I silently tell myself, trying to stay calm. *He won't hurt you. He promised.*

The voice is confident, but my common sense screams louder. People fall out of love. Not everyone keeps their promises.

I slip on my shoes and grab my purse. I'm still wearing what I had on when I left him twenty-four hours ago. One whole day, that was all I had, all it took for him to come for me.

I'll always show up.

When I turn to him, I see he's watching me warily. Any amount of trust I earned by loving him withered away as he slept last night. There's hell to pay, all right, and I'm the one he's going to bill for it. His eyes are full of suspicion. He's a commander, and he believes I've defected.

What's the punishment for a traitor these days?

"Go," he says, motioning toward the door. "Tiptoe."

I tread lightly, holding my breath as I head for the stairs. As soon as I reach them, another door on the floor creaks, opening a bit. I spin that way, terrified, and see Killer's head peek out from the other bedroom. He sees Naz before he sees me and starts to growl.

"Killer," I whisper frantically, calling for him, my heart racing. "It's okay, boy."

The dog looks my way, silencing. His gaze bounces between Naz and me, the usually passive Killer on alert, like he can sense something's wrong.

"Karissa, is that you?"

I almost cry out at the sound of my mother's voice calling from the bedroom. I turn to Naz, wide-eyed, trying to keep my voice steady as I say, "It's fine, Mom. Got some water. Go back to sleep."

I stare at Naz, my eyes pleading with him, as Killer heads back into the room, deciding there's no threat.

"Goodnight, sweetie," she says back. "Sweet dreams."

"You, too, Mom."

I wait for Naz to make a move as his head turns toward the dark doorway. After a moment, he turns back to me, motioning toward the stairs. Relief almost cripples me when I turn back around and walk again.

She's okay.

My mother's still okay.

It's dark down here, just as black as it is upstairs. I blink, still trying to adjust to it, my eyes drawn to the living room when I reach the first floor. All at once the air leaves my lungs in a whoosh as I nearly crumble.

There's blood everywhere. I can hardly make it out in the darkness, a lake of oozing black on the floor, a body floating in the center of it, something sticking straight out of his chest. A knife.

John.

Dead.

I cry out before I can stop myself. Naz's arms encircle me from behind, his hand reaching up, his palm pressing into my neck as strong fingers grasp my chin, forcing me to look away from the mess. His breath fans against me as he whispers, "Don't."

Don't look.

Don't think.

Don't breathe.

Don't.

I chant it in my head, tears streaking my cheeks as he leads me right out the front door. His car is parked nearby. We don't pass another living soul, and I'm grateful for it.

Something tells me a witness tonight won't live to see tomorrow.

I cry to myself the whole way to Brooklyn, my body shaking and teeth chattering. I clench my jaw to keep from making any noise. Bile burns my chest, my throat, scorching my insides, sending me up in flames. I nearly lose it a few times in the car, and Naz says nothing, his gloved hand reaching over and grasping the back of my neck. His touch is firm as his fingers knead the muscles. It eases my headache and calms the fire raging inside of me, but I only cry harder.

Why does his touch affect me this way?

Those vengeful hands killed a man tonight, they took the life of another, and yet they soothe me like nothing ever has before.

I hate myself for it.

When we get to the house, he presses a button on the visor, the garage door opening. He pulls the car in before closing the door again, cutting the engine. He sits there, staring straight out the windshield, his voice detached. "I should kill you."

Despite my attempt to stay silent, I whimper at those words.

"I should wrap my hands around your neck and steal your last breath," he says. "Bleed you dry, drain you of every last drop of that filthy Rita blood. You drugged me... betrayed me... so you could run off, put yourself at risk. You lied to me, when I've done nothing... nothing... to hurt you!"

His voice raises, anger seeping into the words.

"I should kill you," he says again, opening his door. "I fucking wish I had it in me to do it."

He steps out, slamming the car door behind him, and heads straight inside without waiting for me. I break down as soon as he's gone, sobbing loud and hard, gasping as I try to catch my breath. It rushes out of me, purging like a flood, as the tears fall and my chest caves in until there's nothing left inside of me.

Nothing at all.

I fold into myself, curling up on the seat, getting lost in the darkness, in the silence, until my eyes dry on their own and my muscles stop fighting the stiffness, succumbing to the anguish.

An hour passes.

Or two.

Maybe it's even three.

I feel like I've been beaten to a pulp, my bones brittle and on the verge of shattering when I finally step out of the car.

I go inside.

There are no lights on in the house, and I don't hear him, but I seem to know instinctively he's in the den. He always is. I consider going upstairs, going somewhere else, anywhere else, but I'm weak.

I'm weak, and I'm scared, but I'm not a coward. I may have Rita blood in me, but that's not all I am. I'm that man's daughter, but I'm not him. And maybe that makes me stronger than I think.

I stroll that way and peer in. I don't find him at his desk, as I expect. He's sitting on the couch, his head down, cradled in his hands, the gloves discarded on the cushion beside him, lying with a small black gun. I've never seen it before, never even knew he owned a gun. Exhausted, and terrified, I slink to the floor right there in the open doorway, leaning back against the doorframe.

I'm at his mercy now.

"How did you know?" My voice is scratchy, but it surprisingly still works. "How did you find me?"

"Your phone."

I stare at him in the darkness. "My phone?"

"I tracked your phone. I knew it was only a matter of time before you led me right to them."

"You used me." I don't know why that stings so much, but it stirs up my guilt, like it's my fault this all happened. "You used me to find them."

"I tried not to involve you," he says. "I did everything I could not to drag you into it."

"How can you say that?"

"Because it's true." The hard edge, the hint of anger, is back in his voice, as he raises his head to look at me. "It would've been so simple to force you to lead me to your mother, and it would've been easy to get rid of both of you. I could've ended this in a day. But then I saw you, I watched you, and I realized..."

"Realized what?"

"That you had no idea who you were," he says. "You had no idea where you came from. And I shouldn't have cared... it shouldn't have mattered... but you reminded me of someone else, someone who died because of who *her* father was."

"That's why you couldn't kill me," I whisper, my voice shaking. "I remind you of her."

"No, I couldn't hurt you because you remind me of her," he says. "I would've still killed you... but you would've never seen it coming. You wouldn't have suffered, not like she did. So I did everything I could not to involve you, so you never would've known. I had Santino steal your school files, I followed you, I searched addresses, but your mother was smart. Had you not moved here, had you not walked into Santino's classroom, looking exactly like a woman we all used to know, I probably never would've even caught her trail."

The guilt from a moment ago amasses until it makes it hard to breathe. "Then why didn't you kill me?"

"You know why."

"Because you fell in love with me." My voice is so quiet I'm surprised he hears it. "You still got your revenge."

"No, I didn't. I punished him, instead."

"What's the difference?"

"Depends on who you ask."

"I'm asking you."

"He didn't suffer," Naz says. "Not as much as I did."

I want to tell him I don't think he would have suffered either way, but I don't think it's worth the breath. Killing us wouldn't have affected John as much as I think Naz believes. Not all men hold the ones they love so closely. If my father could so easily walk away, could live his life surrounded by white picket fences in suburbia, knowing his family was struggling to live, removing the burden of us from his world would've just been a blessing.

Naz knows that deep down inside. He's told me himself—only a coward leaves his family. Nobody mattered more to John than himself.

Maybe that's what stopped Naz, the truth that my father didn't really care about me. Maybe it wasn't love that saved me. Maybe it was the lack of it.

I don't know.

"I hate you," I whisper. I feel it in my gut, and I can't deny it. I can't ignore it. I'm so angry, so hurt, so consumed that the hate feels like lava, settling in the pit of my stomach. My world was a sunny sky before him, a pretty picture my mother drew for me, and he painted it all black with the truth, splattering it with red from the bloodshed.

I hate it.

I hate him.

"I know," he says quietly. "You said you wouldn't… you said you *meant* it… but I know you do."

"But I love you, too… I don't know how I still can. I hate you, but I still love you somehow. It's just… how can I feel both ways?"

"Easily," he says. "The opposite of love isn't hate, Karissa. It's indifference. You're a passionate person, and love and hate… it's not a far stretch from one to the other. They both take passion, someone getting under your skin and consuming you. And I ate you alive, sweetheart. You never had a chance."

A chill flows down my spine as he stands up. I watch him warily when he turns my way, seeing the darkness lurking in his eyes. "What am I supposed to do now?"

He steps toward me, reaching into his pocket and pulling something out. I watch incredulously as he drops it on my lap, stepping right over me like it's nothing. I glance down, blinking with surprise when I see that it's my engagement ring.

"You set a date for the wedding," he says. "That's what you do."

Epilogue

Vitale.

He traces the name again and again, the rough texture of his hands skimming along my back. It's as if he's branding me with his touch, claiming me as his with the signature of his fingertips, an ironclad contract forged with blood, sweat, and tears.

My tears, usually.

It was almost my blood, too.

According to Greek Mythology, people were originally created with four arms, four legs, and a head with two faces. Four hands to touch with. Two mouths to speak. Fearing their power, Zeus split them into two separate beings, condemning them to spend their lives in search of their other halves.

I learned that from Plato's *Symposium* during my time in Santino's class.

It's a beautiful concept: your soul mate, a part of you, existing in the world inside of another body. People spend their entire lives searching for the one, the one who can complete them, but I never had to look. Mine started chasing me before I was even born.

I once thought the reality couldn't be as fascinating as the fantasy, but I was wrong. *So very wrong*. It might be the case for other people, but they don't know Ignazio Vitale. They haven't met him. They haven't seen what I see in his eyes.

He's my other half.

Maybe the stories got it wrong, I think.

Maybe Cinderella didn't live happily ever after.

Maybe, come midnight, she wanted to run away.

Maybe her prince wouldn't let her.

Mine didn't.

Vitale.

No sooner I figure out what he's writing along my back, his hand leaves my flesh, the bed shifting as he rolls over, finally turning away from me. I breathe a deep sigh of relief, but it doesn't last long.

The moment he pulls away, I start to miss his touch.

For as much as I hate him, I also love him.

I love him.

I love him.

And I fucking hate that, too.

He's a monster, wrapped up in a pretty package.

But I find myself wondering at times like this, when I feel the distance between us, if maybe in his eyes, the real monster is *me.*

Coming Fall 2014

The thrilling conclusion to Naz and Karissa's story.

TORTURE

to her

SOUL

Acknowledgments

To Sarah Anderson, the only person who knew I was writing this book as it was happening. You endured my rants and supported the story since day one, somehow managing to not strangle me when I flounced the manuscript for like two weeks, declaring I was never looking at the damn thing again. You have the patience of a saint.

To my family, for their endless support and acceptance that some days, when the characters were talking, the dishes just weren't going to be done (or the laundry... or the cooking... or really anything). To my spawn, for occasionally surviving off of nothing but pizza for the same reason as above. I owe you a nice dinner (that someone else cooks). To my brother, the first person I ever signed a book for, and to his wife and kids... I couldn't ask for a better support system with you guys. My entire family rocks. Love you all.

To my mother, who would've probably read this book and then gave me "the look" that mothers give their children. I miss you. And to my father... if you read this book, let's never talk about it, okay?

To my best friend, Nicki Bullard, who keeps me sane through the insanity. I honestly couldn't ask for a better friend. You're the best "assistant" around. Here's to many more road trips and book signings and crazy memories in the future. Love you to pieces, bitch.

I want to give some love to the bloggers out there, who dedicate so much time to books out of love for reading. You all are phenomenal, and I wish I could name you all, but trust me when I say authors appreciate you more than you'll ever know.

(Special shout out to my wonderful street team, and to Heather Maven, for working tirelessly for the books she loves. Much love also goes to Author 101 on Facebook... you ladies are wonderful.)